Two Boys

ISBN: **0-9650495-8-2**
ISBN 13: **9780965049580**

Owl of Athene Press
www.owlofathenepress.com

Cover design by CreateSpace

Author photo by Don Walker, Boulder, CO

Two Boys

Susan L Metzger

2012

Introduction

This novel is a vivid account of the human relations—some of them malicious—the friendships, and family situations that generate childhood sexual abuse and its range of outcomes. Susan Metzger has a gift for describing intimate encounter, and her story-telling will ring as true with professionals treating young people or families as it will with the lay reader. This is a novel for anyone who wants to understand the varieties of human desire, sexuality, and friendship more deeply while being "caught" in a good story. Metzger's tale is on sound ground psychologically—never losing its soulful, human quality.

One of the novel's strengths lies in its depiction of the aetiology of illness (rather like a case history) whether in the character of Johnnie, C.K., or their neighbor, Harold Panzerov. Some of her best writing is about sexual encounters. Metzger has a gift for sexual imagery and colorful sexual interaction that does not so much titillate as take the reader inside the transaction—perhaps one might add—in a socially redemptive way—since these are human couplings that most will have only imagined.

With the advent of same-sex marriage, the abolition of "don't ask, don't tell," and similar cultural change, this is a timely work. "Boy love," as it is called, has always been around. As we know, ancient Greek culture made place for it. Forms of such relatedness may be "returning" with marriage legitimation a possibility. Persons so inclined, perhaps genetically, will need to find partners somewhere, somehow. How is this to happen? How is conventional culture to understand and manage it?

As with heterosexual relatedness, many questions arise as to what constitutes abuse and how same-sex relatedness is to be managed by those participating in such unions, professionals assisting them, and the public at large. With a vast vice and pornography industry controlled by the underworld, we are forced to realize that

our conventional culture with its Judeo-Christian underpinnings has not been "good" at sex—of any kind. This new area, featuring the "return of the repressed" in same-sex relatedness, presents additional challenges to sanity and public order, and Metzger has explored a few of them in her novel. This is where I see her work contributing: She has captured well the mind-set of both victim and perpetrator in illicit same-sex transactions and, situationally, contrasted it meaningfully with "good ol' fashioned" boy/girl lovemaking.

Although she doesn't present us with an "acceptable" same-sex union as a contrast—nonetheless—this story may help us infer what a licit same-sex transaction *might be* by showing us what it is not—thus helping consciousness grow. We've a long way to go to understand the range of human relations that now confronts us, but Susan Metzger's work is a wonderful, engaging contribution.

Thomas J. Kapacinskas, JD, NCPsyA.

Author of: "Initiatory Knowing: Reflections on Simone Weil and C.G. Jung" in *Intimacy: Venturing the Uncertainties of the Heart* (Spring Journal Books).
Past Assistant Professor University of Notre Dame
Past President: Chicago Society of Jungian Analysts
Founding Member & Faculty Member:
    C.G. Jung Institute of Chicago
    Inter Regional Society of Jungian Analysts

Foreword

Two Boys is based on a real daycare center molestation case in a small town in the Midwest in the mid-1980's. It was similar to the well-known McMartin case in California and accompanied by a rash of similar occurrences across the country, most notably ones in the Rogers Park area of Chicago; Niles, Michigan; Jordan, Minnesota; Boston, and Miami. All these cases took place during the same 3- to 5-year time span.

My former husband, Thomas S. Ryan, is a psychologist and was the executive director of The Child Sexual Abuse Treatment and Training Center of Illinois (CSATC) in Bolingbrook, Illinois. Since we lived in the same town in which this case occurred, he was asked to provide guidance to the local therapists who were interviewing the child victims at this daycare center.

With both an MBA and an MS in Counseling Psychology, I've had fairly extensive experience working with therapy and corporate groups. This led to my becoming involved organizing and running the parents' support group. As a result of Tom's and my involvement in this case, I became familiar with many of the horror stories reported by the children and the children's parents. Beyond that, I became a student of cult behavior, attended many workshops and read whatever I could get my hands on.

To add depth to the character of C.K., several of the members of a homosexual pedophile therapy group that were being treated at CSATC gave their permission for me to review their case records with their names expunged. Three of the men provided me with their personal journals as well. In addition, Tom provided me with a great deal of insight into the minds of homosexual pedophiles.

My hope is that by weaving the story of *Two Boys* around these facts, I will help parents and adults who were molested as children better understand the damage done by these heinous acts. I also want to provide hope to those who have suffered at the hands of

such abusers. So many victims of child abuse believe the abuse is a result of their being bad children. Otherwise, why would a respected adult do this to them? Maybe this story will help them understand that it was not their fault.

Many people still believe that none of these events took place. The details *are* difficult to believe. Yet, there was tremendous consistency among the children's testimonies in similar cases across the country. There is the argument that the therapists interviewing the children asked leading questions that caused the children to imagine things rather than recall them. Granted, there were flaws in the interviewing techniques in the early cases so that the children's testimonies were judged as unreliable. The prosecutors and interviewers in subsequent cases learned a great deal from those errors and conducted their interviews in ways that avoided leading questions. There were too many victims and their parents telling similar stories to many different interviewers, all separately from one another, for this to be the case.

This is a work of fiction that is based on a real event.

Susan L. Metzger

INSTRUCTIONS FOR READING *TWO BOYS*

Silly as this may seem, it appears necessary. Although I was comforted to learn that William Faulkner originally color-coded the four different voices in *The Sound and The Fury* so that readers could keep them straight (this was later abolished), I resist labeling each "voice" change and have, instead, used a fleuron to denote a switch. Even so, many readers may be confused, especially in the early chapters.

The chapters alternate between C.K. and Johnnie. Johnnie's viewpoint begins the novel. C.K.'s is the second chapter, Johnnie's the third, and so forth. No one chapter contains both characters' points of view. Within each chapter are both the child voice and the adult voice. Often, the chapters open with the adult voice of either Johnnie or C.K., whoever's chapter that is, but not always. Each time there is a fleuron, the voice switches to the child or back to the adult. In Part One, the child voice of Johnnie is six and half years old. In C.K.'s opening chapters, he is eight. The adult voices are those of men in their mid-forties. In the midst of some of Johnnie-the-child parts, there are lines and paragraphs in present tense that are italicized. These denote Johnnie's flashbacks to the daycare center. There are no italicized sections for C.K., because C.K. is conscious of these memories. Johnnie is not.

The one exception to this pattern is Chapter Fifteen about their neighbor Harold Panzerov. This is written in third person omniscient point of view, not in Harold's voice at all.

SLM

THANKS

I owe sincere gratitude to Thomas S. Ryan, my marriage partner for nineteen years, who is a clinical psychologist and was Executive Director of The Child Sexual Abuse Treatment and Training Center of Illinois, which treated child sexual abuse victims, their families, and molesters exclusively. It was his extensive knowledge, which he often shared with me, that heightened my awareness of this issue.

I also am grateful to Jerry Lowell, the therapist at the agency who ran a molester's group consisting of homosexual pedophiles. Jerry arranged for me to view name-expunged case records and personal journals of these men. These men later read what I had written and said I had "nailed it." I would thank them as well, but I do not know their names.

Thanks to Stu Dybeck, Gwen Raaberg, and Jamie Gordon, all instructors of mine in Western Michigan University's MFA program, for coaching me through this. And to Joe Moleski, a visiting lecturer in the same program, who convinced me to believe in this novel and in myself as a writer. Thanks to C.A. (Kip) Crofts, U.S. Attorney of Wyoming, and James Simmons, J.D., PhD for the accuracy of the legal processes and terminology.

Thanks also to Beverley Sutton, who enlightened me on the value of this book to women molested as children. She told me that she had always figured it was her fault that her uncle had molested her as a pre-teen and beyond, and it wasn't until she read this story that she realized the abuse was his fault, not hers.

A huge "thank you" to Tom Kapacinskas, Jungian Analyst, for reading this novel, making suggestions, re-reading, and then writing the Introduction. It is a treasure.

And sincere gratitude to Kirkus Reviews for such an encouraging review of this book in its manuscript form.

Susan L Metzger

PART ONE

1

Yesterday, I received a clipped-out newspaper article at my psychiatric clinic. With it was a brief note from a neighbor who lived along the road adjacent to the farm on which I grew up. It said, "Dear John, I thought you'd like to know. Had to look you up in the Chicago phone book at the library. Yours truly, Harold Panzerov." The subject of the article was my best friend, C.K., who was sixteen the last time I saw him. The clipping was from last week's *South Bend Daily News.* It reads as follows:

> Clive Kendrick Bookout, 45, a former resident of South Bend, with one week left on death row at the Indiana State Penitentiary, is scheduled to be put to death by lethal injection a week from today for the murder of a 12-year-old boy. Known as C.K., Bookout has two prior convictions for molesting a child when he was 18 and has been implicated in as many as 19 other sexual assaults against children. Five years ago he was convicted of molesting seven Indiana boys under the age of six. He was taking part in a work-release program when the murder occurred last year. He was born July 20, 1978 to Gloria Bookout Davis and Walter Bookout. Walter Bookout has been attempting to secure a Governor's pardon for Clive, but at this point he has been unsuccessful. Bookout is to be put to death at 7:20 AM next Tuesday, November 18th.

The first time I met C.K. was the most joyous day of my childhood. We were both pure, innocent, and unaware of the harm that had befallen us, I because I didn't remember and he because he didn't care.

I was six and a half years old in 1985, an only and lonely child. We lived on a small horse farm in northern Indiana, and

my parents were both professionals, my mother a philosophy professor at the university and my father a clinical psychologist in Chicago. He commuted just twice a week, staying several nights at my grandmother's home in a Chicago suburb. I watched all the educational TV programs for kids, and although I was considered a precocious child, able to read before age four and capable of conversation with any adult, I recall longing for a brother, a close cousin, a neighbor, or even, God forbid, a sister if she were my own age. Most of the children on *Sesame Street, Mr. Rogers' Neighborhood,* and *The Electric Company* were accompanied by other kids during their activities. I wanted that too.

"It's a beautiful day in the neighborhood," sang Mr. Rogers on the TV. He was talking about pet rats. A skinny lady told him how smart they are. I wonder why he talks so slowly, I thought. I wanted to watch him forever.

I sat at Daddy's feet. He sat on the couch and read the Sunday paper. Mommy was supposed to be fixing breakfast in the kitchen, but I could hear her talking on the phone in there. I heard her hang up. "Oh, no! That was our last hope, and they—the Nicholses—are going away for the day and can't take him either." She stood in the doorway with a pancake turner in her hand.

I'm bad. But that's good.

I wanted to be gone and wished I were at Grandma's house. She always wanted me. Mommy was beautiful with her long yellow hair. She had on jeans and a tee shirt. She looked mad, and I knew it was my fault. Gosh darn it. I knew I was bad. I squirmed. Maybe Daddy would know what to do.

He brought the newspaper down real slowly. He smiled a little. Then he nodded his head once. "Guess we can't go, then," he said and put the paper back up.

"Do you think we could take him along? I mean, if Ted and Judy wouldn't mind. But they would mind, huh, since they don't have kids?"

Daddy brought the paper down again. "How ridiculous. Expect a six-year-old to tag along for eighteen holes of golf?"

"Since I've never played eighteen holes of golf, I don't know. Couldn't he just walk along with us? Collect balls or something? I don't want to cancel this. It's our big chance to try golfing for real, not just the lessons. And with some very interesting people. What do our horoscopes say for today? Find them. In the entertainment section."

"That's where they belong," Daddy said. He smiled at me. "Let's see here. Leo, right?" Mommy sighed hard. "Plans with acquaintances go awry today. Make the most of time with family members, especially children. Jupiter in Virgo brings unexpected benefits." He winked at me. "Better call them and cancel. We'll do something else, just the three of us." He put his hand on my hair and messed it all up.

———————————

Looking back, I'm still amazed that my mother, with a doctorate in philosophy, let herself be influenced by daily astrological predictions, and further, that she didn't catch on that my father had made that one up. I could tell. But she took a deep breath, clenched the pancake turner, and returned to the kitchen phone.

———————————

Big, black Tucker came over to me and leaned his soft hard body against me. I fell over with him and hugged him. He licked my face real slow. He loved me and I loved him. *Black is the best color.* I wiped the dog spit on my shirt. I put my cheek against his neck. He rolled over so I could rub his belly. The fur was thin and soft. I found the right spot and rubbed faster. His back leg started to go. This always made me laugh. My mother said dogs think they're scratching their own itches.

Mommy brought breakfast out, so Daddy and I went to the table. She still looked mad, so I ate all my pancakes. I cleaned up every last piece. When she picked up my empty plate, she didn't notice how clean it was. I really was good. *We like you best when you're bad.* She started

5

to walk away. Gosh darn it! Then I knew how to make her happy. I said, "Let's go for a walk down the dirt road. I'll ride my bike!"

My mother loved going for walks down the dirt road, which was really a country gravel road that was about two miles long and went past the north perimeter of our farm. It led past a couple of old cattle and sheep farms and a few newer houses, and ended at the four-lane bypass. Very few of the neighbors knew one another because our houses were so far apart. When we did encounter a neighbor, very little was said about the nearby town or what was going on in it. It was as though each family out here lived in its own little world.

I believe I'd just learned to ride my bike a week or so earlier. My mother had shamed me into doing it by proclaiming that most kids could ride a two-wheeler in kindergarten, and here I was about to enter second grade and couldn't do it yet. A whole week had gone by, and I hadn't ridden it a second time. I much preferred going to the library, working puzzles, and watching TV.

Mommy stopped. She had the plates in her hands. Her mad face started to smile. "Really?" she said. Her eyes got soft. "You want to try your bike again?"

I nodded hard. My stomach started to glow. I jumped up and down. She smiled bigger and got taller. "Leland, you'll come along, won't you?" I kept jumping. "Why are you so excited?" she asked me.

"I don't know," I said.

"Leland, Johnnie wants to try his bike again. Let's go!" She bounced into the kitchen. She bounced through the house and got everyone's shoes. Tucker started bouncing too, so Josie and Tilly woke up and bounced. They always knew when we were going out. Daddy still sat and read, but he was turning the pages faster. Mommy came back and dropped Daddy's shoes by his

feet. I was the first to have mine on. Velcro is faster than laces. Daddy set the paper down, but he kept reading it while he put his shoes on.

"Let's go, Leland!"

"Let's go, Daddy!"

The dogs ran to the front door, then back again. They whirled and twirled and ran to the door again. Mommy and I went to the door. Tucker was first in line. His tail wagged so hard it hit Josie and Tilly in their faces. Josie's and Tilly's tails whacked Mommy's legs. Daddy came down the hall. He tried to smile.

Mommy opened the door and the dogs ran out. The sun made sparks fly from their black coats. They whirled and twirled some more. Mommy got my bike out of the garage and we walked over to the dirt road. Daddy walked slower behind us.

"Here, Johnnie. Daddy and I will stay on either side of you until you get going." She held my bike for me. I got on. The gravel looked mean. I pushed on the left pedal, then the right one. Mommy ran sideways with her arms out, and so did Daddy.

———

I recall that my parents looked like some tropical birds performing a mating dance. Their arms were stretched out like wings, and they ran faster and faster as I picked up speed on my bicycle. When I hit the deep gravel on the edge of the road, the handlebars turned perpendicular to my forward direction, and I crashed to the ground.

My parents instructed me early on that I was never to swear. However, they said that if I was pretty angry, I could say, "Darn." If I was angrier yet, I could say, "Gosh darn." And if I was as furious as I could get, I could say "Dagnabbit." which was the cuss word used by some octogenarian cowboy in old westerns. Why they thought "dagnabbit" expressed more anger than "gosh darn," I don't know. They did explain that all three were derivatives of "damn" and "God damn," neither of which I was ever to say until I turned twenty-one.

——— ———

"Dagnabbit!" I said. *I hate you, Jack.*

Daddy picked me up and held me. "Everyone falls down when they're learning," he said.

"Try again, sweetheart," Mommy said. She picked up my bike and held it for me. I didn't want to get on again, and my knee hurt.

"I want to go back home." I felt like crying, but I knew she'd be sad about the walk down the dirt road. She frowned. "No, I'll try again," I said.

We did the same thing, and they did the bird dance again. I went farther this time because I stayed up longer. The road started going up, and my legs got tired. I stopped. "I'm tired," I said to Daddy.

"We can leave the bike and just walk," said Mommy. She smiled big.

"Do you think that's fair, Christine?" Daddy asked.

"It's okay," I said. I didn't want to be bad.

"C'mon, Leland. How about just to the pink house and back?" Mommy looked at me.

Daddy took my hand. "You know how much Mommy loves walks down the dirt road."

——— ———

The dirt road led past a cow farm, over a one-lane railroad bridge, another small farm, and then an abandoned, pink Cape Cod on the right. During the two and a half years we'd lived there we'd never seen anyone at the pink house. The paint was past fading, most of it had peeled off, and the windows were very dirty with the old white trim exposing bare wood. Behind the house was a small cow barn with large holes in the roof. To the side stood a faded, pink, two-car garage with no doors. Inside, debris was stacked high against the back walls. Piles of junk lay scattered around the yard, and the grass was tall and seedy.

Guilt abided in me strongly in those days because I'd been conditioned by some previous events to believe I'd been a "bad"

child, and I remember suggesting we walk to the hill beyond the pink house to please my mother. She and my father didn't even look at the house as we passed, but I saw an old brown pick-up parked in the back. The truck's dreariness blended in so well with the buildings and yard, I never really turned my head to look at it. I was looking at the hill beyond it, anticipating the beginning of the end of the walk down the dirt road.

At the base of the hill beyond the pink house was a small valley with a pond on the right and a swamp filled with cattails on the left. Tucker, Josie, and Tilly leaped into the pond, flushing several quacking mallards, and a great blue heron lifted itself out of the edge of the cattails with its gigantic wings. We stood and watched as it labored into the air.

———

Mommy said, "You must be tired. Let's head back." She leaned down and gave me a hug. She said, "Thank you." I squeezed her hard and didn't want to let go. Her cheek on my cheek felt good. Her arms and her body felt like warm magnets. I wanted to stay that way. She let me go and my arms slid off her. She took my hand and began walking.

We walked back toward the pink house. Daddy walked beside Mommy, and Mommy held my hand and Daddy's hand. I looked at the pink house and thought about the pick-up truck. Now, a small black car was in the driveway.

"A car," said Mommy. We walked faster.

A lady was in the front yard, raking. She looked kind of like Mommy, but she was short. She had curly hair. She didn't see us. We watched her, but she didn't look up. I looked at the yard. Mommy and Daddy looked at the yard. We kept walking, almost past the pink house.

"A boy," said Mommy.

We stopped.

"Johnnie, it's a boy," she said. We walked back to the pink house.

He was kicking at a clump of dirt. He didn't see us, and I just watched him. His hair was straight and long and almost white. His jeans and his red tee shirt looked too big for him.

"He looks about your age," Mommy said. "Why don't you go say hello. See if he's going to live here." She sort of pushed me at him. I didn't like that, so I didn't go. My chest was pounding. My head felt funny. I wanted him to like me, and I wanted him to live here. I wanted a neighbor to play with. So, I started walking to him.

He looked at me. He didn't smile or anything. His eyes were blue like the sky. Then he grinned. Big. I looked into his eyes.

He is across from me, crying. We are at Little Friends Daycare Center, at the long lunch table. But it's not lunchtime. All the children are sitting there. Scared. Tears run down his face. He sobs, looks at me. All the children have bowls. Mine is coming. Liquid, with rabbit. Pieces of fur. It's Fluffy. We're all bad. The hand comes to me with the bowl. My pet bunny! The bowl is in front of my face. Smells sick. He watches me. The hand sets the bowl down. I open my mouth to scream.

"Hi. Who are you?" he asked me. His face was blurry. I couldn't get air. I sucked in. I wanted him to like me. I made his face be clear.

"I'm Johnnie," I said. I live down the road. At the horse farm." I pointed. My arm was shaky.

"The horse farm?"

"Uh huh," I said. I swallowed. My throat was all dry.

"I'm getting a pony as soon as we move in," he said.

Yes! It was true. A friend. A neighbor. I liked looking at him. "When?" I asked.

"I ain't sure," he said. He looked at his mother. "I think in a few weeks. Ma! When're we movin' in?"

Mommy came up. "Hi! What's your name?" she asked the boy.

"C.K," he said.

Seekay, I thought. I liked the sound.

"What do the C and the K stand for?" Mommy asked.

"Clive Kendrick," C.K. said. He sounded very polite. I thought his real name was ugly. I liked "Seekay," though.

"Oh," said Mommy. She acted impressed. "Is Kendrick your last name?"

"No. Bookout is."

"Oh, so you're C.K. Bookout?"

"Uh huh," he said and looked at his shoes.

His mother came up. She was friendly. She said, "Hi! Do you live along here?" I liked her smile. She looked like she was laughing, but she wasn't. "I'm Gloria Bookout." She shook hands with Mommy. Daddy was there now too. They all shook hands and said their names. Mrs. Bookout wiggled a lot.

"Come meet Walter," she said, and Mommy and Daddy followed her to the back of the house. Mr. Bookout was rolling up a big piece of wire fence. He was taller than Daddy and had light brown hair.

"We have kittens," said C.K. He raised his eyebrows.

"Really?" I answered. "Where?"

"C'mon," he said and ran toward the barn. I followed as fast as I could, but I couldn't keep up. I felt wobbly.

"How old are you?" I asked. I was breathing hard. We stood in the big doorway of the barn.

"I'll be eight next month—July 15th. How old are you?"

"I'll be seven in January." I didn't want to say "six and a half."

"Oh," he said. He sounded disappointed. I was embarrassed. I wanted us to be the same age. I think he did too.

I followed him into one of the stalls. He stopped and pointed at the corner. We tiptoed the rest of the way to the kittens' nest. He kneeled down in front of them, and I looked over his shoulder. The brown mother lay on her side. She curled her paws and let them go. She kept doing this and purred real loud. Eight tiny kittens drank from her belly. Their heads were very big and their bodies and feet were small.

"Their ears and eyes is still closed," said C.K.

I could see that their eyes were closed. "How can their ears be closed?" I asked.

He pointed to one tiny ear. It looked thick, like there was no hole. "See?" he said.

11

I nodded, even though I wasn't sure.

"They's just two days old," said C.K.

"They're," I said.

"Huh?"

"*They're* just two days old," I said. Mommy said people who talked like he did weren't educated. I wanted to help him.

"That's what I said," he said and laughed a little.

"*They're* not *they's*," I said. Then I got real scared because I thought he might get mad at me.

He looked at me. "Whatever. Ain't they cute?"

"They really are," I said, and I kneeled down next to him. I stared for the longest time. There were hundreds of pink paw pads. The whiskers looked like glass threads. Two days old. They were brand new. The mother cat stopped purring. She looked at us, and I could tell she didn't like us. She stood up all of a sudden. Some of the kittens hung on with their mouths. When they fell off there were a bunch of little suction sounds. They all started mewing with tiny voices. All of them together. It almost hurt my ears. The mother ran out of the stall fast. We looked back at the noisy kittens. Their heads bobbed up and down. When one kitten's mouth touched another kitten, it went poke, poke, poke at it, and then the kitten mewed some more.

C.K. said, "I guess she didn't like us starin' at her babies. Is them all your dogs, the black ones?"

"Yes. Flat-Coated Retrievers," I said. I liked my dogs and I liked to tell people what breed they were.

"Black-coated retrievers?"

"No. Flat," I said. It was hard to say "flat" real loud without spitting on him. Mommy said that was always a problem for her at dog shows. Most people didn't know what kind of dogs they were.

"I never heard of 'em. We have a Golden Retriever, but she's crazy. Ma and Pa keep hoping she'll run away. She jumps on everybody, and she's real nervous."

C.K. looked at the kittens again and picked one up. I picked one up too. It was ugly when I looked at its face. Its head was big and its body was tiny and squirmy. It was very light and had the

softest fur. I held it up close to my eyes and watched the wrinkled face nod and bump my thumb. I didn't like it. It sort of scared me because it was so ugly. I wanted to throw it back in the nest. I looked at C.K. He was holding his kitten's body in one hand. He held its head in the other hand.

"I wonder how far we can twist their heads around without killin' 'em," he said.

"Yeah, I wonder," I said. I started to twist mine, slowly, and he began to twist his. *The younger the animal, the closer it is to God. It's best to kill the youngest ones.* So far, nothing was happening. We looked at each other's kitten, and then we looked into each other's eyes. He smiled and I smiled. We started to laugh. I felt so happy. He looked happy. We continued to twist, real slowly. Nothing happened. For the longest time. Nothing. Even though we kept twisting. Slowly, real slowly. He stared at his kitten and stopped smiling. I stopped laughing and just watched mine too.

When I felt a crack, the tiniest little crack, I screamed and threw the kitten back into the nest. I leaped up and wanted to run out. But C.K. was still twisting and didn't look at me.

"You're going to kill it!" I said.

He looks up at me. His face says nothing. Then, he twisted the head hard. When he opened his hands, the kitten was dead. I watched for it to breathe or squirm, but it didn't. I looked into the nest to see if I could see my kitten. I was afraid it would be dead too, but all of them were squirming and mewing, and I couldn't tell which one was mine.

C.K. was still kneeling. He looked down at the dead kitten. I didn't know what to say, and he didn't move. Then he started shaking a little. I just looked at him, but I couldn't see his eyes. He shook harder, and then he looked up at me. His face was all scrunched up, and tears ran down his cheeks.

I put my hand on his shoulder and said the only thing I could think of. "Let's bury it. We can have a funeral." I had just been to my grandpa's funeral, so I knew all about them. He nodded and stood up. He wiped his face on his sleeves.

"You got a shovel?" I asked.

"Yeah, this way," he said. He walked out of the stall. I followed him. We'd forgotten about our parents. When we walked out the barn door, we saw them standing in the back yard. We hurried back into the barn. C.K. held the kitten close to his belly so they wouldn't see it.

"Johnnie!" Mommy called. She'd seen me. "We're going now."

C.K. and I looked at each other for the longest time. I wanted to run into the barn and hide. And I wanted to run to Mommy and Daddy at the same time. I couldn't decide which to do. So, I just stood and stared at C.K. and the kitten at his belly.

C.K. started looking all around the barn. He ran over to some big barrels. They had lids sitting on top, loose. He pulled a lid part way off and said, "We'll put him in here for now."

I had to stand on my tiptoes to look into the barrel. It was very dark and looked empty. I didn't want him to drop the kitten in because it would hurt the kitten. "Wait!" I said. I saw a pile of loose hay. "Let's put some hay in first." I ran and grabbed a bunch of it. He pulled the lid all the way off and stood back while I dropped the hay in. "There," I said.

"Johnnie!" Mommy called.

C.K. dropped the kitten in. We lifted the lid together and set it on top real quietly. Then we ran to the barn door. We walked out of the barn together like nothing had happened.

The four parents were talking, and Mr. Bookout was throwing sticks for Josie.

"What are the dogs' names?" asked C.K.

"That's Josie," I said. "The big one is Tucker, and the other one is Tilly. Josie is the mother of both of them."

"Oh," he said. "They all look the same to me."

We stood halfway between the barn and our parents. Mommy had started taking small steps backwards. "Let's go, John," she called.

I was a little shaky, and I think C.K. was too. We walked, slow, towards them. We pretended we were bored. But we didn't have

14

to pretend very long. They kept on talking and talking, and they didn't pay any attention to us. We stood and listened to them talk.

Mrs. Bookout said, "C.K. will be in fourth grade this fall. How about Johnnie?"

I held my breath and hoped Mommy would lie. "Second," she said. I wanted to hide. I didn't want C.K. to know I was so far behind him. I wanted to hit Mommy. I wouldn't look at C.K. "His birthday is January first, so we had to hold him back. It's too bad because I know he'd be happier doing third grade work. He reads at the seventh grade level already. At least that's what his test scores indicated." That was better. At least C.K. would know I was smart. I looked at him to be sure he was listening. He was. "So, if you've been working at the plastics factory for twelve years, what did you do with C.K. when he was little?" Mommy asked.

"Daycare," said Mrs. Bookout. She started swaying back and forth.

"Where?" Mommy asked. "I guess that's a silly question since there's only one daycare center in town."

"Little Friends," said Mrs. Bookout. She had a funny look on her face.

"Johnnie went there, too," said Mommy. Her hands were in fists.

"Do you believe what they say happened there?" Mrs. Bookout asked. She swayed harder.

"Yes," said Daddy. He sounded mad. He looked at C.K. and me. We looked at him. "We ought to talk about this another time."

"Did the police ever call you?" asked Mrs. Bookout.

"Another time," said Mr. Bookout. He sounded quiet and mad. He looked disgusted. Tucker leaned against him. I thought he was mad at Tucker, but he was stroking Tucker's head, hard and fast.

The four parents looked at the ground for a long time. C.K. and I watched them. No one said anything.

Finally, Mommy said, "When will you be here again? Maybe the boys could play some more."

"Every evening and weekend till we move in," said Mrs. Bookout. "We usually have pizza. Johnnie could join us."

"Okay," said Mommy. "I could walk him down tomorrow evening. How would 6:30 be?"

"I may need you to be at home for a phone call then," said Daddy. "Let's make it tentative," he said to Mrs. Bookout.

Gosh darn! Mrs. Bookout looked hurt. Mommy said, "I'm sure he can come down even if it's a little later." She smiled at Mrs. Bookout.

I looked at C.K. and he looked at me. We jumped up and down for a while, then we ran away and hid behind a big tree. He looked at me with a serious face. "We can bury the kitten tomorrow, okay?" he whispered right in my face. I nodded my head once. He held out his hand. I grabbed it and shook it hard. Then we both ran back.

Mommy and Daddy had started walking home, and I ran to catch up. I turned back and waved at C.K. He waved at me.

2

Yeah, man, I killed Ricky. The shrinks here—they want me to talk about my parents, my upbringing, the daycare shit, Johnnie, the boys I molested. Yeah, all that shit happened. Who gives a fuck? I don't give a shit, so why is it so important? Makes no difference now anyway. I'll be dead in a week. My lawyer says the governor might pardon me. Why the hell should he? Who the hell am I? I killed my beautiful Ricky. I should die.

But he made me do it. He broke my heart, man. It was so good. He loved me. I loved him. We was best friends. Did everything together. Best buddies. Little kids are supposed to be loyal. And he was. For a long time. Well, what the fuck, it's all over now.

They say my ma's nearly starved herself to death, and my pa's doin' what he can with lawyers and shit. They've been great parents, can't deny that. They's doin' what they can. Always have. Yeah, they always tried hard. Ma worked in that factory all her life, and Pa, once he became foreman, he put in twelve hours a day at the plant. Had a real nice home growin' up. Lived out in the country. Had a dog, cats, chickens. And Johnnie.

The shrinks want me to remember my childhood. Relive it. Feel it again, shit. Stuff just happens, and you go on. Like the daycare crap. They say I was victimized. Victimized, my ass. So, they did bad stuff to us. We weren't hurt by it. We all grew up. What's the big deal? I guess there was one kid who committed suicide—threw himself out of a car when he was seven. But that could've been from somethin' else. Yeah. Oh, and I guess there was one put in a mental hospital cuz he became "catatonic"—all rigid and shit. But maybe he would've been like that anyway, too. Who knows?

The shrinks keep sayin' if I don't recall my feelings—relive 'em, fuck, I won't change. Well, there just ain't no feelings to relive. I don't know what they's talkin' about. Everything was okay, that's all. My parents' divorce? Most kids' parents got divorced back then.

So, they didn't get along, they went their separate ways. They were happier, so who was I to complain? No big deal.

Johnnie? Yeah, Johnnie was special.

———

My great grandpa died and left this old pink house a couple miles outa town. It was a mess. The whole insides had to be tore out. There was all kinds of garbage in the yard. The plumbing didn't work. All the paint was peeled off. Awful. It took Ma and Pa a year to get to own the house. Some homestead law or somethin'. Then we sold our house in town and had two months to move into the pink one. So, every evening when Ma and Pa got home, we went out there to work on it.

We took Tigger with us right away cuz she was gonna have kittens again. We was only there one day and she had 'em. Up in the barn, in a stall. That was her seventh litter, so I didn't care much. Ma made me take food up to her twice a day, though. So, I looked at the kittens then. This time they was all tiger kitties, like her. Other times there'd be a white one or a black one, or grey and white. Not this time. The daddy must've been a tiger too, that's what Pa said.

We'd only been goin' out there for a few days. Pa was tryin' to roll up that whole stretch of cow fencing. Ma was rakin' the front yard, tryin' to get all the junk up so she could mow the grass. She told me to "just go play." She said that a lot. So, I was standing in front of the garage. There was little mounds of dirt where moles or something had dug. You could see where their tunnels was. I knew Ma's lawn mower would hit the mounds, so I was tryin' to knock 'em all down. Some of 'em was real hard, so I had to kick at 'em a few times.

I was gettin' pretty good at this, havin' a fun time, really. I looked up, and there's this kid. He looked scared and just stared at me like I was a snake or somethin'. Back behind him was his parents, watchin'. I figured maybe he lived around here. He looked my age. Maybe he could be a friend. I grinned at him. But geez, he didn't smile back. He did this weird thing. He spaced out or

somethin'. He looked at me, but it was like he didn't see me. Then he got this real scared look on his face. Looked like he was gonna scream or somethin'. Then he like woke up and was pretty normal. I asked him who he was. Said he lived up at the horse farm. That was a fancy place. Ma said some rich people from Chicago lived there. They was professors or somethin'. She never said nothin' about no kid, though, so I didn't figure this kid was from there. But he was. He seemed pretty nice. I liked his hair. It was black and kinda curly. You could see the curls even though it was cut so short. He had a good face and looked like a regular kid.

We didn't get to say much before all our parents came over. I told him I was gettin' a pony, but he didn't seem to care.

When I told him about the kittens, though, he looked excited. So, we ran off to see 'em. They was only two days old and funny lookin'. We stood lookin' at 'em, and he got this crazy idea to try and twist their heads—just for fun. To see how far they'd twist. He threw his back into the nest, and something happened to mine. Maybe it was dead when I picked it up. It was probably sick or somethin'. Oh well.

Johnnie seemed all upset about it and wanted to bury it. Have a funeral. That seemed like fun, so we planned it. It was fun to have an adventure. Then, Johnnie's parents wanted to go. His ma said he could come back the next evening. I wished he could stay that evening. He seemed to like me.

After they left, Ma and Pa started arguin' about Little Friends again. Ma asked, "C.K., what happened there? Mr. Ambrose says they did do bad stuff to the kids. Why don't you tell the truth?"

Pa said, "Leave the boy alone. Nothin' happened to him. People are just makin' stuff up to cause trouble. Jack and Bernice are good Christians. You think they'd hurt kids? 'Sides, C.K. would tell us if anything happened. Wouldn't you, son?"

I nodded. I couldn't tell. If I did, Jack would know and kill my parents, even though he was in jail. He'd showed us he was strong enough to bend those bars. He could just put his hand out and stop traffic. He had special powers. He knew all kinds of things—just through the air. With no one sayin' nothin' to him. He just knew

cuz he had ESP. He showed us on that dog—showed us how he'd kill our parents. Put stuff on a cloth and hold it over their noses till they fell asleep. Then while they was still alive, he'd cut their hearts out. The heart would beat for a while, then stop. The dog died by then. Of course, the heart belonged to Satan, and Jack gave the dog's heart to him. Said he'd give our parents' hearts to him too. Anyway, I didn't want my parents to die like that, so I never told what happened there. None of the kids did, far as I know.

Ma said the Ambroses seemed like real nice folks, even if they did talk too proper. Pa didn't say nothin' and went back to rollin' fence. Ma went back to rakin'. I went back to kickin' mounds of dirt for a while. Then I ran back up to the barn and peeked into the barrel where we'd put the dead kitten. We was gonna have a funeral the next day when Johnnie came over. It was still there. I was happy.

3

I woke up before Mommy and Daddy in the morning. All I could think of was C.K. and the kitten. I ran down the hallway to their bedroom. They were still sleeping. I put my mouth near Daddy's ear and whispered, "Daddy, how much longer till evening?" He sat up a little and looked at me. He looked real sleepy. Mommy mumbled something about talking till three in the morning.

"I still don't see what harm there would be," she said more clearly. She rolled over and looked at Daddy.

I didn't know what that meant. It sounded like something I shouldn't know about, so I didn't ask.

"Just limit it to an hour this time. Please," said Daddy. "Let me talk to some people." I thought this was about C.K. and me. Daddy and Mommy were very grumpy. Daddy had to go away to Chicago for a meeting. He was going to be gone for three days.

How do children, especially "only" children, spend all their time, day after day, in the summer? I know I spent some time in front of the TV, but my parents were too aware of the need for other kinds of mental stimulation. I mean, what is there to occupy a child's mind? As adults, there's so much, but a child, it seems, just doesn't have that many concepts and memories to call upon.

So, when I think back on my childhood, I can't imagine what I did each day all summer. My mother was a faculty member of the Philosophy Department at the university, and when she was gone, Pam came. Pam was a woman in her thirties who had a developmentally disabled brother. She made a career of helping the handicapped. Consequently, she made little money and worked for us whenever she could. Besides, she genuinely liked me. She always brought something interesting—a new game, a special cookie recipe we'd

Susan L Metzger

make together, a movie video to watch, or a new book. Sometimes she took me places, such as church functions, family picnics, and even special events for her disabled students.

But on the days my mother spent at home with me, I can't imagine what I did. She says now that she read to me, that we went to the library, to playgrounds, and out to a fast-food hamburger restaurant for lunch. Still, day after day? Intellectually, I understand that a child's mind is simply occupied by such elementary tasks as exploring the differences in color, weight, and size of various objects, and I know my parents provided me with all the most well-reviewed educational toys on the market, but when I try to remember my childhood, I can't remember what kept me occupied and stimulated.

I attended a private school in South Bend about sixteen miles away. There were two problems with this. First, all the friends I made in school lived so far away, their parents were not very eager to drive them to our house to play, although they did occasionally. And secondly, I didn't have the opportunity to meet playmates in our small town because my parents didn't socialize with the town's residents, nor did they enroll me in any of the children's activities there.

Consequently, all my play time with C.K. took place during the summers, on weekends, and occasionally after school.

This day was the longest in my life. Mommy had all sorts of paper work to do. I played with my toys and watched TV. Mr. Rogers talked extra slow this day. I kept running in to Mommy's office to ask her how much longer till we'd go to C.K.'s house. She finally got mad and took me to the movies.

When we got home, I wanted to go straight to C.K.'s. Mommy said, "After supper." I didn't want to eat, and it was macaroni and cheese. That was my favorite. Mommy was grumpy again. She said, "Johnnie, this has been a very trying day for me. You can eat later. Let's just go to C.K.'s house now." And she put my macaroni and cheese in the refrigerator.

I couldn't stop jumping. "Do you want to ride your bike?" she asked.

"No. I'd like to skip there." I meant it. She laughed and hugged me.

We skipped down the dirt road together. Tucker, Josie and Tilly skipped, too. When we passed the farmhouse on the right, a puppy ran out to us. We had never seen it before. The lady in the house ran out, calling her. "Lassie, Lassie! Here puppy puppy!" It ran out in the road. Tucker and Josie and Tilly went over to it. It rolled over on its back with its hind legs hanging open. Our dogs sniffed it, and it wagged its little tail real fast. When it got up to run, Tucker put one big paw on its back. It couldn't move.

The lady screamed at us. "Get that big dog off her! He'll kill her!"

Tucker wouldn't kill anything. He liked the puppy and was licking its face with his big tongue. Mommy grabbed Tucker's collar and tried to pull him away. Tucker wagged his tail so hard Mommy could hardly hold him. She picked up the puppy with her other hand. She held it until the lady came up to her. The puppy licked Mommy's face. I petted it, and it licked me too.

The lady was mad. "You always let those damned dogs run free. Come here, baby," she said. She took the puppy from Mommy.

"These dogs wouldn't hurt anything," said Mommy. She sounded gentle, the way she talked to the lady. "I'm sorry if we scared you. These are very friendly dogs. I'm sorry. Really." She held her hand out to the lady to shake. "I'm Christine Ambrose. We live at the horse farm." She pointed.

I could tell the lady wanted to stay mad. But she shook Mommy's hand. "I'm Linda Boggus." She held her puppy to her and petted it. It was very cute. Black and white with sort of bluish eyes.

"What kind of dog is that?" I asked.

"A Border Collie mix." She was still mad, but I think she sort of wanted to be friendly. "What are these? Long-haired Labs?"

"Flat-Coated Retrievers!" I said.

"Never heard of 'em. Are they some kind of Lab?" she asked Mommy.

"No. Actually they're a separate breed. There are Curly-Coated Retrievers too. They're both rare and almost no one's heard of them. They're very friendly."

"We just got Lassie here last night. I'm going to have to think of a way to keep her from runnin' out in the road or she'll get hit. That Jenkins boy down the road speeds through here. How long you lived here?"

"About two and a half years," said Mommy. "I'm sorry we haven't met you till now. Just poor timing, I guess."

"Guess so." I could see now that the lady was about Mommy's age. At first I thought she was about fifty or sixty. She just looked old. She had funny short hair, and she wore an old lady's dress.

"When is your baby due? Mommy asked. I looked at the lady's belly. I guess it was sort of big.

"Another month."

"First one?" asked Mommy.

"Yes." Mrs. Boggus looked friendlier now.

"Well, this is Johnnie. He's my first and only. He's on his way down to the Bookouts to play with C.K. Have you met them yet? I think they're planning to move in in a month or so. In that old, pink house."

"Oh, yes. I know Gloria from way back. So, she finally got possession of that place, huh?" Then she leaned closer to Mommy and sort of whispered, "She was quite the boozer. Walter started takin' her to church. He did a lot of drugs. They seem okay now? Maybe the church straightened 'em out, huh?"

Mommy looked scared. "Well—we just met them yesterday. They seemed okay. Quite nice. I'm glad to know that, though."

"Her grandfather owned that place. Lived there all alone. He was a drunk too. Let the place go all to hell. It's just sat there now for fifteen—twenty years."

Mommy didn't know what else to say. Lassie started squirming to get down. "Well, nice meeting you," said Mrs. Boggus.

"You too," said Mommy, and started walking again. Mommy walked a lot slower now. She didn't look very happy. But I was.

———

As one traveled down the road, the Panzerov's house came after the Boggus' on the right side. It wasn't really a farm, but there was a small, blue pole barn, a large garden, and a shed where Mr. Panzerov kept a couple goats and some chickens. As I recall, he also had a yellow dog that was rarely seen and a fat orange cat.

Mr. Panzerov supposedly had been injured on the job when he was still quite young and received Workers' Compensation for the rest of his life. He walked with a very slight limp, and I never understood how he got away with this. He did all kinds of work on his property and cared for acres of yard in grand style. His lawn was as impeccable as a golf course.

He had three obese daughters who were still quite young, maybe pre-adolescent to adolescent, and I overheard my father, on more than one occasion, intimate that Mr. Panzerov probably committed incest with all of them. My father was a psychologist who specialized in the treatment of child molesters and sexually abused children. Every time he saw a fat, unhappy woman, he concluded that she was a victim because one way to repel men's sexual advances was to be fat and unattractive.

Anyway, Mr. Panzerov was rather rotund himself, and when he walked, his belly seemed to lead the way. He always wore a white shirt and denim coveralls. His dark hair was combed neatly over a receding hairline, and his jowls were large and meaty. No one seemed to know anything about Mrs. Panzerov.

<hr />

After we passed the Panzerov's, I could see C.K.'s house. "May I run ahead?" I asked. Mommy nodded. Tucker ran with me. I ran into the yard. No one was there. I looked back at Mommy, but she was so far back. I was a little afraid to go up and knock on the front door by myself. I'd never done it before. I went up to it. It was very tall. I knocked, but the noise was too soft. No one heard me. I tried again. It was a little louder, but it hurt my knuckles. Finally, Mommy came and knocked. She knocked hard.

Mr. Bookout opened the door. He was chewing and swallowing. "C'mon in. We're just finishing dinner," he said. Tucker tried to go in.

I grabbed his neck and almost went for a ride. Mr. Bookout stopped him and shooed him out. Poor Tuck. He looked sad. Mommy was behind me and said, "Bad dog. Stay."

The house was a mess. There were boards and white dust all over the floor. The walls weren't really walls. They were just boards with spaces. White chunks of stuff were all over the floor, and nails, and hammers, and saws. The windows had those fat blinds that open and close with a string. They were all yellow and had lots of dust on them. And it smelled funny.

"Hello?" It was Mrs. Bookout in another room. I walked toward her voice. She was in the kitchen, except it wasn't really a kitchen. All the cupboards were on the floor. The white sink was brown and had nails and pieces of wood in it. The walls were like the walls in the living room—just up-and-down boards. The whole house sort of looked like a skeleton inside. Mrs. Bookout and C.K. sat on upside-down buckets. They were eating chicken from a red and white box.

C.K. looked happy to see me. He set his piece of chicken back in the box. "I'm full now, Ma. Can I go play?"

"You finish your supper," she said. She grabbed the piece of chicken out of the box and handed it back to C.K. "And eat your cole slaw and potatoes." She smiled at me and rolled her eyes.

"But I'm not hungry," said C.K.

"You little brat," she said. "You eat that or I'll whip you." She smiled at us again.

C.K. didn't look scared. He sighed and looked at me. He shrugged and grinned. He took a little bite of the chicken leg. His cup of coleslaw and bag of fried potatoes weren't even open.

Mommy and Mr. Bookout came in. C.K. sighed again real loud and set the chicken leg down. "Pa, I'm full. Can I go play now?"

Mr. Bookout smiled. "Sure, son. Have a good time." Mr. Bookout was always quiet and never got mad.

"How'm I supposed to discipline that boy when you say 'yes' to everything I say 'no' to?" Mrs. Bookout said. She sounded mad. Then she giggled and smiled at Mommy.

"He's ate enough," said Mr. Bookout. C.K. waited. "Go on son, go play."

C.K. ran out the other side of the room, and I followed him. We ran down three rickety stairs and out the back door. We ran up to the barn, and we stopped in front of the barrel. We stood there and stared at it for a long time. Tucker had come with us. He sat down between us. He looked at C.K., then at me, then back and forth. He looked like he wanted to say, "What now?" His feathery tail swept the barn floor. He wagged it all the time, no matter if he was sitting or standing or lying down.

C.K. started to pull the lid off. "Wait" I said. "Where are we going to bury it? Do you have a shovel?"

C.K. slid the lid back on. "We'll need a cross, too," he added.

He stood there with one finger hooked over his bottom teeth. He stared at the floor. Then he shook his hair out of his eyes. He looked real serious. "We could bury him out back behind the woods. There's a field out there with one big tree in the middle. We could bury him there."

I nodded. I felt real serious too.

"We'll hafta steal a shovel outa my dad's truck," he said. "And there's pieces of wood all over the place we can make a cross with."

I nodded again and followed him. We walked out to the old pick-up truck. It had a white box on the back that covered the whole truck part. Its door was lifted open. We both stood on the back bumper and held on to the top of the tailgate. We looked inside. It was as messy as the house. It had boards and tools and nails and stuff all over the floor. There were three or four different kinds of shovels. We both pointed at one that was long and had a point. "That one," we said and giggled.

"Keep a lookout," said C.K., and he climbed in. Without making a sound, he pulled the shovel out. He pushed the handle at me to take it. I held the handle, and he lifted the shovel part over the tailgate. I kept looking toward the house, but no one came out. C.K. hopped down from the truck and carried the shovel to the barn. I followed him.

"Where you going with that shovel?" yelled Mr. Bookout's voice. "That's my best spade."

We froze and turned around to look at him. He was standing just outside the back door. C.K.'s face had no expression on it. He held the shovel. I sure didn't know what to do. I waited for C.K. to say something.

"We's gonna dig worms to go fishin'," he said.

I nodded my head. I was scared. C.K. had lied. Mommy always told me that if I told the truth, she would never punish me. I had tried lying, and Mommy always knew. I decided it wasn't worth it. Even if I did something wrong and told the truth, Mommy and Daddy wouldn't punish me. I liked it that way. I wondered now what would happen to C.K. And I had nodded my head, so I had lied too.

"Okay," called Mr. Bookout. "Just don't lose it."

"We won't," said C.K.

"No, we won't," I called. I felt my heart pound. Mr. Bookout went back into the house. "Whew!" I said to C.K. He didn't say anything.

"One more thing," he said. "Black paint." He handed me the shovel and started to walk away.

"Wait," I said. "Where are you going? Don't leave me."

"C'mon," he said. I set the shovel down, and I followed him back into the house. He went down into the basement. It smelled terrible, and it felt wet. He turned a light on. There was a shelf with a bunch of old cans of paint. We squinted and tried to read what the labels said. Every single one said "pink." A large one said "white." There were a bunch that had blue or brown paint dribbled down the sides. I saw a small one that looked like it had never been opened. It said "black."

"Here," I said. C.K. grabbed it and put it under his shirt. He turned and started to leave. I followed. On the way out there was a small table with old paint brushes and clear glass bottles of liquid. C.K. took a small brush and kept going.

When we got back to the shovel, Tucker was sitting there waiting for us. I picked up the shovel, and the three of us marched up

to the barrel. C.K. and I slid the lid off, and we looked in. The kitten lay there. It looked like it was asleep, except its head was turned kind of funny. C.K. tried to reach for it, but it was down too far.

"Let me try," I said, and I tried to scoop it out with the shovel. I got the kitten to balance on the very end of the metal part and had to bring it up very slowly. Just when I got it to the top of the barrel, the shovel slipped, and the kitten fell on the floor. Tucker grabbed it in his mouth and ran out of the barn.

C.K. screamed at him, "Tucker!"

I told him to shush or his dad might hear. So we whispered the darn dog's name as loud as we could. "Tucker. Tucker. Here, Tucker." He just kept running in circles. He'd throw the kitten up in the air a little, and then he'd catch it again. Then he'd run in circles some more. We kept calling him, but he wouldn't come. I even went out and tried to catch him, but he stayed away. He'd stand and shake his head. The kitten's head jiggled real fast when he did this.

"Maybe if we just go out to the field, he'll follow us," I said. C.K. said okay and we started to walk.

Then C.K. stopped and said, "Wait. The wood for the cross."

"Oh, geez," I said. I couldn't stand this. I just wanted to get the funeral over with.

He said, "You go on and I'll catch up. It'll just take a second." And he ran back towards the house. I didn't know where I was going, so I just walked. Tucker trotted next to me until I tried to grab him. Then he'd jump away and spin in a circle. He still had the kitten. Darned dog.

There was a bunch of thick bushes in a long row. I didn't see how to get through them. The field was on the other side. Tucker ran up and down the row, and then he ducked low and ran through. I went to that spot. It was like a short tunnel. I had to crawl through it and drag the shovel behind me. The branches had prickers on them, and they scratched my arms. When I got through the tunnel, I was in a big grassy field. Sure enough, there was one big tree out in the middle. I started to walk to it.

I walked a while, and Tucker and the kitten trotted next to me. I gave up trying to catch him, so he stayed closer. We were about half way to the tree when Tuck stopped and turned around. He wagged his tail hard. It was C.K. coming. We waited for him. He was carrying all kinds of stuff, and I could see string hanging down. He walked fast and was puffing.

"I nearly forgot all this stuff," he said. He was smiling real big. I was happy to see him again. I'd been walking alone for a long time. In his arms he had the can of paint, the paint brush, a screw driver, and a bunch of string. The string was hanging down to his knees. I picked up the loops, and he handed me the whole wad of it. We were happy, and we walked to the tree.

When we got there we hardly said anything to each other. I started digging the hole, and C.K. started making the cross. I watched him while I dug. First he shook the paint can. Then he opened it with the screwdriver. Then he took a long piece of wood and a short piece of wood and painted them with the black paint. *We all like black the best.* He set them up against the tree so they would dry. It was windy, so they dried pretty fast. I kept digging, but I got tired, and I couldn't seem to scoop much dirt each time. All we said to each other were things like, "Good thing it's windy. The paint'll dry fast," and "This dirt is hard," and "Yeah." Tucker lay on the other side of the tree with the kitten between his feet. His tail was still wagging.

When the paint seemed dry enough, C.K. put the two pieces of wood together in a cross. Then he took the string and reached into his pocket and brought out a pocket knife. I was surprised to see the knife. My parents sure wouldn't let me have a knife. He cut off a long piece of string. He wrapped it around the pieces of wood in a criss-cross way. I kept digging. Then, he cut two little chunks out near the bottom of the cross, on the edges. He cut one real long piece of string. He tied one end of it there at the bottom of the cross—real tight. Then he tied the other end to the screwdriver. It was a big screwdriver. Then he tightened both of the knots.

The hole I'd dug was under a very big tree branch. The branch hung down so low, our dads probably could have touched it, and

it stretched way out. I stopped digging. The hole was big enough now, so I stood back. C.K. made three or four big loops with the string and held them in his left hand. He had the screwdriver in his right hand. He tried throwing it over the branch. He missed a bunch of times. I tried to help by saying "Almost!" each time. Finally, it went over. He pulled on it until the cross hung upside down just above our heads. Now we needed the kitten.

I saw a small branch sitting on the ground. It was about the same size as Mommy's training dummies she used with the dogs. I picked it up and called, "Tucker, Tucker, mark!" just like Mommy did when she trained him. He leaped up. He forgot about the kitten, and I threw the branch. He ran after it, and I grabbed the kitten. It was horrible, all slimy and wet and cold. I could see its white skin where the fur was parted all over its body and its big head. I hurried to the hole and set it in and dried my hand on my jeans. C.K. took the shovel and pushed the dirt back in on top of the kitten. When it was all back in, he stomped on it. Tucker was back with the branch in his mouth. He wagged his whole body. He wanted me to throw it again, so I did.

"How about some rocks?" I asked. "Are there any out here?"

"Probably," said C.K. We walked out into the field and found a few rocks. We put them on top of the grave. Tucker was back with the stick, but I didn't throw it anymore. C.K. and I sat down next to each other in front of the grave. Tucker lay down next to me and chewed on his branch.

All the children are here. Probably fifty or sixty of us. Bernice is wearing a black robe with a hood. Jack doesn't have a robe, but he does have a hood on. He keeps telling the children to hush.

"Listen to me," *he says.* "Sing this song: Ten o'clock news just said, 'God has died.' Ten o'clock news just said, 'God has died.' Ten o'clock news just said, 'God has died.' Everybody, come on now. *He sings it very slowly this time and some of the children try to sing along.* "Ten. O. Clock. News. That's right. Good. Just. Said. 'God. Has. Died.' Very good. Now everyone. Ten o'clock news just said, 'God has died.'" *All the children begin to sing this over and over, and soon we are swaying together in time to the music. We sit in a circle around the grave. The whole big circle of children sways*

back and forth, singing. None of us smiles or looks at each other. We just look at Jack and keep singing. Bernice is in the middle. A dead chicken lies on the ground in front of her. It's one of the ones we hatched and raised at the school. A hole is already dug for it, and a black cross sits next to it. She places the chicken into the hole and pushes dirt over it with her hands. We all stop singing. When the hole is all filled in, she holds the cross up in the air. She stands tall and holds the cross above her head with both hands.

"Satan, we love thee. In thy name we sacrifice this creature that we loved. We love you above all. Bless us, Satan," she says. Then she slowly turns the cross upside down and sticks its top end into the grave.

"Children?" Jack demands.

"Bless us, Satan," we say together.

C.K. and I stood up. Tucker stood up and sniffed at the grave. C.K. untied the screwdriver and pulled the cross down.

This seemed like a dumb funeral to me. I wondered if it was the way they did it in C.K.'s church. It sure wasn't like Grandpa's funeral.

"Why did you hang the cross upside down?" I asked.

"That's just the way to do it."

"My Grandpa's funeral was different. We all sang songs about Jesus and prayed, and a minister said a bunch of stuff."

C.K. shrugged. "I guess that's how they do it at our church too." He walked a little ahead of me with the cross and all the other stuff. I pulled the shovel behind me.

4

The best damned thing about Johnnie was that he liked me. No matter what I did, man. Even if he disapproved of something, shit, he might let me know how he felt, but he didn't dislike me for it. Ma was always on me for somethin'. Then she'd yell at Pa for it. Pa just let her be mad and went and did what the hell he wanted. Sometimes it seemed like he just didn't care.

The real problem with this society is the rules. Too many of 'em, and they don't make no sense. Like who you can love and who you can't. We're talkin' about love, man. Love. Who cares who loves who? It's the love that counts. This country sucks. In Sweden and places like that, shit, you can love whoever you want, and no one interferes. I should've moved to Sweden when I was eighteen. Or twelve! That would've been even better. Get the hell outa this shithole.

I remember the look on Johnnie's face the second day he came over. He was all beamin' and glowin'. He was really happy to see me. And Ma wanted me to sit there'n eat! Shit. I wanted to go play. We had this cool plan to bury the dead kitten. Pa understood.

Johnnie had this churchie idea for a funeral, but I liked the way we'd done it at Little Friends. So, I did it that way. I knew it was "bad," so I didn't talk about it much—just did it. He went along with it, but he did that weird spaced-out number again. I didn't care. He liked me and I liked him. It was the start of a great friendship.

———

The funeral was over. I don't think Johnnie liked it. I think he wanted to do it like his grampa's. I thought it was fun, and now I had this cool black cross of my own. I'd always wanted one. I led the way back to my house. "I gotta figure out what to do with this cross," I said.

Johnnie said, "Yeah, you don't want your parents to know about the kitten."

I was thinkin' about a place to hide it. Probably the barn. I led the way to the barn door. Johnnie dragged the shovel all the way. He set it against the doorway and followed me in. I looked around the barn.

"Way up in the rafters might be good," I said. There was a ladder that went way up to the hayloft. I set the other stuff down and put the cross and twine into the front of my jeans. Johnnie followed me to the ladder, and I started climbing up. I was nearly to the top, and then I looked back. Johnnie was standing on the third rung and just lookin' up at me.

"Come on," I said.

"I'm scared," he said.

"You can do it," I said. "It'll be fun up here." He still looked scared. He took three more steps and stopped. I had to talk to him all the way up. It took a long time. Finally he got there. Then he was real happy.

"You're a good leader," he said. "I never climbed a ladder before."

We looked across the hayloft. It was dark way in the back, and there was loose hay all over the floor. There was some pitchforks standing against one wall, and next to them was a big roll of baling twine. We turned back around and looked over the edge. His dog Tucker was down there whinin'. The dog put his front feet on the ladder and looked up at us. Then he hopped up and down and whined some more.

"Poor Tuck," said Johnnie. "He wants to come up too." He treated that dog like a friend.

I started looking for a place to hide the cross. There was some old bales of hay stacked way in the corner. I went over to them, and Johnnie followed me. It was dark and hard to see. I held the string and let the cross fall down behind the bales. Then I tied the end to the string on the top bale. That way I could get it out later.

I was glad to have it hid. Johnnie didn't say nothin', so we started to go back down. That is, *I* started to go back down. I went

half-way down and looked up to see if he was comin'. He hadn't even stepped onto the ladder yet. "Oh, geez," I said. "Not again." He was froze. "C'mon, you can do it. It's just like goin' up except it's backwards." He wouldn't even talk. Geez, I thought. Now what? So, I went back up and showed him how to grab the top step with his hands. I suppose the tricky part was steppin' off the hayloft onto that first step. It scared me too the first time. Like, what if you slipped and missed the step? But I had to act like it was no big deal.

"Watch. It's easy," I said and showed him where to put his hands and then his first foot. I went down a couple steps. He grabbed the top rung with his hands and then really froze. He couldn't take the first step. And he couldn't get back. He was all sorta twisted and froze. His feet was on the hayloft and his hands was on the ladder.

"I can't," he said. He sounded calm the first time he said it.

So I kept encouragin' him. I could tell he wanted to come down. He just couldn't move his legs. The way he was was worse than gettin' back or goin' down. Then I started gettin' mad. "Just move your right foot over to this step here," I said and patted the board. "I'll hold your foot if you'll put it here. Come on."

"I can't." He was startin' to sound really scared.

"You can't stay like that."

"I can't move." He started to cry.

"You have to," I yelled at him.

"Get my mommy!"

"Your mommy? What's she gonna do?"

"Mommy!" he started yellin'. He was startin' to shake. I thought, oh geez, what if he falls?

"I'll go get help," I said. "Don't move." And I hurried down the ladder. I wondered, should I get his ma or should I get my pa? His ma might not let him come over again, so I decided my pa would be better. I ran to the house and walked in the back door real slow. Ma and Christine was talkin' about havin' babies. They looked at me.

"Gotta go to the bathroom," I said. They smiled and went on talkin'. I went up to the second floor. Pa was whackin' at a wall.

I put my hand on his arm. "Pa, you gotta come out to the barn. But don't tell Ma and Christine. Johnnie's stuck on the hayloft and can't get down. He's cryin'. You gotta come. But don't tell, okay?"

We went out the front door so we didn't have to go past the mothers. As soon as we got outside, we walked real fast. I explained, "Pa, he wanted to go up there and I told him 'no.' He wanted to see what was up there, and I said 'no we shouldn't.' But he went up anyway. I followed him only part way up. I never even made it to the hayloft, and he decided to come back down. He got scared and is sorta stuck up there—between the ladder and the loft. He's cryin'." We hurried into the barn. Thank God he was still there, in the same position. Twisted and cryin'.

"Hold on, son!" Pa yelled to him. He ran up the ladder and grabbed Johnnie around the middle. He brought Johnnie down in front of him and set his feet on one of the steps. He kept his arm around him all the way down. So Johnnie really did climb down by hisself. I thought that was good.

When they was all the way down, Johnnie stood there lookin' real white, and his face was all blank. He couldn't even say, "Thank you" to Pa. He did try to smile, but it looked goofy.

Pa said to him, "You okay?" Johnnie sorta nodded yes. "You know you shouldn't go up there. There's no rail to keep you from fallin' off. You could've been killed. The same is true for both of you." He looked at me hard.

"We won't do it again, Pa. I promise," I said. He put his hand on my head for a second. Then he walked away. He stopped at the door.

"How was fishin'?" he asked.

"We ain't gone yet," I said.

"Poles are in the house, you know."

"Thanks, Pa," I said. He kept walkin'.

Johnnie still looked kinda bad. "What would you like to do now?" I asked. He shrugged. "We could go fishin'. If you want."

"Sure," he said. He still looked white.

I put my hand on his shoulder. "Sorry I scared you," I said.

"Sorry I was a chicken," he said. He smiled a little.

I put my hands under my armpits and flapped my elbows. "Bawk bawk!" I said. We laughed. We headed for the house to get the fishin' poles. "Want a cupcake?" I asked.

"Sure," he said. We ran into the kitchen. Ma had a box of chocolate cupcakes on top of the refrigerator. Her and Christine was still talkin' about babies. And breastfeeding. Ma thought it was gross. Christine said it was the best thing for the baby and the mother. She was tellin' Ma why. Ma had a funny look on her face. I reached for the cupcakes.

"Wait a minute, young man. Ain't you the one didn't finish your supper?" Ma said.

"Aw, Ma, please. Johnnie ate his supper and can have one. He won't eat one unless I do, right, Johnnie?" Johnnie nodded yes.

Ma crunched up her shoulders and got that silly look on her face. She rolled her eyes at Christine and said, "I suppose." We took the cupcakes and ran out again.

We barely got out the door when I remembered. "Wait. The fishin' poles." I started laughin'. "We gotta go back in." Johnnie started laughin', too, and we could hardly walk we was laughin' so hard. We went back in the door and I stopped again. "Wait, " I said. I couldn't talk I was gigglin' too hard. "I don't know where they are!" We both bent over and laughed so hard it came from our bellies. We couldn't stand up and had to lean against the wall. Johnnie's face got real red and tears ran down. He couldn't talk.

"Let's—let's—" I couldn't talk either. Real fast, I said "Let'sgoaskPa." We bent over again. Tears ran down my face, too, and I couldn't catch my breath. I waved my hand for him to follow me. We sorta fell through the kitchen, squealin' and gaspin'. Ma and Christine watched us, and they couldn't help laughin' too.

"We need to go in about ten minutes," Christine called to Johnnie.

We hurried upstairs to where Pa was still whackin' at walls. We was still gigglin' about nothin'.

"Pa, where are the fishin' poles?" All of a sudden that sounded real funny to me, and I looked at Johnnie. He looked like his face was gonna burst. It did and we bent over again and laughed. My

nose and my eyes was runnin' now, and I sniffed hard. Johnnie burst out again. It was awful. We just couldn't stop. I looked at Pa, and he was laughin' too.

"Just inside the back door," he said. "What's so funny?"

"Everything!" I said, and we ran out. Down the stairs, through the living room and back through the kitchen. Ma and Christine stopped to look at us again. We waved as we ran past them.

"They're right there!" said Johnnie. We'd been past 'em four times and hadn't seen 'em.

"Oh, geez," I said. We grabbed two of them and ran out. "The pond's that way," I pointed back behind the house. We ran all crooked, tryin' to carry the fishin' poles and laugh at the same time.

We had to walk real careful through a patch of raspberry brambles. They kept grabbin' our clothes and sometimes our skin. Johnnie got scratched a few times. I was afraid he might start cryin' or somethin'. But he was pretty brave. We went through some more woods and bushes, and finally we got to the pond. We'd stopped laughin' by then, but I felt like gigglin' some more. We set the poles down and I showed him how to pull the line out at the ends. He'd never fished before. I showed him the hook and the bobber. I started to show him how to put a worm on.

"Oh, no," I said.

"What?" He looked so serious I couldn't stand it. I burst out laughin' again. This was so funny. After lyin' and everything about using the shovel to dig worms, we never did it and here we was needin' worms and we didn't have any. And no shovel, either.

I was belly laughin' again. "No worms!" I burst out. "And no shovel to dig 'em." Johnnie cracked up. We laughed so hard we fell to our knees and then rolled on the ground.

"No worms!" he blurted out, and then he made a funny snorting sound. I laughed so hard I couldn't breath. He got all red in the face again.

I nearly blew my nose on myself. Every noise or word or snort we made made us laugh harder. We just rolled on the ground and

laughed. Finally, I think we just ran out of energy. We just laid there and breathed. It was so good to have a best friend.

I think we just sorta spaced out for a while. It was warm out, and we just laid there. Then Johnnie screamed. Then he giggled. I opened my eyes and sat up. Tucker had found us. His whole body was waggin', and he was lickin' Johnnie's ears. Johnnie went "blaaaah" and wiped his ears with his sleeve. Tucker came over to me and licked my face and ears too. I guessed it was time to go. We picked up our poles. We both sighed at the same time. Then we giggled a little and walked back.

Ma and Christine was outside callin' us. We hadn't heard 'em at all. They looked mad and said they'd been callin' us for ten minutes. Oh well.

Johnnie went home, and I didn't know when he would come again. No one said nothin'.

5

Every day, as I deal with my clients' emotional problems, and when I think back on my and C.K.'s childhoods, the beauty of defense mechanisms never ceases to awe me. When something is too emotionally painful or unacceptable to us, our psyches cope by defending against it in various ways. If we are suffering from low self-esteem, we'll go buy a fancy car that says "I'm special." If we were stripped of our power as children, we'll become body builders or black belts in karate. If our mothers or fathers told us we were stupid as children, we'll fly into a rage when our boss says the same thing. And if something happened to us that was so horrible and unacceptable to remember, we may conveniently repress it or be incapable of remembering it.

———————

Every week, Mommy or Daddy took me to see Louise. I knew she wanted to talk about what happened to me at Little Friends. And every week I told her that they fed me some bad food once, and I threw up. That's all I knew.

This week, I was excited to tell her about C.K. "And he went to Little Friends too." I thought this would make her happy. Every time I went to her office, she had me pound on clay and punch the Jack punching bag. I knew she'd be happy to have this to talk about. I watched her face when I told her. It got all bright.

"Really?" she asked. "How do you know he went there?"

"His mother told my mother."

"Oh." The bright face went away.

"He's very nice. He has new kittens. His grandpa died and left them an old pink house, and they're tearing it all apart so they can fix it and move in. I'll have a neighbor!"

"Do you remember seeing him at Little Friends? Did you and he play together there?"

"No. I don't remember ever seeing him before."

"Oh." She looked sadder. "Well, tell me all about him."

"He has real blond hair and he's real nice. But he's older than I am. That's too bad. But we laugh a lot." I tried to think of more. I tried to think of something she'd like. It was hard. All I could think of were the good things. "He's brave, and he knows a lot about kittens and about climbing ladders and fishing." Then I remembered the dead kitten.

"What's the matter?" she asked. "You look real serious all of a sudden."

"Oh. I don't know. I just thought of something."

"Would you like to tell me about it? You don't have to, you know. But I'm very interested and excited about your new friend. I know this is very important to you—to have a neighbor. Did he do something to make you sad? Or scared? Or mad?"

"Well, sort of, " I said. "Sad. And scared. And mad, I guess."

"Wow. That's a lot of feelings."

"Yeah," I said and laughed a little.

"Was it funny, too?"

"Oh, no! He killed the poor little thing."

"Poor little thing?"

"A kitten. A little kitten. Just two days old."

"Really? He killed it?"

"Twisted its head real hard."

She made a painful face. "Why did he do that?"

"I don't know. Well, you see, we were sort of playing this game—" How was I going to tell her this? "It's pretty complicated. It was an accident."

"Oh. An accident. Well, that's good. I'd hate to think your new friend would kill a kitten on purpose. That would be pretty awful."

"Yeah," I said. I started thinking about C.K. Maybe there was something wrong with him. I started thinking about how he twisted the head, even when I told him to stop. I started getting

scared about him. I decided to not tell Louise any more. I didn't want him to be bad.

"Well, is there anything else you'd like to tell me about him?" She always looked at me like she loved me. I loved her.

"He lies to his parents."

"Ooo. Really? Like, what about?"

"Nothing important, I guess. Just stuff like his dad asked what we were going to use the shovel for. And he said we were going to dig worms to go fishing. That was a lie."

"Really? What was the shovel for?"

"To bury the kitten. We had a funeral for it."

"Well, that's nice. Where did you have the funeral?"

"Out behind his barn. In a field. Under a tree."

"Want to tell me about it? Did it make you sad?"

"No, not sad. It was kind of funny because Tucker took the kitten away and wouldn't give it back. I had to trick him by throwing a stick. Then I got the kitten back." She nodded and looked interested. "I dug the hole, and C.K. made the cross. It took a long time because we had to wait for the paint to dry, and I wasn't very good at digging a hole."

"He painted the cross? That's nice. What color did he paint it?"

"Black." Louise's eyes got bigger and she wrote something down. I could tell she felt real serious, but she was trying to look happy. She smiled and said, "Go on. I like your story."

"What did you write down?" I asked. She didn't write things down very often.

She acted like she didn't know what to say. Then she said, "Sometimes you say things that are very interesting to me, and I want to remember to think about them again, so I write myself a reminder."

"Oh," I said. I knew she thought the black cross was something special. I wondered for a second why C.K. wanted to paint the cross black instead of brown or white or pink. But I didn't care. That's just what he wanted.

"Go on," she said. "Tell me about the funeral."

"Well, after we got the kitten back from Tucker, I put it in the hole, and we covered it up. We put rocks on top, and C.K. put a rope on the end of the cross and threw it over the tree branch so it would hang upside down, right over the grave. Then he took it down again and we went back to his house. That's all." I could tell Louise wanted to write something down again. She picked up her pen, but she didn't write.

Then it was time for Mommy to come in. Louise always said I could tell Mommy what we talked about; but she said I didn't have to. She said what I told her would be our secret unless I wanted to share it. When Mommy came in she looked a little different than the other times—sort of worried and happy at the same time.

Louise said that we'd had an interesting discussion. "Would you like to tell your mother what we talked about today?"

"Just C.K., Mommy. I told her about my new friend."

"Yes," said Mommy to Louise. "We're pretty happy for Johnnie. Ever since we moved in we've wished for a neighbor for him to play with. And now it looks like he has one." Mommy smiled at me. "So, what wonderful things did you tell Louise about him? The torn-up house? The kittens? Their fishing pond?" She looked at Louise. "He's teaching Johnnie how to fish. I don't even know how to fish."

"That's wonderful," said Louise. She looked at me to see if I would tell more. I wasn't going to. "Anything else, then?" she asked. She always asked this before she and Mommy talked alone. She always said she'd keep secret whatever I wanted her to. Mostly I believed her. I went down to the kids' room to play with the toys. When Mommy came to get me, she didn't look very happy, and she didn't talk very much.

I didn't play with C.K. for a few days. Mommy said they were probably busy. At suppertime the phone rang. Mommy said it was for me. I knew it would be either Grandma or Daddy. "Hello?" I said.

"Hi, Johnnie, this is C.K. We just got a phone. Ma said I could call you and see if you can come play."

Mommy watched me. She was smiling and looked like she expected something to happen. "It's C.K.," I whispered to her. She nodded hard and smiled big. "He wants to know if I can go play."

"See if he can come up here. I can drive down and get him."

"My mommy wants to know if you could come here. She can come get you," I said.

"Just a minute. I'll ask my ma." When he came back he said, "Okay, I can come. When?"

"When?" I asked Mommy.

"In a few minutes. As soon as you finish eating," she answered.

I was so excited. C.K. and I hung up, and I started wondering if he'd like it at my house. I ate real fast. Then we got in the car and drove down to get him. I was thinking about my best toys. I had a lot of them and was pretty sure he'd like them.

When we got there, C.K. was standing in the front yard. He ran and jumped into the back seat. "Where are your parents?" Mommy asked.

"In the house," said C.K.

Mrs. Bookout came out the front door. She was bouncing and smiling. "When would you like me to bring him back?" Mommy asked.

"We can pick him up on our way home, if that's okay. About nine o'clock?"

"Fine. Leland should be home any minute, so I've got to run. Maybe we can chat when you stop later?"

"Sure. You behave yourself," Mrs. Bookout said to C.K. "Don't be a brat."

"Geez," said C.K.

When we got to my house, Daddy was just getting out of his car. I jumped out of the car and ran to him and leaped. He always caught me and swung me around. That feeling zipped through my stomach. He hugged me a long time and set me down. Then he saw C.K.

"Hey, Buddy, how're you doing?" He sounded friendly. I kind of thought he didn't really want me to play with C.K., but he seemed friendly now.

———————

It's such a predicament to know something is not good for your child when your child is so thrilled about it. I know, now that

I have kids of my own, what my parents were struggling with. C.K. was not the kind of child they would have chosen as my best friend, and yet I'm sure they shared my joy and enthusiasm. Sometimes they encouraged our camaraderie, and other times they discouraged it. I saw no pattern, no rhyme, nor reason to these ups and downs. I suppose it depended on what was on their minds at that moment. This day, my father was initially disappointed to see C.K. at our house, then changed his attitude when he saw my joy.

———————

"Daddy, look! C.K. came over. I'm going to show him all my toys. He gets to stay until nine o'clock!" Daddy smiled and laughed with me. Mommy came up and gave Daddy a hug.

"You had supper?"

"No, I didn't stop. Is there anything?"

"Sure is," she said, and they walked into the house. He had his arm around her.

"Are they always this nice to each other?" asked C.K.

"Yeah, pretty much," I said. "Aren't yours?"

"No. They's always fightin' about somethin'. Sometimes Ma throws frying pans at Pa."

"Really? What does he do?"

"Nothin' much. Ducks and walks away."

I couldn't imagine that.

6

Johnnie's parents was so different. They didn't call Johnnie names. Or each other names. And his dogs didn't jump on me. And his house cat never had kittens.

"How come she ain't had any kittens?" I asked him when he showed me his cat. She was Siamese and her name was Emily.

"My mom had her spayed," Johnnie said.

"Oh, yeah, Brandy, the Golden Retriever, she's been spaded. I didn't think cats got spaded."

"That's funny," said Johnnie. "Our girl dogs haven't been spayed. I guess we're opposite." He laughed.

"Yeah."

"So, what do you want to do?"

"I dunno," I said. Show me around your house."

———

That damned house had more books than a fuckin' library. Every damn room had at least one wall full of book shelves. His ma and pa's room had one whole wall from top to bottom filled with books. Johnnie's room had half a wall full of books. Then the parents had a "library." All four fuckin' walls had books, from top to bottom. The kitchen had a section of books, mostly cookbooks and books on natural foods and "eating healthfully." When we walked into his parents' bathroom, I couldn't believe it. I opened one of the cupboards and guess what! Books. Johnnie said they was all humorous books. What the hell for? So they could laugh while they shit? Even the laundry room had two shelves of books.

———

"Don't you guys ruin your eyes readin' all them books?" I asked.

Johnnie shrugged. "I don't think so. Daddy got glasses when he was five, and Mommy doesn't wear them at all. She reads as much as he does."

"What about you? You wear glasses?"

"No. Mommy thinks I got her eyes."

"Geez," I said. We were standing in the library. There had to be a million books in there.

"Don't you like books?" he asked.

"Yeah, they're fine. I just don't know how you read so many."

Johnnie shrugged again.

I said, "Ma says they want to put me in the gifted program at school. She said Pa was an honor student in high school. I guess me and you's both smart, huh?" We giggled. I held out my hand for him to "give me five." He did. It felt like we was brothers. I liked bein' smart.

We went up to his room. It didn't really look like any boy's room I ever seen. It was too beautiful. It had a whole wall of big windows, and his curtains was the same material as the bedspreads. The material had a neat pattern—he called it a "geometric pattern"—mostly dark blue with red and yellow and white shapes—triangles and squares and stuff. I coulda spent the whole time just followin' the shapes. My bedspread had baseball bats and footballs on it, and my curtains was just yellow. The bedspread used to belong to my cousin Fred. He was in the Army now.

The walls was all white. He had a big desk with drawers and a chest made of the same wood. Even the bookshelves matched. It was just beautiful. I was afraid to touch anything. There was a telescope by the windows and a long row of shelves with all kinds of toys and games.

"What would you like to do?" he asked.

"Wow. I don't know. There's so much here." Just then Johnnie's ma came in.

"Have you had supper, C.K.? I'm warming up some stew for Dr. Ambrose. Would you like some?"

That sounded great. Ma'd made liver for supper, and I hate liver, so I was hungry.

"Okay," I said. "Johnnie, is that okay? I'm starvin'."

"Sure," he said. "Maybe I'll have some more." His ma looked at him like she didn't believe him.

"I thought you hated my stew," she said to him.

"I liked it tonight," he said.

"Mm hmm," she said and raised her eyebrows.

Except for my rich Aunt Clare's house in Connecticut, this was the nicest fucking house I'd ever been in. 'Cept for all them damn books. They sort of cluttered the place up.

They had this huge, modern kitchen in the same big room as the dining area. On the other side of the dining area was a screened-in porch. It was really a balcony that overlooked their pond. There was another porch just like it off the master bedroom upstairs, right above the dining area. But it was all done in rustic wood, so it didn't come off like snobby and shit. The first time I sat in that dining room, I decided, damn, I would do whatever it took to be rich enough to have a house just like this when I grew up.

Johnnie's ma shooed us into the bathroom to wash our hands. Johnnie showed me which soap to use and which towel to use. Then we went and sat down at the table with his pa. We each had a placemat with flowers all over it and a cloth napkin that matched. I thought, wow, I better try 'n' remember what Ma told me about table manners. I took the napkin and put it in my lap. Then I tried to remember to not put my elbows on the table.

Christine brought this big shiny pot to the table and started dishing stew out. Oh boy, beef stew, I thought. I was real hungry and couldn't wait to put a nice big juicy piece of meat in my mouth. She dished some onto Leland's plate first. It smelled real good. Then she took my plate.

"Are you real hungry?" she asked. "Do you want a lot?"

Susan L Metzger

"Yes, please," I said. So she put about four big spoonfuls on my plate. I had my fork all ready to stab a nice big piece of meat. I looked at the plate of stew. My fork was in the air, all ready. I looked and looked. No meat. First I thought maybe she'd just missed it. Then I looked at Leland's plate. I thought maybe he'd gotten it all by mistake. He didn't have none either. I looked at Johnnie's plate. None there neither. I cleared my throat so he'd look at me.

I whispered, "Where's the meat?"

He whispered back, "There isn't any. We're vegetarians. We don't eat meat, except Mommy lets me have cheeseburgers at McDonalds sometimes. Every once in a while Daddy has a steak, but not too often.

"What's the matter, fellas?" Leland asked.

"C.K. was looking for meat. I told him we're vegetarians."

Leland laughed. "Most of the time, anyway. C.K., this is very good stew. See those brownish squares in there? That's fried tofu. It's very good and is almost like meat, except it's made from soy beans. It's a lot more healthful for you than meat. Try it."

I saw lots of carrots, peas, potatoes, green beans, broccoli, and then the brown squares. First I ate some potato, then a carrot and some peas. I hate broccoli. Then I got sorta brave, and I stabbed a brown square and put it in my mouth. It was sort of chewy. It tasted pretty good, but I swallowed it fast. Then I ate some more potatoes, peas and carrots, and green beans. Then more tofu. I sort of got used to it. Pretty soon the plate was all cleaned up except for the broccoli. At least there was milk to drink. That was normal, any-way. It wasn't such a bad meal. I felt better. And I kept my elbows off the table the whole time.

I said, "Thank you, Christine, that was very good."

She laughed. "Wait till you try my soy burgers. You'll love them."

Johnnie groaned. "McDonald's is better," he said. They all laughed, and Johnnie and I went back up to his room.

We got out his He-Man figures and his Castle Greyskull. He said he'd be Skeletor and I could be He-Man. That was nice, but I really liked being Skeletor better. We played for a while. He didn't

do a very good job at bein' Skeletor cuz he just wasn't evil enough. I'd practiced with my cousin Skip. He was twelve and really knew how to be the "evil Skeletor." So, I showed Johnnie.

Every once in a while his ma or pa walked past his door and stuck their heads in. "How you doin'?" they asked.

"Fine," we'd say, and they'd walk away. One time, though, I know they was both outside Johnnie's room. I could tell cuz first his ma poked her head in, then his pa did, and they was both headed in the same direction. I could hear 'em whisperin' down the hall. I don't know what they thought we was doin'. That's one thing I can say for my parents. They didn't spy on me.

After a while, when I was sure Johnnie was gettin' the hang of bein' evil, we decided to go outside. I wanted to see his pony. He said he was a nice pony—Stitches was his name—but he didn't like to ride very much. It was kind of a long walk out there. He showed me his English saddle. He said it was a real good one cuz it was made in Germany. But he said his ma was gonna sell it cuz he never used it. He had a riding teacher and everything. Mostly, he said, he liked to ride for about five minutes, and then he was ready to get off.

His barn was all on one floor, not like mine. Mine had a first floor, a hayloft, and a basement where horses or cows could come in and out. His barn had a huge indoor riding arena at one end and eight big stalls at the other end. Their hay was all stacked in big square piles at one end of the arena. Johnnie said we could climb on them. He said the bales was stacked a certain way to make the pile real sturdy.

We climbed to the top. His goofy dog, Tucker, came too. Tucker got to the top before we did and looked like King of the Mountain. Funny dog. He stood up there and looked down at us. His floppy ears sorta hung across his face and made him look stupid.

"Look how stupid your dog looks," I said.

Johnnie smiled and said, "Duuuh," and made a goofy face. We started laughin' again.

I said, "Duuuh," and held my paws up and wiggled my rear end just like Tucker.

Johnnie did a "He he he!" belly laugh, and I burst out laughin' harder. We both bent over and fell on our knees. We looked up at Tucker, and he was still doin' it. God, did we laugh hard. He looked so stupid. Tucker musta thought somethin' was wrong cuz he came and licked our faces. We finally made it to the top and just looked around. I knew this would be a special place. We sat there a long time and didn't say nothin'.

The next pile over was lower. The way someone had taken bales off it left a sorta little room. We went down there and sat in the little room. It looked like we could make a cave out of it if we could move some bales around. We talked about it and figured we'd only need three more bales. I went to pick one up like I seen my Uncle Jerry do at his farm. I grabbed both pieces of twine in both hands. When I went to lift it, nothing happened, except my arms felt like they was gonna pull right out, and the strings hurt my hands.

"Damn!" I said, just like Uncle Jerry.

Johnnie sorta gasped. "Do you swear?" he asked.

"No. Not really. Sorry." I thought it sounded cool, but I guess he didn't like it.

We started tryin' to move the bales around together. We'd grunt and groan and laugh. Laughing made it harder. But we made such funny noises, it was hard not to laugh. So, we'd get one end up and push the whole thing over. Then push and pull it to where we wanted it. After we moved the three bales and all our gruntin' and goanin' and laughin', we finally had a cave. We climbed in together. For a while we pretended we was cavemen. We talked to each other in grunts and sign language. The only words we said was "fire" and "kill."

Johnnie climbed out to go kill some food. I was kneeling in the cave. He said I looked like one of his ma's dogs in a cage, and he pretended to lock the door. I woofed and panted. Then I said for him to get in. I wanted to see what I had looked like. I climbed out and he climbed in. I locked the pretend door. He woofed and panted like I did. Then he did his weird thing again. He just spaced out, like he didn't see me. This time I tried talkin' to him.

"Johnnie, what's the matter?" I whispered.

He didn't answer. He just looked right through me.

"Johnnie, wake up! Say something." Nothin'. He looked kinda sad, like he'd done somethin' bad. He just kept starin' ahead. So, I just sat and watched him. He'd blink every once in a while, but five or ten minutes musta gone by and that's all he did. I didn't know what to do. Finally, I reached through the door and touched his shoulder. "Come on," I said.

He blinked once and looked at me. He was still spaced out for a few seconds, then he smiled and crawled out.

"What was you doin'?" I asked.

"Doing? Being a dog, same as you." He smiled. "What do you want to do now?"

I didn't know. I didn't like what he just done and kinda wanted to go back to the house, or at least outa the barn. "How about your pond? Let's go see it."

"I'm not supposed to go down there unless Mommy or Daddy comes with me. It's really a peat bog, and the edges fall into the water sometimes. They said I could fall in and get stuck."

"Well, what do you use it for?"

"Mommy trains the dogs in it. And we skate on it in the winter. There's fish in there, but Daddy says they're real little and nobody would want them. He swam in it once. The water's real warm, but it's slimy crawling out because of the peat. He says maybe he'll make a dock some day, with a ladder so we can get in and out." We walked back to the house. "Maybe Daddy will take us down. I can ask him."

We found his pa in the library. He had a magazine open and was talkin' on the phone. He didn't see us or hear us, so we stood in the doorway and listened to him.

"Well, according to Smythe, no one has come up with any cure for the true sociopathic pedophile. We're talking about the guys with no conscience. I know his mother abandoned him when he was in fourth grade." He listened for a while. "I still think he did it without a conscience, and treatment is a waste of time. He belongs in jail. Forever." He listened again, and said "Yeah" and

Susan L Metzger

"Uh huh" every once in a while. "Of course I'll meet with you and Burgess in Boston. Just let me know when."

When he hung up, Johnnie asked him to take us down to the pond. His pa said as soon as he went to the bathroom, he'd do that. He walked out of the library. I stood lookin' at all the books again. I looked at the magazine he'd been readin' out of. It said "*The Journal of Interpersonal Violence*." I wasn't sure what "journal" meant, and I knew what "violence" meant, but "interpersonal" meant nothin'. It sounded kind of spooky. It was hard to believe he was readin' stuff about violence. He seemed like he wouldn't know about it at all.

To this fuckin' day, I remember what Johnnie did down at his pond, man. I remember not wantin' to play with him after that. I was sure somethin' was wrong with him. He about scared the hell outa me. It made no sense. At the time, anyway. Now, I guess I realize how fucked up we both were. Him more than me. I guess. At the time, anyway.

Johnnie's pa led the way down to the pond. We walked down some steps that was made out of railroad ties. They was pretty far apart, so we had to take two steps for every step down. Leland kept tellin' us—me, really, cuz Johnnie knew this all already—about how you can be walkin' along the edge of the pond, and the peat can just break away and fall in the water. So, he said we shouldn't walk right on the edge. He said there was a couple of places at one end, and on the island, where the ground seemed just fine, and then all of a sudden one day, his foot went through, all the way up to his knee. He said he didn't go down there by hisself anymore.

"Could all of me just fall through?" I asked. I wasn't sure I wanted to go down there.

"I don't think you're heavy enough, but I'm not sure. That's why we never go down alone. You boys remember that, okay?" We nodded hard.

Johnnie's three dogs came along, of course. When they ran next to us, I could feel the ground shake. Josie went sniffin' along the bank, tryin' to catch frogs. A frog would leap and she'd snap her teeth at it, but she never caught one. Tucker and Tilly leaped in and swam out to the island.

I could hear a big ole bullfrog croakin' off to the right.

"Can we try to catch him?" I asked.

"You can't catch them," Leland said. "You can't even see them. At least I've never been able to find one to see it. All you do is hear them."

"May we try?" I asked.

"Sure, we can try," he said. So, we started walkin' toward the bullfrog. I followed behind Leland, and Johnnie was behind me. We tiptoed through the tall grass. The bullfrog would stop croakin', and we'd all stop and wait and listen. We didn't say a word. As soon as he croaked, we'd start again, tiptoein' real careful.

We was headed right for him, and it sounded like we was gettin' real close, when Johnnie shouts real loud, "My ball! My blue ball!"

Leland and I turned around and there was Johnnie smilin' real big and holdin' this blue dog ball up for us to see. "I found it," he said. He looked real happy.

"The bullfrog," I whispered. I didn't care about no blue ball. We was so close to the frog—a great big, huge bullfrog.

Then, to make it worse, we hear Christine off behind us. "The blue ball!" she yells. She came traipsin' through the grass grinnin' big as Johnnie. "Tucker!" she yells, "Your blue ball! Tucker!" Tucker came swimmin' back from the island. He came out all drippin' wet and ran right up to her. It seemed like he was grinnin' too. So much for the bullfrog.

Christine took the ball from Johnnie and started wavin' it around in front of Tucker's face. Tucker got all excited. She kept makin' a motion like she was gonna throw it in the pond for him to go get.

"Don't throw it in the pond!" Johnnie screamed.

"It'll float," Christine said.

"No it won't!" Johnnie looked real scared about it.

"Of course it will," she said, and she threw it into the water. It didn't float at all. It sank like a big hunk of rock. Tucker jumped in after it, stupid dog.

I guess I'd heard about temper tantrums before. And maybe that's what Johnnie was doin'. But somehow I think this was different. First, he yelled, "Dagnabbit!" Then he jumped up and down and screamed. He started yellin', "No, no, no!" And he just jumped up and down so he could stamp both his feet at the same time. He kept screamin' until his voice got all hoarse. He was cryin' at the same time, too. He'd yell at his mother, "Why did you do that! My ball! It's gone!" Then he'd scream some more in that hoarse voice and stamp both his feet at the same time. I thought he wouldn't ever stop. He was like a wild, crazy, hurt animal or somethin'. I began to get a little scared, like maybe he'd never stop. Maybe he'd just do this forever. I looked at his ma and pa. They almost looked glad that he was actin' like this. They just stood there watchin' him be mad.

Christine said something dumb like, "I'm sorry. I really thought it would float. I'm glad to see you expressing your anger." That was weird. I decided the whole family was weird, and I wanted to go home. So, I started walkin' backwards to sorta move away. Then I turned and walked away fast. I almost reached the steps.

"C.K., wait!" It was Johnnie. I felt like runnin' away from him, but I stopped. He was runnin' right toward me. "Wait," he said. "I'm sorry. My mother just made me so mad. I knew that ball wouldn't float. I've been looking for that ball for a long time. It's really neat because it's solid rubber. And now it's gone." He started cryin' again, but then he swallowed real hard and made hisself stop. I guess I understood. My ma threw my favorite shirt in the fireplace once cuz I left it on the floor. I wanted to grab it outa the fire, but she made me just stand there and watch it burn.

"Maybe she'll get you another one," I said.

"Yeah, probably," he said. He was wipin' the tears off his face. I didn't know what else to say, so we walked up the stairs. When we got to the top, Ma and Pa was there. They was lookin' around, tryin' to find us.

"Where you been?" Ma asked.

"Down at the pond," I said.

"Well, we gotta get goin'. Get in the car." Leland and Christine showed up just as I was gettin' in.

"Bye, C.K." they said. "Maybe you can come back tomorrow."

"Sure," I said. I know I said it kinda soft. I looked at Johnnie. He looked sorta embarrassed. "Bye," I said to him. I kinda wanted to pat him on the shoulder or somethin'.

"Bye," he said. "See ya."

We drove away.

PART TWO

7

Four years later, when I was in fifth grade and C.K. was in seventh, two major events shook our relationship. The first was his parents' divorce. The second was Harry. Perhaps an underlying third event was his earlier arrival at adolescence than mine.

The first event that seemed to eventually lead to Walter and Gloria Bookout's breakup was the arrival of Ladonna at our horse farm. "Cross-Eyed Ladonna" is what we fondly called her behind her back. She came to our door one day looking for a place to board her horse. I remember how beautiful she was. She had shiny, shoulder-length, dark auburn hair and the voluptuous body of a 1950's movie star. She was friendly and outgoing, had a beaming smile, and crossed eyes. I remember being smitten the moment my mother opened the door and Ladonna was standing there.

———————

"Hi," she said. She had sparkly white teeth and pretty pink lipstick. I saw that her eyes were crossed, but I didn't care. I was staring at her hair. I'd never seen hair this color. It was a red-brown and so shiny, there seemed to be a gold halo around her head. She kind of wiggled like Mrs. Bookout, but she was bigger, and her chest stuck out more.

My mother said, "Hi. Can I help you?"

"Walter Bookout and I work together, and I'm lookin' for a place to keep my horse. He said you might have room here. He said this is a real nice place." She had a southern accent. "Oh," she said and giggled kind of like Mrs. Bookout, "my name's Ladonna Michaux." She held out her hand to shake my mom's hand.

My mom shook her hand and said, "I'm Christine Ambrose. Are you new to the area? You have a southern accent." My mom didn't like southern accents. She said people that had them

sounded unintelligent. She also said she was wrong, and this was just a prejudice of hers.

"Oh, no," said Ladonna. My mother's from Kentucky, but my father's from France. I guess I just picked up my ma's way of talkin'. I grew up here. Lived here all my life."

Some doctor told my mom and dad that there were a lot of "second generation Appalachian folks" here. He said their parents had come here to harvest the fruit crops north of us in Michigan, and then they stayed. My mom didn't like them very much. I don't think my dad did either, but he didn't say much. My mom called them "hillbillies" once in a while and got mad when they drove their old run-down cars too fast. She said all the women were fat and disgusting. Ladonna wasn't fat and disgusting.

"Tell me about your horse," said my mom.

"She's a black mare. A walkin' horse."

"A Tennessee Walker?"

"Uh huh, and she's real sweet. I wanna breed her next Spring."

"Well, I don't know if we can accommodate a foal," said my mom. "But we'll see. A mare and foal really need a double stall, and we don't have one."

Ladonna looked disappointed. "Well, maybe it could just be born out in the pasture?"

"My mare foaled out in a pasture when I was a kid, and they were both fine."

"You've had a foal before?" Ladonna perked up and got all excited. "Daryl and I can't have children, and I guess I'm just so excited about this, I really want to find a way."

My mom started liking her better. "I'm sorry to hear that. How long have you been married?"

"Ten years. There's just nothin' they can do."

"Well, I'm sorry." My mom waited a second. "Come out to the barn and I'll show you around." She and Ladonna walked away. I hurried and got some shoes so I could follow. I was sort of out of breath by the time I caught up. I walked behind them for a while and just watched Ladonna's butt. Her jeans were real tight, and she just looked good. Her beautiful hair sort of bounced as she

walked. She was real curvy. I couldn't take my eyes off of her. I guess I must have looked kind of stupid. When they talked, I just stood there and watched her. I watched her pink lips talk. And I watched her hair swish around on her shoulders. And I kept noticing how big her chest was. It just stuck out real far. And I guess I noticed her eyes once in a while. They were a real pretty blue, but one would cross, and then when she looked a different way, the other one crossed. But I didn't care.

My mom asked her when she wanted to move the horse in, and she said that evening if it was okay. My mom said sure. They seemed to get along and laughed and joked around.

"Do you have a trailer?" Mom asked.

"No, but Walter said he'd get her for me. He's gonna bring me some hay too, until I get my own—twenty bales or so to get started."

"We can sell you hay. Most of the boarders here buy it from us. But that's very nice of him."

"Well, he's just that kind of guy." Ladonna laughed like she wasn't sure my mom liked her.

"Yes, he seems very nice. How long have you two worked together?"

"Oh, about six months. He's my supervisor. He's the one that interviewed me for the job. God! I was so nervous. But he really put me at ease. He's so nice." She giggled and wiggled some more.

"Yes, he seems to be. I don't always know what he's thinking, though. He's quiet but always so pleasant." My mom was serious, but Ladonna just giggled again.

———————

She was my first love, and I used to watch out the window for her car coming up the driveway. Then I'd run out to the barn and hang around her. It probably drove her nuts, but she was always respectful. When she spent a lot of time brushing her mare, I'd get Stitches out and groom him too. I even tried riding a few times when she was riding, but I only got in her way.

Walter Bookout was there quite often, which was fine with me because he usually brought C.K. It was funny how he always explained his reasons for coming over, though. Clinically, he was exhibiting the defense mechanism justification. It worked for him, but even as a kid, I probably sensed the truth. He either had to repair a piece of tack for Ladonna or brought sacks of grain or those huge bags of shavings for her stall. She had a VW Rabbit, and he had a pick-up truck, so it appeared logical that he did these things for her. Besides, our barn was on his way home. C.K. and I were happy to climb to the top of the hay pile and talk. We were too young to catch the glances of affection between them or the brushing of one against the other. I guess we probably saw those things, but they didn't register.

Of course, most practitioners in my field realize that children have the uncanny ability to know when these sorts of things are going on. Maybe C.K. and I sensed it, but I have no recollection of that. I was infatuated with Ladonna, and she could do no wrong. Even when she announced to my mother that she and her husband were divorcing, I knew her husband was the one at fault. I only saw him one time at the barn, and I didn't care for him.

One morning she arrived before I left for school. This was unusual, so I ran out there. My mother thought it odd, too, and went upstairs to get her shoes. I entered the barn a few minutes before she arrived and slid open the big door. Ladonna's mare stood in the aisle on the crossties, and as Ladonna brushed her, she was sniffling.

———

"Hi, Ladonna!" I said.

She jumped. Her eyes were red and her face looked all streaky. She turned around right away and started brushing the mare's rear end. Her back was to me. I wished I hadn't come and didn't know what to say. I almost turned around and left.

"What're you up to this morning, Johnnie?" she asked without looking at me.

"I was just getting ready to leave for school. I saw your car." I was just about to ask her if she was okay, and then my mom came in.

"Honestly!" Ladonna said under her breath. She heard my mom, but she still didn't turn around.

"Good morning, Ladonna. Everything okay?" my mom asked.

"No, everything's not okay," she answered and finally turned around.

My mom saw her red eyes and streaky face. "Oh, what's wrong?" she asked.

Ladonna started to cry real hard. She put her face in the mare's long mane. She grabbed a hand full of it and just hung on. "It's Daryl. We're splittin' up."

My mom said, "Johnnie, go get in the car. I'll be right there. Did you brush your teeth? Go do that first. Don't forget your lunch. Go."

I didn't want to go. I wanted to help take care of Ladonna. Actually, I got a little excited, like maybe she could be mine now. Kinda goofy, I knew. I opened the big sliding door far enough to squeeze through and slid it shut. I started to go back to the house, but then I realized I could hear them talking. So, I stood there and listened.

"What happened?" my mom asked.

"Oh, it's been comin' on for a long time. We just been tryin' to work out a settlement so the lawyers don't take so much. Everything was goin' okay until he told me this morning he wants my aquarium. And he wants me to sell her and give him half the money. I can't sell her. She means everything to me. And that aquarium is mine. I've had it twelve years, since before we was married." She cried real hard now. Then she said, "And here I am thirty-two years old. I ain't got no kids. I just never get pregnant. Maybe it's his fault. You know? Maybe with some other man I could have kids. Damn! I don't know where he gets off thinkin' he can have my aquarium. But it's her that really matters. I want to breed her this spring."

It was all quiet then, but I could hear more sniffling. I figured my mom was giving her a hug or something. I wished I could give her a hug.

"Did he pay for her?" my mom asked.

"He paid part, maybe a quarter. My mom helped me too, and I used money I been savin' for two years."

"Well, I doubt a judge would just make you sell her. Why not just give him the aquarium, and maybe he'll change his mind about the horse."

"Yeah, maybe. It's just we're tryin' to not pay the lawyers so much. Now this. What a jerk. Maybe he'll settle down. Oh, gosh! I better get to work. It's almost seven thirty."

"Let me know what happens, okay? Call anytime," my mom said. I ran for the house before she came out.

We never saw Daryl again, and Ladonna kept the mare. Nothing was said again about the divorce. One day she announced that it was over, and that was that. My mother and father were pleased with her as a boarder. She was helpful, considerate, and never complained. We had other boarders, too, and everyone seemed to get along. Being that our stable was small—just eight stalls, the people formed a close-knit group and stayed for years.

Walter Bookout didn't come around much anymore, so I started spending more time down at C.K.'s house. Things were changing there.

C.K. had been coming to my house so much, I think it must have been months since I'd been to his house. Then he called one Friday after school and asked me to spend the night. My mom and dad said "sure" and looked happy about getting rid of me because they wanted to go out "on a date" together. They'd been doing this weird thing about making dates together, and it seemed real important to them. I didn't understand it.

Anyway, they dropped me off at C.K.'s. I had my clothes for the next day and my nightshirt and my tooth brush. I probably wouldn't use them, but it made my mom happy that I took them.

C.K. met me at the door. He looked serious. I knew something was wrong. "What's the matter?" I asked.

"Ma and Pa. They just had a big fight. Ma hit Pa in the shoulder with that big iron skillet. I thought I heard a crack, but he won't go to the doctor. He's sittin' in the kitchen with ice on it."

"Where's your mom?"

"She's up in the attic, fixin' a bed for him up there. I think he's gonna live up there from now on."

"Wow," I said. "What was the fight about?"

"Ladonna. Ma thinks Pa's seein' her on the side."

My stomach got all tight, and for a minute I hated Mr. Bookout. How could he? "Is that true?" I asked.

He shrugged. "I don't know. I don't think so. I don't think Pa would do that."

"No, I guess not," I said and relaxed.

"Pa said he knows someone who saw Ma walkin' outa Wrench's Saloon with some man about a month ago. She said it was a lie, and she wouldn't cheat on him. He said his source was very reliable. But he said he hadn't brought it up till she accused him of seein' Miss Cross-Eyes—that's what Ma calls her. And he says that ain't true."

This was pretty interesting. This kind of thing just never happened at my house, except maybe for my grandma. She'd been married three times and was seeing someone else now. But it wasn't this kind of stuff. She got mad at her last husband, but it was because he lied about money. That was boring compared to this.

"Why did she hit him with the frying pan?" I asked.

"She was screamin' at him that it was true about him and Ladonna cuz her sister—her sister works at the plant too—saw him and her—Ladonna—kissin' in the parking lot after work."

I got mad again. No man should be kissing Ladonna.

"But Pa denied it and said they was just friends and that he ain't never kissed her. Ma screamed, 'Oh, yes you did!' and whacked him real hard in the shoulder. I heard it crack."

"Wow. What did he do then?"

"Just walked outa the kitchen, then came back in with his shirt off and got some ice and put it on his shoulder. He's been sittin' out

there ever since. That's when I called you to come down. He said it was okay, and so did Ma. They ain't talkin' to each other, except Pa told her he'd start sleepin' upstairs from now on."

"Wow." I followed C.K. to the kitchen door, and we peeked at his dad. He was sitting on a chair, holding a bag of ice on his shoulder. He didn't see us and just stared out the window. We tiptoed away. "Let's go to your room," I said. He nodded and we went upstairs. It was messier than usual. His bed wasn't made, and there were clothes all over the dresser. Usually his bed was made. It was larger than mine, a double bed, and when I spent the night, we slept in it together. I set my bag of stuff down on the chair. We heard some banging and shuffling upstairs in the attic where his mom was fixing things up for Mr. Bookout. I thought about Mr. Bookout kissing Ladonna and felt mad again. I wasn't sure it was true. His mom was kind of goofy sometimes, and I figured she might be making it up.

C.K. said, "Let's go outside. I don't want to be in here."

"Sure," I said. I didn't like it either. We went out to look at his chickens. There must have been forty or fifty of them now. A couple years ago he'd gotten fifteen baby ones. Five had died, and he raised the other ten. Now, after a couple years, there were all these. And his family had been eating eggs all along, too, and had given a bunch to us. C.K. said once that a hen can lay as many as 260 eggs a year. I didn't like birds very much. I liked animals with fur better, especially Flat-Coated Retriever puppies. Chickens were pretty ugly, except when they were tiny chicks. I thought they were extra ugly when they started getting their first feathers. They looked so spiky, and you could see their bumpy skin. Creepy. And the big white roosters scared me. They'd chase people. But here we were, walking through the chicken flock. The five white roosters looked at us, like they dared us to come closer. I looked the other way. That's what C.K. told me to do. That way, they don't feel challenged to fight. But I was scared anyway. I wondered why we'd come here. "Why are we in here? What do you want to do?" I asked.

"I don't know." He was sort of kicking at the ground. "Want to shoot some of 'em? There's too many."

"Shoot them? With what?" I couldn't believe he said that.

"Pa's .22 revolver. It'll be fun. My ma and your ma could cook 'em. They'll be glad to have some free chickens, I bet."

He looked like he really wanted to do this. I was happy to see him look brighter, so I said okay. We went back to the house to ask his dad for the gun, but when we went into the kitchen, Mr. Bookout was gone, and C.K. couldn't find him anywhere in the house. His truck was still in the driveway, though. C.K. finally asked his mom where he was. She was in her bedroom now, changing the sheets on her bed.

She said, "How the hell should I know? And I don't care, either." She started screaming. "I hope he never comes back! He's no good, you know. Maybe he'll never come back. What the hell do you want him for?"

"Nothin'," C.K. said and walked back to me. I had waited in the doorway of her room.

"Do you know where he's gone?" she screamed at him. "He's probably out with Miss Cross-Eyes!"

"Let's go," he said to me, and we walked away.

"He's no good, you know!" she screamed again.

We hurried out the back door. C.K. headed for his dad's truck. He opened the door and pushed the seat back forward. There were three rifle cases and two smaller cases with pistols in them. C.K. reached for the bigger pistol case, a black, hard plastic one with a black handle. He opened it. The case was lined with red velvet. Inside, there was a long-barreled pistol with a wooden handle. Below the barrel was a small cardboard box. C.K. picked it up and rattled it. It sounded full of bullets. He put the box in his left hand and grabbed the gun. He slammed the truck door and led the way to the chicken coop.

He walked in very long strides, and I had to run to keep up with him, even though we were the same height now. He stopped in the doorway and handed me the box of bullets.

"Open it," he said. He seemed sort of spaced out. I watched him slide the little button on the side of the gun forward, and the cylinder fell out to the side. He held his palm out. "Hand me six bullets," he said.

I opened the box and tipped six golden bullets into his hand. I knew he'd done a lot of shooting with his dad, but I'd never been with them. My parents weren't crazy about guns, even though we had a 12-gauge semi-automatic shotgun. They did some skeet shooting with it, but mostly, my mom used blank popper shells in it for her dog training. They had let me shoot it a couple times, and I wasn't too bad. I'd hit several clay pigeons. But I'd never touched a handgun before. My mom and dad said more people accidentally get shot with handguns than ever get protected from criminals with them. So, I was nervous about C.K. having this gun. But he sure seemed to know what he was doing. He slid the bullets right into the little holes and shut the cylinder with a firm click. It sounded like something from a police movie. When he said, "Let's go," he sounded like he was *in* the police movie. It was sort of like I didn't know who he was right then.

I watched him walk through the dark coop. I stood in the doorway and waited to see what he would do. He was headed for the yard out the other door where the chickens were fed. That's where most of them stayed and pecked for food. There was only one small window in the left wall, and it was all covered with white dust. I could barely see the four big garbage cans under the window where they kept the feed. There were three rows of shelves on the right side where some of the hens had nests and laid eggs. The floor was covered with dried poop. C.K. stood in the far doorway. There was sunshine all around him, and I could only see his outline.

He stood looking at the chickens for a long time. He kept sort of rolling the pistol around in his hands like he was waiting for something. Finally, he turned and looked at me like he was waiting for me, like he couldn't do this unless I went with him. I don't know why, but I walked over to him. When I got there, he kneeled down in an aiming position. He shot once, and the chickens all squawked and flapped their wings and scattered all over the place. They kicked a lot of thick dust into the air, but I stared into it and looked for a dead chicken on the ground. When the dust cleared, there was no dead chicken. I was relieved. The chickens were all over the yard. Some were behind the garage, and four of them had

flown up into the big oak tree. Some were under the car and truck, and a lot of them had flown towards the barn.

C.K. looked up at me and grinned. "This'll be a lot more fun now cuz they's all spread out." I didn't say anything and just watched him. "C'mon," he said and started circling around the oak tree. "C'mon," he said again, waving me to him. He seemed to need me by him, so I went.

We looked up and saw four hens sitting on the lowest branch. They looked down at us every once in a while, but mostly they seemed confused, like they wondered how they'd gotten up there. Their heads turned this way and that. They'd stretch their necks out long and look straight down at the ground at their friends. I felt sorry for them because they couldn't figure this out.

"This is perfect," C.K. said. He stood and leaned against the tree with one shoulder. He aimed the pistol with both hands straight up at the closest hen. Her red and brown feathers sparkled in the sun, and she fluffed herself up. She shook all over and then settled down again.

"CRACK!" went the gun. The hen sat still for a moment, then she toppled off the branch. She hit the ground with a soft thud and bounced a little. Blood oozed out of her head.

"Bulls eye!" C.K. shouted. He glanced at me and smiled. He went over to her and looked down. He placed his hand on her breast. "Dead!" He looked proud. "C'mon, let's get another one." He sort of put his arm on my shoulder and urged me back to the tree trunk. I didn't like this. My stomach started feeling funny.

We looked up at the other three hens. They had no idea what was going on and were still craning their necks to see the other chickens on the ground. C.K. took aim, and I shut my eyes. I heard him take a deep breath and hold it. I waited for the shot. Instead, he said, "Here, you shoot one."

I nearly jumped. "No," I said. "You go ahead. I don't want to."

"It's fun. Here. I'll show you how."

"No, really, I don't want to."

"Yes you do. You just don't know how fun it is. Here." He opened my hand and put the gun into it. I felt all trembly as I felt its heaviness.

71

The gun is huge and heavy in my hand. Jack closes my fingers around it and puts my other hand underneath to hold it up. In a cardboard box are all the baby chicks the children hatched in the incubator. And Jack has just found a nest of baby robins that he brought along. We are out in the woods. The baby robins have huge pink mouths that open wide. Their heads and bodies are dark grey and ugly. The baby chicks are soft and yellow.

There are ten children. We're the ones that won the dance contest, where we danced to Michael Jackson music in front of the video camera with our clothes off. There's Angie and Jessica, and the rest are boys. The cameraman liked the way I moved my shoulders, so I was one of the winners. Now I get to help give Satan the baby birds. He'll be very pleased with us.

Jason gets to go first. He chooses a robin. Jack places it on a tree stump. It opens its huge mouth. Jack shows Jason how to hold the gun and how to pull the trigger. He takes Jason up real close and helps him aim at the robin's head. Jason pulls the trigger, and the robin falls off the stump. Jack picks it up and smiles. He sets it down by a big paper bag and claps his hands. We all clap too, but not as loud as he does.

Clive is next, and he chooses a baby chick. It keeps falling off the stump because it can walk fast. So, Jack breaks its legs. Clive shoots it real quick. We clap. Jack sets it by the bag.

Now it's my turn. I choose a robin because they're so ugly. The gun is in both my hands. The robin opens its mouth. I understand that it's hungry and wants its mother to feed it.

"Shoot, Johnnie," Jack says.

"This is bad," I say. "I don't want to."

"Yes, you are bad. That's why Satan loves you. If you don't do this for him, then what will you be?"

I can think of no way out. I must pull the trigger. Poor bird.

I decide to close my eyes. Somehow, it won't really be my fault then. I shut them as tight as they'll go. I feel the cold metal trigger under my fingers. It is very hard to squeeze, then BANG! I feel the power of the explosion in my hands.

"Aw, you missed!" said C.K.

I felt like I'd been dreaming. There was a flurry of squawks and flapping wings and loose feathers flying above us in the tree. Three brown chickens flapped to the ground.

"You musta hit the branch. Geez, Johnnie."

"I'm sorry. I really didn't want to shoot one anyway. Can't we do something else?"

He bent down to pick up the hen he'd shot. "I suppose. Let's take this into my ma first. Maybe she can cook it for supper."

We went into the kitchen, and he handed the chicken to his mother. She just glared at him. She took the chicken and set it in the sink. "You been messin' with your pa's gun again?"

"I thought you'd like a fresh chicken for supper." He said it so innocently, like he really meant to do her a favor.

She glared at him some more. "Put that gun back where you got it." She turned away from us and started washing some dishes. C.K. stuck the pistol in his belt, and we walked back outside. He started walking down the driveway, away from his dad's truck.

"Aren't you going to put it back?" I asked.

"I will. When I feel like it." We walked to the end of his drive-way and turned right down the dirt road. We just walked for a long time without saying anything. Finally, he said, "I'm glad you're spending the night."

8

Shit, Ma's always said Ladonna was the cause of everything that went wrong in our lives. She says it's when Pa started lyin' and when I started goin' bad. She says everything was great between her and Pa until Ladonna put her horse up at Ambrose's barn. She says she remembers it to the day—the day that horse arrived. Pa started workin' late and running out in the middle of the night. He'd be gone for two hours—to buy cough drops and shit like that, even when he wasn't coughing. "Said his throat kept gettin' dry," she told me later, when I was all grown up. She laughed when she thought about it. "It was in the middle of the summer when it was real humid out. Ridiculous!" We laughed about it real hard together a couple times. She'd say, in this squeaky voice, with her face all scrunched up, "It was in the middle of the summer—when it was real humid out!" Then she'd burst out laughing, and so would I. I don't know, man. It seemed real funny at the time, when she'd talk about it like that.

I guess I was about twelve when Ladonna came. I sure as hell wasn't interested in girls yet, so the whole thing seemed damned goofy to me.

I mean, I didn't get it when all of a sudden Pa started takin' me up to Johnnie's place all the time. Ladonna was always there, and she and Pa talked a lot and stacked hay and hauled bags of grain in. I didn't give a damn about her and was glad to spend the time with Johnnie. We spent most of our time on that damn hay pile.

Where we had our fort, way at the top, you could look way down at people ridin' their horses. Sometimes four people was ridin' at the same time. Seven people boarded their horses at

Johnnie's. Most of them was women and just two men. They ignored us, and we ignored them, except when we pretended they was the cavalry of the Evil Sorcerer's Tribe. They had terrible magic powers and were coming to get us. So, we decided to escape out the bottom of the earth. We made this really neat, kinda wide—four bales square—tunnel straight down through the center of the pile. It was easy to do at first cuz we just lifted four bales out and then four more and then four more. Well, it wasn't that easy, but we was able to lift them out together. But once the tunnel—Johnnie called it a "shaft"—got deeper, we couldn't lift the bales out no more. We'd get down there and try and lift one together. We'd get it about as high as our chests, but that wasn't high enough to lift it out. Then Johnnie had the brilliant idea—Johnnie always had brilliant ideas—to use ropes to pull 'em out.

We went around the barn looking for strong ropes, but all we could find was the horse lead ropes, and they was too short. Then Johnnie said we could use lunge lines—those long, flat, canvas straps they put on a horse's halter. The person stands in one place, and the horse runs around him in a circle. Johnnie ran into the tack room and came out with two of his mom's lunge lines. Each one had a snap at one end and a loop handle at the other end, and they was a light tan color and real long, so he had to hold them in loops like a cowboy's lariat.

We took them to the tunnel. Johnnie tossed them both down to the bottom and jumped down after them. He looped a lunge line around the end of one bale, put the snap end through the loop end and pulled it tight. He did the same thing on the other end of the bale. Then, with the snap ends in his hand, he climbed out again. He handed me one snap and grinned.

"Now we can just pull them up." He looked very satisfied with his idea. I was proud to be his friend. We began to pull, but it was harder than we thought. Johnnie looked like he was trying to fig-ure this out. Then he looked up above us and grinned again. "We can make pulleys!"

I looked up into the rafters, which was only about four feet above our heads. He threw his snap over one of the rafters. I stood

there and waited. "Throw yours over, too." He looked annoyed that I didn't get it. So, I threw mine over. He grabbed it and handed it to me. "Pull," he said. We both pulled at the same time, and the bale started to come up. Brilliant.

We did another bale, and then another, and spent almost the whole day pulling bales out of the shaft. We had to figure what to do with all them bales we pulled out, though. There was a bunch. We piled eight of 'em right around the top—to hide the entrance from spies—and the rest we put at the front of the haystack. The whole top of the pile was almost flat, so when we put the extra bales along the front edge—with spaces in between 'em—it looked like a castle.

We had an old cooler Pa'd given us. We kept apples and pop in there. And we had some other cardboard boxes with food and other stuff, like horseshoes, and magic markers, and cardboard and paper to make signs. There was a tape measure, a hammer, a stapler, a big role of masking tape, and a scissors. We ate all our lunches up there, and when it was real warm out, our parents let us spend the night. We had sleeping bags and pillows. I tried to figure a way to make a campfire up there, but Johnnie freaked out when I suggested it. I guess there really wasn't a way without burnin' the place down. But it's something I thought about a lot, like if we had big sheets of aluminum foil and a whole bunch of rocks and gravel. I think we could've had a fire. But Johnnie said "NO, NO, NO! Absolutely no way!" So, I gave up.

One day my cousin Skip got left at my house for a day cuz his parents had to be in court all day or somethin' for my Uncle Bud—he'd got caught with a stolen car or somethin', I don't know. I liked Uncle Bud, but his breath smelled bad all the time. Anyway, Skip was there. He looked kinda dirty or raggy or somethin', but I didn't care. He was four years older than me and knew a lot of neat stuff. Pa took us up to Johnnie's.

No one was around when we got there. Christine's car wasn't in the driveway, and nobody was in the barn. Pa sorta stood around and looked down the long driveway every few seconds. Then he talked to the horses. I took Skip up to the top of the hay pile and

was startin' to show him the tunnel when I heard a car honk, a friendly kinda "toot toot." I sorta wondered who it was and got worried Johnnie might get mad at me showin' someone else our castle. But I heard Ladonna call, "Hi, Walter! Sorry I'm late." And then I could hear her talking some more, but I didn't listen.

"Guess how we got all them bales out, " I said to Skip.

He looked down the tunnel for a long time. Finally he shrugged.

"I dunno. You couldn'ta lifted 'em all out. 'Specially the ones down low." His hair was hanging down across his eyes. I could smell his b.o., but I was sorta spaced-out, looking at an orange stain on his old white tee shirt. The stain was in the shape of a sword. It was a single-edged sword. You could tell cuz one edge was curved. Johnnie would think it was cool. I wanted to remember to show him.

"C.K.!" Pa was calling me from down below. I went over to the edge and looked down at him and Ladonna. I could smell Skip come and stand next to me. We climbed down and stood in front of Pa and Ladonna.

Pa said, "We're gonna run down to the tack shop and get a halter for Ladonna's horse. Do you want to come with or stay here?"

"Who's that!" Skip whispered loud in my ear. He meant Ladonna. Pa looked at him and grinned just a little.

"Skip, this is Ladonna Michaux. She works at the plant and keeps her horse here."

"Hi," said Skip. He stood there looking stupid, kinda like Tucker.

"That's quite a fort, ain't it?" she said.

"Castle," I mumbled.

"Yes, ma'am," Skip said. He straightened his back and cleared his throat.

"So, you wanna stay or come?" Pa asked.

I said "stay" at the same time Skip said "come."

Pa said, "It's gotta be one or the other." I laughed a little, but I didn't want to go for no ride to the tack shop. The tack shop was boring.

Just then Johnnie walked in. "Hey!" I shouted. I was glad to see him, but I was a little scared he'd be mad about Skip. He was dressed nice—tan slacks and a blue polo shirt. He looked at Skip. I could tell he was wondering who he was. I was trying to read his face to see if he was getting mad or not. I think he was trying to decide, too.

"This is Skip," I said. "You know—my cousin?"

"Oh, yeah. Hi." He seemed to relax.

Skip said, "I'd like to go to the tack shop. Can't C.K. stay here now that Johnnie's home?" Pa nodded. Skip just stood looking at Ladonna. He sorta weaved back and forth like he was trying to think of somethin' to say. Ladonna looked at Pa and gave one little laugh. Pa and her turned to go, and Skip followed them. His eyes was glued to Ladonna's backside. He still looked like Tucker. Speaking of who—came bounding in. He trotted over to Johnnie and put his big head under his hand to be petted. He sat down next to Johnnie's left leg and leaned on Johnnie so hard Johnnie almost fell over.

"Geez, Tuck!" said Johnnie. He kneeled down and gave Tucker a big hug. He hugged that dog a lot. Tucker licked his face all over and Johnnie laughed. He stood up and wiped dog spit on his shoulder. He said, "What do you want to do?"

"Mmm, I dunno," I said, thinking about the tunnel. We needed to start digging through the dirt at the bottom. I couldn't figure out how we was gonna get the dirt out. I mean, where was we gonna put it? "Want to start digging?"

"Sure," he said. "I have to change clothes, though. My mom took me to a Philosophy Department brunch. It was awful."

I got down, and we went to the house. I waited in the kitchen while Johnnie went up and changed. Christine was cleaning up dishes from breakfast that morning. Just some plates that already looked clean. All they ever ate for breakfast was fruit. Fresh fruit. Never canned pears or applesauce—the good kind.

"How are you doing, C.K.? Where's your dad?"

"Him and Ladonna and Skip—my cousin—went to the tack shop. I guess Ladonna needed a halter."

"Tell me about Skip. How's he related to you? How old is he? Why did he go to the tack shop with them?"

She was being real friendly, but geez! Which question was I supposed to answer first? She did this a lot.

"Well," I said, trying to remember them all. "Skip's, I guess fifteen or sixteen." Then I couldn't remember what else she'd asked. I always felt kinda nervous around her. Around Leland, too. Sometimes it seemed like they didn't like me a whole lot. But they was always real nice. "What else did you want to know?"

She laughed. "About Skip. Tell me about him. Is he from your mom's family or your dad's?"

"Uhh. His ma is Aunt Mincie. Aunt Mincie is Pa's sister."

"Aunt Mincie? What an unusual name. What is it short for?"

Her dang questions. "I dunno. It's just Aunt Mincie."

"I mean," she said, "is Mincie a nickname for, um, gee, I can't imagine what longer name Mincie would stand for. Mincibell? Inmincible? Mincerella?" She started giggling real hard. "What is it? Do you know?" She laughed harder. "How about Minced Meat?" Her eyes was getting all watery and she stopped washin' a dish. She was laughin' pretty hard. I started laughin' a little, too. Mostly cuz it seemed the polite thing to do. I didn't see what was so funny. I liked Aunt Mincie. She always worked hard—she had two jobs, and she always looked like she needed to go to sleep.

Christine looked at me. Maybe she saw I didn't think this was so funny, and she slowed down a little. "I'm sorry, C.K." She wiped some tears away with the back of her wrist. "You know how some things just strike you funny sometimes? Minced Meat Bookout!" She burst out laughin' again. I was wishin' Johnnie would come back. I decided to go up to his room. He was takin' a long time. I got up and started to walk out when Christine said, "Where are you going, C.K.? I'm sorry. Did I offend your aunt? I'm not, really. I just think the name is funny. No, not funny, really. Different, that's all. You know how sometimes a new word just sounds unusual to you? Oh, boy!" she said, more to herself. She blew some air out real hard. "Am I stressed out or what?" She looked at me. "Have

you had breakfast? Would you like some pancakes? I'll make you some." She was real serious now.

"No," I said. "I had breakfast. Thanks, though." Johnnie walked in. Thank goodness. "What took you so long?"

He looked puzzled. "I didn't take very long. I just changed clothes and came down." I followed him out the door, and we ran out into the driveway and headed for the barn.

My mind was back on gettin' the tunnel going. "So what do you think about gettin' the dirt up? I was thinkin' maybe we could tie a bucket to a lunge line and pull it up just like the bales."

He grinned at me. His face looked bright. "That's what I thought, too. Let's go!" We raced to the barn door. I won. I always won races. We was the same height, but he just couldn't run as fast. Course I was older, so that's probably why. Johnnie never looked upset about losing. He seemed to expect it.

Without talkin' much we got two horse buckets. We didn't need to talk a whole lot to know what the other one was thinking. Maybe we had E.S.P. together.

———————————

I like to think about us—how we communicated. Shit, it just flowed, you know? We never had to ask, "Huh?" or "What do you mean?" We just knew what the other wanted and what the other was thinking. And feeling, I guess. I mean, like, I knew when he was happy and shit like that. We, like, respected each other's minds, if you know what I mean. Neither of us thought the other was better. I mean, we was different. He was pretty smart for his age—dreamed up inventions and shit like that—like the pulley. And he was real smart in school. But I got lots of A's too. Pa gave me ten dollars for every A, so I managed to get plenty of 'em. Somehow, though, Johnnie was—I don't know—I don't want to say he was smarter than me. Shit, maybe he was. He read more fucking books. But I was older and two grades ahead of him in school. I don't know what I'm trying to say, man—I just mean we seemed equal or somethin', even though we was so different.

I went in the feed room and got the big, metal grain scoop. Johnnie got the long-handled spade. Then we marched into the tack room, and each of us lifted a canvas lunge line off a hook. We each had a bucket and put the lunge lines in them. I saw a metal hoof pick and threw that into my bucket just in case we ran into stones while we was diggin'. Then we walked to the far side of our castle where people took bales down to feed the horses. They sort of made steps for us to reach the top. We lugged all the stuff up with us and carried it to the edge of the tunnel.

We still hadn't said a word. Johnnie threw the snap end of his lunge line over the rafter, and so did I. We each attached a bucket with the digging tools in them and lowered them to the bottom. Then was the fun part. In order to get to the bottom, we had to push our arms and legs against the sides of the tunnel and let ourselves down a little at a time. I always felt like a mountain climber doing this. Coming up was harder, but really fun. We had tried holding onto the bales' strings and putting our feet in the cracks between the bales, but after a while the bales got loose and worn down at the corners, so we did it like mountain climbers instead. We agreed we didn't want to ruin our tunnel, so we took good care of it.

It was kinda dark down there cuz it was so far down, but we started digging at the bottom. Johnnie dug with the spade, and I scooped up the dirt with the grain scoop and put it into a bucket. We filled both buckets. We still hadn't said nothin' to each other. When they was all filled up, we climbed to the top of the tunnel and pulled the buckets up. Then one of us finally had to say somethin'.

"What're we gonna do with all the dirt?" I asked.

We stood there looking at the buckets, then looking down at the floor of the barn. We looked at each other and shrugged. "How about in the manure pile?" I asked.

Johnnie thought about it. "I don't think so. They sell it to people for their gardens. How about the woods?"

Everything the Ambrose's didn't know what to do with they put in the woods—old rotten bales of hay, watermelon rinds, an old lawn mower. The woods was so thick no one could see into it from the barnyard. I used to try to imagine what would become of all that stuff. Johnnie's mom said it was all biodegradable and would disintegrate and become part of the soil—that's why it was okay. She said they'd never put plastic or glass out there. I had trouble with the lawn mower, though. How long would it take for that to disintegrate? I asked Pa once, and he said "five hundred years." I knew Christine was a little strange, so I just figured she'd have to haul it outa there one day. But Johnnie's idea to put the dirt in the woods seemed okay.

We got the big wheelbarrow and dumped the two buckets of dirt in. Then we went back down the tunnel to get more dirt. We'd just gotten down there and was beginnin' to dig when a voice shouted down the tunnel to us, "Hey, what you guys doin'?" It was Skip.

"Diggin' out dirt to go deeper," I yelled. Without even asking us, he came down the tunnel—the wrong way, puttin' his feet in the cracks and crunchin' the corners of the bales and pullin' on the strings. "Geez! Be careful! You're pulling it all loose!" I shouted at him. He didn't care.

"Man, your dad's girlfriend is dynamite," he said. His eyes was all big, and he was breathing kinda hard.

"She's not his girlfriend," Johnnie said. He sounded mad. I'm the one should've been mad.

"Yeah. She's not his girlfriend," I said, tryin' to sound madder than Johnnie. "Besides," I said, "she's cross-eyed. Pa wouldn't want someone who's cross-eyed."

"That doesn't matter," Johnnie said, loud. That surprised me. Quieter, he said, "She's very pretty."

"Pretty Cross-Eyed Ladonna," Skip said, real dreamy-like. I thought he was gonna drool or somethin'. He looked like Tucker again.

"Pa don't have no girlfriend," I said. "He's married to Ma."

"Don't matter," said Skip. "Your Pa's real sweet on her."

"He is not," I said.

"He is not!" shouted Johnnie. What was with him?

"Pretty Cross-Eyed Ladonna," Skip said again.

"Get out of here," Johnnie demanded. "This is my barn, and I want you to leave." I just looked at him. I never heard him sound so mad.

"I saw him kiss her," Skip said. He leaned real close to me and opened his eyes real big, right in my face.

I put my hand on his chest and pushed him back. "Yeah, get outa here," I said. "What do you care, anyway?"

"Cuz I'd like to have her for myself, that's why," Skip said, leanin' into my face again. "Beautiful Cross-Eyed Ladonna. I'd love to have her all to myself, with no clothes on, and push my prick into her cunt. Ooooh, how sweet. She's got a great ass."

Johnnie kicked him in the shin and started to punch at his face. Skip just put his hand around Johnnie's neck and held him back. The three of us was all crammed into that small space at the bottom of the tunnel. I kicked Skip in the other shin and tried to pull his hand off Johnnie's neck. Johnnie kicked him again, and so did I. I pulled down hard on Skip's elbow, and he let go of Johnnie. I kept kickin' at his right leg, and Johnnie was kickin' at his left one. Skip started yelling "Ow!" And we kept on kicking. He tried swinging a fist at Johnnie's head, but the wall was too close and he hit his elbow on the hay. Johnnie ducked. But when Skip swung the other way with his other fist, he hit me on the side of the head. At first I thought I was gonna fall down, but then it wasn't so bad, and I kicked him real hard just below the knee. Johnnie kept kicking too. Finally, Skip started to climb up the tunnel—the wrong way, grabbin' at the strings. I could see corners breakin' off the bales where he put his feet. He pulled on the strings harder, and some of the bales got loose. Hay was fallin' down on us. He got high enough that he could kick at our heads, so Johnnie grabbed the spade and started pokin' it real hard at Skip's butt. He got him once in the balls, I think, cuz Skip started moanin', and he bent over. We stopped attacking him then. We waited a long time. Skip just stayed bent over, moaning. Finally,

he climbed real slow to the top. He disappeared, and I didn't see him again until Christmas.

I looked at Johnnie. We was both breathin' real hard. I was all sweaty, and Johnnie was all red in the face. He looked furious. "I hate him," said Johnnie. "He better not touch her. She's very nice." At first I thought maybe Johnnie was sweet on her, but I guess he really just thought she was nice. She *was* nice.

"I like Cross-Eyed Ladonna," Johnnie said. "She's a good boarder. And she's having some hard times. She's divorced," he whispered.

I was surprised he also called her "Cross-Eyed Ladonna." It seemed sort disrespectful. "Really?" I asked. "How do you know?"

"She told my mother one day—a few years ago. I overheard them talking. Daryl tried to cheat her out of stuff. Like her horse."

"Cross-Eyed Ladonna loves her horse," I said. "That would be terrible." It was funny how we both started callin' her "Cross-Eyed Ladonna" after that. You wouldn't think we would, since it was pukey Skip that named her that, and it was an insult to call her that. But it stuck. There was somethin' easy about the sound. It was easier to say than plain "Ladonna." It kinda made her more special. Maybe it was like a pet name. We never just called her Ladonna any more, and the way Johnnie said it, it sounded like he liked her even more because of her crossed eyes. We heard her tell Christine once that she'd been born like that, and her ma and pa couldn't afford the surgery. And now she just worked in a factory and didn't have extra money. So, we all just got used to her eyes bein' that way, and Johnnie sure didn't care.

I don't know where Skip went after that, maybe back to my house. I didn't care. We kept on diggin' our tunnel.

That night, I stayed at Johnnie's, and we slept on top of our castle. It was supposed to rain hard and maybe have thunderstorms, so when Pa asked Christine where we'd be sleepin', she said, "In the house." But later the forecast changed, and it was only supposed to drizzle, so she let us sleep in the barn.

We was sound asleep. Tucker, Josie, and Tilly was all with us. Sometimes we had to help them climb up the hay pile, depending

on how the boarders had taken hay from the side of it. Sometimes there was good steps all the way up, and sometimes there was walls we had to climb. Tonight the dogs was able to climb up by themselves. It was good to have them up there to protect us in case a spy from the Evil Sorcerer's Tribe came.

I was havin' a dream about Uncle Bud tryin' to start his motorcycle. Skip was there, all stinky and dirty-lookin'. His eyes was all wide like when he was followin' Cross-Eyed Ladonna. Instead, he was lookin' at his pa's motorcycle. Uncle Bud kept jumpin' down on the starter peddle, and it would sorta purr loud for a few seconds and then die. Then he'd do it again. And again and again. But it never would start. Skip just kept starin' at it all stupid-lookin'. I guess Uncle Bud was gonna let him drive it by hisself. And I was just standin' there watchin', I don't know why. Just watchin' Uncle Bud jump up and down and the motorcycle purrin' and stoppin', purrin' and stoppin'. It almost caught once and purred for a longer time. I woke up then and heard the purring right next to me. Except it wasn't purring. It was Josie growling. Real low, way down in her throat. Her ears was perked up, and she'd growl a little, then stop, then growl a little more and stop. Tucker was sound asleep next to Johnnie, and Tilly was behind me, asleep too. It was pretty dark, except for the big light outside the barn that stayed on all night. It shined in through the little windows that was way up high in the arena. They was very dirty—I don't know how anyone ever cleaned them—but some light did shine through.

Josie was lookin' toward the far side of the hay pile where the stairs was. I listened for a while, but I didn't hear nothin'. She'd lift her head and growl a little. Then she'd put her head back down. When her head was down, she wagged her tail. I couldn't figure this out. I poked Johnnie. "Wake up," I whispered. "But shhh! Don't talk. Something's in here."

Johnnie woke up real quick and sat up. He looked around. Then he looked at me like I was tryin' to trick him, like he was sayin', "Yeah, sure." Then Josie growled again. Tucker and Tilly lifted their heads up, too, and perked their ears. We all looked over by the stairs. I imagined the spy from the Sorcerer's Tribe was

coming to get us. My heart started pounding. Then all three dogs stood up and wagged their tails. I looked at Johnnie. He screwed up one side of his face and shrugged at me. We sat still and listened. The dogs stood still and listened, too.

Mostly, we heard nothin', then every once in a while, I could hear somethin' like a half meow from a cat—a sort of "me-, me-." Then there'd be nothin'. Then more half meows in a row. Then nothin'. The dogs sat down but still listened. Josie cocked her head from side to side every once in a while. I wondered if one of the barn cats was trapped behind some bales of hay.

"Do you think it's a cat?" I whispered.

"Must be," said Johnnie.

"Maybe it's stuck. Should we try to find it and get it out?"

"I don't know, " said Johnnie. I tried to figure what he was thinking.

Shit. Now, of course, I'd know the sound of fucking a mile away. I have to laugh when I think about us back then—so naive. Of course, by then our memories of all the ass fucking at the daycare center was pretty much gone. But then, most of that was kids screamin' and shit. Not many sighs and groans of pleasure. Maybe from the adults. But we sure didn't listen to those—their groans of pleasure. I can still remember poor little Johnnie lyin' face down on that green rug. Damned old Jack rammin' his dick in Johnnie's poor little ass. Johnnie was screamin' and moanin', and damned old Jack was gruntin' away, enjoyin' his damned self. I suppose them was sighs of pleasure, but we kids never paid attention to that. We was so damned terrified.

We didn't say a word, but we both got out of our sleeping bags. I grabbed the flashlight, and just as I turned it on, we heard this loud gasp and a low moan. We stopped and listened. "Must be cats fighting," said Johnnie. "That big white tom cat must be in here. Let's go chase him away."

"Maybe it's a trick by the Evil Sorcerer's Tribe," I said, mostly kidding. But I was a little scared. I started imagining one of them great big guys with chain mail and a huge sword hiding on the stairs. He was makin' cat noises just to get us to come near him. Just when we'd get about half way down the stairs, he'd grab us both by the neck and carry us off to his king. Something poked me in the ribs, and I screamed loud, "Ahhhhh!"

"Shhhh!" said Johnnie. "That was me. Shine the light over there." He pointed toward the stairs. I shined it over there, but all we saw was the barn wall. We tiptoed over to the edge.

"Wait. Stop." said Johnnie. "Did you hear that?"

I listened. I could hear a rustling. Then a soft snap, sorta like the elastic of my underpants. "What is that?" My heart was poundin' real hard. All I could imagine was the evil warrior snapping a hay bale string to keep his balance. I pictured him perched on the edge of a step, tryin' to stay close to the pile so we wouldn't see him when we shined the light down there. I imagined him losing his balance and grabbing a string to hang on. Maybe the snap was him losin' his grip on it, and maybe he fell off. I thought I heard some more rustling.

"Quick!" whispered Johnnie. "Go shine the light down there."

"Here—you do it," I said and handed him the flashlight.

We creeped over to the edge. The dogs stood at the edge, too, and wagged their tails. Johnnie shined the light down to the floor. We didn't see nothin' but loose hay, like usual. Then he shined it over against the back wall. Two yellow eyes shined back. We both screamed and ran back to our sleeping bags. Tilly took off after the eyes, and we heard all this hissing and cat growls. There was a bunch of scuffling and more cat growls. "Tilly!" Johnnie yelled. "Stop it! Come here!" Tilly always chased the barn cats. It started sounding real bad, like she'd gotten hold of the cat and was bitin' it or somethin'. Johnnie ran over to the sound and tried to shine the flashlight on the animals.

I was sure I heard more shufflin' and scufflin' down below. It sounded like something said, "Damn!" but I figured it was just the cats—you know how cats can sound like humans sometimes.

Johnnie got over to Tilly and the cat, but then the cat got away and ran off. Tilly ran down the stairs after it, and Johnnie kept yelling for Tilly, but Tilly wouldn't come. He gave up and walked back to me. He shined the flashlight right in my eyes and laughed a little.

"Cut it out!" I said. As we walked back to our sleeping bags, my eyes was sorta all splotchy cuz of the light, but when I looked at the big open doorway of the barn, I thought I seen two people hurry out. It sorta looked like my Pa. And a woman. Sorta looked like Cross-Eyed Ladonna. I blinked hard and looked again, but there wasn't nothing there. I felt all jumpy from the cats and the growling. I still wondered if the evil warrior was waiting for us on the stairs. My heart pounded. I figured I was just seein' things cuz of the flashlight in my eyes. What would Pa and Cross-Eyed Ladonna be doing here at this hour, anyway? I was jumpy.

Johnnie started getting back into his sleeping bag, but I knew I couldn't go back to sleep. I was too nervous. I didn't dare tell him what I thought about the evil warrior on the steps. He'd laugh. "I'm hungry," I said. I thought maybe I could convince him to go back into the house and sleep there.

"There's all kinds of stuff in the cooler," he said. "Remember, my mom gave us sandwiches, and pop, and Snickers. There's cookies, too—chocolate chip. And apples." He shined the light on the cooler. He was only part way into his sleeping bag. He got out of it. "I'll get you something. What do you want?"

"Well, I really have to go to the bathroom. Number two. I better go in the house."

"Do it in a stall. The boarders do. I've done it out here a couple times, too. When no one was here. Just cover it with shavings."

Doggone him. "Alright," I said. "If you have to know—I'm a little scared." I waited for him to say somethin', like maybe he was, too, but he didn't. He just waited for me to say more. "Didn't you think about the evil warriors? With all those noises?"

"Maybe, a little," he said. He was just being nice to me. He really wasn't scared.

"Well," I figured one of 'em was waiting on the stairs for us—gonna wait till we got down there—it was him makin' all those

noises—as bait for us. Then, when we went lookin' for the noises, he was gonna grab us and drag us to the evil king."

He was startin' to get into this. "Like this?" he giggled and jumped up and grabbed me by the neck. He tried haulin' me off toward the stairs. I was laughin' and screamin', "No, no!" and tryin' to fight him off, but really lettin' him drag me. He pretended we was in front of the Evil Sorcerer himself.

"Mighty sir!" he said to the wall. "This is one of the leaders from the Other Side. One of our spies was successful in capturing him. What would you like done with him, sir?" Johnnie let me go and leaped over to the wall. He was now the Evil Sorcerer. In a deep, slow voice he said, "Throw him to the lions."

Tucker, Josie, and Tilly stood there waiting. Their tails was waggin' real fast. Johnnie threw me at their feet, and they attacked. I tried to pretend I was being eaten, but their tongues licked at my ears and my mouth and my eyes. I couldn't stand it no more, I was laughin' so hard. They tickled—a lot!

9

C.K. mentioned a number of times that his dad gave him ten dollars every time he received an A on his report card, and he said he earned many A's in Math, Science, History, and English. I never could figure that out because his spoken English was so poor. Yet, when I was in graduate school, I taught some Freshman Composition courses to earn extra money. I was amazed how, for much of the population, spoken English differs from written English. My parents spoke the way they wrote, but I learned that most people don't. It finally made me realize that even though C.K. and his parents and extended family, and even Ladonna, sounded unintelligent, they were really quite smart and capable of learning to write correct English even if the cultural norm was to speak it incorrectly. I thought that once a person learned the proper way to write, it would carry over into their spoken words, but that does not seem to be the case. I wish I had realized this then. I think I just came to the point where I knew C.K. was smart, and I became accustomed to the way he and others in our community talked.

I remember the time I was in Mrs. Bookout's car with her and C.K. We'd gone to the grocery store and were hurrying back to their house where Mrs. Bookout's friend, Marge, was to meet us with her son, Harry. From there we were all going to a birthday party at the roller rink. C.K. had mentioned Harry, but more as a kid he was forced to play with from time to time and someone in whom he seemed uninterested.

Harry's only positive attribute, as far as I can recall, was his uncanny ability, at age eleven, to fix cars. Other than that, I despised him. He talked incessantly, knew more about decadent adult activities than most adults, and enticed C.K. with his evil ways.

C.K. and I were in the back seat of Mrs. Bookout's car. She'd just turned off the highway onto the dirt road when her car jerked a few times. Then it died. She tried to restart it a bunch of times, but it wouldn't. She started swearing. Then she finally told C.K. to run on down to their house and see if Harry and Marge were there and to call Dave's Garage to see if someone could come fix the car. I wanted to go too, but she said for me to stay with her. I don't know why.

My farm was right there, and I said, as politely as I could, "Mrs, Bookout, you can call from my house."

She said, "No. Just stay there, Johnnie." Every once in a while she muttered, "That damned Walter. Damn him, damn him." I guess she probably thought I couldn't hear her, but I could. I couldn't do anything except wait for someone to come rescue us.

I sat in the back seat and watched the top of the hill in the dirt road for C.K. Or, maybe he wouldn't come back, and Dave would pull up behind us in his tow truck. So, I looked out the back window every once in a while. It seemed like hours, and no one came. Mrs. Bookout just stared straight ahead with her hands on the wheel, muttering and gasping and sighing. She'd let the wheel go with her right hand every once in a while and drum her fingers on the side of it. Then she'd grab it again and hold on. She didn't say a word to me. I thought about it and decided I should stop watching the road for C.K. I really wanted to just walk home, but I didn't dare ask. Mrs. Bookout looked like she was made of stone and wouldn't even hear me if I did. So, I waited. I figured C.K. probably got home, told Harry and his mother what happened, and they called Dave's Garage. And Dave probably had something else to do first, and then he would drive his tow truck out to help us. So, I waited for Dave. I finally turned around on my knees on the back seat and rested my head on my arms. That way I could stare out the back window and watch for the tow truck. I watched all the cars and trucks go by on the highway. I watched the hill in the distance for Dave's blue tow truck, but it never came.

"What's this?" Mrs. Bookout said.

I turned around and looked out the windshield. C.K. and another boy were walking towards us.

"What's he bringing Harry for?" she asked. I knew she wasn't asking me, so I didn't answer.

As they got closer I could see that Harry was a little taller than C.K. and his hair was only a little darker blond, but it was much longer and hanging in his eyes. He kept flipping it back over the top of his head with one hand. He was carrying something in his other hand. It looked like tools. C.K. had some too. What were they carrying tools for? Maybe they thought Mrs. Bookout could fix the car, or maybe Dave had told them to bring tools, and he would be coming any minute. I jumped out of the back seat and ran to meet them. I didn't run right up to them because I wanted to get a better look at Harry first. His face looked sort of thick, but his body looked normal. He was looking at C.K. and talking with his mouth open real big, and he waved one hand around in the air. C.K. was looking at me. At least he wasn't looking at Harry.

Harry was so busy talking he didn't see me when they stopped in front of me. "And he went down the slide like a greased pig and never touched the hand rails and never put his feet down, and when he got to the end he went right off and skidded on his butt, oh, I don't know, ten feet, or maybe more, and got dirt all up his shirt and he was sayin' 'oh, fuck, godammit, mother-fuckin' shit, jesus christ,' and shit like that, and his ma was standin' right there watchin' and listenin' to him and she didn't say a word, she just stared at him and gave him that evil look, you know, like she was gonna kill him, and he looked up at her and just grinned like he dared her to say somethin' to him, and—"

"Shhh!" said C.K. "This is Johnnie, my best friend. Johnnie, this is Harry."

Harry looked at me. He had small eyes that looked like he wouldn't let them open all the way. I made mine go bigger, so maybe he would, too, but he didn't. He just looked at me. "Hey!" he said. He smiled a little, and then he turned back to C.K. "You know what he did? He looked up at her, stared right at her, stuck

his tongue out, then said, 'Ma, you're a fat-assed pussy,' then he went back to go down the slide again—"

"C.K.!" Mrs. Bookout yelled. "What the hell are you doing? Did you call Dave?"

Harry finally shut up and followed C.K. over to Mrs. Bookout. What a jerk.

"When's Dave coming?" she asked.

C.K. said, "He can't come for two hours cuz he's got four other calls to go on. Said he's swamped. Harry said he can fix it. His ma didn't mind, so we went out and got Pa's tools. Harry says he can fix it."

"Oh, right," said Mrs. Bookout and rolled her eyes. She looked at us all real mean. Harry walked over to her car. Mrs. Bookout had left the door open, and Harry reached inside, down under the dashboard, and pulled real hard on something. The hood popped up about an inch. He walked around to the front and fiddled with something under the front edge. We heard a snap, and he lifted the hood up. He unscrewed something and lifted a big round pan-looking thing off and set it on the ground. He took its lid off and looked inside. "Air filter's pretty dirty. When's the last time you had it changed?" He looked up at Mrs. Bookout.

"How should I know? Walter's supposed to take care of the cars."

"That's probably not the problem," he said. He stood up and started unscrewing more things under the hood and setting them on the pan thing. He picked something out and blew on it real hard. Then he held it up to the sky and looked into it. He held out his hand to C.K., and C.K. handed him the tools. Harry really went to work then, banging here and there, unscrewing things, and putting them back. Then he tried to start the car.

Mrs. Bookout saw him start to get in. "You can't drive! Besides, it's a stick shift."

"I ain't drivin' it. I'm just startin' it. Maybe." Mrs. Bookout acted like she was going to pull him out. Then she just stopped and watched. When he turned the key, the car tried to start, but it just wouldn't. He tried three times. Finally, he got out and said, "It's the fuel filter. You need a new one."

"Do you have one?" Mrs. Bookout asked. We all looked at her like she was stupid.

Harry looked at her with his little pig eyes. His face was real serious. "My ma can drive me down to the parts store and get one."

"Well," said Mrs. Bookout. "Should I stay here or come with?" Somehow, it seemed like she was the kid and he was the grown-up. It was weird.

"Don't matter," said Harry. "I'll need some money to buy it, though."

Mrs. Bookout looked at him and then at her car. She turned and looked down the dirt road and then back at Harry. "Well," she said. "How much is it?"

"Mmm, fuel filter for this car will run ya between ten and twenty. Better give me twenty-five, just in case."

Mrs. Bookout went to get her purse out of the car. "Damned Walter," she said. She went through her wallet, then dug into the bottom of her purse. She put some bills on the seat and started counting change. "Twenty-one dollars and eighty-three cents."

"That should do it," said Harry, and he took all the money. He stuffed it into his pockets. "Let's go," he said, looking at each of us. He was smiling big as he started to walk back to C.K.'s house, but he kept his head turned to see who was going to go with him.

C.K. stood by my side and didn't move. I stood by him. Neither of us wanted to go. It was like we were magnets to each other. Harry walked slowly, still looking back and still grinning. We didn't move. All of a sudden Harry's grin disappeared and he stopped. His little eyes got smaller and sorta looked like Tucker's whenever my mom scolded him for something. Heaven knows why I felt sorry for this jerk, but right then, I did. I nudged C.K. a little and said, "Let's go." I took a step and C.K. followed. Harry grinned again, and his eyes went back to normal.

As soon as we caught up with him, he started talking. He talked to C.K. "So, I hear your pa's got a girlfriend, that's what my brother Duke said, he said he saw your dad kissin' some red-head lady at work, and they was holdin' hands in one of the hallways, said she's real pretty, but as soon as they saw Duke, they let go of

their hands, like no one's s'posed to know. I guess that must be a bummer for you, huh? Your folks splittin' up. My ma and pa split up ten years ago, I was just one. I saw him once a couple years ago. He came to the door and knocked. Shit, I didn't know who he was and wasn't gonna let him in, but Ma let him in and he just stood and looked at me for a while, didn't say nothin' to me, just stared. He looked kinda nice, but then Ma asked him for a buncha money, and he walked out the door again, that's all I ever seen of him, I hope you get to see your dad again, but it's not like I miss him or nothin' cuz I never got to know him, 'sides, I got three big brothers and they's just like a pa, 'cept they's always drunk or smokin' dope, but they share with me, that's how I know they love me, ya know? You done any dope?" He stopped talking, and he turned and looked at me with those little eyes. Those eyes—they were like they belonged to some animal—a weasel or a possum. I hated him.

"What's dope?" I asked. Grandma called a person a "dope" when she didn't like him. I didn't know what he was talking about.

"You know what dope is, don't you, C.K?" he asked.

"No, I don't. Why're you saying all those things about my parents?" He looked sad and mad. "They're not splitting up!"

Harry waggled his hands in the air and said, "Whoooaaa. Aren't we upset." Then he laughed real hard. "Your pa's gettin' pussy, and I bet you don't even know what that is, do ya?"

C.K. didn't answer, so Harry looked at me and grinned in my face. "Do you know what it is, huh? Ha ha ha!" God! I hated him. None of his words made sense. Something about cats and C.K.'s dad, and about dopes. It was like he was from another planet.

We were right by our barn now, and I just wanted to go home. I just wanted to get away from this creep. "I think I—," I started to say, but then I thought about C.K. and how he'd be left with Harry and have to go to the roller skating party with him alone if I went home. I liked to roller skate, but how would we get rid of this creep? I looked up at my house and saw my mom's car there. I wanted to run to her and have her hug me. I never wanted to see Harry again.

———

Harry had been at Little Friends too, I later learned. Two of his older brothers were there as well. The pre-school made extra money by letting older kids come in the afternoons for after-school care, and many were used as "junior counselors" during the summer. I bring this up now because I recall how I felt about Harry that day, even though I didn't remember his being at the preschool. I must have had contact with him and with his brothers. I do remember some older boys and how they helped Jack with the little kids, though I can't clearly remember faces and which ones were Harry's brothers. I just remember big boys.

What I'm talking about now, though, is this awareness or intuition that I experienced when I was with Harry. Granted, his personality and behavior alone were enough to alienate anyone, but there was more. There was this intense hatred and fear—a deep-seated terror, maybe, that I felt when I was with him. These thoughts bring to mind a dream I had last night, probably triggered by this present effort to recall these childhood events.

In my dream, I was here in my office waiting for my next client and catching up on some paperwork. The client was a new one, a Mr. O'Cull, who, according to my secretary, claimed he needed only one appointment. I'd heard that before and figured he wanted a prescription for something I wouldn't want him to have and hoped he could pay as little as possible for it. Normally, my secretary announces a client over the intercom, but in this dream, Mr. O'Cull simply appeared in the doorway, seeming to have never even opened the door. His appearance was that of a decent businessman. He had on a dark suit, a reddish tie, and was holding a briefcase; his face and body were average-looking, though his dark, curly hair was a bit too long, and his eyes were rather large, giving him an innocent appearance.

I was startled by his sudden presence, but then was put at ease by his manner and dress. He came forward and shook my hand. He sat in the chair across from me and began talking. I kept straining to understand him because I could catch only half of his words. The rest were either garbled, lacked coherence with his other words, or they were just spoken too softly for me to make them out. What I

97

did understand, however, was terrifying. He was very intense in what he said, and he seemed very intelligent. I got the sense that he was a professional of some kind and very educated. But he was accusing me of murdering his son, and he cited many examples of irrefutable proof of this. He was extremely confident in what he said, even though I continued to strain my ears to understand him. He still used incoherent words. Dreams are like that sometimes.

As I sat there and listened to him, I was panic struck because there seemed no way out for me. I watched him talk and noticed that his appearance began to change. It was like watching a movie of the Wolf Man or some other horror film. Mr. O'Cull's eyes began to grow smaller, his hair began to turn blond, and the waves in it became straight.

Suddenly, I had an urgent need to urinate and excused myself. I ran to the men's room, nearly tripping over my own feet. I burst into the restroom, barely making it to the urinal in time, and gratefully relieved myself. Afterwards, I was shaking with fear and glanced at myself in the mirror as I washed my hands. In the mirror I saw not my own image but that of Harry. Then I awoke.

———————

"Look out!" C.K. said. Up ahead was a big cloud of dust on the dirt road and a rumbling sound. "It's Ken Jenkins!" C.K. and I leaped off the side of the road, but Harry just stood there and watched. It looked like he was going to dare Jenkins to run him over. Ken Jenkins started honking his horn, but Harry stood there and stared at him, grinning real big. I hated that grin. I don't think Ken Jenkins had any intention of slowing down, and Harry finally figured this out and leaped off the other side of the road just in time. Ken Jenkins just missed him and never did slow down.

"God damned mother fucker!" Harry shouted. There was so much dust, I could hardly see Harry.

"What a nut!" I said to C.K.

"So's the other one," said C.K., shaking his head. I wondered who he thought I meant. We all waved our arms in front of our faces so we wouldn't breath in the dust, and we kept walking.

"Jesus mother-fucking Christ!" said Harry. "Who the hell does he think he is, some asshole from Mars? He nearly killed me! Shit! Who is that, anyway? I ought to have Duke go get him. Where does he live? Duke'll get him alright. Flatten his nose and make him wish he'd never seen me standing in the road. What the hell did he think, anyway? Jesus Christ. Did you see that? He nearly killed me! What an asshole. Damn!"

"Why'd you just stand there?" C.K. asked.

Before Harry could answer, we heard a whimpering sound up on the bank. I couldn't see my house anymore because of the hill. Tucker was standing there. He was wagging his tail low but hard, and his ears were way down. He was happy to see me, but he wasn't sure he should be there. My mom had taught all three dogs not to go beyond the boundary of our property—unless she gave the "okay" command—so Tucker was torn between coming down to be with me and staying where he was.

I was so happy to see him. "Come on, Tuck!" I called. He leaped down the bank and ran right to me. He plopped his butt down at my side and leaned against me. His heavy body felt good against my leg. I petted his big head.

"Here, boy," said Harry. He held his hand out to him. Tucker always loved everyone, but his ears went flat against his head, and he scooted back away from Harry and went around to my other side. "What's wrong with him?" he said and tried to pet him again. Tucker scooted away and went behind C.K. This was real odd.

"It's okay, Tuck," I said. I took hold of his collar and led him up to Harry. I petted Tuck on the head and said, "It's okay. He's nice." Harry held his fingers out to Tucker's nose. Tucker sniffed at them like they smelled bad, and he tried to back away again. Harry reached his hand out to pet him on the head. Then, instead, he made a fist and punched him straight in the nose.

Tucker went, "Ooof!" His face all scrunched up, and he leaped back. He backed way away and sat down. His eyes were all squinty, and he looked confused.

"What'd you do that for!" I screamed at Harry. "You jerk! He was just starting to trust you." I couldn't believe it. What was with

this guy, anyway? I wanted to kick him—just get him out of my sight. Tucker sat next to C.K. and looked like he'd been punished. I wanted to punch Harry in the nose. I had my fist all tight, ready to do it, too.

C.K. said, "Cool it, Johnnie. Harry didn't mean it."

"Didn't mean it!" I couldn't believe C.K. was taking sides with this jerk.

"Yeah," said Harry. "He deserved it. Why won't he let me pet him? What is he, weird like you? Huh? The dog's crazy. All I wanted to do was be nice to him. What'd your ma do to him? Train him weird? Like she trained you weird? Your whole family's weird. That's what my ma said. Said you guys think you're so smart and rich and la de da, like you think you're special or somethin'. You're really just stupid. Like your stupid dog. Stupid! And you're a wimp, too, isn't he C.K.? Why didn't ya go ahead and try to punch me, huh? You knew I'd whip ya, that's why, huh? You're just stupid." His fists were up, and he was sort of bobbing up and down on his toes.

"We gotta get ma's car fixed," said C.K. "Let's go." He started walking. Harry stood and glared at me. I was going to just let the two of them go on. I really wanted to go home, anyway. My stomach felt sick. Harry finally turned away and followed C.K. After he reached C.K. and walked with him a few steps, C.K. turned his head back to look at me. His face didn't say much, but he waved his hand low behind his back for me to hurry and come along.

I didn't know what to do. I sure didn't want to be around Harry anymore, but then I didn't want C.K. to have to put up with the creep all by himself. I started to go with them. Then I started to go home. Then I just stood there trying to decide. Finally, I slipped my fingers under Tucker's collar and followed them. Tuck trotted along by my side, happy to go with me anywhere. Harry never turned around, but he started talking at C.K., using a bunch of swear words and babbling on about something dumb. Tucker and I mostly caught up to them but stayed back a ways.

One time, I heard Harry say my name, and C.K. told him to shush. C.K. glanced back at me. Harry turned around and looked at me, too, but they kept walking. We reached the back property

line of my farm and then started to go over the bridge. It was an arched bridge that was made of huge wood pieces that looked like railroad ties, but they were longer. Underneath the bridge were railroad tracks. Harry and C.K. stopped in the middle of the bridge. They were talking and pointing down at the tracks. I didn't want to just stand at the beginning of the bridge and wait for them to keep going, so Tucker and I slowly went up to them. At first I thought neither of them was going to talk to me. My stomach felt sicker than ever, and I still wanted to go home.

Harry turned and looked at me. His little pig eyes got smaller, and he smiled. "Hey. Sorry I hit your dog. He offended me, that's all. Sorry." He held out his hand to shake. I didn't want to touch it. I had to think about this a minute. He was a creep and I hated him. Why would I want to forgive him? Tucker wagged his tail just a little, so I let go of his collar.

Harry patted his leg and held out the other hand to him. "Here, boy," he said. "I'm sorry." Tucker put his ears way down and sort of crept over to Harry. Harry stroked his head. Tucker let him pet his head, but he didn't sit next to him or lean on him.

"Lassie! Lassie! Here, girl! Come!" It was Mrs. Boggus, screaming at her Collie. Their farmhouse was just on the other side of the bridge. She must have seen us up there. "She's in heat!" she screamed at us. "Don't let your dog near her!" I could tell she wanted to run after Lassie, but she was in her yard with two tiny little kids in one of those plastic swimming pools. The older kid was standing up in the pool, and the little one was sitting in it. She screamed at Lassie some more, but the Collie wouldn't listen and kept running to us.

"Grab Tucker!" I said to Harry, but Tucker had already turned to listen to Mrs. Boggus, and then he saw Lassie. He shot away so fast, no one could have held him. I watched Mrs. Boggus leave her kids in the swimming pool and run after Lassie. I ran after Tucker.

C.K. and Harry and I all ran over the bridge, yelling at Tucker, but he wouldn't listen. I could see him sniffing under Lassie's tail, and she seemed to like it. She held her tail way to one side. Tucker jumped onto her back, and then it looked naughty. I could tell it

was naughty when he made his hips bump against her butt real fast. Mrs. Boggus got to them and tried to pull on Lassie's collar, but Lassie wouldn't move. Then she started batting at Tucker's face. But Tucker didn't seem to care. He stayed there for a few minutes, and then he slid down Lassie's side so both his front legs were on her right side. But they were still stuck together at their private parts. Tucker looked uncomfortable and sort of confused because he couldn't stand right. Finally, he lifted one rear leg over Lassie's back, and they stood there back to back, or tail to tail, stuck together. Mrs. Boggus kept pulling on Lassie's collar.

"You boys keep pulling on 'em while I get the hose. That's supposed to get 'em apart." She hurried off to the other side of her house.

Harry said, "One of your babies is drowning." We all looked at the little pool. The littlest kid had slid down in the water and was on his back kicking his arms and legs in the air. The other one, a girl, just stood there sort of smiling and giggling. Mrs. Boggus ran to the pool and grabbed the baby out of the water. It made terrible noises. It wheezed and sputtered and made a low, croaking sound. Mrs. Boggus turned it on its stomach and started pounding on its back. I thought she might break it. The baby was trying to breathe, but every time Mrs. Boggus hit it, it gasped and started to cry. Then it would try to breathe again.

Bernice is pounding little Jennifer on the back. Jennifer is naked and limp and dripping with the muddy water. Clots of chicken blood and guts are sliding down her body. One long, white feather is stuck in her hair, almost like she'd been playing Indian. Jennifer falls to the ground and digs her fingers into the mud. Her white skin looks extra white between the streaks of mud that cover her buttocks and back. More white chicken feathers are stuck in the mud around the water hole. Suddenly, Jennifer makes a horrible honking noise, then tries to cough; honks again, then coughs and cries and wails, "Mommy! Help!"

"You know your mommy's at work, Jennifer," *says Bernice, stroking the little girl's back.* "She knows you're being baptized, and she's very glad we're able to do it today. You know we can only do three children a day. You're one of the special ones today. Satan is very, very pleased. He will*

be very good to you now that you're baptized in his name." Jennifer coughs lightly and whimpers a little. She's breathing normally now and starts to shiver, even though it's very hot out. The sun has begun to dry the ends of her hair, and little hard, corkscrew curls are starting to form.

I'm next. The hole in the ground is about as large as one of our big trash cans at home. I can't see how far down it goes because the water has blood and mud in it. It's very dark. I see a couple of small bones with some flesh still on them. I don't know if they're from a rabbit or a chicken.

I'm excited and scared. I get to give myself to Satan today. Lots of good things will happen then. I'll be very happy. I'll get to go to K-Mart and steal toys. I'll be able to have sex with one of the older boys. I'll get to feed the chickens. And I'll get to choose which chicken is a gift for Satan. Satan will love me even more. And I'll get to choose two candy pills instead of one.

One of the teacher's aids takes Jennifer to the shower. She seems fine. She's smiling. Jack takes my hand. "You ready, Johnnie? This is your special day. Want to feel the water? It's nice and warm." I put my hand in it. It isn't as warm as bath water, but almost. "It has all the things in it Satan loves. Blood, bones—what else?"

"Pee pee?" I ask.

"That's right. Do you want to put some more in there? Satan loves golden showers. Can you go now?"

I tug on my penis a little and try to pee. A few drops come, but that's all. "That's all I got," I say. I look up at Jack's big face. He has nice blue eyes and nice brown hair.

"And what else does Satan love?"

I think a minute. Blood, bones, golden pee pee—Oh, yes, "Poo poo!" I say, proud of myself.

"That's right!" says Jack smiling. "And whose poo poo is in there?" he coaxes.

"Yours!" I say, happy.

Jack looks happy too. "That's right! You're very smart! And why is Satan happy that it's mine?"

"Umm— Because you're the head guy?"

"And what's the name for the head guy?" he chuckles. I can't think of it. I look at Jack. He's pushing his lips forward into a little point. "P—Pr— Preee—" he says and waits after each sound to see if I can guess.

"Priest!" I shout.

"Yey! You got it!" he says and hugs me. I love him. I hug his neck and press my face into his big, warm cheek. He smells good, like perfume. But I don't want to let go. I'm afraid of the water. I hold onto him tight. He explains, "Johnnie, you don't need to be afraid of the water. The water won't hurt you. It will wash away all the awful God things in your body so you can be all fresh and clean for Satan. Don't you think that will make Satan happy? And love you all the more? And do nice things for you? You know what you get to do afterwards, don't you?" I shrug my shoulders, but I think I know. He says, "A toy? A toy from K-Mart? This afternoon. You and me and Jennifer."

"What about Toby?" I ask. He's waiting to go in after me. Bernice is pushing him on the swing right now.

"Oh, yes, of course. Toby too. But Toby has to wait till you're done. So, as soon as you go in the water, then Toby gets to go, and then we all go to K-Mart."

I look at the water. I don't want to make Jack mad. "Okay," I say. I think about Jennifer and the horrible croaking sounds she made. I decide that I'll be stronger. I take a couple deep breaths for practice, like my Aunt Paulette showed me once when she tried to teach me to swim. I feel strong and brave. I look at Jack. "Okay," I say.

He guides me to the edge of the water hole, and I feel my feet gush in the mud. I curl my toes over the edge. The water plays with my toes. It's warm. I see several bones, some wet white feathers, and some pieces of Jack's poo poo floating on top. I take a deep breath and hold my nose closed with my fingers. Jack's hands grip my arms as he lifts me up and holds me above the middle of the water hole. Quickly, my feet, knees, thighs, butt, back, shoulders, neck, chin, mouth, eyes, and hair go under. Jack puts his hand on my head to hold me down. My heart pounds. I raise my arms and hands, trying to feel the air. They bump pieces of poo poo and a bone. I hear Jack talking in a low, steady tone. He goes on and on. I'm running out of air. I feel his big hand on the top of my head, holding me down. I want to get up now. I want to breathe. My chest starts to hurt. I start kicking, try-ing to get up. I reach higher with my hands, grabbing fistfuls of air. Jack's hand is bigger and stronger now on my head. I can't get away from it. I try moving to the side, but the hand follows. I'm going to have to breathe

in. I don't think I can stop it. No, no! I scream inside. Don't breathe! Don't breathe! I can't help it. Huuuuuuuuh. I feel water go into my lungs. I cough it out. But more comes in. I'm going to die! I'm only half aware of Jack's hands under my arms, grabbing my body, pulling me up. I feel daylight. I try to breathe, but nothing happens. I try to cough, but nothing happens. My chest and throat just stop. I can't get them to do anything. I go to sleep.

Honk! Wheeeeze. Honk, honk, wheeeeze! Is it Jennifer? My head is spinning. I try to open my eyes, but the sky and the trees and the grass go round and round. Then, air. A little. I cough hard, make a horrible noise. Then more air. I cough. A little more air. I open my eyes and see mud. And I look at my arm. It has red and brown splotches on it, with little clear rivers running down. Air. Oh, the air in my chest feels cool and so wonderful. My heart is still pounding and I feel very tired and weak. I feel the sun on my back and on my legs. It feels good.

"Johnnie, you were great. You are clean now. Satan will love you forever and give you all the toys you want and make you feel good whenever you want. I'm very proud of you, Johnnie." I want Jack to hold me. I turn over and look at him. I hold my arms out to him to pick me up. But he steps back. "You belong to Satan now. Let's get you cleaned up." He stands tall and reaches for my hand. My legs are shaky, but I stand up. Once more I reach for him to hold me. But he lets my hand drop and pushes on my shoulder, pushes me forward to go into the school.

10

Yeah, shit, Johnnie had them spells or whatever they was. Like I said, hell, we'd be in the middle of something and he'd just space out. You couldn't talk to him or nothin'. They lasted only a minute or two and then he'd, like, wake up. I told my school nurse about it once, and she said it sounded like some kind of fits—you know, epilepsy or somethin'. She thought he might be on some kind of medicine for it. But I asked him once if he took any pills, and he said no. So, I don't know what was going on.

As for Harry, well, he was okay. At first I didn't like him at all. He was a damned motor mouth, never stopped talking. And he talked about stuff I didn't know nothin' about—drugs and sex and shit like that. Actually, now that I think about it, he really made me uncomfortable. Any time I had the choice between playing with Johnnie and playing with Harry, I chose Johnnie. Johnnie was steady, man, you know, like a friend is supposed to be. And Harry, well, he was hard to take with all his jabbering. But there was something—oh, shit, I don't know—bad, like, you know—exciting, maybe. Yeah, that's the word—exciting. But I guess it sorta scared me at first. I didn't know what to do with him. I didn't know how to talk like he did, and I guess I sorta *did* want to talk like that, and sorta not, too. Johnnie was solid. Yeah, solid. I can't believe I'm comin' up with all these good words. But they fit, man, you know? Shit. Harry was "exciting" and Johnnie was "solid." Yeah.

———

That time we was walkin' back to my house so Marge could take Harry to get the fuel filter for my ma, there was all that commotion with Linda Boggus's baby trying to drown and Tucker and Lassie stuck together. By the time Linda Boggus got her baby breathing right, the dogs had come apart again. Linda Boggus

didn't seem to care, though, cuz of her baby. I guess the baby was okay. It was out in the yard with her a few days later.

Watching them dogs "do it" brought back a memory of Little Friends, though. It kinda freaked me out when I thought about it. Harry and Johnnie had been there too, but I didn't say nothin' to them right then. Besides, Johnnie was havin' one of his spells. And we just never talked about it, anyway. It always kinda seemed like he just didn't remember.

It wasn't the dogs with their tails stuck together that reminded me of the animal suits. It was when Tucker was on top of Lassie's back. When we was at Little Friends, Jack and Bernice had all these animal suits—monkeys and dogs and cats, rabbits, squirrels, skunks, and some funny bird suits. They didn't have any feathers, so it was hard to believe they was birds. But all the suits fit little kids, and they all had the part between our legs cut out—you know, where our private parts was. And Jack and Bernice would get all the kids to take all their clothes off and get into the suits and then ask us if we knew how the animals made babies together. They'd have the camera there, the one that spit the pictures out. And we'd always start with the dogs cuz some of us had seen dogs do it. Harry always wanted to go first. And he always got the Dalmation suit. Sally usually had the lady Dalmation suit. We'd all have a suit on, and we'd all line up, and Jack pretended he was an animal trainer. He had a big bullwhip that he snapped real loud. It scared us all. One day he hit Tommy Jones on the back with it. I don't think Jack meant to hurt him, but maybe he did. Tommy cried a whole lot. It went right through his squirrel suit. Bernice was real mad at Jack cuz there was a big red line across Tommy's back. She took him into the kitchen and put cream on it. She kept callin' Jack "mother fucker."

Anyway, we all had to march in a real straight line all through the school and then down into the basement. They had a bunch of cages, and we each had to go into a cage and be locked in there until it was our turn. Some of the kids hated the cages and cried and screamed to get out. I kinda liked it. It was a safe place, and it was better to be in the cage than out of it. They had all the

lights out, so it was dark in the cages, but then they'd have one light shine right on the middle of the floor. And then one pair of animals at a time would come out of their cages and try to make a baby. Jack called it "fucking." But the way he said it, none of us used that word.

Harry always went first. Him and Sally. Sally didn't want to go first, but she always had the lady Dalmation suit on, so she had to be with Harry. They'd go out to the middle, with the light shinin' on 'em. They'd lay on their backs. Bernice had a big jar of Vaseline. She'd get a big glob on her finger and rub it between Sally's legs. Sally cried a little at first. We could see Bernice's finger going up inside Sally and she'd just rub her like that for a while and put her finger in and out. Sally'd stop cryin' after a while and just lay there.

While Bernice was doing that to Sally, Jack would start rubbing Harry's penis. He'd spit on his fingers and then rub up and down on it. And then his penis would stand up straight. Harry never complained and seemed to like it. Then, after a while, Bernice would ask Jack, "Is it time?" and Jack would say, "Yeah." And Bernice would make Sally get on her hands and knees. Then Jack would bring Harry over to Sally. Harry would be on his hands and knees too, right behind her. Then Jack would say to all the children, "This is how dogs fuck. You'll get to do it too. Satan will love you for doing this." He'd sorta hurry and say this to us, then rub Harry's penis some more. When Harry's penis would start to go down, Jack would have to use more spit and rub it again.

Then, he'd scoot Harry up behind Sally and try to push Harry's penis into Sally's hole. Sally didn't like that, but Bernice held her so she couldn't move. It never did work because Harry's penis would go limp, and Jack would try to get it stiff again. The best he ever did was get it aimed at Sally, and Jack would grab the camera. Then he'd lay down and take pictures of them, some of them up real close to their butts, and some from way back, and some more from the side.

Then he'd say, "Okay, that's good. Satan loves you very much and he'll bring you all kinds of toys." And then he'd give each one

109

a quick hug and send them to their cages. All the cages had pad-locks, and only Jack knew how to open them.

The one animal-suit day that I was thinkin' about when Lassie and Tucker was "fucking," I had the monkey suit on. And some girl I didn't know had the lady monkey suit on. And we was second that day. When Jack came and unlocked our cages, I watched Harry. He sat in his cage cross-legged like an Indian and just sat back and enjoyed the show. He could relax now. I could remember, though, real clear, the look on his face. It was different than the other kids'. They was all scared. Harry didn't seem to be. But his older broth-ers was there, too. Maybe that's why.

Anyway, I'd done this before, but I'd always had a rabbit suit or a bird suit on and had to do what Harry'd just done. I never liked it, but it wasn't horrible. It didn't hurt or nothin'. It just felt creepy, like we knew we shouldn't be doin' this. But Jack and Bernice kept tellin' us it was a good thing that would make Satan happy, and then we'd get more toys and candy. So, I went out into the light. I didn't like all the other kids watchin'. A lot of them was still cryin'. And so was the new girl with the lady monkey suit. Jack was sorta draggin' her by one arm and tellin' her she'd like this.

"You know what?" he said to the girl. "You get to do some-thin' different cuz monkeys are primates, and primates can do it different ways, like people. People are primates. You ever see your mommy and daddy fucking?" The girl looked real scared and didn't know what he was talkin' about. She just whimpered and had a hold of her monkey tail with both hands. I couldn't see her face very well cuz of the mask. And when Bernice tried to get her to lie still so she could put the Vaseline between her legs, she screamed and tried to run away. Jack caught her and brought her back to Bernice. Then he got the bullwhip and cracked it once right in front of her. He didn't say nothin', just cracked the whip. The girl shut up and laid down. She spread her legs out like Bernice told her to and let Bernice rub her.

I laid on my back and let Jack put his spit on me and rub. It was a weird feeling. It felt bad and I hated it, but it felt good too, especially when my penis stood up. That day, I was afraid Jack was

gonna bite it off cuz he leaned down and went to put his mouth on it. I jumped back, but he put his big hand on my belly and told me this wouldn't hurt. "This is what Satan wants me to do. Maybe tomorrow I'll let you do this to me." And he put his mouth on my penis and sort of licked it and made his mouth go up and down. It felt good, but I was still afraid he would bite it off. After a while, I guess I just didn't think about it. And when Bernice asked if it was time, Jack said, "Yeah."

When he led me to the girl, Bernice had the girl just stay where she was on her back with her knees apart. He told me to lay on the girl and put my penis in her hole. I didn't want to lay on the girl. I didn't want our faces to be together, even with the masks on. So I said, "No."

"I'll get the whip," Jack said.

So, I tried layin' on the girl without touchin' her. I knew Jack would try to push my penis into her hole, so I waited for him to do that. I was up on my toes and my hands, like a push-up. But Jack took so long puttin' spit on my penis and rubbin' it some more, that my arms got tired. So I let my knees come down on the floor between the girl's legs. That helped a little. But he was takin' so long, and my arms finally got so tired, I had to lay on her. She started cryin', and I could feel Jack fiddling with my penis. The girl shouted "Ow!" once real loud, so I pushed back up on my hands and toes.

"God damn it!" Jack shouted. "I just about had it. Clive, don't you do that again, and you," he looked at the girl, "don't you yell again. That didn't hurt! Bernice, you get the camera. Clive, let yourself come down now." He was pulling on my penis now, and I felt it get soft. This never did work, and I was pretty sure Jack wanted the boys to put their penises inside the girls. It just never happened, but I guess they was happy with the pictures they got. "A little closer to her, Clive. That a boy! Got the camera, Bernie?" And they took a bunch of pictures. I was real glad to get back to my cage. The girl cried some more in her cage, and then she went to sleep.

Johnnie had grabbed Tucker, and Lassie went home. The three of us kept walkin' to my house. Harry was smilin' real big

and not sayin' nothin' for a change. I looked at him and thought about him at Little Friends. I didn't like him at all right then and was real glad Johnnie had decided to come along. I thought he was gonna go home before we even got to the bridge. That stupid Harry punched Johnnie's dog right in the nose. I couldn't believe it. So I think it was real big of Johnnie to keep comin' along. I hoped he would. Harry said he was a wimp, and for a minute there I kinda thought so too cuz he wouldn't punch Harry. I could tell he wanted to, but he didn't.

So, I was thinkin' about us kids at Little Friends and feelin' all sorta freaked out, and lookin' at Harry made it worse. I was feelin' kinda jittery. I wished my ma hadn't said we should all go to the party together. I didn't even want to talk to Harry. But he was walkin' right next to me, and Johnnie had gone back to walkin' behind us with Tucker. Harry looked right at me once. He had these tiny little eyes that was kinda creepy. I looked right at him. I didn't have nothin' to say, and I guess he didn't neither. But he got this real strange smile on his face, like he was enjoying some secret or somethin'. He was creepy, that's for sure. And he didn't look away, neither, you know how you'll look at somebody and then you both look away? Well, I started to look away, but he didn't.

I turned around to see Johnnie. He smiled and made his eyebrows go up. I wanted to walk with him and get rid of Harry. "Harry," I said. "Keep goin', okay? I just wanna ask Johnnie somethin'." Harry stopped and looked a little mad. "Go on," I said. "I'll catch up in just a second." Then I whispered, "It's about his stupid dog." That was a lie, but it got rid of him for a minute. He nodded and walked on.

Johnnie walked up beside me. He let Tucker go, but Tucker stayed with us. Johnnie looked happy. His face was all bright, and he waited to see what I was gonna say. "Harry's a creep," I said.

"Geez! Where'd he escape from, some mental hospital?"

Once Johnnie said that, I realized Harry *was* kinda crazy. I got goose bumps. He reminded me of that creepy movie about the guy who seemed so nice but was really murdering people all over town, and no one thought it was him cuz he was so nice. "I'd like to

get rid of him and just you and me go skating," I said. "I just don't know how."

Johnnie thought for a minute. He always came up with good ideas, so I figured he'd come up with somethin' now. But he kept thinkin' and didn't say nothin'. Finally, he said, "I don't know. He's going to fix your mom's car. Is he? I mean, can he really do it? Does he really know how?"

"I think so. That's all his brothers do is work on cars. And he's with them most of the time, I think. His ma works three or four jobs and ain't never home."

"Okay. Well, I don't know. Maybe he can go alone with his mom to the parts store, and you and I can stay at your house. But then we still have to go to the party with him, right? Will he have other friends there?"

"I don't know. It's all cousins and relatives."

"Wait. Are you his cousin?" Johnnie looked shocked.

"Yeah, some kinda cousin—second or third cousins. Ma explained it once, but I forgot. Let's see. Her brother is married to Aunt Candy, and her sister married a guy named Bill. And Bill's daughter from his first marriage married a guy named—"

Johnnie started gigglin'. "And they found this creepy baby on the side of the road one day, picked it up, and said, 'Oh, yuck!' But they kept it anyway and named it Harry, right?"

I started gigglin' too. Harry heard us laughin' and turned around. He looked mean. We shut up real quick. "Let's catch up to him," I said. I didn't want him to do nothin' else weird cuz he was mad at us. So, we sorta jogged up to him. He still didn't say nothin', which got me kinda worried cuz he always talked a lot.

Now we was in front of the Panzerov's. All three fat daughters was out in the garden pullin' weeds. They had a yellow dog named Sparky that always came out barking and snarling. And today it did the same thing. They yelled and yelled at it, "Sparky! Sparky!" but it ignored them. Tucker stepped out in front of us. He looked like a majestic king, the way he stood. Sparky turned and ran.

"Cool dog," said Harry. "Tucker, here Tucker." He patted his leg for Tucker to come. But Tucker went in a circle around by

Johnnie instead. "That really is a stupid dog," he said to Johnnie. Johnnie didn't say nothin'. Good for him.

Finally we got to my house. Marge was inside drinkin' coffee. She had on her same old green stretch pants and a big loose blouse with black flowers all over it. She had long, straight brown hair that hung down in front of her shoulders. Ma said it looked stringy. She thought Marge should cut it and get a permanent. And wear some make-up and lose weight. You could see all kinds of lumps of fat under her green pants.

"Sure took long enough for you to get here," she said. She had a real strong southern accent, Johnnie told me later. I don't think he liked southern accents. She didn't sound bad to me. She sounded just like my Gramma Bookout. Johnnie said dumb stuff sometimes.

Then Harry started in. "Gloria's car just needs a fuel filter. I took the old one out, it's pretty dirty, and I checked the radiator hose connections, they was okay, and the spark plug wires was all connected right, the jets in the carburetor took some blowing out, oh, yeah, and two of the spark plugs needed their gaps reset, and I did that, and it really should start with a new fuel filter, it was really the only thing left that it could be, and that's how fuel filters acts when they's all plugged up—the car just stops runnin', so I got money from Gloria, and you gotta take me down to the parts store so I can get a new fuel filter, and then we can stop by her car, I'll put it on, and the car should start right up, and then we can go to the party."

"Okay," said Marge, and we followed her to her car, except I really didn't want to go.

I said, "Marge, Johnnie and I'll just wait here. Johnnie gets carsick pretty easy, and there's no sense us goin' to the parts store."

"Okay," said Marge, and she and Harry got in the car and drove away. What a relief!

Yeah, I'd really had it with Harry that day. And I felt real close to Johnnie, you know? Somehow, seein' the creep together with

the angel, so to speak. Shit, Johnnie sure was an angel. Too bad I wasn't. Johnnie and I sat and watched cartoons for a while, and I was happy to be with my best friend. But after a while—hell, I don't know—a half hour or so, I started thinkin' about that damned black cross I'd hid in the barn. I'd taken it out a few times when Johnnie wasn't around. I think he really didn't remember stuff from Little Friends. I'd say things every once in a while, like about the cross, like askin' if he'd like to play funeral, and he'd just look at me funny, like he didn't know what I was talkin' about. Well, shit, and when Tucker and Lassie was fucking, I thought about askin' him later if he remembered the animal suits and the fucking at the daycare center, and then I decided not to. I sorta knew he didn't remember. Shit. It's too bad we all didn't just forget, I guess. But it wasn't that bad, when you think about it. We all came out alive, nobody was really hurt. They was just playin' with us. Yeah, ha! It was a different kind of playin' from what most kids do, but shit, like I said, no one was hurt. It never really bothered me.

———

"Wanna play funeral?" I asked him. We was watching a *Bullwinkle* cartoon, and it was pretty dumb, and I just kinda wanted to see what he'd say. He gave me that funny look again, so I didn't say nothin' else. "How about goin' up to your barn? We oughta check on the tunnel, see if anybody's been messin' with it."

Johnnie had trouble pullin' hisself away from the TV sometimes, so it took him a minute to answer. It was sorta like he had to slowly pull his eyes off the screen. Finally, he looked at me. "I'm sure the shaft's okay. Don't you like this?"

"It's kinda dumb," I said.

Johnnie thought about that a minute. "You think so? I love it. But sure, let's go. I can take Tucker home, then, too. My mom's probably wondering where he is."

I had this urge to go out and get the cross and take it with us. Johnnie went out the door and started callin' for Tucker. Tucker was over by the chicken house. He was funny. He just sat outside the pen and watched the chickens. He reminded me of Tramp in

Lady and the Tramp, the way his head was cocked and his ears up. Funny dog. I liked Tramp. I liked Tucker, too.

"Just a second," I said to Johnnie. "I'll be right back." And I ran and got the cross. I stuck it in my pants, under my shirt so Johnnie wouldn't see it.

"Where'd you go?" he asked, when I got back.

"Just checking on Miss Kitty. Her kittens is due any day, Ma said."

Johnnie said, "Oh," and we started walkin'.

We walked on up to Johnnie's. Johnnie wanted to go see his ma first, so we went in the house. His ma was on the porch reading a book.

Johnnie said, "Hi, Mom. Mrs. Bookout's car died, and Harry's fixing it, but his mom had to take him to go get a fuel filter. So we came here." Christine looked up from her book. "I had to come here because Tucker followed us to C.K.'s house. But he wasn't bad. He only came when I called him. Anyway, I just wanted to say 'hi!'" He grinned at his ma. She smiled a little, and then looked sorta confused.

"Harry's fixing the car? How old is Harry?"

"Eleven," I said. "He knows all about cars cuz his brothers works on 'em all the time. We was surprised too."

"His brothers *work* not *works* on cars. And we 'were' surprised, not 'was.'" Christine was always correctin' my English. Her way sounded funny to me. I'd gotten used to Johnnie talkin' that way, but that was just Johnnie. No one else I knew talked like that. Well, maybe some teachers.

"Okay," I said. "But he really does know what he's doing. His own ma trusted him. That's why she took him to the parts store."

"Harry. What's Harry's last name?"

"Um." I had to think about that. "Johnson, I think."

"Johnson? Is it Johnson?" she asked.

"I think so. Why? Do you know him?"

"I might, " she said.

I don't know how she woulda known him, but I didn't care. "Johnnie, we probably ought to get goin'. They could be almost

done by now." I explained to Christine, "We just came by to check on our tunnel. My ma's car is just down by the highway." We got up to go. Johnnie went and gave his ma a big hug. I didn't see him do that too often. He squeezed her real hard.

"You okay?" she asked him. She looked worried.

"Yeah," he said kinda soft. I guess he really didn't want to go be with Harry again. But we had to. And I had to get rid of this cross. It was pokin' my belly, especially when I sat down. Johnnie and his ma looked at each other for a long time. That was weird. I started to just go, and then Johnnie followed. But he looked back at his ma one last time and gave a little wave. I sorta felt like a creep makin' him go be with Harry. But I had to get rid of this cross. I was plannin' to stick it between some hay bales halfway down the tunnel.

When we got out there, we went right to the arena where the hay was. We stood in the doorway, and I said, "I can just go up there real quick and see if everything's okay."

We didn't see Cross-Eyed Ladonna's car there, so when she said somethin', she scared us half to death. We both jumped. "Hey, Johnnie, C.K! How you guys doing?" She'd been in one of the stalls. "Oh, did I scare you? I'm sorry." She laughed. "You both jumped about a foot in the air! What're you up to? Somethin' you shouldn't be doin'?" She laughed some more. Then another woman appeared. It seemed like I'd seen her before, but I couldn't think of where. She was kinda short and had chopped-off-looking black hair, kinda like a man's. She reminded me of how a lady mole might look. Her nose was long and pointy, and her eyes was kinda beady-looking, but she was still kinda pretty.

Cross-Eyed Ladonna said, "Mary, this is C.K. and Johnnie. Johnnie lives here, and C.K. almost lives here," she laughed. "But he really lives down the road. He's Walter's son."

"Nice to meet you," Mary said. Her voice was quiet and slow. She reached out and shook hands with each of us.

"Mary's real interested in horses and is gonna take some ridin' lessons from me." Mary stood there and smiled. "I was just showin' her how to clean a stall. Very important." She laughed again. "So, what're you guys up to?"

This was my chance to go hide the cross, so I said, "Johnnie, you can talk to them while I go check on the tunnel. Then we better get goin'." Johnnie nodded and seemed all sorta googly-eyed like he always got around Cross-Eyed Ladonna. I think he really liked her, like maybe even for a girlfriend, but she was way too old.

I ran and climbed the hay pile as fast as I could. I pushed my arms and legs against the walls of the tunnel and went down about halfway. I stuck the cross between two bales that wasn't pushed together real close, and then as I went up, I counted how many bales there was to the top. Nine. I was relieved to have a good place for it. I also felt a little excited cuz now I wanted to do some stuff with it.

When I got back to Johnnie and Cross-Eyed Ladonna and Mary, Mary was back in the stall, and Johnnie was talkin' to Cross-Eyed Ladonna about his science project at school. Somethin' about DNA. "We better go," I said. I gave him a little punch on the arm. "Come on." He left Cross-Eyed Ladonna sorta like he left his ma—real slow.

11

When I met Mary in the barn later that day, I had a reaction similar to the one I'd had from meeting Harry. It was, again, a more intuitive sense of fear combined with an underlying terror. At my core, I knew she was evil, but it wasn't something tangible. I was aware that she was similar to Harry but couldn't have defined it. I reacted by wanting to shrink back from her. The reason I didn't, of course, was my opposing feelings for Ladonna. I was smitten, no doubt, by my first love, and I remember the giddiness, shyness, and warmth when I encountered her. Besides, she was beautiful, and I'd probably think so today.

That day was one of the more emotional ones of my childhood. Between the horrors of Harry, watching Tucker mate with Lassie, feeling terribly jealous of the mild interest C.K. had in Harry, and running into the opposing forces of Mary and Cross-Eyed Ladonna, I was getting frayed at the edges. When we reached Gloria Bookout's car, the fuel filter had been replaced, and the car was ready to go. In fact, Harry and Marge had just left and told Gloria they'd meet us at the roller rink.

Mrs. Bookout was annoyed because we had just gotten there. "Where've you two been? I was just about to drive down to the house." She was standing outside the car with her hands on her hips.

"I had to take Tucker home," I said, as politely as I could. "He followed us down to your house."

"Oh. Okay. Well, they just left." She seemed to forgive us.

And boy, was I happy that Harry was gone. C.K. seemed glad, too, and we slid into the back seat. C.K. started giggling.

"What?" I whispered.

He whispered to me, "Do you think Marge'll try to skate?" He held his hands down by his legs and made big round shapes with his fingers, then moved his shoulders back and forth like an elephant. I burst out laughing. "Shh," he said. He didn't want his mom to know what we were laughing about. Then he put on a real straight face. "Are you gonna skate, Ma?" he asked. I put on a real straight face, too, which wasn't hard when I thought about Mrs. Bookout skating. She'd look pretty good.

"I might," she said. "Why? I bet you think I can't, don't you?" She sort of sounded like she wanted to fight about it.

"I just never seen you," he answered.

"There's a lotta things you ain't seen me do, and skatin's just one of 'em." She sounded mad now.

"Okay, sorry," said C.K.

"You oughta be. Think you're so smart sometimes."

"I was just wondering," C.K. said softly. He looked at me and shrugged.

"I saw that." She was looking at us in her rearview mirror. "Johnnie, don't you take his side. He's always givin' me a hard time."

I guess we both figured that we ought to just shut up until we were alone. I tried to look out the window, but it was the same old scenery. I looked down at the seat and saw my fingers drumming the upholstery. I felt funny—kind of nervous or shaky. I let my head fall back against the seat. It was weird because I felt all alert and full of energy, but I was tired, too. The ride seemed to go on forever, and I wanted it to go on forever. I wanted to roller skate with C.K., and I wanted to just go to sleep, all at the same time.

When we got there, I didn't want to get out. C.K. just sat there too, and Mrs. Bookout sat there and let the car run for a while. I don't know why *they* felt that way. It was their family's party. Finally, Mrs. Bookout turned the car off. She grabbed her purse and sighed and said, "Okay, guys, let's go. Lock your doors." She waited just a second, then said, "Did you hear me, C.K.?"

"Yes, I heard you. I can't lock it until I'm out."

"Don't you talk back to me, you smart mouth! You are really bugging me today." She looked at him real mean. I thought he'd been very polite.

"I'm not talkin' back. I just answered," C.K. said.

"You are talkin' back, and you ought to be damned grateful I even brought you to this party. Now go in there and skate." She gave him another mean look.

Geez! I thought. When I wasn't around C.K.'s parents for a while, I forgot how unfair they could be. And C.K. always looked like his feelings were hurt, but he never said anything against them. Sometimes, he even stuck up for his mom or dad when I said I thought they weren't being fair. Like now, when we got into the roller rink, and Mrs. Bookout was pretty far behind us, I said, "Why's your mom acting so mean?"

He said, "She's not mean. She's just upset about the car."

I said, "Oh." Then I looked around for Harry. He was already skating with another boy, an older boy with slicked-back hair. I was relieved. Now, if we could just avoid him, I'd be happy.

We went to the counter and asked for skates. I wore size six and a half, and C.K. didn't know his size. Mrs. Bookout was behind us talking to a lady. "Mrs. Bookout," I called. She looked at me. "What size shoe does C.K. wear?"

"He should know. Doesn't he know? C.K., how come you don't know?" She was looking real mean again.

C.K. said, "I wasn't there when you bought these shoes. You just brought 'em home, remember?"

She came over and grabbed his arm. "If you talk to me like that in front of my friends once more, you're grounded for a month. You figure it out," and she huffed away.

"Here, give me one of your shoes," I said. He handed one to me, and I looked inside for the size.

"I looked when she first bought 'em and couldn't find it," he said.

I looked on the bottom of the sole, and it wasn't there, and I looked on the inside of the tongue, and it wasn't there. It wasn't printed on the inside of the sides, either. Then, way in by the arch,

there was a little skinny tag sewn on. I turned it up and had to open the shoe real wide to see it. A number seven was on it. "Seven," I said, showing him.

"Wow. I couldn't find it. Thanks. Seven," he told the man behind the counter. The man gave us our skates, and we went to a bench to put them on.

"How can your mom buy you shoes and you not be there to try them on?" I asked. "How does she know they'll fit?"

He shrugged. "I guess she just knows." I looked at his feet and wondered if the shoes really fit him. Whenever my mom took me for shoes, the lady always measured my feet first, brought out three or four pairs, and had me try them all on. She'd push on my toes to see how much growing room I had, and she'd feel the sides to see if they were too wide or too narrow. Then my mom would push and feel. And finally, we'd decide which were the best ones. How could Mrs. Bookout know if the shoes fit C.K. if he didn't try them on?

"Hey, chicken shit!" It was Harry. He'd skated onto the carpeting and stood in front of us. The older boy was next to him. The boy had on a black t-shirt with the sleeves rolled up and tight blue jeans. "Where's your stupid dog?" Harry laughed. "You should see this guy's wimpy dog," he said to his friend. Then the two of them rolled away. Harry was waving his hands and talking non-stop. My heart was pounding.

"Just ignore him," C.K. said. We finished tying our skates on. "Race you to the floor!" he said and scooted off. He got there first and glided out onto the shiny wooden surface. I'd had almost a year of lessons as part of my PE class at school and caught up to him real fast. We coasted along the floor together.

"Who's that other guy?" I asked.

"His name is Bruce. He's kind of a creep. Gets into a lot of trouble. They kicked him out of school last year and now his mother has to send him to the church school—she has to pay for him to go there."

"Is he a cousin, too?"

"Yeah, but I don't know how, or why. I don't like him, and I don't see him very often. I just stay away from him."

Lucky for us, Harry seemed real happy to be with Bruce, and they ignored us. We skated for a while, and then the mothers called us to come eat. We ate a bunch of pizza and then birthday cake. The kid whose birthday it was was only five years old. He couldn't even skate. But that was okay. The pizza and cake were real good.

We watched C.K.'s mother. She and Marge were whispering to each other. Then they came over to us. Mrs. Bookout said, "C.K, I've got to go with Marge into town. There's no reason your pa can't pick you up here after work. Here's a quarter. Go call him and tell him to come get the two of you when he gets off." She looked at her watch. "That'll only be forty-five minutes." She looked at Marge like they had a secret. "I've gotta go now. Bye." She gave him a quick kiss on the cheek and hurried away with Marge.

C.K. stood there with his hand still out and the quarter sitting in it. I don't know why, but I felt scared. I guess I was still worried Harry and Bruce might do something to us. Then I got mad. How could she do that? My mom would never just leave me. C.K. stood there and watched her go. He had no expression on his face, but his mouth was sort of open like he was about to say something. "Come on," I said. "Let's go call your dad." I put my hand on his shoulder for just a second. Then I led the way to the phone. He didn't know his dad's work number, so we had to look it up in the phone book. I read the number off to him while he dialed.

"Hello," he said. His voice was real quiet. "Can I speak to Walter Bookout?" Then he listened. "Okay," he said and hung up.

"What?" It sounded to me like I was screaming at him. I really wanted to get out of there now. "What happened?" I demanded.

"They said he's working on the line and can't come to the phone."

"That's all? How are we supposed to get a hold of him?"

C.K. shrugged.

I said, "Well, call back and tell the lady to tell him to pick us up here."

"Yeah," he smiled. "Good idea." He went to pick up the receiver and stopped. "She only gave me one quarter."

"Geez!" I said.

"Well, she probably only had one. You know, after paying for the fuel filter." We stood and looked back in at the roller rink. Most of the people had started skating again. Bruce and Harry were skating too.

"Can you ask one of your relatives for a quarter?"

He thought about that for a minute. He seemed to be sort of squirming, like he really didn't want to. Then I remembered this special calling card my mom had given me. It let me call home, but only home, without a quarter. But the card was in my desk. I had memorized the number a while back. Now, if I could just remember it. Oh, yes, the numbers spelled "toll" when you turned the card upside down. So, it was my home number plus 7701. Yes! I was pleased with myself.

"I'll call my mom and then she can call your dad," I said.

He scrunched up his face. "How? You got a quarter?"

I decided not to tell him how and just do it. "Magic," I said and made my eyebrows go up and down. He grinned. I dialed "0" and then my home number and waited for a beep. My mom had rehearsed this with me a bunch of times, so I remembered what to do even though I hadn't done it yet. I really didn't know if it would work, so I was sort of holding my breath. I heard the beep and then dialed 7701. I waited. Then it began to ring.

"Hello?" She sounded kind of sleepy. I didn't care.

"Mom, it's me. We're stuck at the roller rink. Can you call C.K.'s dad at work and tell him to come get us? Mrs. Bookout had to leave and gave C.K. just one quarter, and it's gone."

"She just left you there?"

"Yes. Can you call Mr. Bookout for us?"

"Well—no, I'll come and get you. I'll come now." And she was there in five minutes.

As soon as we got in the back seat and buckled our seat belts, she asked, "So, C.K., your mom just left and didn't say why?"

"Yeah, sort of," said C.K.

My mom normally would have asked C.K. a whole bunch of questions, but this time she didn't, and we rode back without saying anything else, except when she asked if we wanted an ice cream cone, and we both said no.

"C.K., do you want me to take you home or to our house?"

C.K. said, "Your house would be nice."

When we got home and my mom turned the car off, she asked, "How about a sandwich?" My mom was always trying to feed us. I think she thought it made her a good mother. We told her we just had pizza. "Watermelon?" she asked. We told her we just had birthday cake. "C.K., would you like to call your dad?"

He shrugged and sort of mumbled, "No." She looked at him like she loved him. I think she did. When he stayed over, she always gave him a hug goodnight.

"You guys might want to check on Stitches. He cut his leg on something, and we have him isolated in the small pasture. There are carrots and watermelon rinds in the refrigerator. I'm sure he'd like a treat."

"Sure, okay," we said and went in the house. We grabbed the bag of watermelon rinds and a couple carrots and walked out to the barn. No cars were there. When C.K. was here, I liked it best when no boarders were in the barn. It was more like our own place then.

Stitches nickered when he saw us coming. He walked with a limp straight to us and pushed the plastic bag around with his nose. He gave C.K. a shove as if he were saying, "Hurry up. Give me those treats!" C.K. laughed and gave him a piece of watermelon rind. He slurped and munched it, and lots of juice ran out of his mouth. He swallowed and practically dove into the bag for more.

"Geez!" said C.K., and he handed him another piece. Even though C.K. told me four years ago that he was getting a pony, so far he didn't have one. Stitches nearly took his fingers off, grabbing for it. We put the rest on the grass for him and gave him a pat on the neck. Then we raced for our castle. As usual, I was trying to keep up with C.K. I was going faster than usual. I thought maybe I could actually tie him today, and I ran as fast as I could. The barn had three aisles, sort of in a U shape. The arena was next to the U. We were just tearing around the first bend when C.K. crashed into Mary, and they both went flying. She screamed, and C.K. screamed. I was a little behind C.K., and I saw it coming, so I didn't scream, at least not as loud as they did.

"Damn!" said Mary. She rubbed the back of her head. She was lying on her back with her legs and other arm all spread out.

C.K. had crashed against the wheelbarrow and was lying on his side. He leaped up. "I'm sorry!" he said. "Are you okay?"

Mary squinted her eyes and kept rubbing her head. "I don't know," she said. "I really whacked my head."

"We didn't know you was here. We didn't see no cars," C.K. said. He looked sort of scared. "Are you hurt?"

"I've got a goddamned goose egg on my head. Ow!" she said and pulled her hand away. "Maybe you two could get me some ice." She was sitting up now and rested her elbows on her knees. She looked up at us like she was wondering what we were waiting for. We ran for the house. I let C.K. go ahead of me. I just didn't feel like racing. Something about Mary made me feel funny inside. A bad kind of funny. So, I just walked.

C.K. ran into the house, and he and my mom rushed back out with ice before I even got there. They ran out to the barn, but I walked. When I got to them, Mary was sitting in a lawn chair, holding a plastic bag of ice on her head. She'd smile a little and then wince again.

"Let me drive you to the hospital," my mom said. "What if you cracked your skull?"

"No, it's not cracked," Mary said. "I'll just let this ice set here a few minutes."

Something about seeing my mom standing next to Mary made me feel sick. I couldn't say why. I felt like throwing up. I left C.K. standing there and walked into the arena. I climbed to the top of the castle. C.K. waited a few minutes. Then he came up, too.

He had a strange look on his face, like he was scared. I said to him, "It was just an accident. You didn't mean to knock her down."

"Yeah," he said, real quiet. And then he didn't say any more. We went to the front of the castle and sat down with our legs hanging over the edge. I could hear my mom and Mary talking out in the aisle. I still felt sick, so I didn't say anything else. And I felt very tired. C.K. looked kind of white and tired too. We looked out the two big doors of the arena. The view out across the dirt road was

into a woods full of pine trees. They used to cut Christmas trees out of there. It was one of my favorite things to look at. The woods seemed to go on forever because you could see so far into it.

C.K. was staring out there, too. I think we sat there for an hour. After a while I didn't hear my mom and Mary anymore, and my stomach felt better.

C.K. stood up. "I guess I better go home now." He said this to the woods.

I stood up, too, but I couldn't think of anything to say. It just seemed like it was time for him to go. I wanted to go in the house and watch TV.

"See ya later," he said to my feet. He turned and waved his hand at me behind his back. He walked across the castle to the stairway.

"See ya," I said.

12

Yeah, damn it, every time Cross-Eyed Ladonna was around, Johnnie got all goofy and just hung around her. Pissed me off. We'd be right in the middle of doing something cool and she'd walk in the barn. He'd drop whatever we was doin' and go talk to her. It was bad enough she was takin' my pa away from my ma, but then she goes and takes Johnnie away from me. Damned bitch. I think about her now, I could—well, I won't say what I'd like to do. I mean, I didn't think these thoughts then—what I'd like to do, but when I think back on it, the bitch had a lot of damned nerve coming in and fucking with my life.

But shit, Johnnie didn't mean nothin' by it, and I guess Pa didn't neither. They was just innocent victims of that selfish bitch. I got to see her as my enemy. And then, she'd throw me off guard cuz she was always so nice to me. I mean, real nice. She took Johnnie and me to the zoo once and bought us goddammed tee shirts and zebra pencils, and took us out to lunch. She was always smilin' and teasin' us. It was hard to stay mad at her. She laughed a lot. And never got mad. At nothin'. Even years later, Pa'd treat her like shit, and she'd just pout a little and walk away. Next time I'd see her, she'd be all smiles again. Not like Ma. Ma'd scream and throw things at the drop of a hat. Sometimes I think that was better. Shit, at least I always knew what Ma was thinkin'.

With Pa, you could never tell. He was always nice. Sometimes he could be damned firm, but he never raised his voice or swore or nothin'. He'd lie and do shit like that. And tell you he'd be some place or do somethin' and then never show up. But shit, all pa's is like that, and besides, he was probably tryin' to, you know, balance out the way Ma was. When you think on it, they was really good together—for me. I mean, I had it all. What one wasn't, the other was. Too bad that fucking bitch screwed things up. I probably wouldn't be here on death row today if she hadn't come around.

Like I was starting to say a few minutes ago, I'd like to have killed the bitch.

To make matters worse, she brought that witch Mary around.

The first time I saw Mary, that day in Johnnie's barn, it sure seemed like I'd seen her before, but I couldn't remember where.

But she was kinda pretty, even if she did sorta look like a mole. It was weird how I liked her and didn't like her all at the same time. And then later, after we was done skating and Johnnie and I was racin' to the castle and I ran into her and knocked her down, I about freaked out. Somehow, seein' her on the floor and hurt and knowing I'd done it to her, and seein' her look at me like she was gonna burn me up with her eyes, I wanted to run screamin' out of there. I don't know why. It was like I'd seen her look at me this way before or somethin', and I got real scared.

Finally, after Johnnie and I just stood looking at her for a long time, she screamed at us to get her some ice. I ran out of there as fast as I could. I figured I'd let Christine take care of her. Johnnie was somewhere behind me, but I didn't really care where he was. I just wanted to get away from Mary.

When I told Christine what happened, she didn't even know who Mary was. And she got all worried Mary would sue her or something. So, she got the ice and kept asking me questions the whole time, so I had to run with her back out to the barn. I kept tryin' to answer her dang questions, but then she'd ask a bunch more, stuff like, "Is she bleeding?" "Does she know anything about horses?" "Is she working somewhere full-time?" "Was she able to walk?" I couldn't answer any of 'em, so I just ran along with her.

When we got back to the barn, Mary was still sitting on the floor. Christine got a chair for her and helped her put the ice on her head. Mary kept groaning and making faces. She couldn't seem to keep the ice on her head cuz it hurt. One time, when the bag slipped and she had to push it back on, she looked at me real mean. I mean, *real* mean. I'd seen that look before about something real bad, but I couldn't remember what. I wanted to run

away as fast as I could. But I was afraid to run away cuz then she might get even meaner cuz I was the one who knocked her down. So I just stood there.

When Christine said, "You can go, C.K. I'll take care of Mary," I was so glad. I wanted to race away and find Johnnie, but I made myself walk slow, like I really didn't want to leave poor Mary. When I reached the hay pile, I felt tired, and climbing up the stairs was hard. This was weird. It was like the tiredness had just come and taken me over. I had the idea that maybe the Evil Sorcerer's Tribe had finally took over our castle and put a spell on me. I imagined that, when I got to the top, I'd fall asleep and some of the warriors would come and carry me away. But as soon as I saw Johnnie sitting up there, I forgot about the warriors.

I was glad to sit down next to him. But I felt all jittery inside and still afraid of Mary. I could hear her and Christine talking back by the stalls. Johnnie and I sat and listened to them and waited for Mary to leave. We didn't say nothin' and just looked out them big barn doors into the woods. It was real pretty there. The sun was setting behind the trunks of the pine trees. It was a big, dark orange ball. We watched it disappear. I'd watched it before like this, and it always seemed to go so fast when it was setting. When it's up in the sky you can't see it move at all. After a while, I didn't hear Mary and Christine no more, and I just wanted to go home. Johnnie seemed tired too, so I left.

I stepped down the bank to the dirt road, and headed for the bridge. I walked over it, and went past the Bogguses. I wondered how Mrs. Boggus's baby was, and I wondered if Lassie would have Tucker's puppies. I wondered how long it would take Lassie to make 'em. I figured half a year or so. When I reached the Panzerov's property, I saw just Mr. Panzerov out in the garden. His three fat daughters must have been in the house. He stood up when he saw me and waved. "How's your mom?" he called. He always asked me that. And whenever she was out workin' in the yard, even when Pa was there, he'd come over and talk to her. She didn't like him cuz he always wanted to talk to her about his injury. She didn't care about his injury.

When I got to my driveway, my ma's car and my pa's truck was both there. That made me happy. That meant they was both home at the same time. I liked that.

I walked in the front door and was hopin' they was bein' friendly with each other. Pa was sittin' on the couch lookin' at the TV, but the TV wasn't on. Ma was on the phone in the kitchen. It had one of them long curly cords on it, and she walked out into the dining room to see that it was me.

Pa looked real serious. "Where you been, boy?" He asked it real slow and low, but I knew I was in trouble.

"Where the hell've you been!" Ma screamed. She had her hand over the phone.

I shrugged. I didn't see what the big deal was. I was almost always at Johnnie's. "At Johnnie's," I said. I couldn't believe they didn't just know that.

"You was supposed to call your Pa at work! I gave you a quarter!" Ma screamed some more. Then she took her hand off the phone and said, real polite, "He just walked in the door. Thanks." And she walked into the kitchen to hang up the phone. When she came back out, she was carryin' her big wooden spoon. She was always threatening to beat me with it, but she never did. "Why didn't you call him!" When she screamed like this, her voice got all scratchy and cracked a lot. It was hard to listen to her. I wished she was a radio and I could turn the volume down. "Tell me why!" She stamped both her feet and held the spoon in the air.

"What'd you do with the quarter, son?" Pa asked. His voice was still real quiet. But when he was serious like this, and the reason I could tell I was in trouble, was cuz his forehead got big deep wrinkles in it, and one corner of his mouth sort of tucked in like he was gonna chew on it.

"I gave you the goddamned quarter to call your Pa, and you didn't do it!" I imagined her nose was a volume knob and her tongue was a slider thing for adjusting the tone. I wanted to reach out and turn her nose, then take the tip of her tongue and slide it all the way to the left to get the scratchy sound out.

I looked at the two of 'em, her all jazzed up and him all quiet. I wondered why he didn't rub off on her. Maybe some day they'd even out. I could feel my heart pound, but I knew that if I said what Pa wanted to hear, he'd protect me from her. "Pa, I called, and the nice lady said you was on the line and couldn't come to the phone."

"Didn't you tell her you had to reach him?" Ma shrieked. I wanted to put my hands over my ears. It was like someone was poking nails inside 'em.

I shrugged again. "I didn't think it would make any difference. She said you couldn't come off the line for a phone call."

"So, you just hung up, right? Right? I'm right, ain't I? You little shit. He must have gotten your brains, Walter. Times like this, I know it for sure. So, how the hell was your Pa supposed to know to pick you up? Huh? Answer me, Stupid!"

"Gloria, don't call him stupid. He'll think you mean it."

"I will call him Stupid cuz he is stupid, just like you."

"Well, it's true. They ain't supposed to take us off the line for anything unless it's an emergency. And then, they don't believe you that it is. Like the time my ma fell down the stairs and Pa called me at work. He had to call four times to convince 'em." Pa was raising his voice a little now.

"I'd like to whip the both of you till you bleed!" Ma screeched. "Well," she said, lookin' at me, "just so you know, we been callin' everybody that was at the roller rink and all the neighbors, even Mr. Panzerov. And nobody knew nothin'."

"Did you call Johnnie's?" I asked.

"You damned smart mouth. You are really gettin' a mouth on you. I didn't think you would, and everybody said, 'Just wait till he gets to be about eleven or twelve. You won't believe it's the same kid.' And they was right. Sometimes I think I don't even know who you are!"

"Of course we called Johnnie's," Pa said in his gentle voice, "but no one answered. We figured they was gone. We thought maybe they was out lookin' for the two of you, too."

"Oh," I said, remembering Mary and how I'd knocked her down. "Christine was out in the barn helping a lady that fell."

"Did she fall off a horse?" Ma asked. She seemed to like stories about people fallin' off horses. She always wanted to know all about it when it happened.

"No, I—" I knew they'd take this wrong. "I knocked her down—by accident! I didn't mean to."

"How the hell did you do that? Did you hurt her?"

"Well," I said, looking at my shoes. I was trying to figure a way to tell this and still make me look good. "Well—" I couldn't think of nothin'. I guessed I'd tell the truth and see what happened. "Johnnie and I was racing to the castle, and this lady didn't have a car parked out there or nothin', so we didn't think no one was in there. So, we was runnin' around the corner, and bam! I hit something and fell against the wheelbarrow. We both got knocked down, not just her."

"Who is she?" asked Ma.

"I don't know. Some creepy lady. Christine didn't know her either." Then I remembered she was Cross-Eyed Ladonna's friend. Pa would know her. "Oh, you might know her, Pa," I said. "She's good friends with Cross—I mean Ladonna."

That was sure the wrong thing to say. It was out of my mouth, and then I knew Ma would get mad. But I was a little bit glad cuz I was sorta mad at Pa for seein' Cross-Eyed Ladonna so much. I didn't think they was sweet on each other. They was just friends, but it made me mad that other people thought that stuff about 'em.

"Oh, I knew it!" Ma shrieked again. She threw the spoon at him. It bounced off his chest, hit the couch, and fell on the floor. I wanted to leave. "That damned bitch!" She turned to me. "What d'you know about her? Is Pa seein' her? Have you ever seen 'em kiss or hug?" I looked behind me at the front door and imagined running out and never comin' back. I imagined them searchin' and searchin' and callin' all the neighbors again and all our relatives and tryin' to find me. But I'd be gone. To California or some place like that. "Answer me!" she screamed.

Pa said, "Leave the boy alone. It's none of his business. Go on, son, you can go to your room."

I didn't want to go to my room. I wanted to get out of the house. "Mind if I check on Miss Kitty?"

"Go ahead, that's fine," he said.

I flew out the door and started to run to the barn. Then I stopped and decided to wait in the dark outside the front window and listen to the two of 'em through the screen. I kneeled down low beneath the window ledge. They couldn't see me there.

"He needs to be punished, Walter. You always let him off. How's he supposed to learn right from wrong!"

"So, where did you and Marge go? Did you meet some guy at Wrench's? People say they seen you there with some guy named Sonny." Pa still spoke in his low, quiet voice.

Ma kept screamin'. "What are you doing? Accusing me of stuff so you don't have to feel guilty about that bitch Ladonna? And who's this 'creepy woman' C.K's talkin' about? You screwin' her too?" Then I heard Ma gruntin' and squealin' like she was throwing stuff at Pa. I heard some scufflin', so I stood up and looked in. Pa was just tryin' to hold her away from him. He never hit her back, but I didn't want to watch, so I ran out to Pa's truck. I pushed the seat back and grabbed his flashlight. I really did want to check on Miss Kitty.

The barn was real dark, except right in the entrance where the security light shined in. In the back, where Miss Kitty always had her kittens in one of the stalls, it was dark as could be. I shined the flashlight right where her nest usually was, and sure enough, there was three little kittens. Miss Kitty was licking her behind, and I made the light go right on her. Then I saw this dark, shiny wet thing oozing out of her butt. It came out slow at first, then sorta shot out. It was a new kitten. Miss Kitty licked and licked at it real hard and started eating the slimy sack. It was gross, so I left.

Damn, I guess that was probably the first time I really thought about leavin' home—I mean, the first time I was serious about it. I didn't want to go back in that house, ever. What I really wanted to do was go up to Johnnie's and stay with them. And never see my pa

or ma again. Well, at least for a couple years or so. Until they appreciated me again. Like when I was a little kid. Pa was always happy to see me then, and so was Ma. They took me places and bought me toys. Pa was always throwin' balls for me to bat and takin' me to the YMCA to shoot baskets. And Ma, even though she was busy a lot, she always hugged me and told me she loved me. Now that I was gettin' older, they seemed to be into their own shit more. They used to seem glad when I was at Johnnie's. And I guess I liked bein' with Johnnie more than them.

I walked back to the big, open barn door where the light shined in. I didn't know what to do. I thought about goin' back in the house and knew I didn't want to do that. I figured Ma was still tryin' to hurt Pa, and Pa was just pushin' her away. He'd probably leave—say he had to go get something at the store—and then he wouldn't come back. Ma'd probably talk on the phone and then watch TV or go to bed. If I went back in there, she'd yell at me more and ask questions about Cross-Eyed Ladonna.

What I really wanted to do was go to Johnnie's. But if I did that, Christine would call my ma and ask if I could stay over, and Ma would say, "Tell him to get his ass back home." I hated it when she talked like that, especially to Christine and Leland.

Then, I thought I could go to the castle. That would sorta be like bein' with Johnnie. I liked that idea, but I needed to think about it a little more. I walked out under the light and looked around. Those darned moles had been at it again. I could see their tunnels runnin' along under the grass, and every couple yards there was a clump of dirt. I walked heel to toe on top of the tunnels and squashed them flat. It felt good to step on top of their round roofs. As I let my weight come down, I could feel the tunnel crumble, and my foot would sink down onto the tunnel's floor. I went heel to toe, heel to toe and crushed the tunnel—foot by foot. Sometimes I imagined I was inside the tunnel and I could see it crumble. I wondered where the moles was runnin' to as I crushed their little city.

When I got to a mound, first I'd kick the dirt away and then I'd scoop it together with my toe and pack it down into the hole real tight. I figured the moles wouldn't be able to dig it out again, or they'd get so tired, they'd give up. First I wrecked one mound and packed the dirt in real tight. Sometimes, there'd be two or three tunnels comin' off one mound, and I'd have to go back. When I thought I was done, I walked all over the yard and found some tunnels I'd missed. I was pretty sure I'd wrecked the whole mole city, and I felt good.

I was standin' there, admiring my good work, when I saw Pa walk out to his truck. It was dark where he was walking, and I knew he could see me cuz I was standin' under the light. But he didn't look at me. I waved at him and started to run and call to him, but he seemed real set on gettin' out of there, so I stopped and watched him go. I wondered where. I hoped he really was just goin' to the store and would be back in a few minutes. But I knew better. Maybe we'd see him tomorrow afternoon after work.

I listened to the engine start. Then the headlights came on. I watched the lights back down the driveway and then turn when he backed out onto the dirt road. He shifted gears, and the back tires spun the gravel a little, and he drove away.

"Well, now what?" I said out loud. I walked over to the kitchen window and looked in. Ma was on the phone again. She was punching the air with her fist. No way was I going back in there. I thought maybe I could just stay out in the yard until I saw her go to bed. But then she'd come in my room in the morning and wake me up, and yell at me cuz I hadn't come in last night. "Shit!" I said out loud, and I headed for the castle. I still had Pa's flashlight, but I didn't turn it on.

The road was real peaceful. I had a lot of energy and wished I could just walk all night. I wished this was the road to California. For a while I pretended it was. I pretended I'd never seen Panzerov's place or Boggus's. I pretended the bridge was the one going over the Mississippi River, and the hill going up to Johnnie's was the beginning of the Rocky Mountains. I climbed the bank up to Johnnie's barn. I was surprised to see the whole place lit up—the

indoor arena, the stall area, and even the driveway lights was on. "Darn it!" I said. I wanted to be in the dark castle by myself. "Now what?" I was kinda wishin' Tucker would hear me or smell me and come lean on me. I liked his big old dog body. I could talk to him about Ma and Pa and about not goin' home. He'd be leanin' hard against my left leg with his great big face lookin' up at me like he loved me more than anything on Earth. He was a good dog.

"Tucker, Tucker!" I whispered. I waited a while and tried again. "Tucker, Tucker." But he didn't come. So, I went closer to the barn. I was standing in the dark, away from where the light came out, so no one would see me.

When I looked into the arena, I saw a horse walk past the door with a person on the other side. All I could see was the person's legs. The rest of the person was behind the horse's neck. The horse was all sweaty, and it looked kinda like Cross-Eyed Ladonna's mare. Then they went past the door and behind the wall where I couldn't see 'em. When they came around the other side of the circle, I could see that it was Cross-Eyed Ladonna. When she got halfway around the other side, I heard a girl's voice, and Cross-Eyed Ladonna stopped her horse and turned around. Mary came running out. Then it hit me.

Mary was from Little Friends. She was one of the witches, the official witches. "Damn, that was eight or nine years ago," I whispered to myself. I got chills all up and down my back. She made me feel icy, like I'd just turned into one of them big ice sculptures, except the sculpture was me. The way she walked out into the arena like that was just the way she used to walk into the big play-room at the daycare center. She wasn't there very often, but when she was, all the teachers acted like she was somethin' special. They had some name for her like High Priestess or somethin'. And she only showed up like two or three times a year. Cross-Eyed Ladonna handed her the horse's lead rope. Mary walked the horse, and Cross-Eyed Ladonna ran out of the arena into the stall area.

Even though I felt frozen, I decided to sneak up closer. There was one glass window on this side of the barn for the tack room where they kept all the saddles and bridles and brushes and stuff.

There was a phone in there, and in the winter there was a heater in there too. I walked real slow cuz my feet made a crunching sound on the gravel. When I got up to the window, I saw that it was open, so I had to be real quiet. If Ladonna saw me, she might call my pa and he'd come and take me home. I really wanted to spend the night in the castle.

I got up pretty close and could see her in there. She was talkin' on the phone. Somebody must've called her. I could see her noddin' her head and smilin' real big. She hung up and sorta ran back out to Mary and the horse. I walked back out away from the barn so I could see into the arena again. She'd gone up to Mary and was talking to her, and it looked like she was askin' her something. Mary didn't look as happy as Cross-Eyed Ladonna did, but she nodded her head a couple times. Cross-Eyed Ladonna was explaining something to her, and Mary was listening. Then Cross-Eyed Ladonna ran out again. She went through the barn and out the other door to her car. She got in it and sat there with the light on. She was digging into her purse. She pulled out a comb and combed her hair, and put lipstick on, and then put something on her eyelids.

Pretty soon some car lights started comin' up the driveway. The lights came right at me, so I laid down real flat on the grass. I could see it was a pick-up truck, but I couldn't see the color or nothin' in the dark. Cross-Eyed Ladonna stuffed the things back in her purse and jumped out. The truck pulled up next to her, and she got in. When the light came on in the cab, I could see that it was Pa.

Cross-Eyed Ladonna got in and put her arms around Pa's neck. They sat there and kissed. A long time. With the light on. I felt sick. I wished they'd at least shut the door so the light would go off. I wanted to look away, but I couldn't. Pa started rubbin' her back. She was leaning way over, and he started rubbin' her butt. "Shit!" I whispered. Finally, she sat up and shut the door. Pa drove around the turn-around. I was laying right in the middle of it. He drove right around me and then went down the long driveway. So, Ma was right. I almost felt like runnin' home and telling her.

I thought that if I did, she'd like me again, and then I could sleep in my bed. Then I thought about sleepin' in the castle alone and about the Evil Sorcerer and his tribe. I knew it was all made up, but I was starting to feel kinda scared. Yeah, I was pretty sure Ma'd be real nice to me if I went and told her what I just seen.

I got up on my hands and knees and was just about to stand up when all of a sudden them big bright lights that light up the outdoor arena came on. They lit up everything out there, including the whole turn-around and me. Then Mary came walkin' out with the horse. She started walkin' the horse around the turn-around. I laid down flat again. Maybe she wouldn't see me. Sometimes the grass in the turn-around was pretty tall, but they'd just mowed it. I put my arms around my head and tried to go as flat as I could. I could hear the crunchy clip-clop, clip-clop as they started around. They was about half-way around when they stopped.

"Who's that!" Mary shouted. That's all she said. I just laid there. Maybe she'd think she was just seein' things. Then the horse started blowin' and snortin', and its hooves was scufflin' in the gravel. Darn horse, I thought. "Who is that!" Mary demanded. "You're scarin' this horse half to death. Get up!"

I thought about just runnin' away into the dark and maybe she wouldn't know it was me. Yep, that was the thing to do. I sure didn't want to get stuck there talkin' to her. So I stayed bent over and ran toward the dirt road as fast as I could.

"Clive Bookout!" she shouted. I started to stumble, but I caught myself and kept goin'. I had to slow down when I got to the edge of the bank, though. I didn't think she could see me cuz it was dark over here. I put my arms around a big tree and stood on the other side of it. Maybe she'd think I was gone. I didn't want to trip on the way down the bank. There was a bunch of big branches on the ground there and some raspberry brambles. You had to be real careful goin' down the bank unless you was on one of the paths. I didn't think there was any path right here. So, I stood there and hugged this stupid tree and waited.

"I know who you are," she said. She sounded real cold. "I know who your master is. I know you want to please him. You don't

want to cause your parents any trouble now, do you?" She always used to say that at Little Friends. She said she'd burn our houses down when our parents was asleep in 'em. She took a bunch of us out to that old cabin in the woods and showed us what a burning house was like. First she put a couple dolls inside, and then she set the cabin on fire. We all stood there and watched it burn. She told us the dolls was screamin' just like our parents would if she had to burn one of our houses down. She said their skin was melting off their bodies and their hair was all burned off, but they could feel everything and was screamin' and cryin' to get out. But they couldn't get out cuz she'd locked the doors.

When the cabin had all burned down, she showed us the dolls. They was all black, and their clothes and faces and hair was all burned off. There was just some melted plastic left. She said that's what our parents would look like if she had to burn them. But she'd only do that if we were bad and refused to do what her and Jack and Bernice told us to do.

Okay, damn it, so we was scared at the time, and we believed her. But she never did burn nobody's house down. And she never really hurt none of us. Parents and teachers, and even the god-dam President of the United States, threatens stuff all the time and never does it. You just learn that that's how the world is. No big deal.

So I stood there and hugged that tree and wondered if I should try running down the bank. Even if I did trip, what was she gonna do? Follow me with the horse? The horse was still jumpin' around. I could hear her sayin', "Whoa, easy girl," and patting it on the neck. She didn't say nothin' else. It was like I kept waitin' and she kept waitin' and nothin' was happening. I felt pretty stiff, and I was still cold. I curled my fingers around the chunks of bark on the tree and ran my fingertips up and down the grooves. I listened and

tried to decide what Mary was doing. I didn't hear nothin' now. Maybe the horse was eatin' grass. Maybe Mary was walking quiet toward the tree to get me. Maybe she'd tied the horse to the fence or maybe she'd let it go. Maybe she was on the other side of my tree and was about to grab me. That idea was enough. I looked down the bank. I could hardly breathe. I kept imagining her skinny hand reachin' around and grabbin' my arm. My eyes must've got used to the dark cuz I could see better. There was a couple big branches, but I figured I could leap over them and be down to the road in about four big steps.

I was sure she was on the other side of the tree and would burst around it any second, so I jumped away from the tree. I took the four big leaps down the bank. My right foot got caught for just a second on one of the branches. But it didn't stop me. I barely felt the road under my feet, and I took off running as fast as I could.

When I got to the middle of the bridge, I stopped and turned around. There was nothin' in the road. No woman, no horse. Mary hadn't followed me. But I was still scared and kept running all the way home. There was one light on in the Boggus's house. The Panzerov's house was all dark. And when I got to my house, all the lights was on. As soon as I saw my house, I started thinkin' about what I was gonna say to my ma.

I knew she'd still be spittin' mad, and she would scream and yell at me as soon as she saw me. I had to figure out what I could say to stop her before she could start in on me. If I could just get the door open and say, "I just saw Pa with Cross-Eyed Ladonna, and they was kissin'," that might do it. I sorta jogged up the driveway and through the gate and decided to go in the front door. I figured she'd be in the living room watchin' TV, and I could catch her off guard. Yes! That would work. She'd listen to me, and I'd tell her everything I seen, and then she'd cuss about Pa and Cross-Eyed Ladonna, and then she'd hug me for a long time and tell me she loved me, and then I could go to bed.

I pulled the front screen door open and had my mouth all ready to say, "I just saw—" I stepped into the living room and expected to see her sittin' on the couch. But she wasn't there. I

knew she must be in the kitchen, and the plan would still work. I hurried through the living room, around the bend through the dining room, and when I came into the kitchen I saw her standing over by the refrigerator with a big whiskey bottle tilted back to her mouth. She was takin' a long drink of it. I'd never seen her do this.

"Ma!" I said. I sorta sounded like I was the parent scolding the kid.

She brought the bottle down real quick, and the brown whiskey sloshed around inside. She screwed the white lid back on. Her eyes was all red and puffy-lookin'. She looked at me, and it was like she couldn't focus on me.

"Where you been?" she said. Her words was all slurred. And then her eyes got real watery and she started cryin'. She held her arms out and came over to me. She hugged me real hard and kept cryin'. We was about the same height now, and I could feel her hot, wet face on my neck. She kept sobbin', kinda soft. She'd sniff and then sob some more. But all she did was hold me for the longest time. She was sorta leanin' on me and gettin' heavy, so I started to shift around. I didn't think I could hold her up.

She finally pulled away. She put both her hands on my shoulders and looked right at me. She looked all soft and kinda sweet. Then I felt her fingers get tight on my shoulders, and it started to hurt a little. Her face sorta went from bein' soft and mushy to serious and mad. She shook me once, just a little. "Where you been?" Then her fingernails really dug into my shoulders, and she started shakin' me real hard. My head waggled back and forth so hard I couldn't hold it on straight. "Where you been!" she screamed. I ducked down and twisted away from her. I went to the other side of the kitchen and stood against the counter.

"I went up to Johnnie's. I hate it when you and Pa fight!"

"How was I supposed to know where you were?" she screamed at me. And then her face went all soft and mushy again and she sorta bent over and started cryin' some more.

"I saw 'em kissin'," I said. I said it low and soft like Pa would.

"Where?" she sniffed.

"Up at Johnnie's. I was gonna sleep in the barn, but Cross-Eyed Ladonna and that Mary woman was there. Then Pa came." I stopped for a minute to see how she was takin' this. She just stood there and looked a little stupid, but she was listening. So, I went on. "When she got into the truck, they started kissin'. That's all. Then they drove away."

"She went with him?"

I nodded.

"What am I gonna do?" she said. Her face got all wrinkled like she was startin' to cry again. She did cry little tiny cries and walked out of the kitchen real slow. Her shoulders was sorta hangin'. She left all the lights on and went into her room.

I turned the TV on, but they was just showin' the news. I tried to watch it for a while—somethin' about Iraq and oil and goin' to war. I tiptoed to Ma's room and saw that she was layin' across her bed sideways. Her clothes was still on, and she had a pillow under her head, and she was asleep. I turned her light off, and then I went back and turned all the other lights off and went to bed.

13

You know how you can think back on certain segments of time in your life, and a general feeling accompanies those memories? I like to call them *feeling clouds* because I can't isolate and identify one specific emotion but, rather, a set of them. Childhood summers are a good example. If we recall a certain summer, say, when we were eight years old, and we recall some of the things we did and the people we did them with, a whole set of emotions goes with that recollection—a *feeling cloud*—a certain character or quality that we can't quite define but which we're aware of when we think of that chunk of time—something like the aroma we smell in a field of flowers. We can't pick out each one, but we have a definite sense of the whole thing.

Most of us can recall a few isolated events from our pre-school years, especially if they were particularly meaningful. But personally speaking, I cannot recall a *feeling cloud* about Little Friends. None of us recalls many events before the age of three or four. This may be a defense mechanism against the frustrations and disappointments that commonly occur during those early years. However, starting at around age four our capacity for recollection improves. For instance, if someone asks if you remember kindergarten, you'll probably remember several images and a *feeling cloud* that accompanies those images. But if you're asked to recall first grade, there's a marked increase in recollection of people and events. It increases again for second grade and on and on throughout our development until the images and *feeling clouds* become quite focused and accessible.

When I think back on the first summer with C.K., when I was six and a half, I recall excitement and completeness combined with a *smidgen* of disturbance. I needed a friend, and I got one, and some of the memories remind me of things I did not want to recall. Then, throughout my seventh, eighth, ninth, and tenth

years, I recall a *feeling cloud* of happiness and satisfaction combined with *noticeable* disturbance. C.K. and my friendship grew and gratified both of us. Then, that summer when I was ten and a half and C.K. was twelve, the feeling cloud shifted. It was one of fear, turmoil, jealousy, and anxiety. But not entirely. All those emotions were mixed with a set of the same emotions I'd experienced for the several preceding years. So, the feeling cloud had many components, one of polarity or opposing forces, one of swinging back and forth between comfort and disruption, and one of joy because of my friendship with C.K. It was a time of change and transition.

After that day that C.K. knocked down Mary in the barn, I didn't hear from him for about three days. This was weird. Usually, he'd call in the morning and want to come up for the day because his mom and dad both worked, and if he didn't come to our house, he had to go to his grandparents' house, and that was boring. I'd gone there with him a few times and thought it was fun because we could walk into town and go to the Dairy Queen. There was a park with swings and slides down by the river, and we could walk there. He didn't think it was any big deal because he'd grown up in town. He was happy to be out in the country where he could go fishing whenever he wanted.

Anyway, after three days, I called him. He was happy I called, but he said he was going to the movies with his mom because she had a few days off of work, and they were just doing some things together. I told him to call me when he got back from the movies, but he didn't. After supper, I called again. He said Harry was there, but I could come down too. I said, "No."

He said, "Oh, come on. Harry's not so bad."

I said, "No. When's he going home?"

"I think he's spending the night. Our mothers arranged it. You could come too."

"No, that's okay," I said. "Call me in the morning after he leaves."

"Okay."

And we hung up. I hated Harry. Why did C.K. put up with him? He knew he was a creep. I felt like crying. So, I went and played my favorite video game. It was C.K.'s favorite, too, so I felt even crummier. I put that one away and took out another one that C.K. had never played. It wasn't as much fun, but I felt better.

I guess heartache is painful no matter what one's age or what the gender of the loved person is. Little did I realize this was one of many love triangles I would experience throughout my lifetime. The one with my mother and father was the first and most basic. This one with C.K. and Harry was the second, and though not nearly as powerful as those occurring in adult love relationships, it was by far the more crushing.

My mom tried to feed me macaroni and cheese, my favorite, but I couldn't eat much. She caught on that things weren't cool.

"Where's C.K. today?" she asked. She was looking at me like she was trying to look right inside me to see what was going on in my brain instead of just listening to my words. She did this a lot. I didn't like it. It always felt like she was going to discover something I wanted to keep a secret. I looked down at my plate so she couldn't look into my brain through my eyes.

"That creep Harry is at his house."

"Oh." She looked out the window. I could tell she was thinking something serious. "Did C.K. ever find out his last name?"

I shrugged. Who cared what his last name was? "Why do you want to know?"

"Oh," she said, like she really didn't want to tell me what she was thinking. She started looking around at the dishes, looking for something to do instead of answering me. I just looked at her like she looked at me, trying to see into her brain. Finally, she looked straight at me. "I just heard that he might not have had the best upbringing." She waited to see if I knew what that meant.

147

"I don't think he did," I said. "He doesn't have a dad, and his mom is gone all the time, and he spends most of his time with his older brothers, and all they do is drink, take drugs, and work on cars."

Her eyes got real big. "How do you know all this?"

"He told us, me and C.K. Well, mostly he told C.K., and I listened. It doesn't bother him, though. He seems to like it. He swears a lot. And he talks too much. But he can fix cars. So, I think he's pretty smart." Why was I sticking up for him?

"But you said he's a creep."

"Well, he is a creep." I didn't know what I was trying to say anymore. "Yes, he's a creep." I looked at her hard.

"Well, then why does C.K. choose to play with him and not you?"

"I don't think he did choose. I think his mom did. Mrs. Bookout and Marge are cousins or something."

"Doesn't Mrs. Bookout know about Harry?"

I shrugged. How would I know?

"Maybe I should say something to Gloria—Mrs. Bookout," she said, and then she sort of spaced out while she cleared the table. I went up to my room to read.

About an hour later the doorbell rang. I figured it was someone from the barn looking for my mom, so I kept on reading.

"Johnnie!" my mom called. "Come down. C.K.'s here."

I set my book on the bed and ran down the stairs. I figured C.K. and Harry must have had a fight and Harry left, or Marge decided to take Harry home, or Harry got sick and had to go home. As I scrambled down the stairs and made the bend at the landing, I saw C.K.'s legs and shoes standing by the front door, and when I reached the bottom I saw the rest of him. I also saw Harry. I stopped. I couldn't decide whether to act happy to see C.K. or mad because Harry was there. In my house. This scum was standing in my house. I wanted to open the door and shove him out. My mom was holding a bouquet of wild daisies.

"See what Harry brought me?" she said, holding them out at me. She was smiling.

"I know we ain't supposed to pick wild flowers," explained Harry. "But that one field back there had so many of these, we didn't think it would hurt nothin' to pick a few." He grinned at my mom.

C.K. said to me, "We're goin' fishin'. Wanna come along?"

I looked at his face. He was my friend, my best friend. I liked his face. I liked the way he looked at me, and I could tell he really wanted me to go. "Sure," I said. "I'll get my shoes." I ran upstairs and got them. When I came back down, C.K. and Harry were already outside. I could see them through the open front door. They'd brought fishing poles and were fiddling with the bobbers. They had a rusty coffee can with worms and another bucket with fishing stuff in it.

"Can we fish here?" C.K. asked. "We couldn't catch anything by my house."

Oh, thanks a lot! I thought. You and Harry can't catch anything at your house, so you want to use my pond. I wondered how much he really wanted me along. But when I looked at his face, I could see that he really did want me along. He had a smile that I don't want to call "sweet," but I guess that's what it was.

"I better let my mom know," I said. My parents were always reminding me how dangerous the ground of the peat bog was. I promised them I'd always let them know when I was going down there. I ran in and told my mom. She said she'd keep an eye on us from the window.

I went back out and told them it was okay, and I got my fishing pole out of the garden closet. Harry had the can of worms and started walking down the long stairway to the pond. I thought about warning him about the peat, then decided not to. C.K. and I walked side-by-side down the long path made of railroad ties and dirt. There were lots of tall pine trees on both sides, and at the bottom, the path was flat and went through some thick bushes. Past the bushes there was a lot of tall grass and weeds and then the pond. Under all the grass and weeds was the peat. The pond spread out both to the right and to the left. My parents told people it took up about seven acres. There was a long island in the middle,

and sometimes we took the canoe out there. The ground on the island was just like the ground around the edges. It would shake if you jumped on it or if the dogs ran by. Every once in a while my dad's foot went through the ground, and one of his legs would sink all the way past his knee. He never had both legs go through at the same time, though.

As we walked down the stairs, I looked at C.K. and smiled. It was good to see him. "We haven't been fishing in a long time," I said.

He smiled and nodded. "I know." We stayed together and walked down the stairway, taking the same steps at the same time. We watched Harry till he disappeared through the bushes. We each held our pole by the handle, with the rest of it riding on top of our shoulders. I liked the way mine bounced and bent behind me as we went down each stair. As we passed under one pine tree, C.K.'s line got caught on a branch. The line was hooked around a little broken-off piece and snagged on the bark there. No matter which way he turned or lifted it, it wouldn't come unhooked. I finally turned my pole upside down and pushed his line with the handle of my pole, and it came undone.

By the time we reached Harry, he was putting a worm on his hook. He didn't look up at us. He just started talking. "These is very good worms. They's better than nightcrawlers, really, cuz nightcrawlers is too big. The fish don't want to grab 'em, and they don't taste as good neither. That's what my brother Bob says, anyway, and he's been fishin' for nineteen years. Almost every day. He and my Uncle Ned used to go fishin' every afternoon after work and sometimes in the mornings, too, especially in the summer. They'd smoke dope in the mornings and drink Budweisers in the evening. Caught a lot of fish. My ma hardly had to go to the grocery store. That was a few years ago cuz Bob got mad at Uncle Ned and won't fish with him no more. Something about he had to buy the dope and Uncle Ned bought the beer, but the dope cost more, and Uncle Ned wouldn't buy it. Bob got pissed off and wouldn't fish with him no more. But he learned a lot about fishin' from him. Like, fish like beer in the evenings and dope—maryjewanna—in

the mornings. They had a can like this with dirt, and they'd mix some maryjane into the dirt and let it all sit overnight. And in the evenings, they'd put the worms on the hook and then dip them into some beer for exactly one minute, then cast out. They said it worked more than ninety percent of the time. What kinda fish you got in here?" He looked at me with his possum eyes. They were so little, I couldn't tell what color they were.

"I'm not sure," I said, trying to remember what my dad told people. "Bass, catfish—I don't know, something else."

Harry nodded his head. "Good. Wish we had some beer. Got any at your house?"

I shrugged. "Maybe. I guess I could ask my mom." He smiled. I looked at C.K. "Want to come?"

He looked at Harry, who was still fiddling with the worm, then back at me. "Sure." He looked happy as we walked back up the steps. "You think she'll give you some?"

I didn't know. "Maybe, if she knows what it's for."

My mom listened to our reasons. She looked sort of unsure, but then she took a can of beer out of the refrigerator and poured a Styrofoam cup half full and gave it to me. We took it down to Harry. He dipped the hooked worm into the cup and timed it on his watch. When one minute was up, he cast his line way out into the water. I was amazed how far it flew before it landed.

C.K. and I stood and watched. After just a couple minutes something pulled the bobber down. Harry yanked on his pole and reeled in his line. He walked to the very edge of the peat to pull the fish out, and a big clump of it broke off under his feet. He fell back and landed on his butt. The chunk of peat fell into the water.

"Jesus Christ!" he shouted. He kept a hold of his pole, and the fish was splashing around on the water. I wanted to laugh, but I didn't. He didn't say anything else and got up. He held the fish in the air. It's skin shone in the sunlight, and it jumped and struggled to get free. It was about ten inches long. "Not bad," he said. He reached down into his bucket and took a net-like bag out of it and put the fish inside. Then he set the bag in the water.

"See? It works." Then he gulped down the beer, handed me the cup, and said, "Get more."

I didn't think my mom would give me more, but I took the cup from him and started up the stairs. C.K. stayed with Harry, which was okay with me because I knew my mom would say no, and I'd be right back. But she didn't exactly say no. She asked if we caught a fish.

I said "Yes, in just a couple minutes. The trick seems to work." I didn't think she'd buy it.

She opened a bottle of non-alcoholic beer and poured the same amount into the cup and gave it to me. "Where's the other beer?" she asked.

"Harry drank it," I said.

She handed me the cup. "This is all now. I know that fish like worms soaked in beer. My grandfather did it all the time. See if this beer works."

I took the cup down to Harry and handed it to him. He already had another worm on his hook. But this time, he tasted the beer first. "It's phony beer," he said. "It won't work. Watch." He dunked the worm for one minute, cast it out, and we waited. And waited. Nothing.

C.K. got bored and started making grass chains. He picked a long blade of the swamp grass. He tied a loose knot in one end, then threaded another piece of grass through the hole in the knot. He tied a knot in that piece, then threaded another one through the hole in that knot, until he had a long chain. Then he tied the first piece to the last one to make a big circle. He held it up to me with a proud look on his face.

"That's really cool," I said. "Now all we need is a frog to jump through it."

He grinned real big and said, "Yeah, let's find one." We got up and started searching through the grass.

"I see a few over here," said Harry. He had been standing totally still with his line in the water for a very long time. I thought, if he doesn't believe the phony beer will work, why does he keep trying? "Chase 'em away from the pond, and then you can prob-

ably catch one. Otherwise, they'll just jump in the water. They can swim real fast and get away from their hunters in the water, but if you get them on land, especially in deep grass like this, they can't go very fast. Especially these pond frogs, they're just stupid when they're away from water. If each of you comes up on one side, I'll throw something in the water, and then maybe they'll jump away from the water, you know what I mean? But be real slow. You know, I really shouldn't be talking cuz I'll scare the fish away. So, just do it, if you want a goddam frog. Why aren't you two fishin', anyway?"

C.K. and I looked at each other and shrugged at the same time. We giggled, but we didn't answer Harry. Then I went on the far side of the frogs, and C.K. came up on this side. We saw them—three of them—all greenish black and shiny with gold eyes—regular pond frogs, not bullfrogs. They were as still as they could be. We each moved real slowly and got pretty close to them. Harry was watching. He had found a short, thick piece of branch and was getting ready to toss it. I looked at him and nodded. He tossed the stick in the water right in front of the frogs, and sure enough, they jumped away from the water, into the grass. We walked after them. One went off to the right, and one to the left, but we followed the one that went straight. C.K. was on one side of it, and I was on the other. I wondered how we would get close enough to actually grab it. Then I had an idea and took my tee shirt off. I held it out flat, and when I got a little ways away from the frog, I tossed it on top of him. We pounced on the edges of the shirt and captured the frog.

"You grab him," said C.K.

"Me? Why? Are you afraid?"

"I don't like slimy things. Here, I'll hold all the edges down, and you can reach under and grab him."

I started to do that and stopped. "Frogs don't bite, do they?" We started giggling.

"I don't think so. Harry, do frogs have teeth?"

Harry shook his head "no," but he didn't say anything.

I didn't want to, but I slid my hand under the shirt. I touched the cool, tight skin once—it wasn't slimy—and the frog jumped. It made the shirt pop up in the middle. We started laughing.

153

I touched him again, and he jumped. It looked so funny, the shirt popping up in the middle like that. We got to laughing real hard, so I kept just making the frog jump instead of trying to catch it because I didn't really want to take hold of it.

"Grab it," said C.K. He wasn't laughing so hard anymore.

I clenched my teeth and made myself grab the frog's body. It wasn't so bad. I wanted to let go when it started wiggling. I could feel its toes pushing on my hand. C.K. lifted the shirt, and we looked at him. His back legs stretched out straight, and his front hands sort of hung on to my first finger, like it was afraid and was holding on for dear life. Its eyes turned this way and that. I kind of liked him. Every once in a while he'd bring his back legs in to his body, then stretch them out straight again.

C.K. picked up his grass ring and held it up about a foot off the ground. I set the frog on the ground and aimed him at the ring. When I let go, he just sat there.

"Poke him in the butt," said C.K.

I touched his butt, and he jumped right through the ring. "Catch him!" I said. C.K. started to, but then he pulled his hand back.

"You come do it. I don't want to touch him."

"Geez!" I said. "He won't hurt you." I went over to the frog and threw my shirt on him again, and we did the same thing to catch him. We had the frog jump through the ring about ten times, and then the frog seemed to get tired. I had to poke him three or four times to get him to jump, and it wasn't so much fun anymore.

Harry finally said, "See, non-alcoholic beer doesn't work. Can't you get some more of the real stuff?"

"No. My mom won't give me any more."

"I'm hungry," said Harry. "Where are we having lunch?" he asked C.K.

C.K. looked at me as if to ask, "Can we eat here?"

"I guess so," I said, and we picked up our stuff and went up to the house.

My mom seemed happy to make us lunch. Usually, when I was done eating, I just got up and left, and my mom put everything

away. My dad always said I should be made to clear off the table, and when he was around for meals, which wasn't too often, I did take my plate and glass out to the kitchen. So, when we were done, I got up to leave, and then I couldn't believe it. Harry starts clearing the table. My mom was in the kitchen when he went out there with all our plates and glasses. He had stacked all the plates and set the three glasses and silverware on top.

"Thank you very much, Mrs. Ambrose," he said. "That was a very good lunch. I especially liked the banana cake. You made that from scratch, didn't you?"

My mom looked surprised. "Yes, I did. Well, thank you very much. You're a very polite young man."

And then she looked at me as if say, "See how well-mannered he is? Why can't you be like that?" She smiled at him and took the dishes he held out to her. "Thank you," she said and looked at him like she liked him a lot. I hated him. But I saw that he could be nice. And then instead of being obnoxious and asking, "Well, what now?" he just stood around the kitchen like he wanted to talk to my mom.

"So, you know the beer trick, huh?" she said to him.

"Yeah, but it don't work with phony beer."

"Doesn't."

"Huh?"

"It doesn't work with phony beer, not 'it don't work with phony beer.' Say 'doesn't,' not 'don't.'"

"Yes, yes! You're right, Mrs. Ambrose. Sorry. I know my English could be better. I'll try harder. Thank you for correcting me. I really appreciate it. I wish my ma would correct me more often. Johnnie's pretty lucky to have a mother that's so smart and educated."

My mom smiled at him. "It's really 'a mother *who's* so smart, not *that's* so smart.' That's a tougher one. Use 'who' when you're referring to people and 'that' when you refer to everything else. It's more respectful." She was being so gentle with him. I couldn't believe it. "When's your birthday, Harry?"

I thought, oh no, here comes the astrology. He said, "November 6th. Why?"

"Oh," she said. "So you're a Scorpio. Your ruler is Pluto of the underworld. But that's not bad. You'll be very involved in emotional relationships with girls when you get older, and you'll probably have some difficulty with them. But you'll also be able to be honest with yourself and not fool yourself into believing things that aren't true, and that's very good."

"Oh. Good."

I'm still unclear why my mother was so nice to Harry. Maybe she felt sorry for him. Maybe she felt she had fallen short in her mothering of me, having sent me to Little Friends for over a year, and mothering Harry compensated for that—helped her feel better about herself as a mother. Or maybe she felt some kind of strange connection with him because her grandfather also soaked fishing worms in beer. Maybe it was because he seemed interested in astrology. Maybe it was because he was so polite to her and was trying to be a better person. Maybe it was all those things put together.

C.K. said, "Want to go back outside now?"

I headed for the door. I could tell Harry wanted to stay and talk to my mom. "We'll be out in the barn, Harry," I said, and C.K. and I left him there.

We raced to the barn as usual. I wasn't nearly so far behind him this time. In fact, he sort of got a head start, and I stayed the same distance behind him the whole way. Cross-Eyed Ladonna's car was parked in front. C.K. slowed way down before he reached the finish line at the barn door. Then he stopped and looked into the barn without going in. This was odd.

"What're you looking for?" I asked.

"Mary. I don't like her. Do you think she's here?"

I didn't know. I knew I wanted to see Cross-Eyed Ladonna, though, and I walked into the barn to find her. C.K. waited out-

side. Cross-Eyed Ladonna was in the second stall with the wheel-barrow and pitchfork. I stood in the doorway and watched her sift the turds out of the wood shavings. "Hi!" I said.

She turned around and smiled. "Johnnie. Hey, fella! How you doin'? I ain't seen you for a couple days." I wished she didn't say *ain't*. But she was beautiful, so it didn't matter a whole lot.

"I'm fine. How are you?"

"Well, I'm okay. Considering I'm shoveling shit!" She laughed in that deep way that I liked. "Sorry. I probably shouldn't say words like that in front of you."

"That's okay." I didn't care at all. She sure was pretty. Her hair was always so shiny and silky-looking. And her eyes were so blue and shaped so pretty. And she had that nice pink lipstick on. I must have been staring at her.

"Is something wrong? Do I have dirt on my nose?" She rubbed at her face and laughed.

"No, no. Nothing's wrong." I felt embarrassed and looked over at C.K. I'd forgotten he was not coming in until he knew if Mary was there. "Is Mary here?" I asked.

"No. She's still at work, but she might come out a little later."

I waved at C.K. to come in. "Coast is clear," I whispered. C.K. came and stood next to me. He glared at Cross-Eyed Ladonna like he was mad at her or something.

Cross-Eyed Ladonna's smile started to go down as she looked at him. "Hey, C.K. How's it going?" She looked at him real serious now.

"Not the greatest," he said. He still looked mad, but he wouldn't look right at her. What the heck was this all about? Then I remembered what Harry and Skip had said about Cross-Eyed Ladonna and Mr. Bookout kissing. I didn't blame C.K. for being mad, and he probably figured they were both telling the truth. And they were both lying. She wouldn't do that with Mr. Bookout.

"Well, I'm sorry to hear that. Anything you want to talk about?" She sounded like my mom.

"No, I don't think so," he said. He looked at me. "Let's go to the castle, okay?"

"Okay," I said and started to run, but he just walked. He still looked mad.

"What's the matter?" I asked.

"Oh—she—nothing."

"What? Are you thinking about what Skip and Harry said about her and your dad? That's not true, you know. She'd never do anything like that."

"Wanna bet?" He stopped and looked right in my eyes. His eyes were watery, and I thought he was going to cry.

"What do you mean?"

"Nothing. Nothing. I don't want to talk about it." He started walking, but then he stopped and whispered, "I saw her kissing my pa the other night. Skip and Harry were right."

"Where? When? Maybe it was someone else. Are you sure?"

"Here, in front of the barn in Pa's truck. I came up here a few nights ago cuz him and Ma had a fight, and I didn't wanna go back in the house. I was gonna spend the night in the castle."

"Why didn't you come to the house? You could have stayed with me. You do a lot anyway. Why didn't you come in?"

"It was real late. And I didn't want my ma and pa to know where I was. It all worked out. But I did see them kissin'. And then they went off together."

I couldn't believe him. I didn't know what to say. We climbed to the top of the castle and started to go down the shaft.

"Hey! I'm here now!" It was Harry down below. C.K. and I walked to the edge of the castle. Harry looked up at us.

"Shit," I said to myself. I didn't want him to know about the castle, and especially about the shaft. I wanted to yell, "Go away!" but I didn't. Instead, I said to C.K., "Does he have to know about the castle? This is ours."

But before C.K. could say anything, Harry was climbing up. "Hey, this is cool. Is this where you guys have that tunnel?"

I looked at C.K. I couldn't believe he'd told the creep about our secret place. "Geez! Why'd you tell him?" I said.

C.K. shrugged. "Cuz it's cool. And I helped make it."

"But it's in my barn!"

Harry walked over to the shaft and looked down. C.K. started climbing down. Harry said, "Wow! Cool! How long did it take you guys to make this?" His beady little eyes were looking at me.

"A long time. There's a certain way you have to go down. Make sure you show him, C.K. We don't need anyone else ruining it like Skip did." I hated Harry, and I was real angry at C.K.

C.K. was at the bottom. Then Harry started to go down. He went part way down and started counting bales. "One, two, three," he said, and he pointed at each bale from the top. "Four, five, six," and he went down further. "Seven, eight—"

"Leave it!" said C.K.

"Nine," he said and reached his hand between two bales. He fiddled and tugged, and finally pulled out a black piece of wood. It had some string around it, and there was another piece of wood tied to it. I couldn't see it real well because it was dark down the shaft.

"Put it back!" C.K. said.

What was going on? C.K. must have hidden something there, and he'd told Harry about it. C.K. looked mad and started coming back up the shaft. Harry kept the wooden thing and climbed back up too. He came right over to me and waved it in front of my face and laughed.

"Want to play funeral?" he said in an evil voice, his eyes getting smaller.

The thing looked familiar. It was in the shape of a cross. Then I remembered that it was the one C.K. made a long time ago when we were little kids. He had made it to bury that dead kitten. I couldn't believe he still had it. Where had it been all this time?

"Let me see it," I said and reached for it.

"Only if you play funeral with us," Harry said. He gave me a sickening smile. This was weird because C.K. had asked a couple times about playing funeral, and it sounded strange, and I didn't know what he was talking about, so I always just said no.

———

I felt jealous right then because, clearly, C.K. and Harry had a secret together. I simultaneously wanted to be part of it and didn't want to be part of it. I wanted to own the secret with them, but there was an element of dread about it This is a perfect example of what I was saying about this strange new feeling cloud that contained polar-opposite emotions. It was exciting but dreadful all at the same time. It was uncomfortable, and yet it was satisfying to be playing with my best friend, even if the horrible Harry was interfering.

"What do you mean, 'play funeral'? What does that mean?" I asked.

"Should we show him?" Harry said to C.K., who was out of the shaft now. He stood and watched Harry holding the cross in front of my face. I hated the sight of it.

I waved my hand in the air at C.K. and turned and went down the stairs. As I walked around in front of the castle to get to the aisle to leave, I heard a car pull up and then some ladies' voices. I heard my mom and Cross-Eyed Ladonna, and I guessed the other one was Mary. I also heard the sound of dog tails wagging hard against the wooden stall doors and my mom telling them to "stay down." They liked to jump on people, even though they were trained not to.

I looked down the aisle and saw my mom, Mary, and Cross-Eyed Ladonna and Josie, Tucker, and Tillie. They were talking, and the dogs were trying to get petted by all of them. One of the barn kittens came scurrying out of the tack room, and Tucker spotted her. He came running at her, and the kitten came running right at me, probably heading for the castle. The cats could climb right up the straight wall, but the dogs couldn't. They had to go around to the stairway. Sure enough, the kitten scrambled straight up the wall of the castle, and Tucker tried to follow her.

"Hey, Tucker!" I was glad to see him. When he gave up on the kitten and saw me, his ears went way down, he dropped his butt low, and he wagged his tail real hard. He was happy to see me and

scooted over to my left side. He sat down real fast and leaned on me. Then he put his big head up against my side and stayed there while I petted him.

"Hey, Wimp!" said Harry. "Catch!"

"What're you doing!" C.K. shouted at him. But Harry threw the cross down at me—over-hand. It came too hard and fast, and I couldn't catch it. It hit my knuckles and bounced into the air. Tucker snatched it in mid-air and ran off with it. First he ran into the arena. He tossed his head and pranced around like he knew he had something special.

I didn't care if he took it and buried it somewhere. I didn't want it. It gave me the creeps. But Harry and C.K. got all upset and slid down the castle wall and ran after him. Tucker knew he was being chased, and he wasn't about to let them take his prize. He ran around in big circles while C.K. and Harry ran after him. They tried cornering him, but he'd bluff them by going one way and then darting the other way. Harry yelled at him, "You stupid dog! You goddam dog! You ass-hole dog!" Then he'd yell at me, "Catch your stupid dog. Catch him! Goddam it, catch him!" But I just stood there and watched. And Tucker kept up the game.

Seeing C.K. join Harry in this was pretty sickening, though. I could hardly believe it was C.K. Why did this cross mean so much to him? I knew Harry was creepy, but C.K? It didn't fit.

Finally, Tucker got hot and tired. He panted hard, and his tongue hung out the side of his mouth. He tried to hold onto the cross at the same time he panted, and the cross kept almost falling out. When it did, he'd toss his head back to get a better grip. When he and Harry and C.K. were at the far end of the arena, he trotted slowly to me and sat down at my side. He leaned on me and dropped the cross in the sand. Harry and C.K. started running at us. Tucker saw this and picked the cross back up. I grabbed his collar and held him. "Sit. Stay," I told him, and he did. As Harry got closer, I was about to tell Tucker, "give," so he would drop the cross in my hand, and then I was going to give the stupid thing back to Harry and leave. I just wanted to go in the house and go back to reading my book.

I put my hands on either side of Tucker's mouth and was about to say "give," when Harry came up, looking real angry, and kicked Tucker right under the jaw. Tucker yelped and dropped the cross, and before I could think, I leaped on Harry and started punching him in the face. I kept bringing my fist up hard under his chin and punched and punched. It surprised him, I think, because he didn't hit me back. He just put his arms up and tried to protect himself. Somehow, I tripped him and fell on top of him. He punched me once in the shoulder, and that made me so mad, I punched him so hard and so fast, all he could do was hold his hands in front of his face and roll over.

I guess we must have been screaming at each other too because all of a sudden my mom and Cross-Eyed Ladonna were pulling us apart. My mom was behind me with her arms all the way around my body, and Cross-Eyed Ladonna had Harry the same way. Mary stood there watching. C.K. stood there with the cross in his hand, and Tucker was gone.

14

Oh, man! That day that Johnnie beat up on Harry! Well, shit, the asshole deserved it—kicked that nice dog right in the throat. Hell, Tucker was just playin'. That's what them damned retrievers do—carry stuff around in their mouths. And that Johnnie! Sure surprised the hell outa me. I didn't think he had it in him. I had a whole new respect for him after that. I wonder what would've happened if them ladies hadn't been out in the barn. Shit! I would've had to break it up. Fat chance. Johnnie was pissed off like you wouldn't believe. Harry really had it in for that dog, so poor Tuck just split. I think his feelings must've really been hurt. Here he thought he was playing some kinda cool game, and then this asshole comes up and kicks him. That was the second time, too. The asshole'd punched him in the nose a few days before that. Damn.

It was a weird time for me. Here I had two friends both wantin' to be with me and just me. One was an asshole and the other an angel. I used to wish I could take half of one and half of the other and put 'em together into one new, perfect friend. But I was stuck with the two of 'em whole.

———

Christine was holding onto Johnnie, and Cross-Eyed Ladonna was holding onto Harry. Harry's face was all puffin' up, and he had blood all over his mouth and comin' out his nose. He was a mess. His shirt was torn and all dirty. Johnnie looked like nothin' had happened. Except he was still real mad. He kept squirmin' and tryin' to get loose from his ma so he could beat Harry up some more. We stood there and watched Christine try to say the right thing to calm him down.

"Johnnie, this won't do any good. Let's talk about it. Here, tell me what happened. And then we'll hear what Harry has to say.

Then we'll work something out." And then Johnnie would nearly pull away and head for Harry again, and she'd have to grab him real quick. She'd put her arms back around him, and he could only move his feet. A couple times she just held him up in the air, but you could tell he was gettin' too heavy for her. Then she'd talk some more.

"I will understand why you did this. You just need to tell me. Will you please tell me now? Did he hurt you? Did he say something wrong?" But Johnnie kept squirmin' and wigglin' and gruntin'.

Finally, I said something. "Harry kicked Tucker. That's why Johnnie's mad."

Then she said the right thing. "Where's Tucker now? We better see if he's okay." It was like she'd shut his switch off. He started turning around to find Tuck. But Christine wouldn't let him go yet. She looked around at the rest of us.

Mary said, "I can take Harry home. I know where he lives."

Christine smiled and thanked her. If she only knew why Mary knew where Harry lived, she wouldn't have been so happy. She held Johnnie looser now and waited till Mary took Harry away. As soon as we heard her car door slam, Christine let go of Johnnie. He didn't say nothin' to nobody but ran around calling Tucker. Christine and Cross-Eyed Ladonna followed him, calling, "Tucker! Here, Tucker!"

I was standin' there with the cross. I'd hid it behind my back. I was relieved no one asked about it. When they was all out of the arena, I went and put it back, except I put it on the other side of the tunnel, thirteen bales down, not nine. Then I went to look for Johnnie and Tuck. I was glad Harry was gone.

I walked to the house and found all of them out in the front yard. Tucker was sitting down, and Christine was holding his mouth way open and looking inside. She let his mouth go shut, and he looked like he was having trouble swallowing. Christine looked worried, and so did Johnnie. Johnnie looked like he was getting mad all over again. Then I showed up.

Christine said, "Oh!" and she and Cross-Eyed Ladonna both looked at me real surprised. "Where have you been all this time?" Christine asked.

I didn't know what to say. Hadn't they seen me out there? I thought they had. "Out in the barn. With everyone else. I was lookin' for Tucker out there."

She said "Oh" again and turned back to Tucker. She got the dogs' water bucket by the front door and set it in front of him. He tried to drink, but he had trouble swallowing. "That does it," she said. "I'm taking him to the vet. Johnnie, you come with me." Then she looked at me. "I'll drop you off at home."

The three of us got in the car, and Cross-Eyed Ladonna walked back to the barn. I sat in the front with Christine, and Johnnie sat in the back with Tuck. I was just as glad we weren't in the back seat together cuz I figured Johnnie was pretty mad at me, too. When I got out of the car at my house, I looked at Johnnie before I shut the door, but he only looked at his dog.

I went in the house. The clock on the TV said 4:10. Pa would be home any minute, and then Ma around 5:00. It seemed real quiet and lonely in there by myself. I thought about callin' Harry to see if he was comin' back. He was supposed to spend the night. I dialed his phone number, but there was no answer. I wondered where Mary really took him. Maybe out to the grave-yard or maybe to K-Mart to shoplift. Or out to that farm with the two-story white house where they hid all the pictures in the chimney. Or, maybe she took him to the Dairy Queen. I kinda wished Christine had took me with them to the vet's. Johnnie and I woulda made up.

I put the TV on. I hardly ever watched it anymore. *Sesame Street* was on, but that's all. I heard Pa's truck and ran out to meet him. He was gettin' his lunch box out of the cab, so I stood on the sidewalk and waited. Then he turned to come in and saw me.

"Hi!" I said. I sure sounded cheerful. "Wanna go shoot some baskets?" He was thinking about something else, I could tell. "How about fishin'? Wanna go fishin'?" He started walking to the house. He smiled at me. "Catch? How about catch with the hardball until Ma fixes dinner?" He smiled at me again and put his arm around my shoulders. He didn't say nothin', and we just walked to the house.

When we got inside, he put his lunch box in the kitchen. He took me by both shoulders and smiled again. "I'm gonna get cleaned up, take a shower." Then he walked away. I went back and watched *Sesame Street*.

I heard something by the front door. I looked up. It was Harry. He was smiling. He had a big gray bag in his hand. "I'm back!" he said through the screen.

I was kinda glad to see him. His face was all cleaned up, but it looked sore on his cheeks and under his eyes. "Where've you been?" I asked.

"K-Mart," he said. He looked real happy. "Look what I got." He pulled out two long, flat boxes, the kind board games comes in. One was CLUE and the other was a Ouija Board. "Wanna play?"

"Yeah! Great!" I said. He started opening the CLUE game. I'd played this once a long time ago with some cousins I ain't seen again. He opened it all up, and I opened all the cellophane bags with all the pieces and cards. He showed me how to play. It was fun, and I figured out that Miss Scarlet committed the murder with the lead pipe in the Library. This was a great game. We played it three times. Harry won the last two, though.

We was near the end of the first game when Ma came home. Pa was still in the bathroom. "Where's your pa?" she asked as soon as she walked in. I pointed at the bathroom. I was getting so close to figuring out that the weapon was the knife. She marched right into the bathroom, and I could hear her talking to him. She was getting all worked up again, so I just didn't listen, and she came out and went in the kitchen. After a while, Pa walked out. He had nice clean clothes on, and he smelled real good when he walked past me. Ma was fixin' dinner. Pa walked right past us, never said nothin', and went out the door. I heard him drive away.

We was playin' the third game when Ma called us to eat. We hurried up and ate and went back to the game. Ma had two beers with her chicken. This was new. Usually she had diet cola. Oh well. Harry was beating me real bad on this last game. He had the person and the room figured out, and I was hoping to figure out the weapon. Then, the door bell rang. It was Marge. I was bummed

to see her cuz I figured she was gonna take Harry away, but she didn't. Instead, her and Ma had another beer, and then they said they was going out for a while and we should go to bed by eleven. We said, yeah, we would, and they left.

Harry finished winning the third game. Then he said, "Let's watch TV. There's an Arnold Schwarzenegger movie on—*Terminator*, I think. I looked it up in the *TV Guide* and sure enough, it was starting at 8:00. We ate cookies and microwave popcorn and watched the movie. When it was over, we tried watching David Letterman. Harry laughed a lot, but I never did understand that show. Finally, he said, "Let's get the Ouija Board out."

As soon as I saw it, I remembered that we'd used it at Little Friends, but I couldn't remember how. Harry said we should turn all the lights out and just use a candle. I got one out of the kitchen drawer and put it into one of Ma's good candleholders. It was dark outside now. Harry set the candle on the floor next to the Ouija Board, and that made it real spooky.

He said, "I learned a new way to play this game."

I felt kinda creepy and scared, but this was exciting. I knew Mary had helped him steal at least one of these games from K-Mart. That's what Jack did at Little Friends. We'd go through and buy something big, then go back in with the bag and put other smaller stuff in the bag and not pay for it. It was our reward for doing something Jack and Bernice wanted us to do. I didn't know Harry was still doing stuff with them, though. After they put Jack in jail, I thought all those teachers and guests—the men we didn't know who just came in to have sex with the kids—just went away. Jack was still in jail, but we'd seen Bernice at different places like McDonalds and the grocery store. Ma didn't believe nothing had happened there, so whenever she saw Bernice, she was real friendly to her. I just tried not to look at her.

"Where'd you get this?" I asked.

"K-Mart. You know, this is a very old game. Some guy named William Fuld invented it in 1890. You know what 'wee' and 'ja' mean? They both mean 'yes'—one in French and one in German, which really doesn't make sense cuz there's a 'yes' *and* a 'no' on

the board. What I really like is the moon picture by the 'no.' I like all them black clouds around it. So, do you remember how to play? Well, Mary showed me how you don't just need to ask yes and no questions cuz see all these letters and numbers? Well, we couldn't spell yet at Little Friends, so they didn't have us use the letters. Sometimes we used the numbers, but mostly the yes and no, remember? And remember how we always had one of the adults or junior counselors play with us? We never got to do it with another kid? Well, I still haven't done it with another kid, but Mary said we're old enough now, and she thought you'd really like playing it with me. So, what we gotta do is ask it some other kinda question, you know, like the name of something—not a question it can answer with just yes or no, and then the spirit we ask spells out the word. See all the letters? Mary said we need to think of somebody dead and ask that guy's spirit something. Who do you want to ask? Who do you, well, did you, know who is dead?" He sat there with the little three-legged pointer board in his hands. He sat cross-legged, and he kept turning the pointer board over and over.

I couldn't think of nobody dead. Johnnie's grandpa, but I never met him. "Only one I can think of is Johnnie's grandpa, but I didn't know him."

"That's okay, we can ask him something anyway. In fact, he'd be a real good one. We can ask him why Johnnie's such a wimp."

A wimp? I thought. After beating you up? But I didn't say that. One of his eyes was pretty swollen now, and I could see a little dried blood in his nose.

Well, shit, I suppose, if someone asked, and people do ask, when it was I first started to go bad, this might've been the moment. It was the first time I decided to do something bad just for the sake of doing it. And it was cool. It felt good. It seemed right, like this was what I was meant to do—like I finally found *me*. I didn't need to run off to no damned California. And I never said to myself, "Okay, this is a bad thing to do, and now I'm gonna do it." It just felt right.

168

"Okay," I said, in the dark. "Let's ask Johnnie's grandpa what makes Johnnie cry."

"Whoa! I thought you liked the dude. But yeah, that's a good one," Harry said. He set the pointer thing on the Ouija Board right under the letters. The light from the candle made the letters and the numbers sorta swim around. "Okay, now put all your finger tips on that edge, and I'll put mine on this edge. Now, remember, neither of us is supposed to make it move. The spirit is gonna make it move. Good. Okay, now ask Johnnie's grandpa the question."

"Wait. How will Johnnie's grandpa know I'm asking him the question? Do I have to say his name or somethin'?"

"Well, I guess so. Yeah, say his name and then ask the question."

"I don't know his name."

"Oh. Well. Just call him 'Johnnie Ambrose's grandpa.' Yeah, that should work. He'll know it's him."

"Johnnie Ambrose's—" I started giggling.

"Wait. We gotta be serious or it won't work. Let's close our eyes and be serious."

"Okay." I closed my eyes, took a deep breath, and got serious. In a low, straight voice I said, "Johnnie Ambrose's grandpa. I'm calling you. We have a question for you. We want to know. What makes Johnnie Ambrose cry?" I had just a hint of feeling bad. Guilty, I guess. I didn't want to hurt Johnnie, and this sorta felt like I was maybe gonna hurt him. But then I felt the pointer board move just a little. I opened my eyes and looked at it. I looked at Harry's fingers and saw he wasn't touching the board at all. His fingers was just right above it. A zing went through my stomach. I liked this.

The pointer board had moved just a little, and then it stopped. Harry said, "Ask again."

So, I did, except slower and louder. "Johnnie Ambrose's grandpa. What makes Johnnie cry?"

Then, real slow, the pointer started to move. Harry said, "Keep your eyes shut." I did, and the pointer kept moving. I peeked once and saw the pointer move toward the left side of the board, and it didn't look like Harry's fingers was touching it at all. My arms and hands felt tingly. I shut my eyes again until the pointer didn't move no more. Then we both opened our eyes. The hole in the pointer board was right over the D.

What things could make Johnnie cry that begin with D? I thought. "Dogs?" I said. We both laughed.

"Drugs?" said Harry, and he chuckled. I didn't get it.

"How about dinosaurs? No, he's always liked dinosaurs. Desserts? No, he loves desserts."

"How about danger?" Harry said, real eerie. "I bet that's it. Oooooh, danger. Yeah, that would make the wimp cry. Let's keep going. Ask the grandpa to keep going."

I thought about how to do that. "Um. Okay. Johnnie Ambrose's grandpa. We'd like you to keep going. Please spell out the rest of the word. What makes Johnnie Ambrose cry?"

We closed our eyes and waited. Nothing happened for a minute. It was a long minute, but I couldn't move or speak or nothin'. We just waited. And then, slowly, it started to move. I kept my eyes shut the whole time this time. It moved about an inch and stopped. We waited for a while, but it stayed where it was.

Harry said, "Let's look."

It had stopped over the E. "Deer?" I said.

He looked puzzled. "I know—demons." He looked at me to see what I thought.

"Maybe," I said. "But he's never talked about them. I know! Decimals! He hated decimals in school this year!" I started laughing.

Harry looked at me. He shrugged. "Let's keep going."

I shut my eyes again and asked the grandpa to go on. The pointer moved quicker now and started toward the front of the alphabet. It stopped near the edge. We opened our eyes. It was over the A.

"Dear?" I said. "Like when you write someone a letter."

"You already said that. Deacon? Does he go to church?"

"No. What's a deacon?" I asked.

"Some guy who helps out in church, like the minister's helper."
I hadn't heard of that. "There ain't no deacons in my church."
He shrugged. "Go on."

This time the pointer board carried our fingers way across
the board. It really felt like it knew where it was going. This was the
most exciting move so far, like it knew exactly where it wanted to
go. It stopped over the T. We opened our eyes.

"Deat?" I said. "What's a deat?"

Harry ignored me and closed his eyes again. He'd left his fingers on the pointer board. I asked the grandpa to go on. This time
it did almost the same thing. It went speeding across the board,
back the other way. It stopped and we opened our eyes. It was right
over the H.

Harry said, in a heavy, breathy way, "Death." He looked at me
real serious. And he just stayed looking at me like that. His funny
little eyes had a eerie light in 'em, and he looked like someone else
with the candle shining up under his chin. He seemed much taller
than me, and his face looked like some grown-up who had caught
me doing something wrong. I felt like running out of the house.
But I told myself this was just Harry, and he looked weird cuz of
the candle. He did look spooky. I mean, real spooky.

"Shit!" I said. "What's that supposed to mean?"

"Death," he said, real heavy. "Does that mean if he sees something dic, he'll cry? Or does it mean that if he himself is close to
death, he'll cry? Or just talkin' about death? You know him. What
do you think? How're you gonna get him to cry?"

"I don't wanna make him cry," I said.

"Well, then, why did you ask the question?" he asked. "I think
you guys are queer together."

"We are not!"

"Shit. Do you want to play this or not?" he demanded. "I know.
Let's ask it if you're a queer."

"No way," I said.

"What, you afraid it'll say 'yes'?"

"Forget it. You think of something to ask it. What dead person do you know?"

Harry said, "How about one of those guys we dug up in the graveyard? Remember? With Jack and Bernice?"

———

Damn. Until he said that, I'd forgotten all about that graveyard shit. Even then, when he reminded me, it was real blurry, like maybe I'd dreamed it or something.

Now, that was bizarre shit they was doin'. I never did understand it. They'd dig up a grave and open the coffin. The dead person'd be all moldy and shit. And then one of the kids would be lowered down into the grave and have to just lie there on the corpse. I never had to do it, but I think Johnnie did. Man, the memories really fade. But they didn't for Harry. He remembered all that stuff like it'd happened yesterday. I think he was still doin' shit with them. With Mary and his brothers. Maybe that's why he remembered it—cuz they was still doin' it. Jack bein' in jail didn't stop 'em. Besides, it was Bernice that was in charge.

———

This was getting too weird for me. "Let's play CLUE again," I said. I wanted to put the lights back on. Harry still looked creepy, even though he was talking more like himself now.

"No," he said. "I wanna ask one of those dead guys somethin'."

"Well, I don't." I got up and put a lamp on.

"What're you a chicken shit, too? Like your queer friend?"

"Why don't you just go home."

Then he didn't say nothin'. He just started putting the Ouija Board away. I stood there and watched him. Then he opened the CLUE box again. He let me go first. We played three more games, but he still didn't say much. I don't think he liked CLUE.

I was starting to feel tired and looked at the clock. Almost 2:00. "I think I'm going to bed," I said.

"Okay," he said. "I'll sleep here." He always slept on the couch when he stayed over. I went upstairs to my room and left him there. One of the windows in my room looked out over the driveway. It was open cuz it was summertime. I took my shorts off and got into bed. Then I heard a car come in the driveway. Then I heard two doors slam and my ma's voice. I figured she and Marge was back, and Marge would take Harry home. I got up and looked out the window. But it wasn't my ma's car. It was some small, foreign car. My ma was with a man, walking to our door. He was short and half bald. He had his arm around Ma, and she was laughing. But I could tell she'd been drinkin' again cuz she was sorta weavin' around. The man held her up straight. I heard them come in the front door. I wondered if Harry was awake. Then I didn't hear nothin' else. I went back to bed.

In the morning, I looked out to see if the man's car was still there, but it was gone. I went downstairs. Ma was still slee-pin', I guess, cuz her door was shut. Harry was sittin' on the couch watchin' cartoons. I wondered if he saw the man or if the man had come in. I sat down on the couch with him.

"Sleep okay?" I asked.

"Okay till your ma and that guy starting moanin' and groanin'. He sure was screwin' her socks off. She was lovin' it, too."

"What're you talking about?" I didn't like the way he said this.

"Screwing. Fucking. Sex. You know?"

I sorta knew, but I knew my ma wouldn't do that.

"You're full of shit," I said. He didn't answer—just kept on watching cartoons.

I wished he'd go home. I'd had enough of him. I started think-ing about Johnnie. I wanted to call him, but I just stayed there and watched TV. Pretty soon Ma came out of her room. She looked kinda bad—all messed up and tired-lookin'. She walked right past us into the dining room. She went to the window and looked out in the driveway. She said, "Damn," under her breath and went in the kitchen and called someone.

"Hi, it's me," she said. "Was my car okay when you left? Was it still there?" She listened a minute. "Can you take me to go get

it? You can get Harry then, too." She listened. "Ten minutes? Fine. Bye." She hurried back past us and went in her room. She came out dressed and said Harry should get his stuff together cuz his ma was comin', and they had to go get Ma's car. She said I could come along if I wanted. I wanted to call Johnnie, so I said I'd stay home.

It all happened so fast, and then they was gone. I was relieved. I could hardly wait to call Johnnie. When I did call him, he said I could come up after three o'clock cuz he was goin' to a movie with some kid named Joey from his school. I couldn't believe it. He never did anything with other kids. Then I got mad. It wasn't my fault he got in a fight with Harry. Maybe Ma would get home soon, and she'd take me to a movie, too.

But she didn't come home. It musta been around noon she called and said her car wouldn't start, and so she was just goin' shoppin' until it was fixed. She said I should go up to Johnnie's and eat lunch there. I told her I was gonna do that anyway. Instead, I watched TV.

———————

You know, things was tough for Ma. Here Pa was goin' out with Cross-Eyed Ladonna, and I think Ma's hours had been cut at work. They was always layin' her off and hirin' her back again. She never could count on the money.

And Pa, it's no wonder he went off with Cross-Eyed Ladonna, she was so nice to him. Ma screamed at him all the time, and Ladonna treated him real nice. They both had a lot of stuff on their minds. And me, shit, I was glad I had Johnnie.

15
- Harold Panzerov -

Harold Panzerov was born the middle son to Russian immigrants Ida and Fyodor Panzerov in New York City in 1948. Harold was a plumpish baby and grew up, as did his brothers, speaking only Russian until he went to kindergarten at age five. His older brother was a math genius and skipped two grades of elementary school. His younger brother, upon entering junior high school, won spelling bees and skipped ninth grade. Harold didn't like math or English and was bullied by his schoolmates for being fat.

Ida, who always maintained a trim figure, worked as the manager of the women's dress department at Macy's while Fyodor worked his way up at a large bank in midtown Manhattan until he became the manager of the Accounting Department. He would spank Harold whenever he found him with candy or cookies, and Ida claimed that the real Harold must have been switched with a fat baby at the hospital when he was born.

Often, after Harold and his brothers went to bed at night, he listened to his parents argue about many things, the most painful of which was him. His mother would say, "I think we should sue the hospital. He can't be ours. You're smart, I'm smart. We're all thin and healthy. Harold is not one of us." She wanted to send him to a boarding school so she wouldn't have to look at him, but Fyodor insisted that hospital nurses took great care in their work, that Harold had not been switched, and it was simply a roll of the dice how the genetics fell.

"How about your obese Uncle Pyotr? Was he switched at the hospital, too?" Fyodor would shout. "He is our son, and we're not shipping him off to any boarding school. What's wrong with you!?"

Ida's response was always the same— grabbed her purse, stormed out of their apartment, and came back an hour later drunk. In the mornings she would pile the breakfast plates high with pancakes and sausage, but on Harold's she would place one tiny pancake and half a sausage link. He was not allowed any syrup. When the boys went out the door to school, she hugged and kissed his brothers but not Harold. For him there was a daily admonition: "Don't you dare eat any candy or cookies today. Promise?"

Fyodor was more fair and played ball in the alley with all three of his sons. Harold's missed catches and the heavy-breathing shuffle saddened Fyodor, but it was the taunts of neighborhood boys that broke his heart. They would laugh at the way Harold ran. "Tubby!" they'd shout, knowing that Fyodor would chase them, shaming both father and son.

By the time he was fifteen, Harold had absorbed so much humiliation that he'd withdrawn into an inner world that was unreachable by others. When his mother was feeling charitable, she would refer to him as "my son the dreamer" to explain his detached behavior. She was so deeply embarrassed by him that when he left home in the middle of the night, shortly after this fifteenth birthday, she was more relieved than worried.

He had seen a TV commercial about the high-paying but physically-demanding jobs at U.S. Steel in Gary, Indiana. The hard work appealed to him, not because he knew what it was to work hard, but because the money would allow him to purchase a nice house in the country one day, maybe have a wife and children. He would be respected.

His size and his impassive countenance made him look older than other fifteen-year-olds, so it was easy for employers to have him around without fear that his looks would give away his illegality. However, he was not prepared for the hot, dirty work and nearly quit on a number of occasions. But driven by his dream, at seventeen Harold was fit and trim and earned a good wage. He met Sally Ann, who worked as a secretary in the main office even though she'd gone to college for two years. He told her he was twenty-one and after three dates asked her to marry him. She

and her sister had been so gently and lovingly raised that they had little to rebel against, so when her parents said she was too young to marry and hadn't known Harold long enough, she hadn't the heart to defy them openly. Instead, just as Harold had, she disappeared one night.

They eloped to Chicago and were happy. When she was due to deliver their first child, she quit her job because Harold was making enough money to support them. She gave birth to a daughter and eighteen months later, another daughter and two years after that, a third daughter. Harold began working some weekend hours to bring home more money, and things were going smoothly for the young couple until Harold took a tumble off one of the towers. It was a simple slip of attention as he looked out on Lake Michigan at a new steamer headed their way. The sole of his boot caught the edge of the metal step of the vertical ladder, and he slid straight down three or four rungs until he caught hold of a side member, twisted his wrist, and dove head first onto the concrete below.

Three weeks later, he woke up with a broken arm, a dislocated knee, and the sight of Sally and the girls sitting at his hospital bed where they'd been the whole while, waiting for his return to consciousness.

At first he wasn't sure who they were. Or who he was. Or where he was. The EEGs indicated he had a fair amount of brain damage, and the doctors were unsure whether he would regain his mental abilities.

At home he was bedridden and dizzy, but Sally Ann was a fine nursemaid, and after a few months, he recalled who she was, who his daughters were, and, once the dizziness subsided, Sally Ann began talking about his going back to work.

She was delighted when he told her he felt clear-minded enough to drive, then terrified when he insisted on driving down the left side of every street. After five near collisions, she insisted that she drive because he had come out of the hospital angrier and more stubborn than he'd gone in, but he refused. When Sally hid the car keys, he became enraged and hit her.

She took him back to the brain doctors, who said that this "was not out of the ordinary" and with time, he might become less violent. That evening, when she didn't make the type of dinner he expected, he threw his plate across the room and punched her in the ribs. Her concern for him dissolved into panic. She'd not been prepared for a violent life. In fact, she'd really not been prepared for adult life at all. This had been the quality that had endeared her to Harold. He felt strong around her. Brave. She had felt protected and strong with him. They had been happy, and now, suddenly, frighteningly, they weren't. One morning she was gone, leaving a note that she had moved to Oregon to live with her cousin and could not take the girls.

Harold's driving improved. He was able to care for his darling daughters and drive to get groceries, but he was never going to be "normal," according to his doctors. He was awarded a large settlement from U.S. Steel, which enabled him to buy a small gentleman's farm several miles outside of South Bend, Indiana. Since he no longer had to work, he tended to his daughters, sent them to school, cultivated a large garden, and bought a few pigs, a cow, a sheep, a goat, and a dog. Although they missed their loving and tender-hearted mother, his daughters got used to Harold's sometimes harsh ways, climbed all over him, kissed him, hugged him, and told him he was the best daddy in the world.

Mary Jo was the oldest, Bonita the middle child, and Joannie the youngest. Mary Jo was eight when they moved to the farm, and she became a surrogate wife to Harold. She did the laundry, cooked breakfast and dinner, and mothered Bonita and Joannie.

Within a year, Harold gained fifteen pounds. The second year he gained another twenty. He looked at himself in a mirror only to shave and simply bought better-fitting clothes as needed. He noticed that the girls were growing rapidly, and he seemed to spend much of his time taking them to K-Mart for new wardrobes, but he didn't mind.

The only time he was lonely was when the girls were at school. He missed sex, but didn't think about it much, and when the urge came on him strongly enough, he would masturbate to memories

of better times with his wife. In the evenings and weekends, Mary Jo, Bonita, and Joannie showered him with affection as they always had. They climbed into his lap to watch TV together, and they kissed him on the lips when they left for school each day.

When Mary Jo was in sixth grade, she climbed into Harold's lap and told him that she needed a brassiere because all the other girls wore them. He said to her, "You're still a girl, darlin'."

"No, daddy, I'm growing up. I'm growing breasts."

"Naw, I don't believe it," he said. "Not till you're at least fifteen."

"My friend Ruthie said you need a bra when your breast fills up the palm of your hand. See?" Mary Jo lifted up her shirt with her left hand, and, as though she were presenting a project at a science fair, she covered her left breast bud with her cupped palm. "See. It fits."

Harold was taken by surprise. He felt a stirring in his groin. He wished he had a sister or aunt or some woman he could ask about this. He wanted to shove Mary Jo off his lap. He pulled her shirt down and took her by the shoulders, angry that she'd caused such forbidden feelings.

Mary Jo was startled. Her expression changed to one of hurt and then to one of confusion. She let her head fall forward and stared at nothing. Then she tilted her plump face to one side and smiled, almost flirtatiously. "But, Daddy, you said I can tell you anything, and you'll always help me." She waited for his response, but he was frozen, suspended. She looked back down and pouted.

Harold couldn't recall ever feeling such guilt and tipped her chin up with his forefinger. When he saw her eyes brimming with tears, he hugged her to him hard. *But dang it,* he thought, as he felt his penis throb. He continued to hold her close and tried to make his arousal go away.

16

Harry really was, pardon my professional language, an asshole. He was one angry, cheated kid. Attacking him was probably the most gratifying experience I had as a youth. To just pound his face for kicking my dog was divine. Revenge *can* be sweet.

By the time we got Tucker to the vet, he was making weird hacking sounds and snorfing through his nose. Dr. Strong, the vet, took us all to his back room right away and X-rayed Tucker's neck. While the X-rays were developing, he smeared some gel stuff on Tucker's neck and used his ultra-sound machine to see if he had "major blockage." He had like a little TV screen with some weird designs on it. The designs moved each time Tucker took a breath.

"I might put an endotracheal tube down him if he gets much worse," he explained to my mom and me. "Right now he is getting enough air." Then he gave him a shot of stuff called cortisone and said this would help get the swelling down.

Tuck was half sitting up and half lying on the table with his front legs stretched out stiff like he was trying to hold himself up. His neck was arched because he was trying to breathe. Each breath sounded raspy. I stroked his head, and he wagged his tail a little, but mostly he was just trying to get air in. I hated Harry. I hated him with all my strength and wished he'd drop dead. The fur on Tuck's big head looked so shiny and black. His ears hung way down close to his neck. I petted them gently.

Dr. Strong put the X-rays up on a lighted board. Mom and I looked at them, and Dr. Strong pointed to one area. He said, "This is the area I was concerned about, but there's no major damage, just swelling. He is having enough trouble breathing, though, that I think you ought to leave him here with me in case it gets worse.

The cortisone won't work for a while yet, and if his trachea closes up much more, I'll have to run the trache tube to save his life."

"Wow," said my mom. She looked real worried. "Are there any risks involved with the trache tube?"

"Well, we always hate to use anesthesia on an animal with breathing problems, and we would have to anesthetize him to get the tube down. But it's our only choice at that point. Unless you'd want to put him to sleep, and I don't think you want to do that, do you?"

"Absolutely not! He's our favorite, and he's one of the best show specials out there right now. No, do whatever it takes to save him." She stroked Tuck's head and started to hug him, but she pulled back because he started hacking again.

"We'll make him as comfortable as we can," said Dr. Strong. He really seemed to care about Tucker, so I trusted him.

I looked at Tuck as we left, but he didn't look at us. He was just trying to breathe. God! I hated Harry. I imagined having some big strong guys hold Harry's legs and arms and head—maybe hold his head back so his throat stuck out. And then I'd get to kick him right where he kicked Tuck, right in the throat. And then I'd watch him try to breathe while his trachea swelled up. He'd hack and snorf just like Tucker, only it would get worse and worse, and he'd turn all blue, and then he'd shudder once and die.

"Want to stop at McDonald's?" my mom asked.

"No, I'm not hungry," I said. She nodded, and we drove home.

I went up to my room and read a book and kept having that daydream about kicking Harry in the throat. Dr. Strong called a few hours later and said he didn't have to do the trache tube thing, but he wanted to keep Tuck another day or two to make sure he'd be okay. What a relief.

The next morning C.K. called. He acted like nothing had happened and wanted to come up to my house as usual. Well, I had a surprise for him. The night before, my friend Joey from my school called and wanted to go to the movies—the 12:00 show. I said yes and was glad to have another friend. Joey was pretty cool, even if he was kind of fat. He was super good at Nintendo and

liked to play sword fighting. So, I told C.K. he could come over after 3:00. He was surprised and sounded disappointed, but I wasn't very sorry. What the heck was he doing telling Harry about our castle, and especially about the shaft? And then he acted so goofy about that dumb cross. I hated Harry.

After the movie, Joey wanted to come over. I thought about it. I thought about how C.K. would feel if I took another friend to the castle. So, I told Joey yes, he could come over. His mom said she'd pick him up just before supper. We played Nintendo for a while, and then the doorbell rang. My mom answered it. Usually I answered it when I knew it was C.K., but I just kept on playing Nintendo with Joey. C.K. came into the living room and was pretty quiet. I introduced him to Joey, and C.K. just watched us play because only two can play at the same time.

Joey was real good at Dungeons and Dragons because he had two older brothers who were real smart. It's a hard game, and I was just starting to learn it. My mom had bought me the books and stuff. So, when we got tired of Nintendo, we got the D & D books out. We tried to explain it to C.K. He seemed interested at first. He liked the names of the guys and places and the sword fighting, but when we explained strategy to him, he seemed to lose interest.

"Have you told Joey about the frog jumping through the grass hoop?" he asked.

"No, I haven't," I said. So, I told Joey. He thought it was funny.

"Want to show him?" C.K. asked.

"I don't know. You want to try it?" I asked Joey.

"Sure," he answered then asked C.K., "Mind if we just finish this one strategy?" Joey was very nice.

"Yeah, sure. Does your mom have some cake or anything?" C.K. asked. "I think I'll go talk to her." He went out to the kitchen, and I could hear him and my mom talking.

Joey and I finished D & D and went out and had cake, too. Then we all went down to the pond. On the way down I told Joey all about the peat and how careful he had to be.

We walked real slowly to the edge of the pond and looked for frogs. I explained the plan to Joey. He thought with three of us it

would be easier. We made a sort of triangle, with C.K. and me on the edge of the pond and Joey between us but farther away. We found a small branch for Joey to throw, and as soon as we found three frogs sitting together on the edge, we motioned for him to throw the branch. He did, and the frogs hopped toward him just like we planned. I had my shirt off and ready. This time, all three frogs stayed together. We got them cornered between us, and I threw my shirt over all three, and Joey and I held all the edges down. The three of them all jumping together under the shirt was really funny, and we laughed a long time.

Then we realized we hadn't made a hoop first. So, C.K. started looking for the old one. He found it, but it was all dry and fell apart. Joey suggested we get some big branches to hold the edges of the shirt down and then the three of us could make a hoop together real fast. We did that, but when we had the hoop all made and went back for the frogs, they were gone. So, we had to start all over to catch frogs. This time Joey wanted to be on the edge of the pond, and C.K. wanted to throw the branch. As soon as C.K. threw the branch in the water and the frogs jumped toward C.K., Joey pushed off the edge to go after the frogs. It happened real fast. A big chunk of peat broke off under his foot, and when he came down on the other foot, his leg sank up to his knee. He yelled and fell forward on his hands. He looked real surprised, and at first I thought he was going to cry when he saw his leg go way into the peat like that.

"It's okay," I said. "It happens to my dad all the time." C.K. and I helped him out. His one leg was all black and gooey. We took handfuls of grass and wiped it off.

So, we started all over and found four frogs this time. We told Joey he better move away from the edge. We didn't want to tell him he was fat. We lost two of the frogs and captured the other two.

I thought it was pretty boring after the first few jumps. Joey seemed to get bored after a while, too. But C.K. acted like he could have done it for another ten hours. Thank goodness my mother called us from the top of the hill. Joey's mother was here to pick him up, so we went back up, and Joey left.

I'd never gotten to show Joey the castle, but I told C.K. I had. At first he looked kind of shocked, but then he remembered that he'd done the same thing with Harry. He said, "Yeah, I guess you could do that." He walked along and just looked down at the ground. Finally, he said, "I'm sorry about showing Harry the castle. I really am." He looked right at me, and he really did look sorry.

I didn't know what to say. I wasn't ready to forgive him. "Maybe we should take it down and build some other kind of fort. And not tell anyone," I said.

We talked about this while we walked out to the barn. It would be a shame to take it down. It was so cool—so special—and it was ours. We walked out to it and stood at the bottom looking up at it. It was so square, and the top looked so much like a real castle with spaces between every bale. But off to the left, where the boarders took bales away to feed their horses, and where the stairway was, it was getting smaller.

"How long do you think it will take them to get all the way to the tunnel?" C.K. asked.

"I don't know. A few months at least."

"Where will we move it to then?"

"Well, more hay will come in from the field—two more cuttings, so I don't know. They'll probably feed this first-cutting hay first. We could build another castle when the third cutting comes in. That should be here all winter because they'll use the other stuff first."

C.K. smiled. "Yeah, let's do that." He looked happier than he'd looked all day. "Want to go up there now? We ain't been down in the tunnel together for a while."

I said, "Okay," but C.K. wanted to go back in the house first and get some more cake to take down there, so we did. We got some Kool-Aid too. We were walking back to the barn with two paper plates loaded with cake and a thermos. We saw two cars coming up our long driveway. The first one was Cross-Eyed Ladonna's, and the second one was Mary's.

"Oh," I said. I could even hear myself sound happy. "Here comes Cross-Eyed Ladonna." Then I remembered that C.K. didn't like her anymore.

He just stopped and looked at them. He said, "Maybe we should go back in the house."

"How about if we hurry and get down in the shaft before they get here?" We had a very long driveway.

"Okay." And we ran as fast as we could without dropping our cake off the plates. We ran into the stall area, made a left turn, and raced for the arena. We ran around the castle, up the stairway, and got to the top before their car doors slammed.

It was real hard to get stuff down into the shaft unless we could tuck it under one arm, or tie it around our waists, or just drop it down there. There was no way we could climb down while holding plates of cake. "Let's hide in the back," I said. So we went way to the back of the castle and ate some of the cake. We left the rest sit there while we went down the shaft.

When we got to the bottom, we sort of didn't know what to do. It was like we didn't know what to say to each other. We used to tell stories about the Evil Sorcerer's Tribe and make up names for the warriors and heroic adventures. But something was wrong. Something was different. We heard Mary and Cross-Eyed Ladonna giggling. They must have come in to get some hay. I really wanted to go talk to Cross-Eyed Ladonna. I always felt happy when I talked to her. I wondered what she was doing—probably cleaning her stall or getting ready to ride her mare. Maybe she was going to give Mary a lesson. That's usually what they did when Mary was here. C.K. was sitting with his knees up and just staring at the ground.

"What do you want to do?" I asked.

"I don't know. How about you?"

"Well, I know you don't like Cross-Eyed Ladonna, but I'd kind of like to go see her. Don't you think she's nice?"

"Yeah, she's nice, but remember, I saw her kissin' Pa. How can I like her after that?"

"Well, I guess so. Are you sure it was she?" I asked.

"Yes! I'm sure. Go see her if you want. I'll wait here."

"No, that's okay."

Then I heard her voice. "C.K.! Johnnie! You guys out here? You guys down in that tunnel?"

I climbed up the shaft. C.K. didn't come. I ran over to the front edge of the castle. She was looking up. She had on a real pretty white T-shirt with pink flowers on it, and her hair was up in a ponytail. The ponytail sort of bounced and swayed when she talked. "You know you got a sick kitty out here? The little black and white one. She's actin' like she don't wanna move. You wanna let your ma know?"

Tomato was my favorite kitty. We had a couple orange ones, too, and a white one with orange spots. Daddy had named this one Tomato. I don't know why. Somebody had dumped off a whole litter of kittens at our farm a couple months ago. We gave them cat food and water, but we never gave them shots or anything because barn cats came and went and got killed on the road or just left. And somebody was always wanting to give us cats. But I liked this one. Her back and sides were all black, and her underneath was all white. Her face was half and half, and the black places matched perfectly on both sides. She had pretty green eyes and one big dot of white on her back, right in the middle. I had asked my mom if we couldn't get shots for just her. I'd seen a few of them die of distemper. They got real tired and didn't want to move, and then they'd die. But most of them grew up and were healthy, and then they'd leave or have kittens. She said no, that then we'd have to get her a shot every year, and then she'd probably run off or get hit by a car, and it just didn't make sense to put money into a barn cat. Then I asked if Tomato could be a house cat, and she said, "No way, Ho-zay." So, I'd hoped real hard that she would never get distemper. I even brought Tomato chicken and tuna, hoping it would make her stronger.

I followed Cross-Eyed Ladonna into the tack room. Tomato was curled up on a red horse blanket on the floor. Her fur looked so pretty. The black was very black, and the white was as clean and bright as it could be. But her coat looked sort of ruffed up. I kneeled down and petted her head. She looked up at me and mewed a little. Her eyes didn't quite want to open all the way, and those grey skin things in the corners were way up and covered part of each eye.

"Think she got kicked?" asked Cross-Eyed Ladonna.

It looked like distemper to me. I stroked Tomato's head, and she purred for a few seconds. Then she went back to sleep. "Maybe. I hope so."

"You hope so!" she laughed. "That's not a very nice thing to say."

I laughed just a little too. "I mean, it's probably distemper and she's going to die. If she got kicked, maybe she'd live."

"This kitty don't have no bad temper," she laughed but looked serious.

"No, no, it's a disease cats get. I think it's a virus, like a cold. Except there's no cure, and they usually die. Some of the other kitties have died from it." My throat got all tight, and I almost started to cry, and I sure didn't want to cry in front of Cross-Eyed Ladonna. I didn't look up at her but said, "I'll go ask my mom," and I ran to the house. I couldn't help crying, and when my mom saw me, she thought something had happened to a person or a horse.

She was sitting at the dining room table with a bunch of papers. When she saw me, she jumped up like you wouldn't believe and sort of screamed, "What happened! What's wrong?"

"It's Tomato. I think she's got distemper," and I started crying real hard.

"Is that all?" she said, and she came and hugged me. "I told you not to get attached to her. I'll come out and see."

When my mom looked at Tomato, she was pretty sure that's what it was. She gave me a hug and looked into my face like she was real sorry. "I hate to see you so sad, but this is how it goes with barn cats. She'll probably die before the day is over. You can help her by making her as comfortable as you can. Don't let the dogs in here, and make sure she stays warm. I think if we took her to Dr. Strong at this point, he'd just put her to sleep. I don't think he could save her." She hugged me real close for a long time, and I felt better. But I was sad.

She went back to the house, and I went and got C.K. When I got down to the bottom of the shaft he was sitting there holding that dumb black cross. "You got that thing out again? What's it

for, anyway? What's this funeral stuff you and Harry keep talking about?" For some reason, my heart was pounding.

He looked at me, but he didn't answer. He had a weird look on his face.

"My favorite kitty—Tomato—she's dying. She's got distemper. Want to come see her?"

He still didn't say anything, but he got up. He stuck the cross into the waist of his pants, under his shirt. Then we climbed up the shaft.

———

Have you ever had a friend, or even a spouse, who you liked for the longest time, and then one day he or she did something that made you see this person in a different light? It might last only a moment, or it might last a day because, mostly, you have liked this person all along and still do. But once that small element of dislike has appeared, it seems to be there forever. It might be a small thing—perhaps you'd never seen this person blow his nose before, and then one day he does it in front of you. After he blows his nose, he opens his handkerchief and looks at what he's blown out. You react internally with disgust and can't quite ever erase that image from your memory. Or maybe it's bigger than that. Maybe he tells you how he cheated his brother out of some money once. That's it. All of a sudden you don't like him anymore for that one small quality or event. But all the other positive stuff is still there, and, mostly, you go on liking him even though there's now a hole in the admiration, respect, or love. Is it no longer love, then, when the admiration and respect aren't there one hundred percent?

———

C.K. and I climbed out of the shaft and came down off the castle. We were just walking around the front of the hay pile when Cross-Eyed Ladonna came into the arena. Mary was behind her, riding the mare. The mare couldn't have seen us because we were around the corner of the castle. We stood there and waited for

them to get all the way into the arena. My mom had told me that horses see things much bigger than they really are when they use their peripheral vision. This is supposed to protect them from lions in the wild. When they see something like that, they jump away or run away unless it's something they're used to. She said horses are really pretty dumb.

Well, I guess Cross-Eyed Ladonna's mare didn't expect to see us there, and she must have thought we were lions or something because she spooked—real bad and real fast. She sort of dropped down and jumped to one side. Mary fell off. She hit the ground pretty hard, but she got up right away.

"God damn it!" she mumbled as she brushed the dirt off her jeans. Then she looked at us and shouted, "You damn kids! Look what you made the horse do! Do you always have to be sneaking around this barn!" She gave us a real mean look.

Cross-Eyed Ladonna caught the mare, and they stood there and looked at us as if to say, "Well, now what?"

"Go on! Get outa here!" Mary yelled at us.

Cross-Eyed Ladonna looked kind of embarrassed. She held the mare's head while Mary got back on. She said to Mary, "It's not their fault. They didn't scare her on purpose." Mary still looked mean and mad. She picked up the reins and gave us one more evil look and rode off.

C.K. and I went to the tack room to look at Tomato. He felt real sorry for her, and we spent a long time petting her and offering her food and water. She didn't want to eat. We talked about how we might make the next castle better. We thought we'd try to make two shafts with a tunnel that connected them. Then we talked about what more we could do for Tomato.

"Have you actually ever watched something die?" he asked.

I couldn't think of anything. Then I remembered the kitten he killed the first day I met him. I was starting to not like C.K. as much as I used to. He was getting weird or something. There was something spooky about him sometimes. It sort of depended on how I looked at him, though. If I looked at him as my best friend, I really sort of loved him. But if I thought about that kitten at his

barn and this stuff with the cross, I didn't like him very much. Right now, I was kind of swinging back and forth. He was being awfully nice to Tomato. But he had that cross stuck in his pants. I didn't get it why he liked that thing so much.

"What are you going to do with that cross?" I asked.

He acted like he was thinking about this real hard. Then we heard the clip-clop of the mare's hooves coming down the concrete aisle. Mary and Cross-Eyed Ladonna were done with the lesson. They walked past the tack room door. The mare startled a little when she saw us, and Mary gave us her mean look again. Then I could hear them putting the horse on the cross-ties in the other aisle and taking the saddle and bridle off.

I heard Cross-Eyed Ladonna say, "Wow! The time has flown. I gotta run. Do you mind finishing her up? She probably ought to walk at least twenty minutes. And then do her stall, okay? I gotta go. Bye." I heard her car door slam and the engine start. Then I heard Mary talking to some other people. One was my mom, but I couldn't tell who the other person was. It was a lower voice but not a man's. Whoever it was wasn't saying much, just "yes" or "no," so I couldn't tell who it was.

I watched C.K. petting poor Tomato. She was barely purring anymore and just slept. I stroked her back while C.K. stroked her head. When my mom said something in the doorway, it scared me. I jumped.

"Johnnie, Harry has come to apologize. He walked all the way from his house—two miles. And he brought a gift for Tucker." Harry was standing there, holding a box of dog biscuits, and my mom had her arm around his shoulders. The sight of her being so nice to him made me sick. My mouth probably hung open. I didn't know what to say. Harry smiled. C.K. turned around and looked at them, then at me, then back at them. "Go ahead, Harry," my mom said. She looked at him sort of sweetly. I nearly gagged.

Harry looked right at me with his possum eyes. His hair looked extra raggy, and his clothes were extra dirty. How could my mother even touch him?

He held out the box of dog biscuits to me and said, "I'm sorry I kicked your dog. Sometimes I get so angry at things, I don't think. I didn't mean to kick him so hard. I think he's really a cool dog. I'm sorry he had to go to the animal hospital, but your ma says Dr. Strong is a real good vet, and Tucker will be okay. I've offered to pay the vet bill, even if I have to mow your lawn and do stuff to help your ma out. She said she has some jobs for me. This is great cuz right now I don't have no way to earn any money. She said I could paint all the fence posts, and that would probably pay Tucker's bill. I thought he might like these when he's all better." He stepped toward me and pushed the box at me. I thought about hitting them with my fist and knocking them on the ground. But I let him give them to me.

"Anything you want to say or ask Harry?" asked my mom. She looked so bright and cheerful, I couldn't stand it. C.K. was still watching us. Part of me wanted to run out of there, and part of me wanted to fly at Harry again and try to kick him in the throat—I had that daydream again where guys held him and I kicked him right where he'd kicked Tucker. And part of me wanted to be nice and do whatever would make C.K. happy. It was hard, but I finally decided to be nice.

I still hated Harry and I didn't forgive him, but I had to say something. "My kitten is dying," I said. "Her name is Tomato. She has distemper."

He stepped over to the horse blanket and kneeled down by her. He stroked her, but she didn't open her eyes or purr.

"Everything okay?" asked my mother. She still looked so bright and happy. I didn't get it. "I've got something in the oven, so I need to run back in. You guys'll like what I'm making. Come in in about half an hour. It should be done." She smiled and left.

Harry petted Tomato some more and then said, "Excuse me a second." He left, and I could hear him out by the stalls talking to Mary. I heard the hooves clip-clop and go out the barn into the driveway. I jumped up and looked out the window. Mary was walking the horse and Harry walked beside her, talking. Harry was explaining something and waving his hands around. Then

they just walked and talked. They walked around the turn-around to cool the horse off. Once, Mary stopped and looked at Harry seriously. He leaned toward her and said something, like it was a secret. Mary looked a little surprised at whatever it was, then she smiled real big and nodded her head. They kept walking and talking, and she looked real interested. Then she looked at her watch, and Harry looked at his. Harry said something, and they both nodded. Mary kept walking the mare, and he came back to the barn.

He came back in the tack room and said, "Mary says there's a real nice pet graveyard on the other side of town. She said she'd take us out there to bury the kitten if you want. She says she feels bad she didn't say something a few days ago when she thought Tomato looked kinda sick. Like, maybe the vet could have made her better then."

"But she's not dead yet!" I said.

"Your ma said she didn't think Tomato would live more than another couple hours. Mary still has to wash the horse and clean the stall and put food out for all the other horses. She's really pretty nice. Poor Tomato. She deserves a nice funeral." And he kneeled down and stroked her some more. He was being kind to her, but I was getting mad at him again because he seemed to want her to die soon.

After a while we got tired of watching her and went into the house. My mom had just baked a marble cake. She was making the fudge frosting now. She gave Harry and C.K. each a beater and me a spoon with frosting. We went and played Nintendo and waited for the cake to cool and her to put the frosting on. I still had nothing to say to Harry, and he didn't say much either. I let the two of them play my best video game, and I just sat and watched. After we had cake and milk we went back out to check on Tomato.

She was lying on her side now. When we left her she'd been on her stomach with her chin on her front paws. I stroked her head. She didn't flick an ear or open an eye. I looked at her closely and saw she wasn't breathing. She was dead. I'd seen dead cats before, and usually someone just put them in a garbage can. But pretty little Tomato looked so peaceful, and her fur was so

beautiful that I really did like the idea of putting her in a pet graveyard. I went in the house and got a shoe box and some old rags. I took a magic marker and wrote "Tomato" on the lid. I took two long ribbons, and went back to the barn. Mary was in the tack room now. Harry and Mary were talking, but they hushed up when I came in.

"Ready to go?" Mary asked.

I laid Tomato in the box. A bunch of the rags were underneath her, and I saved one to put over her. Then I put the lid on, and Mary helped me tie the two ribbons. We all got into Mary's car. There was something about this I didn't like. They were all extra quiet, like they had a secret or something. Mary stopped at the house so I could tell my mom where I was going. I left Tomato's coffin on the front seat and ran in.

"Why don't you just bury her in the woods?" my mom asked me. She looked sort of worried. "How much does it cost to bury an animal in this cemetery?"

"Cost? I don't know," I said. "I think it's free."

"Unlikely. I better talk to Mary." I think my mom was unsure about Mary.

My mom went out to Mary's car. Instead of getting back in, I stood outside Mary's window while my mom talked to her.

"It's only two dollars," said Mary. "I told the boys I'd take them to the Dairy Queen, too, and this place is only a couple miles out of town. An older couple started it on five acres years ago. It's very charming. They play music and everything. And they give you a plastic flower to push in the ground right at the grave." She was smiling now and being very normal. "I know he's upset. I think this might help. I'll have him back in about an hour and a half. Is that okay?"

My mom was smiling back, but she still had a little bit of a worried look. "That's a nice idea." She looked out toward the woods like she was thinking about something else. "Usually, we just bury them in the woods."

"I think this cat was special to him." Mary smiled. "Wanta jump back in, kiddo?" she said to me.

I walked around to the other side and got in the front with Mary. C.K. and Harry were in the back seat. As Mary drove off, I looked out the window at my mom, and she definitely looked uncomfortable. This made me scared. At the end of the driveway, Mary did *not* turn left toward the Dairy Queen. She turned right.

Looking back, I realize that my parents also had a strong, negative hunch about Mary. Or maybe it was more, although I am certain that if they had more than a suspicion about her—if they had ever seen her at Little Friends or if anyone had told them she'd been one of the leaders of that cult, they would have not allowed her on the farm at all. I think they were just as confused as I was. They liked Cross-Eyed Ladonna and were thrown off by her friendship with Mary. On the other hand, they were suspicious of most everyone in the town at that point. Add to that their negative gut feeling, and they did not trust her. I'm surprised, with all that, that my mother let me go. I know she was torn between good sense and gut feeling. It's too bad that she made the wrong choice.

"The Dairy Queen's that way," I said.

"We're going to a different Dairy Queen," said Mary. "This other one is better." And she drove down the highway.

The way we were going was the way my parents took to go to Chicago. C.K. and Harry didn't say anything in the back seat. We must have driven for a half hour. Mary finally turned off the highway onto a gravel road with farms and a few houses. Then she turned again onto another gravel road, and we passed some more farms.

"I thought we were going to the Dairy Queen," I finally said.

"Oh, sorry. It's more convenient to go to the cemetery first. Do you mind?" Mary said.

I shook my head no, but I wondered why she said we were going to a "different Dairy Queen" when she planned to go to the

graveyard first. I looked at her. From the side her nose and lips sort of came to a point. Her black hair was short all over, like a man's. She looked straight ahead and didn't look at me at all when she talked. I didn't know what to say next. I was starting to get a little carsick.

"How much farther?" I asked.

"We're here. Right. Now," she said and turned down a sort of path. There was no gravel or pavement, just some tire tracks in the grass. We were in the middle of a grassy field, but there was a little woods off to the left. The tracks went into the woods. I looked for the house that the old couple lived in and a graveyard, but I didn't see them. Mary drove into the woods a little ways and then stopped and turned the car off. C.K. and Harry got out. Harry acted like he knew where he was, but C.K. looked around like I did, like he didn't know what was going on either.

Mary got out and went around to her trunk. She opened it and took out a big cardboard box. It had some folded black and red cloths in it and a big rope. I could hear other smaller stuff jiggling around in the bottom.

"What's that?" I asked.

"Stuff to help with Tomato's funeral."

"Where's the graveyard? I don't see one. Or the old couple's house?"

"Back this way," she said and walked off, carrying the big box in her arms. Harry followed right behind her, and C.K. after him, and then me and Tomato. C.K. turned around and looked at me once.

"What's going on?" I whispered.

He looked kind of worried. He shrugged and kept walking. I swallowed hard and started to wish I'd just buried Tomato in our woods. This was feeling creepy.

When we were in the middle of the woods, we came to a place where it looked like someone had had a campfire. There were some burnt logs and rocks in a circle, and there were big trees all around us. Mary set the box under a low tree branch near the campfire. Then she sat down on the ground, Indian style. She patted the

ground on both sides of her. "Sit down, guys," she said. Harry sat right next to her, and C.K. sat on her other side, but much farther away. I sat away from her too, next to C.K.

"First of all," she said, looking at me and C.K. "If either of you tells anyone about this funeral, I'll burn your house down."

I started laughing, but then I looked at C.K., and he looked terrified.

Now she says, "And I'll wait and do it when you're at school and your parents are both inside. As I've told you before, children, I'm a real witch, and Jack and Bernice depend on my special powers. Jack and Bernice have special powers too, but theirs are different from mine. Now, remember, you must do as I say. I have the power to lock your house by just thinking about it. I can lock the locks so no one can get in—or out. And I can start a fire by just thinking about it. So, I know you all love your mommies and daddies, And remember the cabin with the burned-up dolls? You don't want your mommies and daddies to end up like that, do you?"

We all shake our heads no. I almost start to cry, and some of the children do start crying.

"Shut up!" Mary shouts. "I hate crying!"

And the ones who were crying stop real fast. A couple of them still sniff and have great big tears rolling down their faces. A few sob big, dry sobs like hiccups.

"Okay, now, everyone understands, right? You don't tell anyone about this or I'll set your house on fire and your mommies and daddies will die. Remember that this kitten is a gift to Satan. He loves it when we give him gifts, especially gifts of death. He will do nice things for you because you gave him this gift." She stands up and goes to the big box. First, she pulls out the black cross. It has a rope tied to the bottom. She tosses the cross over the tree limb and pulls it until it hangs right by her face. Then she reaches into the box and pulls out some red robes and some black robes. "Put these on. Remember these are very special robes. When we wear them, we show Satan how much we honor him. Clive, here's yours. Johnnie, here's yours. Harry. Sonia, Tammy, Jill, Ryan, Jessica, and Chuckie."

We fiddle with our robes and hoods but get them on pretty quickly because we've done it so many times before. But it's easier today. Most times we've been in the basement with candles. It's much easier in the daylight.

Soon, we're all dressed and standing around the campfire. Mary has pulled more wood into the campfire ring, stuffed newspaper in between the logs, and lit a match. She's blowing on it now to get it going.

"Children step over here. Don't get your robes near the fire. Stand in a circle now. Johnnie, want to get the kitten for me?"

I walk up to her with the shoe box. Her robe is all black and has some red designs on it, way up on her chest. I look up to see what they are. The one in the middle is the upside-down star. It's very beautiful. The other two are higher up on her shoulders, and I can't see them. I feel very special standing this close to her and being the one to hand her the sacrifice. She smiles down at me and takes the box.

Inside is the black and white kitten. First Mary spreads out her red cloth underneath the black cross, and then she spreads out a piece of plastic. She lays the limp kitten on the plastic, then reaches into the big box for her beautiful, silver knife.

"Okay, children, stand around me in a circle. That's right." All the black bodies and the red bodies stumble and bump into each other. Some of them have to hold their robe hems up so they don't step on them. A few of the older children are taller, and their ankles and shoes stick out the bottoms of their robes. Pretty soon the circle is made around Mary and the kitten. I can't tell who is under each hood, but I think Clive is next to me.

"Okay, children, let's begin our song." She starts to sing. "God is dead and Satan loves me. God is dead and Satan loves me." We begin to sway back and forth while we sing. "Very nice! God is dead and Satan loves me. Beautiful. Keep going. Harry, will you keep leading the song? God is dead and Satan loves me. Good, now keep it up."

Mary gets her knife and holds it in both hands. She raises her hands above her head and looks down at the kitten. She begins to mumble words I don't know. They sound like magic words. She begins to breathe heavier as she says them. We can't see her face very well because the hood covers most of it. Her hood is the only one that is open at the face. Our hoods are like bags with eye holes. She takes a deep breath, says her magic words, then blows out hard. She does this over and over. The children keep singing and swaying, and the singing gets louder and louder. Then Mary shouts, "Stop!" and we all stop singing.

She says, "To you, Satan, our gift of devotion and loyalty," and she brings the knife down hard with both hands, and it plunges into the kitten. The kitten's body jumps as the knife goes in. I stare at the kitten and want to cry. I expect to see blood gush out, but none does. Then Mary kneels down and cuts the kitten's belly open. She cuts some more inside the kitten, then pulls out a small red glob. She holds it out to show us. "The gift!" she says and slowly carries it to the fire.

"Okay, children. Begin."

And we sing, "God is dead and Satan loves me" as we make a circle around the fire. We stumble and trip on our robes, and pretty soon we have a circle again. Mary stands with the heart stretched out to the fire.

"Now, children. Mmmmm," she hums, and we all make the "mmmm" sound too. Most of us run out of breath and have to take in more air before we hum again. We know that Mary wants the "mmmm" to go on for a while. She kneels down and shuts her eyes and hums. Then she stops, and we stop. She says more magic words and then carefully sets the heart in the fire. She leaps up and claps her hands, and we do the same. We try to laugh and be happy.

I glance over at the kitten. Her guts are all hanging out, and I feel sick. One of the other children, a girl, has pulled her hood off and is throwing up. A couple of the others start to gag and one or two more throw up. Mary ignores them and goes over to the kitten again. She picks up her knife and starts cutting at the kitten's feet and legs. She cuts off toes, mostly, and the tail and head, and cuts the legs into pieces. She leaves the body. Then she begins to hand a piece of the kitten to each child. Each child takes a piece and goes back to the fire. The children who threw up have vomit on the robes where they wiped their faces, but they've put the hoods back on.

Mary hands me a whole paw, a front paw. I run my thumb over the top of each toe and count, one, two, three, four. I do this over and over, feeling the fur-covered knobs. I can also feel the little toe pads underneath with my first finger. They're very smooth and soft. The nails stick out only a little, and I feel each one as I count, one, two, three, four, one, two, three, four.

Mary finishes handing out parts of the kitten and ignores us while she tosses the body into the fire. It sizzles and chokes the fire, but she pokes at the kitten with a long stick. The fur burns away quickly. The smoke gets thicker and darker. It blows at me once and gags me. I run off to the side

and think I'm going to throw up, but then some fresh air blows in my nose, and I'm okay. The rest of the children just stand and hold their pieces. Mary doesn't care what they do now, except she yells at us once, "Don't drop your part of the gift. Hold onto it!" We can't talk to each other, but now and then one child bumps into another, and they whisper something. "No talking!" shouts Mary. She pokes at the kitten's body some more and rolls burning logs on top of it. She glances at her watch, throws a few more sticks and newspapers on the fire and puts her knife and other stuff in the bottom of the box. She takes out a folding shovel from the box and shouts, "Come!"

We line up behind her, each of us still holding our piece of the kitten. She marches into the woods, and every so often she stops and digs a small hole. Each time she does, one of us sets our kitten piece in the bottom, and Mary covers the hole again. We do this until all the pieces are buried. Then we march back to the box, take our hoods and robes off, and toss them into the box.

We stand around and watch while she pokes at the fire to make sure the kitten's body is all burned away. Then she pulls the black cross down. She takes the rope off the end and hands the cross to C.K. Then she tosses the rope back into the box. "Good job, boys."

C.K. found a large rock and pounded the cross into the dirt in front of the campfire. I felt sick, and my head was spinning. I felt dizzy and weak and wanted to go home. I never wanted to see Mary or Harry again. On the way back, Mary pulled into the Dairy Queen. She got me my favorite—a vanilla malt, but I couldn't even take one sip. The smell of it nearly made me throw up. We all sat there for a long time and didn't say a word. I had my window open and felt real spacey like I didn't quite know where I was. It was like I was waking up from a bad dream and couldn't tell whether the dream was real, but I couldn't remember a dream. When I realized I was sitting there with a vanilla malt, I started stirring it with my straw. I took a sip. There's nothing better than the taste of a vanilla malt. I took another sip.

"Is that good?" Mary asked.

I jumped, because I had forgotten about her. And then I realized Harry and C.K. were in the back seat. It was strange. I felt like my mind wasn't all in one piece.

"Great malt, huh Johnnie?" C.K. asked.

I guess I had just been daydreaming or something and forgot that Mary had brought us down here.

I went home and took a nap because I didn't feel very good. Later I realized Tomato was gone and figured my mom had buried her in the woods. She was really thoughtful sometimes.

17

Fuck, I was just torn, I guess. Like I said, Johnnie was my best pal. I guess I loved him. But that damned Harry was a cool guy. Sure, I didn't like some of the shit he did, but he was a hell of a lot more interesting than Johnnie sometimes. I mean, he just knew shit that I didn't. And Johnnie was getting stuffy sometimes, like playing that Dungeons and Dragons crap. I don't know how he enjoyed it, man. You had to be a goddamned genius to understand it. When some of the neighbors said the Ambroses was snobby, I could see why they said that. But they didn't know how much fun Johnnie could be. I loved him, and I didn't want to hurt him, even though that damned Harry made it seem kinda fun, you know, to shake Johnnie up. I'll never forget that fucking funeral with that barn kitten, the black and white one. Johnnie had some weird name for it. I can't remember now what it was—Pomegranate or Raspberry or something like that, I don't know. But yeah, that damned funeral scared the shit outa me cuz of that Mary woman. But worse than that, I got scared shitless when I saw Johnnie's reaction. I thought he was really freakin' out on me this time. I thought maybe his mind was gone and wasn't never comin' back.

———

We was nearly done with the funeral. I thought it would be fun, and maybe it woulda been if Mary hadn't been there. She scared me—gave me the creeps. I think she really was a witch. She knew all kinds of magic words, and she said she could make fires start just by thinkin' about 'em. But the fire that she burned the kitten in—she started it with matches. I don't know. Mostly, I was scared and just did what she said. And so did Johnnie. He looked weird, though, like he did some other times, like the time he was in that dog cage. I think he just spaced out, but it was hard to see

him with the hoods on. But after we took the hoods off, he was like in a trance. I didn't try to talk to him or nothin' cuz I figured Mary would yell at me. He was like that all the way back to the car, and in the car, too. He didn't say nothin', just sat and stared off into nowhere. When we got our malts at the Dairy Queen, he started to wake up a little.

He drank his vanilla one for a while and stared out the window. I hadn't tried to talk to him since we left the graveyard. But now he was blinkin' and lookin' at stuff and turning his head.

"Hey, Johnnie?" He turned back and looked at me real quick, almost like he'd forgotten I was there. "How's the malt?"

"Pretty good. Want to try it?" he said holding the cup out to me.

"No, I got one, too. Remember, you taught me about them."

"Oh, yeah, I forgot." He laughed a little.

Mary watched him the whole time. She'd been watching him the whole way back from the graveyard, and she looked worried. "How're you feeling?" she asked him.

He just looked at her—stared at her, sort of, for a long time. Then, he looked out the window again and never answered. She still looked worried—a lot, like she was trying to think of something to say to him.

"So, what did you think of the funeral for Tomato?" she asked him.

He answered her right away. "I didn't like it. I wish I'd buried her in my own woods." That's all he said, and that's all she said about it. Then she drove us to Johnnie's house. She drove up to the garage and told Johnnie and me to get out. She said she'd take Harry home, and then she drove out again kinda fast. We two stood there and watched them go. When her car had went over the hill, I looked at Johnnie.

He looked tired and still a little spaced. "You okay?" I asked.

He looked right at me and smiled a little. "I'm tired. That's all."

I was worried right then that he wouldn't like me any more. What would I do if he decided he wanted Joey for his best friend

and not me? I wondered how much of the funeral he was there for. I mean, when he spaced out sometimes, it was like he went away—in his mind. It was like he wasn't seeing and hearing the same things I was.

"What did you really think of the funeral?" I finally asked.

He acted annoyed. "Like I said, I didn't like it. Let's not talk about it anymore."

I wondered what he'd tell Christine and Leland. I thought Mary was stupid. Didn't she think Johnnie would tell? But I guess we both really believed she'd burn down our houses with our parents inside 'em if we did.

So, we went in the house and watched old TV shows—*Bewitched, I Love Lucy, Dick Van Dyke, Mr. Ed*. I loved them all, and they seemed to do Johnnie some good too. His ma thought he looked a little pale and asked if the pet graveyard was nice. He just said he wished he'd buried Tomato in his own woods. Christine, of course, asked why, and he just said he thought Tomato would have been happier at her own home. Christine had no idea that Johnnie was protectin' her.

Suppertime came, and I just didn't want to go home. I didn't want to see my ma, and I figured I wouldn't see my pa, unless he came to take a shower and leave again. As usual, Christine invited me to stay, and I called my ma, and she said okay. Johnnie and I didn't do nothin' special, just watched TV and went to bed.

The next morning, Harry called me at the Ambrose's. I didn't know he had the number. Johnnie said it wasn't in the phone book. He wanted to come fishin' again. I told him no and I'd call him in a day or two. Right then, I just wanted to be with Johnnie. I wanted it to be like it used to be. I wanted Mary to go away, and Cross-Eyed Ladonna to go away, and Harry to go away. I wanted Ma and Pa to be like they was, even if they had fights. But they hadn't always fought. They'd go weeks at a time bein' all lovey with each other, and then they'd have a fight. I wanted Pa to take me to shoot baskets and Ma to hug me more. But right now I had Johnnie, and I tried to think of something he'd like to do.

"Wanna go ride bikes? We could go down where they's putting in the freeway. I heard Ma say they's packed the gravel all

Susan L Metzger

smooth now, so it's like one big gravel road all the way from the highway up to Darden Road."

Johnnie really perked up at this, so we told Christine, and she packed lunches and pop for us and put them in Johnnie's back-pack, and we went. My bike was already there, so we didn't have to stop at my house. When we passed by the Boggus's house, Linda was out in front with her two kids. She had 'em on a plastic teeter-totter set. They looked pretty cute. She looked at us kinda friendly and waved, so I said to Johnnie, "Let's stop. We ain't really talked to her since her one kid almost drownded and Tucker did it to Lassie."

"I don't know. I bet she's still mad at me for letting Tucker loose."

"She doesn't look mad," I said and rode my bike right up to her. She looked friendly. "Hi! Is your baby okay after it fell in the pool?"

"Well, nice of you to ask," she said. "Yes, he's fine. Sure scared the heck outa me, though. Say, you're C.K., aren't you?"

"Yes," I said. "And this is Johnnie Ambrose."

"I thought so. You know, usually you boys go by here so fast I never have a chance to get to know you. And we all live so far apart from one another. You sure are growin' up. How old are you now?"

I always hated this question when Johnnie and I was together cuz of him bein' a year and a half younger. People just didn't realize how smart he was, so he was really like my own age. Even though I was almost twelve and Johnnie was ten and a half, I said "I'm eleven and he's ten and a half."

"Eleven?" Johnnie said. "He'll be twelve in just a few days."

"Twelve, huh? Well, I guess you're babysittin' age, ain't you?"

"Well, I guess so." It's something I hadn't thought about before. I didn't know how to babysit. "I ain't done it before, though."

"Well, I could teach you. You certainly are mature enough. You could learn. Come here. Meet Sandra and Billy. Sandra's four and Billy's two." She took me by the arm and led me over to the teeter-totter. Billy had a kind of cool Cubs baseball shirt on and blue shorts. His blond hair was thin and blew straight up in the air.

He was trying to stay on the teeter-totter seat, but he looked pretty wobbly. Sandra looked nice and smiled at me. She was trying to be gentle with her little brother and made the teeter-totter go up and down real slow.

"I'm Sandra, and I'm almost four," she said. She held up four fingers. Her hair was darker than Billy's, and her ma had put it in two curly pigtails. Each one had a big pink ribbon around it. She was pretty cute.

"Yes, punkin. Almost four. One more month." Linda Boggus turned to me. "She's practicing. It's a big deal to turn four. Do you remember?"

I tried to think back. That's when I was at Little Friends, and I didn't want to think about it. I looked at Billy. "How old are you?"

He just smiled and turned away. Linda said, "He's a little young for that. When he's almost three, he'll get the hang of it, I guess. So, C.K. want to learn more? I'd pay you, oh—how about a dollar an hour until you really know what you're doing, and then we'll raise it to maybe a dollar and a quarter, maybe even a dollar fifty if you can, you know, pick up after them, make meals, clean up the kitchen."

"Well, I guess so," I said. I hadn't done none of those things at home, but if someone paid me, I sure would. Sandra was still lookin' at me. I went over to her. "Do you know what my name is?" She shook her head. "It's C.K. Can you say 'C.K.'?"

"C.K.," she said and giggled.

"No big deal, huh?"

"No," she laughed. "That was easy. Want to meet my doll? Her name is Cinderella."

"Cinderella—what a nice name. Do you know the story of Cinderella?"

"Sort of," she said. "I saw the cartoon."

"Well, I should read you the story sometime. Would you like that?" She nodded her head real hard. "Okay, it's a deal. The next time I come see you, I'll bring it with me and read it to you."

"It's a deal," she said and turned away like she was embarrassed. Then I went over to Billy. This wasn't so hard, talking to children. "Hey, guy, can you say 'C.K.'?"

He smiled, then looked at the ground and made a noise something like "shay shay." I said, "Okay, I can be Shay Shay." This was going to be fun. I said to Linda, "Okay, I'll try. Are you going to give me a lesson or something?"

"Sure. How about tomorrow morning? Ten o'clock?"

I couldn't think of nothin' else I was doing. "Okay. I'll be here."

She looked happy and said, "I know the Panzerov girls would want to do it, but—" she stopped and looked around her like someone might be listening. She kinda whispered, "I just don't like people who are that fat. They might teach my kids to be fat, and I don't want that. Besides, they seem kinda strange. You ever met them?"

As far as I knew, no one had ever met them. One was older than me and rode a different school bus, and the one younger than me went to some special school. I didn't know nothin' about the youngest one. I told Linda, "No, I aint never met any of 'em." I glanced at Johnnie. He looked like he didn't get the the whole babysitting thing.

After we started riding again, he said, "You like kids? I mean, you like to talk to them?"

"I don't know. I ain't tried much, just a couple times with some of my cousins. But no one's offered to pay me before. And it really wasn't so hard. I think you just ask them a lot of questions. Just think, maybe I can make enough money to buy a cool sword or something. You know, a real one, and one for you too. Then we can have real sword fights."

"I saw some in an antique store a few weeks ago, and they were forty dollars. How long do you think it will take to make that much?"

We talked like this all the way down the road, and when we got down to the dead end, we had to pick our bikes up and lift them over one of them metal guard rail fences. On the other side, we could see where they'd been workin'. We'd ridden bikes down here before, and you could always see where a road might be cuz it was a great big wide, flat path, but it used to have grass and weeds all over it. Now, it was all gravel and real smooth. We got out on it

with our bikes, and mostly we could ride pretty easy. A few places was soft and had puddles, but mostly it was packed hard. We went to the left and went all the way down to where it ran into the highway. We stood there and watched the cars and trucks go by.

"How many miles do you think that was?" I asked.

Johnnie looked back the way we'd come and shook his head. "About three, I guess." The sun was gettin' hot, and there was no shade, so we rode back to his house. We was glad to go in and watch TV. We walked past the kitchen and heard Christine talkin' to somebody. We walked into the kitchen, and there was Harry.

"Shit!" I said to myself. Things was so nice without him. Him and Christine was talkin' about astrology. They was so deep in their conversation, they hardly looked at us. I mean, they looked at us, sort of to let us know they saw us, but they kept on talkin'. They was sittin' at the little table eatin' cake. Harry had a big glass of milk in front of him, and he looked real happy.

He asked her, "So, you mean there's more to it than just being a Scorpio or a Capricorn or a Libra? What did you say about the moon and what was the other word—ascension?"

She was real patient with him. "We each have a sun sign. You named three of them. There are nine more: Aquarius, Pisces, Aries, Taurus, Gemini, Cancer, Leo, Virgo, and Sagittarius. When you see horoscopes in newspapers and magazines, that's what they're referring to—people's sun signs. It's what sign, or constellation, the sun was in when you were born. But the place of the moon is important, too. Your sun sign is what you aspire to all your life—that is, all the attributes of that sign. But your moon sign is sort of what you must have in order to feel good about yourself. So, say your moon is in Leo, you would probably need to be creative in some way to feel good about who you are. Then there's the ascendant, or rising sign. That's the sign that was right on the horizon when you were born. And the attributes of that sign are what your persona, or your personality, are likely to be."

"That's very interesting. Can you teach me more?"

"Well, I can probably do your chart. But you have to find out exactly what minute you were born. And where you were born."

"I was born here. How do I know what minute?"

"See if your mom can get me a copy of your birth certificate. Then I can send away to a place in California, and they'll send me your chart. Then I'll read it for you. Ask your mom, okay?"

"Yeah, I can't wait. I'll do your next oil change for you!"

"What a deal," said Christine, and they both laughed. Johnnie left the room. I followed him. He went and turned the TV on and looked mad.

"What's the matter?" I whispered.

"Why's she so nice to him? He's a creep! But I guess I can't say that to you since you're his friend. Why are you his friend?"

He almost looked like he was gonna cry. Geez. So, I said, "I know what you mean. He is a jerk sometimes. I was really mad at him when he hit and kicked Tucker. But he's kinda cool, too. He knows a lotta stuff, and he's fine as long as he's not mad at you."

Johnnie thought about what I said and started to giggle. "Yeah, he's great as long as he's not pretending to be King Kong!" I giggled too, then we started watching *Star Trek*. Some space guy had three heads, and all three heads was disagreeing about something.

———

Well, dammit, it was true. Johnnie was my very best friend. I mean, even when he was really down, he could laugh. Here he was all pissed off at his ma, and this kid he hated was over at his house and bein' nice to his ma and foolin' her, and he was mad as hell. But he could still laugh. How could I be mad at him, or think Harry or anybody else could take his place?

———

"Let's go up to your room and make paper airplanes," I said.

I think he really wanted to watch *Star Trek* cuz he didn't answer me right away. The guy with three heads was trying to decide whether to go be with his wife on his home planet, which was about to blow up, or go be with his daughter on another

planet, which was about to blow up, or stay here with the crew of the Enterprise. I didn't care, but Johnnie did, so I waited until the guy decided to go be with his wife. It was kinda sad, but pretty goofy, too, so when a commercial came on, Johnnie got up and turned the TV off.

On the way to the stairs up to his room, we had to pass a row of windows that looked down his driveway. A car was comin' up. He stopped and said, "Oh! Here comes Cross-Eyed Ladonna. Let's just go out to the barn for a minute. I want to ask her something." He looked at me like he expected me to go with him.

"I don't want to talk to her!" I reminded him.

"Oh, I keep forgetting. I really don't think it was she you saw with your dad. Come on. She's so nice."

"You go. I'll go up to your room and start makin' a plane. Where were we in your airplane book? Number twelve?"

He nodded.

"Fine, I'll start on number twelve. But come back right away, okay?"

Johnnie looked a little disgusted. "Yeah. I'll hurry." And he went out the door. As I went up the stairs I could hear Harry still askin' Christine questions and her answering them. Weird. I didn't get it why they liked each other.

I took Johnnie's *Airplane Origami* book off his bookshelf and opened it to number twelve. I got a piece of Johnnie's typing paper and started following the directions. After a few minutes, Harry whispered at the door, "Hey, what're you doin'?" I wished he'd just go away. Johnnie'd be really mad if he found Harry in his room.

"You better get outa here," I said. "Johnnie'll be pissed if he finds you in here."

"Christine said I could come up. Where's Johnnie?" he continued to whisper.

"He's out in the barn, talkin' to Cross-Eyed Ladonna."

"Think he'll tell her about the funeral?"

"I don't know. Probably not. Mary scared the shit out of us enough, he probably won't say nothin'."

"That scared you?"

I didn't feel right talking to Harry about it. It was okay to do some of the stuff with him, but I didn't want him to know that it scared me. Or at least that Mary scared me. "Not really. She's just weird."

"No, she's cool, man. But she's worried about Johnnie spacin' out or whatever it was he was doin'. What was that, anyway?"

I didn't want to tell Harry what I thought about Johnnie's spells. "Nothin'. He just does that sometimes. No big deal."

"Yeah? Well, talk about weird, that dude is a genuine weirdo. Let's just go. We can go to your house."

I thought about it for a minute. Harry always came up with cool things to do. But then I thought about Johnnie comin' back and finding me gone, and I couldn't do it. "No, I told him I'd be here."

"Well, let's go fishin' in his pond, then. I think Christine'll give me real beer now. I'll promise her I won't drink it. She'll believe me."

"We don't have our fishin' stuff here. It's all at my house."

"Let's go get it."

"No, I've gotta wait here for Johnnie."

"Jesus Christ! You guys are fairies together, ain't you? I knew it."

"Shut up about that. We are not!"

"Well, then come with me. Leave the wimp out in the barn with his sweetheart. We'll come right back. And then he can come fishin' too, if he wants."

"It's his pond! What do you mean he can come too if he wants? You go get the poles by yourself. I'll be here."

"Okay, fine," and he left. I finished airplane number twelve and started on thirteen. There was twenty-six in the book. I imagined havin' all of 'em done by the time Johnnie got back—all of 'em lined up on his bed, ready to fly. Maybe him and me could fly 'em while stupid Harry fished.

By the time I started on plane number fifteen, I wondered where in the heck Johnnie was. At this rate, Harry would get back before Johnnie. I decided to finish number fifteen, then go out to

the barn. Maybe somethin' was wrong. Then I remembered Harry had to pass by the barn to go to my house. I hoped him and Johnnie hadn't gotten into a fight. I dropped number fifteen and ran out to the barn.

Cross-Eyed Ladonna's car was still parked out front, so I relaxed a little. If bad stuff was goin' on between Harry and Johnnie, she'd do somethin' about it. I slowed down before I got to the big doorway. I heard some quiet talkin'. When I walked in, I saw Cross-Eyed Ladonna's mare on cross ties. She had one front leg in a bucket of water, and Johnnie was holding up the other front leg. He was bent over with his back to me. Cross-Eyed Ladonna was petting the mare and talkin' to her. The mare didn't like havin' her leg in the bucket of water, and she was tossin' her head and tryin' to nudge Johnnie away. The mare saw me right away and picked up her head and perked up her ears. Cross-Eyed Ladonna turned to see what the horse was lookin' at.

"Hi," I said without looking at her.

"Hey, C.K. How you doin'? I've had some bad luck." She pointed at the leg in the bucket. "My mare cut her pastern, and it all swelled up, so I gotta soak it. I couldn't get her to keep her foot in the bucket, so Johnnie's holding up the other one. See, that way she's gotta put her weight on the leg that's in the bucket. Pretty tricky, huh?" She laughed and gave me a little punch on the arm. "Horses is pretty dumb, ain't they?"

I nodded and walked to the mare's side so I could talk to Johnnie. He couldn't look at me cuz he had to lean over to hold the leg up with both hands. The mare was swayin' and kinda leanin' on him. Cross-Eyed Ladonna held the mare's head, but the mare was too strong and pulled away and pushed Johnnie's butt with her nose. She'd try to hop out of her bucket every once in a while, and Johnnie really had to fight to hold on. The floor was all wet where the mare had tipped some buckets over already.

"How much longer?" Johnnie gasped.

Cross-Eyed Ladonna looked at her watch and said, "Just three more minutes. The vet said to leave it in there for twenty. Three times a day, too. Boy, this is gonna be fun."

Johnnie gasped again and said to me, "Sorry I've been so long. She needed help."

"I'm on number fifteen. Thirteen is really cool. I can't wait to fly 'em." I tried to find the right words to tell him Harry was coming back with our fishin' gear. Then all hell broke loose.

"Boo!" It was Harry in the doorway. The two fishin' poles was wagglin' back and forth, and the bobbers was swingin' around. The mare must've seen 'em before we did cuz she reared up with both front legs. The one leg threw Johnnie forward. Then her rear hooves slid on the wet floor and went out from under her. She fell on her side, but she couldn't get up cuz her head was still tied to the crossties. It happened so fast, I could hardly see it all. The mare was thrashin' around on the floor, tryin' to get up, and her neck was all twisted sideways. There was horse legs everywhere, and the sound of her shoes scrapin' on the wet concrete was awful— sounded like razors on a chalkboard or somethin'. I jumped back, and Cross-Eyed Ladonna let go of the mare's halter. It looked like one of the mare's front legs hit Johnnie on the back, but I couldn't tell for sure. He cried out and rolled off to the side. Finally, the mare pulled back so hard, she pulled right out of her halter. She got up and ran out the back door.

Johnnie was rolled in a ball on his side. I ran over and kneeled down. I tried to see where he was hurt, what part of his body he was holding. It looked like his stomach. He looked sorta white, and he was breathin' funny. He had tears in his eyes, and he acted like he was trying to breathe in, but he couldn't. He could breathe out a little, and he sorta trembled when he did. Then he'd make these little wheezing sounds — little short ones—when he tried to breathe in.

"Got the wind knocked out of him," Cross-Eyed Ladonna said. She picked him up and held him in her arms. She sat on the floor with him. "Relax, sweetheart," she said. "Then you'll be able to breathe. You just got the wind knocked outa you. Relax and you'll be able to get the air in." She sat on the wet floor and held him and rocked him. Pretty soon, his breathing did get easier. His face got pink again, but the tears was still there.

I looked up at Harry. He still stood there with the damn fishin' poles. Cross-Eyed Ladonna got mad at him. "Set those damn poles down—out on the other side of the driveway, and go find my horse. Johnnie'll be alright here in a minute."

Harry just stood and looked at her. He didn't know how to catch a horse. "Go on!" she screamed at him.

I jumped up and unhooked the halter from the crossties, and then I went out the back to find the mare. Harry followed me. "Did I do that?" he asked.

"You can't sneak up on a horse and say 'Boo!' They spook! You freaked her out! It's lucky nobody got hurt. Course we don't know about the mare yet. You see her thrashin' around!" What an idiot. He didn't say nothin' and just followed me. "Go get a lead rope." He went back in the barn. I found the mare out in the small pasture, eatin' grass. I walked around her and looked for more cuts. One hock was all scraped and bloody, but that was all.

Harry brought the rope. I hooked it onto the halter and walked up to her. I petted her long, black neck and talked to her nice. I was glad she didn't try to run away from me. Slowly, I lowered the halter down by her nose, and she let me slip it on. I hooked the latch and pulled her head up with little tugs. She started to follow me. When she saw Harry, she arched her neck and put her ears way forward and blew air out her nose. She swerved way around him like she was scared. I petted her neck some more and told her it was okay. He held his hand out to her, but she just snorted and backed away. I knew I couldn't hold her if she bolted, so I yelled at him.

"Get away! She's scared of you!" He backed away real fast and stood by the corner of the barn. She didn't take her eyes off him, but she let me lead her into the barn and put her in her stall. I took the rope off her halter and shut her door. "Whew!" I said to myself.

As soon as I latched her door, I looked at Johnnie and Cross-Eyed Ladonna. He was kneeling now and pressing on different spots on his chest and belly. He found one spot that made him flinch, but just a little. Cross-Eyed Ladonna stood up and put her arm around his shoulders. He stood up, and they just stood like

that and talked. He looked okay now and started to walk. He saw me and smiled.

He said, "Wow! I never had the wind knocked out of me before. That's awful. I couldn't take any breaths."

I was still real worried if he was okay. "Did she kick you?"

"I don't know. I guess so."

"Or he may have just hit the ground hard when she tossed him like that," said Cross-Eyed Ladonna. "Just fallin' on your chest or back can do it. I think he's okay. He's tough. Ain't ya?" She grinned at him and gave him a big hug. She turned to me. "Hey, guy, thanks for gettin' my mare. She okay?"

Ladonna really was nice. I finally looked at her face. Those crossed eyes were weird, though. I never knew which one to look at. So, first I'd look at one and then the other. Sometimes one seemed to be lookin' at me more than the other, so I'd look at that one. I saw them pink lips Johnnie talked about. They was a pretty color, and I started thinkin' about Pa kissin' 'em. I had to look away again. "Her one hock is scraped," I said, and then I turned away.

I almost forgot about Harry. He was standin' about halfway down the aisle, just waiting. Cross-Eyed Ladonna spotted him.

"You! I'm mad at you. You better get outa here. And until you understand about horses, you better stay outa this barn. Now go on. I better look at my horse, see what damage you done." He had to walk past her. "Go on," she said and pretended to run at him. He scooted away from her, smiling.

Johnnie didn't even look at Harry and headed for the house. He looked to see if I was comin', but it was like he didn't even see Harry. On the way, Harry picked up the fishin' poles and followed us. I walked next to Johnnie, and Harry was behind us. Johnnie walked into his house and went right upstairs. I followed him, and Harry headed for the kitchen.

When we got into Johnnie's room, he picked up each of the paper airplanes I'd made. "These are cool." He grinned at me. He had number twelve in his hand. He flew it, and it glided across his room and landed right on top of his computer. "Smooth," he said. "That's beautiful."

I was happy. I wanted him to try the others. I started to show him number thirteen when Harry appeared in the doorway. He had a large paper cup in his hand. He was careful not to actually come into the room.

"Beer," he said and smiled real big. "The real stuff. Ready to go?"

I looked at Johnnie. I could see the muscles in his jaw get all tight, and he just glared at Harry. "You set one foot inside this room, and I'll kill you." He said this quietly, but I sure think he meant it. "Ready to go where?" He put both hands on his hips and spread his feet out wide. I almost laughed cuz he looked like some cop in a police movie. But he was serious.

"Fishin'," said Harry. He was acting sorta cocky like he had some kind of "in" cuz of Christine.

"Where do you think you're going fishing?" Johnnie asked. He didn't change his pose at all.

"Your mom said we could all go fishing in your pond and use beer to catch 'em."

I thought I better say something. "How about if you fish and Johnnie and I fly these planes? We'll watch you fish. I don't really wanna fish, anyway. It's kind of boring."

Johnnie looked at me and nodded. Harry said, "Fine," and left. We let him go and figured he'd just go fish and we'd come down with the planes when we was ready.

We made five more, so we had nine altogether. Johnnie got a grocery bag, and we set 'em all in there, bein' careful none of the wings got bent. I guess we took kind of a long time makin' the planes cuz by the time we got down to the pond, Harry had already caught seven fish. He held up his net for us to see. He looked happy. I guess I felt a little guilty leavin' him alone, especially since none of us was supposed to be at the pond alone. But he asked for it, and besides, he really did seem to like fishin' by hisself.

We started throwin' the planes back and forth. The wind was mostly quiet, but every once in a while it would come just enough to make the tiny leaves on some of the small trees wave a little. We tried to time the planes with the wind cuz then the wind would lift

a plane and carry it for a long, long time. One time, it took a plane all the way to the middle of the island. I wanted to go get it, and Johnnie said maybe we could take the canoe out there. He went out to the island with his dad a lot, and I had gone a couple times, but Christine had never let us go alone.

"I better tell my mom," he said. "Well, ask her, actually. I think with all of us down here, she'll say yes." He ran up and came back down real quick. He nodded his head while he was runnin' towards me. "We can't take too long, though, because it's almost time for supper." We went straight to the upside-down canoe. We flipped it over and started draggin' it to the water. We got it mostly in the water, and was just about to get in when Harry called to us.

"Hey! Where you goin'?" he shouted.

I yelled back, "Out to the island. One of our planes flew out there."

"I wanna come. I wanna fish from the island."

I looked at Johnnie. He rolled his eyes and looked like he was gonna be sick, but he was faking it. Harry hurried over to us with his pole, his bucket, his net of fish, and his precious cup of beer.

———

Well, I suppose a lot of us has some horrible childhood memory—somethin' that we can't never forget. It can haunt us forever, man. We try to make some goddam sense out of it, but it don't ever come. There's guys in here seen their mothers murdered, or seen their sisters raped, or their dad's throat slit open by some gang—all when they was still kids. Bad stuff. And we think about it and think about it and can't never figure out why it happened. God? There ain't no god. Too much bad shit in the world to be some kinda loving god. No way.

Well, what Johnnie and I experienced that day was one of those bad things. I've thought about it and thought about it, and I can remember it clear as the day it happened. And in all these years I ain't never figured out why it happened. There ain't no goddam reason. Hell.

18

I think C.K. had many more positive associations to his early childhood than he did to his later childhood and his adolescence. I
believe, had he been given the choice, he would have remained a
small child. Things were certainly better for him at home during
our first few years of friendship, before his parents separated. As I
recall, he seemed to like playing the simpler, child-like games and
wasn't interested in the more intellectual activities like Dungeons
and Dragons. I don't think it was because he was less intelligent
than I; he was just happier participating in activities appropriate
for younger children. Babysitting would give him the opportunity
to do that, to re-live his own childhood.

At times I felt like his parent, as though he looked to me for
the positive regard he wanted and needed from his parents but
was no longer receiving. That was okay with me, but it turned the
tables in an odd way since a great deal of the appeal he had for me
was his being a year and a half older. I always felt privileged to be
the person he wanted to spend time with. I think that's generally
true, that kids prefer to be friends with those older than themselves, as though it is some kind of honor to be befriended by the
more mature and wiser.

So, at this point in our friendship, things were changing and
doing odd twists and turns. And, of course, it was all complicated
by Harry and the destructive nature of the triangle. But that was
about to change.

I hated Harry and wished he would die. He kept popping up
everywhere—in my barn, in my room, at my pond, in my kitchen
with my mother. And worst of all, in my and C.K.'s castle. It was
like some horror movie where little monsters keep appearing in

unexpected places, threatening to take over your life and maybe the whole planet. And I wasn't sure exactly what he was after. At first I thought it was C.K., but then he seemed to be after my mother. And at times I thought he was after me because he tried to be so nice sometimes. Each time I thought he was gone, he'd reappear. If it hadn't been for C.K. and the fact that C.K. seemed sort of stuck with him because they were cousins, or because his mom felt sorry for him or something, I would have told him go to hell. I hated him. When he tried to come into my room that day, that was it. Somehow I got real mean and told him to stay out. And he did. He just went away. That seemed sort of respectful, and I sort of even liked him for it.

The one wonderful thing that happened that day was after stupid Harry spooked Cross-Eyed Ladonna's mare and I had the wind knocked out of me, she held me in her arms and rocked me. I had my arms around her, too, and the left side of my face was sort of buried in her chest. Her chest was soft and firm and warm and cushiony, and I didn't want to move from there, ever. Each time she rocked me back and then came forward, my face would sort of mush into them further. Even after I could breathe again, I kept moaning a little and pretending I was still having trouble. I don't know how she knew I was okay again, but she did and made me stand up.

When I saw Harry standing there afterwards, I still hated him, but I also kind of thanked him in my mind. I mean, if he hadn't spooked the horse, I wouldn't have been able to be so—you know—close—to Cross-Eyed Ladonna. So, in a way, I kind of liked him a little right then. But I didn't let him know.

When he tried to come into my room when C.K. and I were making paper airplanes, I really did hate him again and wished he were dead. Those beady eyes and shaggy hair and dirty clothes just made me sick. Then, when he didn't come in and just went away, I felt sorry for him.

Well, when C.K. and I got done making a bunch of planes, I think we both felt sorry for Harry down there fishing all by himself, so we went down. We had told him we'd be down real soon,

but it took us a long time to make those planes. When we got down there, though, he seemed fine. He'd caught a bunch of fish already and was happy. I looked at the back of his thick body in those dirty clothes, and I saw the cup of beer sitting there—I couldn't believe my mom had given him more—and then I started hating him again. There was something just plain disgusting about him.

One of the planes got picked up and carried by the wind all the way out to the island, so C.K. and I decided to take the canoe to get it. We had it in the water, with just the bow up on the peat, and we had started to get in. Then Harry comes along and says he wants to go out to the island, too, and fish. I thought, good grief, he follows us everywhere. I really did start to think I was in a horror movie. I did not want him to come. I wanted to be out on the island with just C.K. It was going to be our own private adventure. Damn him, I thought. I hate him, I hate him, I hate him! I screamed in my head.

I looked at C.K. He was already sitting on the back seat with a paddle in his hand, and I was standing in front of the canoe, getting ready to push it all the way out into the water. His mom had let his blond hair get real long, and it was turning white from being out in the sun. He had his body angled on the seat to look at Harry. The wind had picked up and blew all his hair forward so it completely covered his face. I couldn't see what he was thinking about Harry. And Harry never asked if we minded. He just came bumping along toward us, carrying all his fishing stuff. He had his pole and tackle box in one hand, and he was trying to carry his net and the cup of beer in the other hand, but the net was too full, and he couldn't hold the cup without spilling the beer. Finally, he held the cup with his teeth and sort of wobbled over to us, trying to say, "Wait! Wait! I'm coming!" but it came out, "Hooway! Hooway! Ibe cubbig!"

He was struggling so much and trying to hurry, that, as much as I hated him, it would have been hard to just take off and leave him. So, we waited. He reached the canoe and said, "Hakes hor haetig," and started putting his stuff in the canoe. Then he got in the middle, sat on the floor, and looked up at me as if to say to his

chauffeur, "Well, Charles, let's move along." He sort of waved his hand up and back at the water.

That made me hate him so much again, suddenly I wanted to hit him with the paddle. I wanted to knock him out of the canoe and hold his head under the water until he drowned. I could see it real clearly: I'd have the canoe paddle in my hands, and I'd whack him on the side of the head. He'd fall out of the canoe and sort of get his arms and feet stuck in the peat. Then I'd jump on him and put my foot on the back of his head and hold it under the water. I'd be so strong that he wouldn't be able to get up, but his arms and legs would be jerking around, trying to get free of the peat, and bubbles would be coming up around his head, and then, after a while he'd be still.

But of course, I wouldn't really do that. I set my paddle in the front of the canoe and pushed and shoved at the pointed bow. The canoe was heavy with two people in it already. After a little bit, it slid all the way down off the peat into the water, but it wobbled quite a bit. I sat down on the front seat and started to paddle.

Just before we got to the island, I reminded C.K. to paddle hard so the canoe would get up speed and slide way up onto the land. If it didn't go onto the land very far, the canoe was real tippy, and it was hard to balance when you got out. He paddled hard, and I paddled as hard as I could, and the bow glided right up onto the land. I got out and pulled the canoe as far up as I could, which wasn't very far because it was so heavy with dumb Harry in it.

Harry got out with all his fishing stuff and the cup of beer in his mouth and headed for the right side of the island. C.K. and I went to the left toward the middle of the island. He had the bag of paper airplanes. He set it down next to a small tree that was about as tall as we were, and we went to look for the plane that the wind had carried over.

The grass was tall but not very thick. The stems were round, not flat like lawn or pasture grass. A lot of the bare dirt—the peat—showed through, and in some places there was no grass at all. I always stepped around these bare spots because they looked like the kinds of places that might let a leg sink in. I'd had pieces

of peat break off the edges, but I'd never had a whole foot and leg go down like my dad did. He said I didn't weigh enough. Still, I stepped over all the bald spots.

C.K. wanted to walk right next to me, but I guess I worried too much about the peat and said we shouldn't walk real close together. He agreed. So we walked closely enough to talk, and we looked for the plane. From the shore, it looked like it had landed right in the middle of the island. We looked for a long time, then finally he said, "Here it is!"

It was a really cool plane. It had a nose that bent downward and wide wings that slanted back. The tail was extra cool because it had two sets of little wings, one above the other. It must have been hard to make. I held it up and tried to imagine each fold. It looked pretty complicated. We both stepped back a bunch of steps and flew the plane back and forth for a while. Then we tested all the others. I looked over at Harry every few minutes and saw him reeling in another fish. He sure was happy fishing.

The sun was setting behind the trees. It looked like a big red ball. The sky was all pink and very pretty. I loved being on the island because I could see so much. I looked up at my house. It looked a lot taller from down here, probably because I could see all three stories. There was a tall peak over the porch on the second floor. Right below it was the screened-in porch where the kitchen and dining room were. And under that was the basement that you could walk out of. My house looked sort of majestic, like a tall castle.

Harry yelled, "Come look at this fish, you guys! It's huge!" He sounded really excited. He also sounded urgent, like we had to go see it. C.K. and I set our planes down and hurried over. I tried to run without stepping on any of the bare spots, but it wasn't easy. I tried to make myself as light as possible. When we got to Harry, he was holding up a fish that was as long as my upper arm. He could hardly hold it up. It was fat, too, and flopping around like crazy.

He was smiling bigger than I'd ever seen him. His little eyes disappeared in his head he was so happy. He said, "I wonder if this one'll even fit in my carrier." I looked at C.K., who was sort

of laughing because he was happy for Harry, and I couldn't help doing the same.

———

There's something heart-warming about seeing a soft spot in someone who is otherwise nasty. I remember seeing a film clip of Adolf Hitler when, near the end of his reign, a small girl with blond curls unexpectedly came up to him and held out a half-wilted dandelion. The warmest expression came over his face. He actually laughed a little, not out of any feeling of humor but out of genuine joy. His eyes twinkled as his whole face showed love and warmth. He brushed the girl under the chin once with his fingertips, and then the expression vanished as he turned back to his audience.

My grandfather—the other one, not the one who died when I was six— was the same way. He was a nasty old man, and everyone said he was selfish and hateful. And yet, every once in a while something would warm his heart for a moment, and the purest look would come over his face. It always surprised me as a kid, and I would realize he was actually quite vulnerable. And I would love him for that moment. For instance, when I was maybe fifteen, he was suffering in a nursing home from a myriad of ailments, the least of which was pneumonia. But he was still strong and feisty and very angry about his present plight. When my mother and I entered his room, he was standing in his baggy pajamas looking out the window at the afternoon sunlight. He didn't know we were coming, but my mother had just bought an eight-week-old Flat-Coat puppy, and she thought he'd enjoy seeing it. He'd been a big dog lover, and his own yellow lab had died of old age a month or so before.

He was more often nasty and impatient with me than not, and everyone said he was just a tough old guy who hated everyone and loved only himself. I believed it as a child, and although I'd wanted to love him, he'd made it nearly impossible. He consistently pointed out my shortcomings and complained that I never did well enough at anything. So, I really didn't want to visit him that day, but my mother had insisted. At least she let me hold the puppy,

whose soft, black form was nestled into my arms as we walked into Grandpa's room.

When he turned around to see who'd come in, he looked stern and grumpy. Once he realized it was my mother and I, he still looked grumpy. When I held the puppy out to him, his face did the same thing Hitler's had. It was like a cloud passing swiftly across and away from the sun. It went from dark to light within a moment, and his emotions took over. He smiled from ear to ear, the lines around his eyes wrinkled, and laughing a little, he said, "Oh, baby, look at you!" He held his arms out and I handed him the puppy. He held it up to his face, and it licked him all over his big nose. And there he was—a pure, loving, vulnerable human being. I felt my chest flood with joy just watching him. And I could see that warm spot I'm talking about, the same warm spot I saw in Harry that day when he caught the huge fish.

I didn't want to stand too close to Harry because of the peat, and C.K. stayed back, too, but we looked at the fish for the longest time, and then Harry couldn't hold it up any longer.

"This thing's gettin' heavy! Wow! This will make some terrific supper. My mom'll sure be happy to see this one."

I almost said, "Hey, that fish should go to *my* mom because it was in our pond," but I didn't want to spoil it for him. I was glad he was happy.

"Would you guys help me get it into my carrier?" he asked.

C.K. said, "Sure," and went and lifted the big net out of the water and brought it over to Harry. It was so full of fish already that C.K. had to carry it with two hands. I still stood back while C.K. held the top open. Harry tried to lower the fish into it, but the fish was so big and flopping so hard, its tail just wouldn't go in. Its mouth still had the hook and line attached to it.

Harry finally got frustrated and said, "Jesus Christ, how can I get the damned thing in here and get the hook out too? Johnnie, can't you help?"

Susan L Metzger

"What do you want me to do?" I asked, stepping just a little closer, worried about the peat holding all of us.

"Hold his tail and his body still while I get the hook out, and then we can just drop him in."

There was just no other way. I really didn't want to grab the fish, but I did. I stood on Harry's right side and held the tail with one hand and grabbed the middle of the body with my other hand. The fish was cold and wet and trying to wiggle away. I couldn't keep him completely still, but I kept him still enough. C.K. was on Harry's left side, holding the carrier open. I aimed the tail right into the opening and lowered the fish about halfway in while Harry fiddled with the hook. We were so close to each other that we bumped each other's elbows. I kept thinking Harry might smell badly, but he didn't.

"Damn thing don't wanta come out," he said, as he twisted the hook this way and that. Finally there was a jerk, and I thought he finally got the hook out, but that wasn't what happened.

First there was the jerk, and then Harry just dropped down. I wondered why he was falling on his knees. I thought maybe the fish had bitten him, or he'd poked himself with the fishhook. But it seemed all three of us were dropping, fast. I looked down and saw lots of water. Then Harry fell right through a big hole in the peat. C.K. let go of the carrier, and it went into the hole too. I felt myself start to go down and turned around and fell flat on my belly on the grass. Then I crawled away from the hole as fast as I could. I didn't want to stop crawling. I wanted to get away from that hole, and I crawled across the bare peat spots through the tall grass, almost all the way to the canoe.

I thought about C.K. and looked back. He'd fallen backward onto his butt and was scooting himself on his side away from the hole. I was afraid to stand up. I wanted to spread my weight out as much as possible. I could imagine another hole opening up under me and sucking me down into the water. I yelled to C.K., "Don't stand up! Spread your weight out!"

I lay there and clutched handfuls of swamp grass. I thought, What should I do now? Is the whole island going to collapse?

Should I hurry and get into the canoe? Would I be able to paddle around to the other side and get C.K.? What about Harry? Where was Harry?

I couldn't stand it any more and jumped up. My chest was pounding, and I wondered if C.K. was all right. "C.K.!" I screamed. I looked over where I saw him fall, but I didn't see him now. "C.K.!" I screamed as loudly as I could. Then I saw his head lift up from the ground. He was back by the hole. At first I thought he'd fallen in, too, and all that was sticking out was his head.

"I'm here!" he yelled.

"Are you okay?"

"Yes! I'm trying to find Harry!"

I thought about getting in the canoe and going to get my mom, but by the time I did that, Harry would drown. I remembered the long rope my dad left tied to the front of the canoe, and I thought if I took it off, we could throw it down the hole for Harry to grab. The canoe was only a few feet away, and when I got to it and started trying to untie the knot, I got scared about walking back across the island. What if another hole fell in right under me? How was C.K. getting so close to the hole Harry fell into? I decided to get in the canoe and paddle around to the other side. Yes, that was it. I'd leave the rope tied to the canoe and maybe it would reach down into the hole, and if I fell in, I could keep hold of the rope and pull myself out. I pushed the canoe into the water as fast as I could and leaped in. I paddled like crazy around the end of the island to the other side.

"C.K.! Where are you?" I shouted. He lifted his head up again and waved at me to come quickly. I paddled the canoe's bow up onto the land and jumped out with the rope in my fist. I got down on my hands and knees and crawled over to C.K. He was lying on his belly with his head over the edge of the hole. The hole wasn't as big as I'd thought. I thought it was as big around as Linda Boggus's kids' swimming pool, but it really wasn't much bigger around than a man. I'd hoped that Harry would be able to look up and see a big area of light. I crawled around the hole, across from C.K. I was so scared my elbows shook.

C.K. was calling down into the hole, "Harry! Harry!" He had one arm way down in the water, up to his shoulder. He was feeling around down there.

"Do you feel anything?" I asked.

"No! Nothing." He looked at me. He had tears in his eyes and looked more scared than I'd ever seen anyone. Then he screamed at me, "Go! Get help!"

I started to crawl, but then I got up and ran the few steps to the canoe. I untied the rope from the canoe and threw the end to C.K. "See if you can get this to go down there." Then I shoved off and leaped into the canoe. I never even thought about tipping over. I just started paddling and paddled all the way to shore in what seemed like seconds. The canoe barely touched the land and I was out of it and running up the stairs to get my mom. I flew into the house and then into the kitchen.

My mom heard me coming and said, "Johnnie, it's almost time to—"

She was stirring something on the stove. "Come!" I screamed at her. I was starting to cry now and trying to yell at her to come help, all at the same time. She looked at me and her mouth fell open. She knew it was something horrible.

"What! What's wrong? Is someone hurt?" she said. She looked real scared.

"Harry—" I sort of sobbed a few times and tried to talk, but my throat was so tight, and my mouth just seemed to cramp all up. "Fell—through the peat!"

"Where? Is he stuck?" she said as she turned the stove off and started running to the door with me.

"No. He—." I kept crying and trying not to. "He's gone—fell through—the island. Gone! Under the island!" Then I let go and burst into horrendous sobs. My mom didn't know what to do. First she started to run out of the house, then she came back and hugged me, then she started to run out again.

Finally, she said, "Nine one one. That's what I need to do, call nine one one. What can I do down there? Oh, sweetie, are you all right?" She always called me "sweetie" when she wanted

me to know how much she loved me. She hugged me again and ran for the phone. She asked me, "He fell through the peat on the island and is down under the water, under the island? And he didn't come back up?" I nodded hard and tried to stop crying, but the sobs had taken me over. I couldn't stop for anything. "Oh God, oh God!" she whimpered as she dialed the phone.

Someone answered and she started screaming, "Come quick, a boy has fallen into our peat bog and is under the peat. It's an island. I don't know how anyone will get him out. Yes, yes, it's fifty-two eleven Meadow Road. The pond's at the bottom of the hill. Just tell them to come down there. I'm going down now to try to help. Please hurry!" She listened some more. "The boy's name?" She looked at me. "Harry."

I nodded.

"Harry—uh, I'm not sure. Johnson? What's his last name?" she asked me.

I didn't know.

"It might be Johnson. I'm not positive. Yes, my son's friend. I'll try to reach his mother. No, okay, yes, I'll go down there now. Call his mother later. Yes, I see. Yes, I'll be down there. Life vest? Oh, shit! Maybe. Yes, I'll try to find one. Thank you. Please hurry! Yes, fifty-two eleven. Yes, Meadow Road—on the west side, right near Bulla Road. Good." Then she hung up. She put her hand on my back. "Come, sweetie, show me where he is."

She grabbed my hand, and we ran out the door. My legs felt real shaky as we ran down the stairs to the pond. I couldn't stop the sobs, no matter what I did. I tried holding my breath, and I tried talking, but nothing worked. My mom kept stopping and holding me. That felt so good that I didn't want her to let go, but she always did and would start running again, holding onto my hand. When we got to the canoe, she shoved it out to the water and got into the back seat with a paddle in her hand.

"Get in, sweetie, and show me where he is. Oh, you poor thing. And poor Harry. I hope we can get him out."

I was still sobbing but pointed to where C.K. was and then managed to say, "No. Go around the end." She did. I paddled as

best I could, but my arms felt like my legs now, shaky and weak. When we got around to the other side of the island, the canoe went right up onto the land, and I got out and pulled on the bow. But my mom didn't wait and came stepping through and onto the land.

"Wait," I was able to say. But I kept crying, "You might—fall through—too. You better—crawl." She went right down on her hands and knees, and we both started crawling. "C.K.?" I yelled.

"Here!"

When we got to him, he was still on his belly at the edge of the hole. He had the rope down in the water and was tugging on it and pulling it back and forth across the little pool. He had tears running down his face, and his whole body was shaking. We crawled up near him and got on the other side of the hole, away from each other.

"C.K., dear," said my mom. "Is he really under there? Has he pulled on the rope? Have you felt him or seen him at all?"

He looked at me and at her and shook his head slowly. "No. Nothing. Nothing. I almost jumped in to see if I could find him, but I got scared. What can we do?" He was crying for real now, too.

"The fire department is coming right away," she said. She reached across the pool and took the rope from him. She pulled on it and had to pull hard. When the end came up, it was tied to Harry's tackle box. C.K. had tied it on and dropped it down there. The box was covered with particles of peat, but that's all. She reached her arm down into the water and felt around. "Nothing," she said. "Just water. Where's the piece of peat that used to fill this hole?" Then we heard the sirens. There must have been ten of them, all screaming and whining up our driveway. We couldn't see them, only hear them.

"Oh, how will they know where we are?" my mom asked. "It's going to be dark before too long." She started to get up.

"Don't stand up!" I yelled at her.

"Oh, right," she said and crawled back to the canoe. "You guys ought to get away from that hole. Come over near the edge. If the edge goes, at least you can swim away."

She stood there for a minute and watched for the rescuers. I guess she decided they wouldn't be able to see her on the island, so she got back in the canoe and paddled around to the other side. We crawled to the edge and watched her. She waited in the middle of the water until they came down. She yelled at them and waved her arms, and they saw her. Then she went to the shore and talked to them. Two of the men got into the canoe with her. They had big ropes and some round life preservers. The one sitting in front helped paddle back out to us.

C.K. and I still stood on the edge. We stood close to each other, almost touching. For some reason, we weren't afraid of the peat breaking off here. If it did, we could swim away. We didn't look at each other or say a word. It was sort of like our old e.s.p. days when we didn't need to say anything. We just knew what each other was thinking. I knew he was shaking and crying, and he must have seen me shaking and crying too. Every once in a while when I realized Harry must be under there fighting to find a way out, and that he couldn't have held his breath this long, and he must be dying, my sobs would almost take me over so that I could hardly breathe. They made my body shake in great big heaves, and I couldn't stop them. I wanted to just fall on the ground and go to sleep or faint or something. And then I'd feel C.K. there, and those scary feelings would settle down. We stood close enough that I could feel the heat from him, and that was good. When I concentrated on that, I felt better. So, I just tried to think about C.K.'s heat, and then I could almost stop crying.

We watched the men and my mom paddle around the back side of the island, and when they got close enough, C.K. and I grabbed the bow on each side and tried to pull it onto the land. It was awfully heavy with three adults in it. I was afraid the whole side of the island would break off. I imagined this whole big piece we were standing on was going to break off any second and sink away. I hated this, waiting for the ground to just go out from under me. I wanted to get back into the canoe. But I had to wait.

The man sitting in the front looked like a weight lifter. He was young and had short, dark hair and great big bulging muscles.

231

He and the other man both had on dark pants and white shirts with some kind of patch on the sleeve. The other man, who sat on the floor in the middle of the canoe, was older and kind of fat and had curly red hair.

My mom stepped out of the canoe and said to them, "You could fall through, too. We've been crawling on our bellies and staying away from each other." She dropped to her hands and knees as soon as she got onto the land and led the way to the hole. I could tell the men didn't want to crawl, and they looked at each other and shrugged. The red-haired man got on his hands and knees, but the muscle man, who was carrying the big rope and the two life preservers, walked. He took only about three steps, and his left leg went down into the peat, up to his knee, just like my dad's and Joey's had done. He said, "Jesus Christ!" and pulled his leg out. It was all black and mucky. He went down on his hands and knees then and dragged the rope and life preservers beside him.

C.K. and I watched the three of them crawl to the hole. I leaned near enough to C.K. to bump his upper arm with mine. I felt his warmth again, but then I pulled away when I thought about Harry saying we were fairies. For a second I started to hate Harry again when I thought about his calling us "queer" and how he had punched and kicked Tucker, and then I remembered where he was now.

"I sure hope they can get him out," said C.K.

"Do you think he's still alive?" I asked, and then wished I hadn't. What was C.K. supposed to say? I mean, how could Harry be alive? How long had it been since he breathed any air? So, I didn't wait for an answer. I said, "Don't answer that. It was a dumb question."

He looked me right in the eyes and looked very, very sad. He didn't say anything. We both looked over to the shore at the same time because there was suddenly a lot of noise. We saw a bunch of regular-looking men and some guys in fireman suits. They were dragging three rowboats down the stairs. They put them in the water with a bunch of equipment—more ropes, some big hooks, a big thing that looked like a huge pulley, and some big tanks and

tubes and things that looked like oxygen masks. Four men got into two of the boats, and they started rowing out to us.

When they all began to land, I thought about my fifth-grade American history class and the story of the pilgrims landing at Plymouth Rock. I guess that was kind of dumb, but this is how I'd imagined them all getting out of their boats. The muscle man got up and yelled at the other men to wait. Then he crawled over to them real fast. He warned them about walking on the peat. Most of them waited, and three of them followed the muscle man, all on their hands and knees. It was getting a little funny, and I felt a laugh starting up in my chest, but I made it go away. C.K. must have thought the same thing because he gave one little snort, but that's all. As soon as the three new men got over to the hole, my mom crawled back to us.

She looked real serious. "Let's go back to the house," she said. "You guys don't need to watch this, and I need to try to reach Harry's mother. I sure wish it weren't nearly dark."

We got into the canoe. I got in the back, C.K. sat in the middle, and my mom pushed us off and got in the front. As we went around the island, we all kept looking over by the hole. One guy was up on his knees. He was tying a rope to the big hook. I wondered what they were going to do with the hook. Were they going to throw it down there and try to hook onto Harry? Or was one of those guys going to hold onto the hook and go down there himself?

As we got closer to shore, I started wondering what my mom was going to say to Marge.

She asked C.K., "Do you know how to get in touch with Harry's mother? Does she work? The evening shift?"

"Yeah, she works. I think at Walker Tool and Die, but I ain't sure what shift. She works at Woolworth's, too. My ma would know."

"Where's your mother right now?"

"Probably at home."

We didn't talk anymore, and when we reached the shore, two of the regular-looking men standing there pulled the canoe way up on the land. I was surprised how far they pulled us up. The

firemen were lighting gas lanterns and putting two great big spot-lights into the other boat. I saw them put a large net in and then a long, black, zippered plastic bag. It was folded a couple times, but I could tell what it was because I'd seen them in movies to put dead bodies in after an accident or after someone had been shot. I was starting to feel sick.

When we stood up to get out of the canoe, my legs were shaky again and felt kind of numb, like maybe they weren't going to work. But they did, even though I couldn't feel them very well. My mom stopped by the men and asked, "Is there anything else I can do?"

One of them said, "No, ma'am. We've got everything we need for now." He had a black radio with a long antenna in his hand. Some lady's voice and some static were coming from it.

We turned to go up the stairs, and then C.K. ran over by the bushes. He started throwing up. Just listening to him made me want to throw up, too. I could feel that hot, sick feeling in my stomach, and my mouth started to water. Then C.K. was done and came back to us. My mom put an arm around each of us and held us close to her for a minute. Her body and C.K.'s and mine all squeezed together felt very good. When she started to let us go, I hugged her harder. She got the message and just stood there and hugged us for a very long time until C.K. started to fidget.

"This is terrible. Very terrible," she said. "Probably the most terrible thing you two will ever experience. I'm so sorry this hap-pened." I think she was starting to cry, too, because I could feel her body shudder a couple times while she held us so tight. She sort of gasped as she took in a deep breath. "This next part is going to be the worst. I have to reach Harry's mother." She gave us one last hard squeeze and let us go.

We went up into the house, and C.K. and I stood on the screened porch and watched the pond. We couldn't see the guys on shore, but out on the island we could see them crawling around. Every once in a while a guy would stand up. Then someone would yell at him, and he'd go back down on his hands and knees. They had set up the two big floodlights, but with the tall grass and all the men out there, we just couldn't see much. My mom kept dialing

the phone, but she talked only once, and that sounded like someone at Woolworth's. She called from the kitchen to C.K., "Your
mom doesn't answer. Do you have any idea where I can reach her?"

"Just at Marge's."

"Do you know that number?"

"No. Sorry."

"Well, do you know of any other relatives or anyone who
would know?"

C.K. was thinking and then someone rang the doorbell.
My mom ran to the front door, and we followed her. It was a
policeman.

"Mrs. Ambrose?"

"Yes. Did you find him?"

"Yes, we did, ma'am. He was trapped way underneath. We
finally sent a scuba diver in there, and he found him."

"I don't suppose there's any hope?"

"Well, we always make an attempt at resuscitation. You never
know, but, well—he was just under the water too long. The reason
I'm here is to find out if you reached the boy's parents."

"No, I've been trying, but I don't have his number. And his
cousin's mother isn't home, either. She's the only contact I know."

"Well, just as well, really. The police department will take over
now. We'll inform the family of the death. But if you could give me
some other names and phone numbers, I'd appreciate it."

C.K. and I were standing behind my mother. She turned
around. "C.K., can you give the police officer your mom's number,
and did you think of any other relatives' names or numbers?"

C.K. was very serious. "Yeah, I know some names but only my
ma's and pa's phone numbers."

"That's fine. Here," she said to the policeman, bringing C.K.
around in front of her. "Maybe you two should talk. I'll stay here
with you." She put her arm around C.K.'s shoulder and held him
close. I walked out onto the porch. I kind of wanted to see if they
used the body bag.

———

Yes, they did use the body bag. I'll never forget the sight of the two men on their knees lifting that soggy boy's body onto the black vinyl, folding his arms across his chest and then zipping the zipper from foot to head. The island was far enough away, and the lighting inadequate enough that I couldn't see every detail. But my imagination filled in the rest.

———————

C.K. came out onto the porch, but they had already loaded Harry into a boat and were going across the water to the shore. C.K. did get to see them lift the bag out of the boat and two men carry it up the stairs. There was another guy in front of them holding a lantern and one behind them also holding a lantern. It was all kind of dim and fuzzy and looked like a dreary old-time movie, something my parents would have watched and thought was "excellent."

We went to the hall windows and watched them load Harry into an ambulance, then the ambulance drove down the driveway. They didn't put the siren or the flashing lights on. We watched the little red taillights going over the hill.

19

Damn. I hate thinking back on that. Damn shitty thing to happen to a kid.

———————

When the policeman was askin' me names and phone numbers, I was sorta numb. I knew that Harry had just died, but it didn't seem real. I was glad Christine was there. She had her arm around me, and it felt real good being sorta pressed up next to her. It felt like when my ma used to hold me on her lap and we'd watch TV together, and sometimes she read to me like that. I loved it. And my Pa hugged me more, too, when I was little.

———————

Hell, one of the best things my pa did when I was real little was have me sit facing him on his lap, but way out to his knees. My butt would sorta be right on his knees. He'd hold my hands and make one knee come up and then the other, and I'd wobble back and forth. See, he was pretendin' to be a horse. And then he'd sing, "This is the way the lady rides, ta dee ta da, ta dee ta da." Shit. And then he'd make both his knees come up at the same time, but real slow, and he'd sing, "This is the way the cowboy rides, gally oop, gally oop, gally oop." That was fun. And then he'd make his damn knees go so fast, I'd almost fall off, and he'd sing, "This is way the soldier rides, ta da ta da ta da ta da ta da." And I'd laugh real hard, and then he'd pull me to him and hug me for a long time. Hell, and then we'd start all over again. And then one day he said I was too big to do that anymore. I asked my ma to do it. Fuck. She said no too.

———————

As soon as the policeman was done askin' me about Ma and Pa and where they worked and all the relatives and their last names and where they worked, and all the phone numbers I knew, which was none except Ma's and Pa's at home and at their jobs, he said I could go. I wanted to go out and be with Harry. I figured they was workin' to get him breathing again, like they do on TV. Christine talked to the policeman some more, and I went to find Johnnie. He was out on the screened porch, starin' down at the pond. We watched the men carry a bunch of stuff up the stairs and put it in the ambulance, and then the ambulance drove away. I knew they must be working on Harry in the ambulance, and they was on their way to take him to the hospital. They still had the lights on the island. I couldn't believe that we'd just watched Harry fall through the ground and go under the island. And not come up. I knew they must be gettin' him to breathe in the ambulance. They had all that special stuff to work on him. I'd seen it in lots of movies. They had some thing they put on a guy's chest. It had electricity in it, and it would make a dead guy jump, and then he'd start breathin' again. Harry would be all right.

Johnnie stood there and stared down at the lights. We could hear the men talkin', and one of them was giving orders. We seen one of the spotlights go out and watched two guys crawl with it to a boat. They left the other spotlight on until they loaded all their other stuff into the other boat. Then that light went off, and all we could see was two lanterns, and after a while those went up the stairs, and then the men drove away.

Christine was in the kitchen talking on the phone. It sounded like she was talking to Leland. Johnnie and I just kept lookin' down at the pond, and we listened to Christine.

"Jesus Christ! Why didn't you tell me the island is that bad! Those boys should never have been out there. No one should!" Then she listened a while. "That's not true. The only times I was out there were early fall when it was dry and solid and in the middle of winter, when it was frozen. Johnnie says your foot went through all the time—all the way up to your knee! Damn it. Why didn't you tell me that? I thought it was safe. And now a boy is dead. Dead!"

Then she started crying real hard. "No, I don't want to talk about it some more. I think you better get your ass home. I don't know what kind of liability we have for this. We could lose everything. Why didn't you tell me!" She cried some more, but softer now. "Okay!" she shouted like she was real mad. Then she hung up, sniffed a bunch of times, and blew her nose.

"You guys out there? Better come and eat in a couple minutes. I just need to warm this stuff up." She sniffed some more and blew her nose again. I heard dishes and pans out there. Then she turned the porch light on and started setting the table. I didn't feel hungry at all. What I had in my stomach I'd just threw up down by the pond.

"I ain't hungry, Christine," I said.

"Me neither," said Johnnie.

"I'm not, either," said Christine. "How about if we just eat this fruit salad? We could use these vitamins with all this stress." So, we sat down. She spooned two big helpings of fruit salad onto my plate. I saw watermelon, bananas, blueberries, and several things I'd never seen before. But that's how it was with Christine's food. So far, none of her weird food had killed me, so now I just ate it. Most of it tasted good.

I ate, but I didn't want to look at Johnnie or Christine. I glanced at 'em a couple times, and they was just lookin' down at their plates like they didn't know what to say neither. Then I started wonderin' what Johnnie was thinking. I knew he hated Harry, so I was wonderin' if he was glad this happened. And Christine seemed to like Harry, so I was wonderin' how bad she felt. I think she thought it was her fault, but it wasn't. When the phone rang, it scared us, and we all jumped outa our seats. It was funny for a minute, and we laughed. But then we stopped laughin' right away. Christine ran for the phone in the kitchen. Johnnie and I listened and tried to figure out who it was.

"Ohhh. So the police found you. Good. No, C.K. didn't know Harry's phone number, and you weren't home. It's terrible. The most terrible thing. I should never have let them go down there. Yes, we'd been down there many times. I guess he was standing on

a weak spot. I really don't understand about peat. Most of it's firm as can be. Yes, he's here. Do you want to talk to him? Sure." Then she called out to me. "C.K., it's your mother."

I didn't want to talk to her. I felt real heavy in my chair like I couldn't get up, like my arms was heavy, and my body was so heavy I just couldn't stand. I wanted to just stay at the Ambrose's table and eat fruit forever.

"Are you going to answer the phone?" asked Johnnie.

"Do you think I can stay here tonight?" I asked him.

"Probably. Let's ask my mom."

"I know what she's gonna do—my ma—she's gonna ask me all kinds of stupid questions about what happened. I'd really like to stay here tonight," I said to Johnnie, like I needed to convince him.

"Good. Fine. But my mom's waiting for you to take the phone."

"Oh. Yeah." I made myself lift my heavy body up and go out to the kitchen. Christine looked sorry for me and handed me the receiver.

"Hello?" I said.

"This is sure a goddammed mess you got yourself into! The police said you and Johnnie was with Harry when this happened. What did you do, push him in?"

I couldn't believe she was blaming me for this. "No, we didn't push him in. We *all* almost fell in—all three of us. I'm lucky I got away."

"Well, how do you think Marge feels?"

I didn't know what to say. "Is Pa home?"

"Of course not. But you better get your butt home right away."

"Well—can I stay here tonight? They said it's alright."

"I think you've done enough damage at that house for one day. I'll pick you up in five minutes. Watch for my headlights so I don't have to get out of the car. Hear me?"

I waited a minute to think of somethin' else so I wouldn't have to go home, but I couldn't. "Yeah." What else could I do? She hung up.

When I got into the car, I could smell the whiskey. I'd barely gotten the door shut when she started drivin' off, and she said,

"Can you imagine being Marge? Her and I was just sitting at her house watchin' TV when this cop comes to the door and tells her son is dead. And then he asks her if she knows where I am, and I was sure he was gonna tell me you was dead, too. But he said you and Johnnie was okay. Then Marge had to go off with the cop to 'identify the body.' Identify the body! Can you imagine? She was in hysterics. Thank God Bob was home, and he went with her. Cop told me you was still at Johnnie's house. Don't you ever come home? Why are you here all the time? Ain't your own house good enough for you?"

She stopped at the end of the Ambrose's driveway. Then she pulled out on the highway. We only had a short way to the dirt road. "Is Pa home yet?" I asked.

"You asked me that already. You know I don't know where the hell he is. Somewhere with that cross-eyed bitch!"

And then, when she went to turn the corner onto our road, she ran over the stop sign. It made a loud bang when we hit it and made a horrible scraping noise under the car, and we stopped real fast. We bent the whole thing over, and it was stuck under the car. She couldn't go forward or backward cuz it was sorta holding the car up off the ground. The car was sorta tipped over to my side.

She pressed on the gas pedal real hard, and the engine roared, but we didn't go nowhere. Then something hit me in the face real hard. At first I thought some part had flown off the car, but it was Ma's fist. My nose and my whole top lip stung real bad. I couldn't help it, but I started crying. And I couldn't stop. I looked at her, and she looked real mean. I felt my nose. I thought maybe it was broken. Why did she hit me? Then I started sounding like Johnnie when he was crying after Harry fell in the hole, when he couldn't stop. It was something way down in my chest. It just took over, and I was sort of heaving and gasping. I couldn't make it stop.

I looked at Ma again and she looked about as surprised as I was. Her eyes was all round and her mouth was hanging open. I just looked at her to see what she'd do next. I had my hand on the door handle in case she tried to hit me again. I was gonna jump out. Then her face got all soft looking.

"I'm sorry." She put her hand on my head and pulled me over to her, and she hugged me.

———————

A hug is so damned powerful, ain't it? Especially a mother's hug. Or a child's. Ain't nothin' like it, man.

———————

Three guys in a pick-up truck stopped and pushed our car off the stop sign, and we drove home. When we got there, Pa's truck was in the driveway. Boy was I glad to see that. I ran in the house, and he was standin' in the kitchen talkin' on the phone. He hung up real quick. I was so happy to see him, I ran up to him like I used to when I was little and he would pick me way up in the air. Then I would wrap my legs around his middle, and he would hold me. This time, I just sorta ran into him, and my face bounced off his chest. I had my arms up around his neck, ready to have him pick me up, but then I just hugged him around his waist. And he hugged me back. And he hugged me like that for a long time.

"Something terrible happened," I said into his flannel shirt.

"I know. I know," he said. His voice was soft, and his body was so big. Everyone said I'd never get to be six foot three like him cuz I had a short mother. But I knew they was wrong.

My ma came in, and her voice was all drunk-crackly again. I hated that. "How'd you find out? Where you been? Nobody knows how to reach you when there's an emergency!"

His voice was still quiet when he answered her, "The police told me." We was still hugging, and he said to me, "They said you done a real nice job of giving them names and phone numbers." I nodded my head against him. I didn't want to let go of his waist. I had my fingers wrapped around his belt in the back.

"Well, let's hear what happened," said my ma in her drunk voice.

Pa pulled me off him and said, "Yeah, let's sit down and talk about this."

So, I told them how we'd all been standing together helping Harry put his big fish in the carrier when he just fell into a hole. I told them how I almost went in, too, but I fell on my back and scooted away. And how I'd tried to find Harry and tied his tackle box to Johnnie's rope and put it down the hole so Harry could grab it, but he never did. And how Johnnie ran and got his ma and all those men came and found Harry.

"I think they probably got him to breathe again when they got him into the ambulance," I said.

Ma laughed. "What! After he'd already been dead an hour? You're sure dreamin'. Been watchin' too much damned TV. Why didn't you grab his arm or something when he was going down?"

"I thought I was going to fall in, too."

"Your favorite cousin falls into a hole and drowns and you can't even grab an arm, or even his hair? You could've saved his life!"

Pa looked at his watch and started to get up.

"Where the hell are you goin'?" said Ma.

Pa said, "The church team's got our last practice before the tournament this weekend. They're countin' on me."

"Basketball! Your nephew dies and all you think about is basketball?"

"He's your nephew, not mine, and I won't be gone that long. 'Sides, C.K. ought to go to bed. I'll be here in the morning."

"Fat chance."

Pa didn't say nothin' else to me or her. He just walked out the door again. Now I had to face Ma alone. I almost ran after him to ask if I could go watch. But I stopped. Maybe he was right. I should just go to bed. Then Ma wouldn't be able to accuse me no more about savin' Harry.

"I'm real tired, Ma. I think I'll go to bed. Besides, Linda Boggus asked if I would babysit her kids. She wants to give me a babysittin' lesson tomorrow morning."

"You don't know nothin' about babysittin'. You can't even help your own cousin." She was lookin' real dopey, like she should go to bed, too.

"'Night, Ma," I said and went upstairs.

I woke up in the morning with my clothes and shoes still on. I must've been awful tired last night. The clock said 9:40. I ran downstairs. Ma had left for work. She'd left me a glass of juice and a bowl of cereal. I ate real fast, washed my face and brushed my teeth, and ran down to Boggus's. On the way, I wondered if Linda Boggus knew about Harry. If she thought I couldn't save him, maybe she wouldn't want me to take care of her kids.

I had butterflies in my stomach when I rang the doorbell. She came to the door right away. She was smilin' real big and holding Billy. He had something that looked like grape jelly all over his face and his hands.

"Good morning, C.K. I'm so glad you remembered. Come in. Billy, do you remember C.K.? Say hi." Billy turned his face away and put it in his mother's hair. I wondered if she minded havin' jelly in it. "Sandra! C.K.'s here. Come say hello."

She walked into her kitchen, and I followed her. She put Billy in his high chair and gave him a cookie. He kept watching me and didn't care about the cookie. I smiled at him and he smiled back. Then he turned away. Sandra came runnin' in with her doll.

"Say 'hi' to C.K.," she said to the doll.

The doll said, "Hi, C.K."

I said, "Hi, Cinderella."

"Mommy, I have to go peepee," she said and put her hand in there.

Linda smiled at me and said, "Come on, C.K. No time like the present." I followed the two of 'em into the bathroom. Sandra had on a red and white sorta sundress. I guess that's what you'd call it, and she pulled up the skirt part and pulled down her underpants. I'd never seen a girl's front parts bare. I mean, I guess I saw them at Little Friends, but I didn't remember very well. I was surprised to see no penis and just the small round part with a crack down the center. I tried not to stare.

"She needs a little help getting up here," said Linda, "because the toilet is kind of high." Sandra's underpants were around her ankles, and Linda lifted her onto the toilet. "I like to be here with

her because I guess she could fall in. She hates the potty seat. Wants to be grown up, you know?" I nodded. Sandra pulled on the toilet paper and tore off a long piece. She crumpled it up, and then she held it out to me.

"Want to wipe me?" she asked.

Of course I didn't, but I said, "Sure," and took the ball of paper from her.

"Oh, you can do it, honey," said Linda.

"No. I want C.K. to do it."

"Well, I think you're big enough to do it yourself."

"Please?" she said and smiled at me. Linda shrugged and let me decide.

I tried to push the paper between her legs, but there wasn't room for my hand.

"Scoot her back a little," said Linda.

I didn't know exactly where to wipe. I mean, how far back to go. So I sorta dabbed at the front.

"Back a little farther," said Linda.

I didn't like this at all. I pushed my hand back farther and Sandra's skin touched my hand. I almost jumped. I just kinda pushed the paper under there and let it drop into the toilet. My heart was pounding. "There. All done," I said.

"Thank you," said Sandra. She jumped off the toilet and pulled her pants up. She pushed her skirt down and walked out of the bathroom. She sort of wiggled as she walked, like she was grown up and had just done something real important. I was glad that was over. I walked back to the kitchen. I think I liked Billy better.

He was eating his cookie and just watchin' me and Linda. Sandra had gone somewhere else.

"You ever changed a diaper?" asked Linda.

"Oh. No, ma'am." I guess I hadn't thought about that part. I just figured I'd play with them and stuff. "Do I need to do that?" I didn't like all this bathroom stuff.

"You sure do. Boys don't get potty trained until they're five sometimes. Girls are easier." She got a washrag and cleaned Billy's face off. "Need to go peepee?" she asked him.

He nodded his head real hard. She took him out of the high chair and carried him on her hip to the bathroom. I wondered if babysitting mostly meant taking kids to the bathroom. I didn't think it would be like this. Linda brought a yellow plastic stool over to the front of the toilet, and Billy got up on it. She pulled his shorts down and started to open two big pieces of white tape at the top of his diaper.

"These tapes are resealable. So if he's dry, you can tape it back together." She opened both tapes and let the diaper fall open. "Billy, you just peepeed in your diaper. It's still warm." It looked wet and yellow, and she let it fall down between his legs and pulled it out the back. She tossed it into the garbage can. "Can you do more?" Billy stood there with his little penis stuck out. It sure was tiny—looked like a miniature of mine. He shook his head no. "You have to get him in here quick when he says he has to go. We only make it once in a while. If he's still dry when you get him in here, be sure to hold onto his penis or he'll spray it all over. Maybe you can teach him to aim. By the time Billy gets up in the morning, my husband is gone. And by the time he gets home from work, Billy's usually in bed, so he doesn't get to watch his dad do it very often. Did your pa help you learn?"

I couldn't remember. "I don't know."

"Well, here's a clean diaper. I keep 'em in here." She opened a closet door. There was two big boxes of diapers. "I buy 'em cheap at the farm co-op, but you gotta buy a bunch of 'em at a time. Oh, well. Here. See if you can put this on him." She handed the thing to me. It was such a neat little package—padded stuff with a plastic coating, all folded nice. I opened it up. It was like cloth inside and was shaped like an hour glass. There was elastic on the sides. "The tapes go in back. You can put it on him while he's standing. Spread your legs out, Billy." Billy did, and I fumbled with it and started to put it under him upside down. "Maybe I better show you the first time," she said. She flipped it over, pushed one end between his legs, spread it out and sort of wrapped the top parts around his waist. Then she opened each tape and pressed it against the front.

"There! It's very easy. You'll get the hang of it." I wondered about that. "You can pull his shorts up."

I stood behind him and reached down. I couldn't help it when my cheek touched his head, and then his cheek. I couldn't believe how soft he was. I wanted to touch him some more, just to feel the softness, but I figured that would seem weird. I pulled his shorts up and said, "There you go." He held my hand and stepped down off the stool. He grabbed my little finger and pulled me into the living room.

There was a bunch of plastic toys all over the floor. He sat down by a red box with different shaped holes in it. There was a triangle, a square, an oval, a star, and a bunch of other shapes. He started putting small plastic blocks with the same shapes into the holes.

"This is his favorite toy," said Linda. The TV was on, and Sandra was watching some cartoon with rabbits and strawberries that talked and had legs and arms. I sat down by Billy and helped him. He was trying to get the rectangle into the square hole.

"You almost got it. Try putting it in there," I said and pointed to the rectangle hole. He did, and it went in. He smiled at me and laughed. His cheeks was pink and looked so soft. I really wanted to touch them.

"Well, you want to learn how to fix a meal? Or should we save that for tomorrow?"

That sounded really hard, so I said, "I guess tomorrow. I need to get up to Johnnie's. He's waiting for me."

"Okay. Tomorrow, same time?"

I said okay and started to leave. I wasn't even to the door yet, and Billy started to cry. He held his arms out to me.

"He likes you. He doesn't want you to go. He'd like you to pick him up," said Linda.

I went back to Billy. He was still holding his arms out to me, but he'd stopped crying. I hadn't never picked a kid up before. But I'd seen other people do it, so I put my hands under his arms and lifted him. He smiled right away. Once I had him up in the air, I didn't know where to put him. I brought him over to my body,

and he put his legs around me, and I just held him next to me. He kinda wanted to slide down, so I put my other hand under his butt. It still felt like I was gonna drop him. But he put one arm on my shoulder, and I grabbed my left hand in my right hand to make a sort of seat for him. That worked.

He looked at my face. "Shay shay," he said. I liked this kid. His little body felt good in my arms.

"See Kay," I said.

"Shay shay."

I looked at Linda. She was smiling. "This'll be great. Maybe I can have you all trained by the end of the week. Then I can get out and do some shopping alone. What do you think?"

"I don't know how to cook. So, I'm kinda worried about that part."

"Oh, you don't really need to cook. Just open some jars and some cartons and boxes. That'll be good enough."

"Okay," I said. "I'll come back tomorrow." I handed Billy to her, and she talked to him and took him in by his toys so he wouldn't cry again when I left. When I got out into the yard, I was relieved to be out of there. But I was kind of excited about going back. I liked Billy.

———————

Well, it's true, man. Little boys have always liked me. They're so easy. They always want to do what I do, and they always do what I ask them to do. And they're soft and their bodies are small and firm. They just feel nice. Little girls got minds of their own. They don't like doing "boy" stuff, you know? Besides, they ain't got penises. Ha ha! You know what I mean? Maybe not. Shit.

Anyway, Billy was beautiful, man, and I was happy to get to know him. Sandra was a girl and just got in the way. But I'll get back to that later.

Johnnie was still my best friend, and we had to deal with this horrible thing I was talkin' about. Horrible. And man, it all seemed so unreal. This death stuff. Maybe when you're kids, you just don't get it, I don't know. It was a long time before I believed what hap-

pened. I was sure those guys in the ambulance would've got Harry breathin' again. Shit. They always did in the movies. I mean, why do they put them scenes in the movies if they ain't true?

———————

I walked up to Johnnie's house as fast as I could. I couldn't wait to tell him more about my new job.

Christine answered the door. She looked real serious and asked how I was doing. I said okay. She said Johnnie was in the living room reading and watching TV. I went in there. He had an old *Star Trek* episode on the TV. He was layin' on the couch, reading *Robin Hood* at the same time. He'd said *Robin Hood* was full of swords and bows and arrows, and he was really gettin' into those lately. He didn't hear me come in. So, I sneaked up behind the couch on my hands and knees and said "Boo!"

"Yaaaah!" he yelled and jumped up. As soon as he saw it was me, he smiled and laughed. "Geez, you scared me! The Sheriff of Nottingham was just sneaking up on Robin Hood—he was asleep in the forest. When did you come in?"

"Just now. I started my job this morning. Well sort of. She's not paying me yet, but she's teaching me what to do. I get a cooking lesson tomorrow. Today I learned how to take them to the bathroom. It's not too bad. Billy's cool."

"Yeah? Well, that's nice. When do you start making money?"

"Next week, I think. Maybe you could come help."

"That's okay. I don't like little kids a whole lot. I never know what to say to them."

"It's not hard. You just ask them about their toys and stuff like that."

"Oh. Well, that's good that you can do it. Want to go out to the castle? We could play Robin Hood. I'll get my swords and bow and arrows from my room."

He ran up to his room and brought down the bow and arrows and two swords his pa had bought him at a flea market in Chicago. His pa said they was ceremonial swords from the Knights of Columbus, whoever they were. The swords were cool, though,

with all kinds of pictures and Latin words engraved on 'em, and the edges wasn't sharp. But I think you could still stab someone with 'em. He handed me a sword and the quiver of arrows, and we raced out to the barn. I didn't run as fast as I could have, so it was a tie at the door. No one's cars was there, so we ran straight in. I still slowed down, though, cuz I remembered crashing with Mary. I hadn't seen Mary for a couple days. I was glad of that.

"Race you to the shaft!" said Johnnie, and we ran down the aisle, into the arena. We raced along the castle wall, and we each tried to get around the corner first. Instead we got there together. I was on the outside and put my arm across to touch the bales so he couldn't get through. But he ducked under my arm, so I tried to push him back. We started pushin' at each other and laughin' really hard. He tried getting around the corner first, but I wouldn't let him. So he tried to trip me. Then I tried to trip him. Finally, we fell down and just laughed. He made a high squeaky noise, and I guess I made a funny face, like I was askin', "What was that?" And he laughed at my face. Then he sort of honked when he laughed, and then I laughed so hard that I made a funny "hic hic" noise when I breathed in. Then he made the "What was that?" face, and we both laughed again. Then he started imitating me. Every time I made a funny noise, he tried to make the same noise, and it sounded so funny to hear what I sounded like, that I just about died laughin'. Of course, I'd make more funny noises then, and he'd imitate those, but sometimes he didn't imitate them very good, and they'd sound funnier than the noise I'd just made.

Finally, my sides hurt so bad, I could hardly catch my breath. I said, "Wait! Just wait!" And I turned away so I couldn't see him cuz just lookin' at his funny face made me laugh again. I needed to just breathe. I tried to take deep, slow breaths and not laugh. I could hear him doing the same. When I could breathe normal, and I felt calm, I turned around and looked at him. He tried to keep a straight face, but first his eyes smiled, and he held his lips tight so he wouldn't smile with his mouth, but none of that worked, and both our faces burst out laughin' again, except this time I imitated

his noises. It was crazy, and it went on forever. I didn't think my sides would ever stop hurtin'. But finally we just ran out of energy.

We went to the top of the castle, and Johnnie told me about some of the adventures in his *Robin Hood* book. We acted out some of them with the swords and bow and arrows. Later, Christine buzzed us on the barn intercom to come eat lunch, and we did. We played Nintendo after lunch and then rode our bikes down to the new freeway again. We sat under a tree and watched the big green bulldozers make the earth flat. When the bulldozer drivers took a coffee break, they called us over and let us sit in the drivers' seats. They was real nice. Then we rode our bikes all the way down to the river and back. Christine invited me for dinner. Leland was home for supper, and he seemed real grumpy, so we didn't talk to him much. I got to spend the night, and we went to sleep after we planned out our new castle. Johnnie thought the next cutting of hay would come in in a couple more weeks.

The next morning when Johnnie and I was eatin' breakfast, Leland was there, too. The four of us ate together—fruit and whole-wheat toast. It was good. I'd gotten to like it. Sometimes I missed Ma's eggs and bacon, but Christine said this was better for me.

Leland was drinking coffee and reading the newspaper. He said to Christine, "Yeah, it's here. Harold J. Johnson, twelve. Argus Funeral Home. Visitation today from 1:00 to 3:00 and 6:00 to 8:00. Funeral's tomorrow at 10:00. Want to go this afternoon or this evening?"

"I don't want to go at all, but we must. I wonder if they'll have an open casket."

"I don't know. I don't imagine too much damage was done. They'll probably have it open." Then Leland set his paper down and looked at Johnnie and me. He looked at me, then at Johnnie, then back and forth. He looked like he was trying to say somethin' but couldn't. I looked at his eyes each time he looked at me. They were always a little hard to see cuz his glasses was kinda thick.

He finally said, "C.K., have you ever been to a wake?"

I shook my head no. "What's a wake?"

"It's where they have the deceased person laid out in his coffin. It's a way for everyone to say a final good bye. It's also a way to help everyone realize that the dead person really is gone."

I said, "I can't believe he's gone. I keep thinking they must've brought him back to life in the ambulance."

Leland looked real sad and real serious. "C.K., they didn't. Harry was trapped under the water for at least an hour. People can rarely be brought back after that long, unless the water is very, very cold, which this isn't."

"Johnnie," his pa asked, "what did you think? Did you think they brought him back, too?"

Johnnie was trying to stab a green grape with his fork, and it always scooted away. "Um, I don't know. I thought they might try, and I kind of hoped they would bring him back. But I guess I knew he probably couldn't live. He was in the water too long." He held the grape down with one finger and stabbed it. He looked up at me. "I guess we just never talked about it." Then he looked at his pa and shrugged.

"What are your parents' plans, C.K.? Are they going to the wake today?"

I had no idea. I hadn't talked to my mom except to ask if I could stay over last night. I said, "I don't know if they can get off work. Maybe they'll go tonight."

"Well, it would probably be best if you two were there together. Chris? Is tonight okay?"

She said, "That's fine. Maybe I better call Gloria to see if that's her plan. I have her work number."

Johnnie and I didn't like this conversation, so we went back out to the barn. We was about to climb up the castle when I remembered.

"Johnnie, I forgot! Linda Boggus thinks I'm comin' at 10:00. What time is it?"

He looked at his watch. "Nine fifty-five."

"I gotta go. I'll come back." I ran out of the arena and down to Boggus's.

20

Iwould say C.K.'s interest in children began that summer when Linda Boggus introduced him to her kids and hired him to baby-sit. I was puzzled by his attraction to children, and this attraction was evident from the beginning of his babysitting career. The loss of his parents, the loss of his childhood, the loss of Harry, and then the temporary loss of me somehow solidified his preference for connecting with children. I understand that part of it. He was clinging to his own childhood, and one of the most natural ways to accomplish that was to spend time with children. The sexual exploitation is another issue that took me years to comprehend and even now is somewhat elusive to me in that I cannot relate to sexual pleasure with a child, although from a psychological perspective, it makes perfect sense. If one is only comfortable relating to chil-dren and one is also a sexual being, then that person is most com-fortable expressing him or herself sexually with children. Doing so with adults makes the person uneasy. He is simply more comfort-able doing *every*thing with children.

I've often wondered if he would have gone over the edge had he not lost me at that very crucial time.

———————

I guess we were really trying to *not* think about looking at Harry dead in a coffin later that day. Actually, I didn't mind that he was dead so much because now I didn't have to worry about him popping up in all my special places. But it was horrible because I'd actually seen someone die—sort of. I mean, I didn't get to actually watch him die, but almost. I thought it was really pretty interest-ing. I mean, I knew this kid, and I knew him while he was alive and talking and thinking and still warm. And then I watched him go under the water, and then that warm, alive kid died. And now

there was no life in him. Where did it go? He was just flesh and bones and blood that didn't move anymore, and he was probably cold. His brain didn't work anymore, and his eyes couldn't see, and he couldn't feel or move. He couldn't hear, I guess. Maybe he could. I wondered if they ever tested the hearing on dead people.

But this was pretty neat stuff. I mean, I knew that it was awful and horrible, and Harry's mother and brothers were pretty sad, but I wasn't sad. I sure wouldn't miss him. I wondered if C.K. was sad. I don't think he liked him much either, but he did a little bit. More than I did, that's for sure. I wondered if it would be weird to talk to C.K. about this, about how Harry was alive and now he's dead. I mean, we could talk about what "dead" is. Like, I wondered what was the last thing to go, like hearing, maybe. Could Harry still hear at the very end? Or did all his senses go at the same time?

When C.K. got back from Boggus's, we went back out to the castle. We sat on the edge of the shaft with our legs hanging down.

"How was the cooking lesson?" I asked. I couldn't help giggling.

"It ain't really cookin'. I just gotta open some cans and jars and packages of crackers and make Sandra a peanut butter and jelly sandwich. It ain't bad. Linda said I can come for one more lesson on toys and changing their clothes, and then she'll let me start the job."

He seemed real happy. But I'd been thinking about what it's like to die, and I wanted to ask C.K. about it. But he was so happy about his job. I didn't know how to get started on the dying subject. So, I just waited.

"That kid, Billy, really likes me," he said, looking at me with a sparkle.

"That's nice. What about the girl?"

"Sandra. She's all right. She talks to her doll a lot and makes the doll talk back. She wanted me to have a tea party with her and the doll. I sorta did, but it seemed real dumb."

"What if she wants you to have a tea party every time?"

"I don't know. I'll just have to find a good TV show for her to watch, I guess."

I waited a few seconds, then I asked, "Have you thought about Harry much?"

He didn't say anything for a minute. "Yeah, a little. It's just hard to believe."

"Well, you might think this is weird," I said and laughed a little, "but I've been thinking about dying."

"Geez! You're not going to go and die on me, too, are you?" he joked.

"No. I mean, I've been thinking about what it must be like to die." I looked at him to see if he thought this was weird, but he looked like he was thinking about it too. So I went on. "I mean, it was so weird to be with Harry alive, and then an hour later, he was dead. I've been thinking about what it must have been like—for Harry. I mean, did everything blank out at the same time? Or was one thing left at the end—like touch or his hearing? What did he think about while he was dying? Or could he even think? Do you wonder about that?"

"I guess not. Mostly, I don't wanna think about it. Who knows if he could think or not? Or hear or feel? I guess I hope he couldn't."

C.K. didn't think this was as interesting as I did. Maybe because he liked Harry and they were cousins. Maybe my mom would talk to me about it. She probably would. But I'd probably have to wait a few days, or a few weeks because she was all upset about Harry, too.

C.K. said, "What do you think about goin' to the wake?"

"I haven't thought about that at all," I said. "Why? What do you think about it?"

"I don't like it, the whole idea. Why do we have to go look at him dead? Then, I'll have to think about him dead. I'd rather just think about him alive, fishin' and bein' happy."

I thought about him alive and how he had kicked and punched Tucker and how he'd sweet-talked my mom, and how he'd called me "wimp" and said C.K. and I were gay together. I didn't like him alive. But I wondered how I'd think about him when I saw him dead. I didn't want to go, either.

"Maybe we don't have to go," I said. "Do you think we can just stay home and let our parents go?"

He looked brighter. "Yeah. I like that idea."

I said, "I think my mom and dad *think* we should go. How can we get out of it?"

"Say we're sick? Disappear just before it's time to leave?" he laughed.

"I don't know. Let's go in the house and see what kind of mood they're in. Maybe we can just tell them we don't want to go." So, we went in the house. My mom was putting lunch out on the porch table, and she said she'd just buzzed us on the barn intercom.

My dad came and sat down. He had an open magazine in his hand and read it while he waited for my mom to bring the food. C.K. and I looked at each other. He made a funny face at me, and I giggled. Then I stuck my tongue out at him and flapped my elbows. He laughed, and we just started giggling.

"What's so funny, fellas?" my dad asked. He set his magazine down and looked at us. He looked tired.

We were still giggling. "Do we have to go to the wake?" I looked at C.K., and he made another goofy face, real quick so my dad wouldn't see. It made me laugh more. "We really don't want to go see Harry dead." I couldn't help laughing. I don't know why. C.K. was trying not to laugh, but he couldn't help it either. He tapped my leg with his foot under the table.

My dad folded his arms and leaned back in his chair. He just watched us, like we were monkeys at the zoo or something. I tried to tap C.K. back under the table, but I missed and kicked the table leg. The table jiggled hard and I said "Ow!" Our two glasses of milk almost spilled. "Oops!" I said, and we both burst out laughing. My dad kept watching.

"I know you guys don't know how to deal with this."

I made some funny noise, and said, "Huh?" and C.K. couldn't control himself and started with his "hic hic" sound. It was just too much. I thought I was going to burst.

"Maybe you boys should excuse yourselves until you get things under control, and then we'll talk about the wake," my dad said.

We jumped up from the table and ran into the living room. I thought it would be such a relief to get away and just let ourselves laugh, but once we got away from my dad, it wasn't hard to stop laughing. We took deep breaths, and we were fine.

"Come eat!" my mom called.

"You okay?" I asked him. He shrugged and nodded, so we went back and sat down. She'd put bread and tomato and lettuce and avocado slices and cheese out for us to make our own sandwiches, so we concentrated on that. C.K. couldn't get a slice of tomato to stay on top of his cheese and lettuce, and every time he went to put the bread on top, the tomato slice slid off. We giggled some more about that.

My dad said, "So, what do you think this wake will be like, Johnnie?"

"I suppose like Grandpa's. He'll just be lying there, and people will go and look at him and cry, and then everyone will leave. Oh, and there'll be a lot of hugging going on." I gave one little laugh.

"What about you, C.K.? What do you expect?"

C.K. thought a minute. "Yeah, the same thing Johnnie just said."

"Okay," my dad said slowly. "Do you have any idea what it is that you think will be so unpleasant? People crying? Seeing someone you knew who is now dead? What do you think? What's the worst thing you think could happen there?"

"I know," I said, getting ready to laugh again. "We'll be standing there looking at Harry in the coffin, and his eyes will suddenly open, and he'll say 'Ha ha! I fooled ya!' Then he'll sit up, and everyone will be happy and go home." I giggled a little more.

But my dad and C.K. didn't laugh. And then C.K. started to cry. "I just don't want to see him dead, that's all," he said, and tears came pouring out his eyes.

My dad held his arms out and said, "Come here, C.K.," and C.K. sort of flew over to my dad and landed in his lap. He cried for a while in my dad's shoulder. My dad gave him a napkin to wipe his face and blow his nose, and then he just hugged him some more.

C.K. stopped crying, but he stayed sitting there with his head on my dad's shoulder.

"It's very, very sad, isn't it?" my dad said. C.K. nodded. "And I imagine it's also scary. This is the first time either of you has experienced this sort of thing, and you just don't know what to expect. It would be a lot easier to just not go. Me too. I'd really rather not go. But you know what? They don't have these wakes and funerals for no reason. There are actually some very good reasons to have them. Want to know what they are?" C.K. nodded again, but he didn't lift his head up.

"Well, wakes and funerals take care of two important things when someone dies—denial and grieving. Do you know what denial is?" C.K. shrugged. "It's when you choose to believe that something didn't happen. It's much *easier* to believe it didn't happen. If we can believe it didn't happen, then we're happier. But only for a little while because the truth—reality—will hit us one way or another eventually. By going to the wake or the funeral and seeing that the person really is dead, it's healthier for our minds. We no longer play a game with ourselves. It's kind of painful right then, but if we get the pain over with right away, then we can go on with our lives. If we put the pain off for a later time, then we fight it and fight it, and then it hits us eventually anyway, so why not just get it over with right away and go on? See what I mean?"

"Yeah," C.K. whispered and nodded. He looked like he was four years old, sitting in my dad's lap with his head on my dad's shoulder, all curled up and needing to be hugged.

My dad went on. "As for grieving, well that's necessary, too. It's normal to be sad about what happened. If we can let ourselves be sad for a while, then we sort of get through that, too, and go on with our own lives. Some people grieve longer than others. The people who were closest to Harry and depended on him for things will grieve longer than the ones who didn't know him as well. Grieving is just letting ourselves be sad.

"So, going to the wake and seeing that Harry really has died—you might even want to touch him and feel that the life has gone out of him. He'll feel cold and not like himself at all. So, if

258

you go and see that he really has died, then you probably won't get trapped in a state of denial. You won't allow yourself to play that game with yourself—because you would just suffer later instead of now.

"All of us who knew and cared about Harry will suffer because he left us, and we feel sort of cheated by that. Some of us might even feel angry at him for leaving us, as strange as that might sound. But it's true. This is especially true for children who lose a mother or father. They get kind of mad at the mother or father for going off and leaving them when they needed them so badly. See what I mean?" C.K. nodded.

"I don't know just what your feelings are or were for Harry, but you might think about what I just said. It might help. Johnnie, does that any make sense to you?"

It did, and I said, "Yes. But I'd still rather not go."

"I know. Like I said, no one wants to go because we know it will be sad and painful. But we do it and know that it's the best thing for our hearts and our minds to go and get it over with. Can you guys try and be extra strong for one day and help each other through this?"

C.K. peeked over his shoulder at me. I looked at his eyes and smiled a little. "Yeah," I said. And he nodded. My dad gave C.K. one hard squeeze and let him sit back in his chair. My mom had already sat down.

"I've got some great homemade tapioca pudding for dessert," she said. "You guys finish your sandwiches, and you can have some." She made the most wonderful, fluffy, delicious tapioca pudding. It wasn't from a can or a box, but she made it in a big pan and beat up egg whites and put them in. It was the best.

I think C.K. and I both felt better. We ate our sandwiches and gobbled down two dishes of pudding.

We took another bike ride out to the men on the bulldozers, but they weren't on any more coffee breaks. They did wave to us, though. On the way back, C.K. went to his house, and I went home alone. We had to take showers and change into good clothes for the wake.

My parents picked up Mrs. Bookout and C.K. so we could all go to the wake together. My parents sat in the front, and Mrs. Bookout and C.K. got in the back with me. Everyone was dressed up, and I was glad to see Mrs. Bookout had made C.K. wear a tie.

C.K. sat in the middle of the seat, and we were kind of scrunched together. I looked at him once, and he looked at me. He looked stiff, and I probably did too. We didn't know what to say to each other. My dad was driving.

"How's Marge doing?" my mom turned around and asked Mrs. Bookout.

Mrs. Bookout looked sort of mad at my mom. "Not the greatest. She's been trying to reach her ex-husband—Harry's father—but she hasn't been able to. Not that he'd care. Or come."

"This is so tragic," my mom said, turning back around. And then no one knew what to say, so we were all quiet until we got to the funeral home. People, all dressed up, were going in and out. Three women about my mom's age were standing together, hugging each other and crying. I got a sick feeling and really didn't want to go in there. Somehow this seemed a lot different than when my grandpa died.

C.K. asked his mother, "Who are they?"

Mrs. Bookout said, "I have no idea. They may not be here for Harry. I think there's two or three wakes going on at the same time."

"You mean there's two or three dead people all in there together?" he asked, kinda loud.

"Yeah, I think so. But each one is in a different room."

That made it seem a little better. I didn't feel quite so nervous. I followed my mom and dad up the steps. C.K. walked next to me, and Mrs. Bookout was right behind C.K. We walked in the door, and it seemed sort of like a church. A man in a suit asked my parents who we'd come to visit. My mom told him, and he motioned us to the room on the left. Outside the door there was a black sign with white letters. It said, "Harrry J. Johnson." Next to it there was a wooden stand with an open book on it. My mom and dad signed

their names in it. My dad said C.K. and I should sign it, too. I wanted C.K. to go first, but he backed away.

"No, you go first," he said.

So, I took the pen and wrote my name in cursive. It was kind of squiggly looking, and I wanted to write it over again, but I decided it would look bad to scratch it out and print it, so I left it. I watched C.K. write his name, but he must have seen what a mess I made and printed it from the beginning. As soon as Mrs. Bookout signed her name, we all walked into the room. I looked in there first, and at the back I could see a long, shiny, brown wooden box with the lid open. People were standing in front of it, so I couldn't see Harry. There were flowers all around the coffin, and it smelled funny—kind of sweet.

My parents stopped and turned to us. The five of us stood in a little circle. There was a bunch of chairs lined up between us and the coffin, sort of like people were going to watch a movie or something. I wondered why they were there. Were we supposed to all sit in the audience and just look at Harry? I looked at the coffin again. Someone was standing right in front of Harry's head, but I could see his hands folded on his chest. It looked like he had a suit on, too. I nudged C.K.

"It looks like Harry had to dress up, too." I started to laugh at my own joke, but C.K. only smiled a little and wouldn't look at me.

My mom and dad were nervous and looked around like they were trying to decide what to do. We heard some loud sobs and looked over and saw Marge hugging a skinny woman. I think I had seen the skinny woman with that little kid who had the birthday party at the roller rink. Marge had tears running down her face, and the other woman was trying to comfort her. Mrs. Bookout turned toward them and waited like she was going to go up to Marge next. Pretty soon the skinny woman patted Marge on the back and walked out the door. Then Mrs. Bookout went up to her. They hugged each other, and Marge put her face in Mrs. Bookout's neck and cried. Two men who looked kinda young were standing there. I figured they were two of Harry's brothers.

After a while, Mrs. Bookout and Marge came apart, and Mrs. Bookout motioned for my mom and dad to come over. My mother went over to her with her arms out. Mrs. Bookout could barely introduce them when my mom put her arms around Marge and started crying herself. She kept saying, "I'm sorry. I'm so sorry. I wish I had known about the peat. This is so terrible. You must hate us so much. I wish there were something we could do. I feel so terrible. You poor lady." My mom really sort of flaked out. My dad had his arm on her back and was rubbing it.

"Take it easy, Chris." He put his hand up on the top of her shoulder and sort of tried to pull her away from Marge. "Chris. Chris, you know we'll get together with Marge after the funeral tomorrow." But my mom didn't want to let go of Marge, and she kept saying she was sorry. Marge looked like she didn't know what to do with my mom and had to sort of wiggle away from her. My mom backed away, but she held onto Marge's hand. My dad put his arm around my mom's waist and held her away from Marge, but my mom still wouldn't let go of her hand.

He said, "Marge, I wish we could have talked before this, and I realize now is not the time, either. But we want you to know we'll give you whatever support you need. We feel terrible. 'Terrible' isn't a strong enough word. I don't know what to say. There are no words."

Marge just stood there with tears in her eyes and listened to him. She looked extra tired and sad. She had a black dress on that was real tight around her butt. She had her hair in some kind of bun. Then my dad shrugged and leaned over and gave her a hug himself. "Whatever we can do," he said and pulled my mom completely away from Marge so that my mom had to let go of Marge's hand. Then, some man and woman, who were on Marge's other side, started talking to her and hugging her, so she turned away from my parents. C.K. and I stood close together and watched everybody.

My mom took some tissues out of her purse and gave a couple to Mrs. Bookout. The two of them wiped their tears away. The three adults stood together, and C.K. and I stood off to the side.

My mom and Mrs. Bookout were taking deep breaths and trying to control themselves. Finally, the three of them looked at us.

My dad said, "Well, let's say our good-byes to Harry, and then we can leave." This was the part I was dreading, and zings shot through my stomach. C.K. and I looked at each other and stood closer together. I wanted to hang onto his arm, but I didn't dare. Harry would think we were queer for sure.

My mom led the way behind the back row of chairs and around to the right side of the room. There was a line in front of the coffin, and it was moving kind of slow. My dad got in front of me, right behind my mom. I tried looking ahead of my mom to see if I could see Harry, but someone was always in the way.

Just before the coffin there was a table with a bunch of Harry's stuff. Someone had put his baseball jacket on a hanger on a stand at the back of the table. And there was a fishing pole on the table and some pictures of Harry holding up fish on his fishing line. There was a Mother's Day card he'd made with crayons that said, "I love you, Mom" in different colors. Some baseball cards were there, and so were some car parts—spark plugs, some wires, a big, greasy-looking thing about the size of a soft ball, and some tools. These made me sad.

Then, there he was, lying there in his suit. Someone had put one of his hands on top of the other hand on his chest. At first, he looked like he was pretending to sleep. But then, I could see that his mouth was closed kind of tight and it was sorta stretched out too far, so it didn't really look like him. Someone had cut his hair and combed it to one side. He looked so neat and proper. But he looked kind of waxy and a funny color, like he was really pale, and someone had put pink stuff on his cheeks and forehead. I looked real closely to see if he was breathing, but there was absolutely no movement.

C.K. and I stood with our arms touching, like when we were on the island after Harry fell through the hole. We just stared. Then C.K. reached out and put two fingers on Harry's hand. He turned and looked at me with his eyes big. "Wow. He really is cold."

I wanted to touch him, too, sort of. I started to put my hand out and was about to touch Harry's hand when a lady's voice said, "Hello, C.K. Hello, Johnnie." We looked to our right, behind us, and there was Miss Bernice from Little Friends. I looked up at her and felt like someone hit me in the chest with a big hammer. Then, another head poked around Miss Bernice and said, "Hi, fellas. How're ya doin'?" It was Mary.

All I remember is that I started screaming. One horrible loud scream after another. I couldn't make it stop. The room got all blurry and fuzzy. As soon as my breath ran out, I'd scream again. I felt so afraid, it was like my brain was trying to go into my body to hide. And then it was dark.

The next thing I knew, I was in a bed. I felt very heavy. I tried to lift my hand, but I couldn't. I tried to move my legs, but they wouldn't move, either.

PART THREE

21

That was quite a goddammed summer, man. My first experi-ence with death. My first pal. And the first time I got to see somebody flip out. I mean, for real. Shit, man, that was scary. I always knew there was something kinda weird about Johnnie, the way he spaced out all those times. But this time, at Harry's wake, it was full-out, full-fledged crazy. It was like I'd lost two friends at the same time. Shit. One had died, and the other might as well have. Yeah, the angel and the devil. Both gone—poof!—all in a matter of two days.

Here we was, lookin' at dead Harry and thinkin' about death and not believing it was for real, and then Johnnie just sorta died too. Not really. I mean his heart didn't stop or nothin'. He just sorta left. Went somewhere else—all in his head. Damn.

I was standing in front of the coffin, lookin' at Harry. There he was, dead. I could see that he looked dead, but it sure was hard to believe. He didn't look like himself. He looked stiff, and his lips looked like they wasn't his. I watched his chest to see if he was breathin', and I watched his nose to see if air was goin' in and out. I was sure I could see a little movement. But I guess it was my imagi-nation. Then I remembered what Leland had said about touching Harry so I could tell the life was gone out of him. I did that. I put two fingers on Harry's hand, and he *was* cold. Then I knew, just like Leland said—I could feel that there was no life there.

Johnnie was right next to me, and I was glad, except he seemed kinda weird about death. I mean, he'd been talking about whether dead people can still hear and stuff like that. I thought about that, though, and I thought about tryin' to say somethin' to Harry just in case he really could still hear. And then I wondered

if Harry's spirit was floating right above us all. I figured it was, so either way, if I said somethin', he'd probably hear me. I wanted to tell him that we tried to save him, that I'd tied a rope to his tackle box and threw it down the hole for him to grab, and why didn't he grab it? Why didn't he come back up through the hole? I'd reached my arm way down there, but he never took it. Why didn't he?

And then Johnnie starts screamin'. I mean screamin' like somebody was tryin' to kill him. And then I saw why. There was Mary and Miss Bernice—together. I felt like screamin', too, but I couldn't cuz I was too busy watchin' Johnnie.

He was screamin', "Don't kill the baby! Don't kill the baby!" He was screamin' at Miss Bernice and Mary. They had Bibles in their hands and necklaces with big crosses. Miss Bernice's four kids was there, and they was all holdin' Bibles, too. They looked spooky—their faces, like they was actors in some horror movie. The kids stared at Johnnie, and their faces was just blank. And Mary and Miss Bernice smiled at Johnnie and watched him. He was jumpin' up and down, sort of like he did at the pond that day when Christine threw the blue ball in the water for Tucker.

I wanted to do somethin'. I stood in front of him and put my hand on his shoulder. I tried to get right in front of his eyes so he would look at me, but he looked right through me at the two teachers.

Leland ran over and tried to hold Johnnie, but Johnnie fought his pa and pointed at Miss Bernice and Mary and kept screamin', "Don't let them kill the baby! Don't let them kill the baby!"

Miss Bernice smiled at Leland and said, "Is there anything we can do?"

That's when Christine jumped right in front of Miss Bernice. She was taller than Miss Bernice, and she had her fists up and almost ran over her. She yelled at her, "Yes! Yes! Get out of here! You witch! Get out of here! Don't you think you've done enough damage!" Then she looked around at all the people in the room and yelled at them. "Someone get this woman out of here! She's a witch! She's a murderer!" But no one did anything. They just stood there and watched.

Finally, the guy who talked to us when we came in rushed over and asked Leland, "What's going on here?"

Leland was still tryin' to hold Johnnie, who was still screamin' about a baby. But Leland was pretty calm. He said to the man, "I think you ought to get this woman out of here. She's the one who ran Little Friends. Bad stuff went on there, and some of these kids still remember. Please. Get her out of here. And I now get it that *that* one was involved, too," he said, pointing at Mary.

I didn't think that Johnnie's parents knew about Mary. Actually, I was sure they didn't know about Mary or they wouldn't have been so nice to her. Mary only came to Little Friends once in a while. She wasn't a regular teacher. But I kinda thought they knew about Miss Bernice and Jack, but I was never sure. Until now.

And I knew why Johnnie was so upset. Sort of. I mean, there was no baby there now. But I remember the time in the basement at Little Friends. They had this one guy in a coffin. He was dead. I don't know who he was or nothin', and I think he'd been dead for a long time. And all the little kids was standin' around singin' the songs. And then Mary came in with this little baby. The baby was real little and didn't smile or nothin'. It seemed like it couldn't look at anything, like it couldn't focus its eyes. Mary was real happy and explained to the children that a nice lady in a big store in Chicago had given her the baby to give to Satan. The lady knew that Satan would be so pleased with the gift that he would do wonderful things for the lady and for all of us children. This was the most special gift we could give Satan because it was so young and had just come from God. And now it was our job to deliver the gift to Satan. That's when we all had to stab the baby with the screw driver.

But I don't know why Johnnie thought there was a baby here now. But he sure acted like there was one. He was *still* screamin'. Leland picked him up, and Johnnie kicked and pushed on his pa to let him down.

Christine yelled at the funeral home man, "Aren't you going to do something?"

The man stood there and looked at Johnnie and Leland and then at Miss Bernice and Mary. Miss Bernice said to him, "I know these people. They're a couple of the social workers who have caused us so much trouble. Would you please ask them to leave?"

I really wanted to say something then. You know, to let the funeral home man know that Christine and Leland were right. I started to, and then Bernice looked right into my eyes and pushed me back—just with her eyes. I started feelin' scared then and looked at my ma. I knew if I said anything, Bernice would kill my ma and burn our house down. So I didn't say a word.

Leland said to Christine, "Let's get him out of here," and he started walkin' out of the room, holding Johnnie in his arms like a baby. Johnnie was still kickin' and screamin'. I looked at Christine. She looked like she was gonna punch Miss Bernice. She was breathin' real hard right in Miss Bernice's face, and she had her fists all tight.

Christine turned to the funeral home man and said, "You're an idiot!" Then she turned to all the other people in the room. She pointed at Miss Bernice and screamed. "You're all idiots!" Finally, she turned to my ma and said, "Why don't you believe what happened? You better get C.K. out of here." Then she ran after Leland and Johnnie, and we could all hear Johnnie screamin' as they went out of the building.

For a long time, the whole room was real quiet, and no one moved. Then Miss Bernice turned to my ma and said, "That poor child. We tried to tell them the boy was schizophrenic, but they just wouldn't believe us." Then she put her arm around me. "How are you doing, C.K.? It's good to see you. I'm so sorry about your cousin. What a terrible thing. I understand you tried to save Harry. I can't believe the Ambrose's let you boys play in such a dangerous place." Then she said to my ma, "Can you believe they let the boys play there?"

My ma looked real confused. She smiled at Miss Bernice and tried to be friendly, but then it was as if her face just wouldn't let her smile anymore, and she whispered to me, "C.K., let's go." We hurried out of the room and went out the front door. We went

down a couple steps. Then my ma stopped. "Wait. We don't have a way to get home. Do you see the Ambrose's car out here?" We looked out in the parking lot, but their car was gone. So, we just stood there on the steps. My ma turned one way and then another. She started to go down the steps, and then she came back up them, and then she just stood still. I could tell she didn't want to go back into the funeral home.

"Let's wait until someone comes out. Someone'll give us a ride home." She kept winding the long strap on her purse around her fingers and then unwinding it again. She kept doing this, and we just stood there and waited. It seemed like a real long time. Other people came walkin' through the parkin' lot and went in, but no one came out. Then, who do we see comin' through the parking lot? Pa.

"Pa!" I yelled. I was so happy to see him. I ran to him, and I hoped he would pick me up and hold me like he used to. But then, I didn't want to run into his chest, so I slowed down. I tried to see if he was going to pick me up or not. He had a suit on and looked real nice. He looked surprised to see me runnin' at him, and he started to put his arms out. So I speeded up. I got to him and felt his big hands go around my ribs, then up, up I went. I wrapped my legs around his waist, and he held me to him. I hugged him as hard as I could.

"Hey, boy. You're gettin' too big for this." But I hung onto his shoulders and hugged his neck.

Ma came up to us. "There's weird stuff going on in there. Leland and Christine just had to carry Johnnie out cuz he was screamin' and carryin' on so bad. Miss Bernice and Mary showed up. I think Leland and Christine really believe they did that bad stuff to the kids at the daycare center."

Pa didn't say nothin' to Ma. But he whispered to me, "Okay, son. Get down now. You're too big for this." He set me on my feet.

Ma said, "I really think you ought to talk to Leland about it. Johnnie's been going to a counselor all this time. Maybe C.K. should go."

"He don't need no counselor," Pa said in his quiet, calm way. "Johnnie's just a strange kid. You think Bernice would be out and about if she was guilty?"

Ma shrugged and still looked worried. "They did put Jack in jail. Johnnie was screamin' somethin' about them killin' a baby. That's what that one article said about that daycare in California. I really think you ought to talk to Leland." She had her hands on her hips, and she looked at Pa real serious.

Pa waved his hand. "Hog wash. People don't do stuff like that." He started to walk toward the funeral home. He turned back around to Ma. "I just come to pay my respects."

"Can you give us a ride home? We came with the Ambrose's, and they left," she said.

"Yeah, I'll give you a ride. You comin' back in?"

"No. I don't want to. No one's come out of there for a while. We'll wait in the truck. Tell Marge to call me when she gets home, okay?"

Pa handed her the keys and walked into the funeral home. We went and got in the truck. We sat there for a long time. Then Ma looked at me. "Well? What did happen there?"

I wouldn't dare look at her. "Nothin'," I said.

"Well, then what's wrong with Johnnie? Why was he saying all that stuff?"

"I don't know," I said.

———

Pa never did believe it. I think Ma did, but shit, she didn't know what to do. A bunch of parents sued the board of directors of Little Friends and got money for their kids to go to college. Shit, I didn't get nothin'. I didn't want to go to college anyway, so it didn't matter. And then, oh, I don't know, five years later or so, they let Jack out of jail. He was supposed to be in for life. But fuck, they let him out. On a technicality. Wish my lawyers'd find a technicality for me. Damn. That Jack done worse stuff than I ever done. Five years and bam—out, free. Me—well, you know where I'm headed. Jack killed kids. Babies, really. I suppose there must've been three

or four of 'em that I remember. Babies don't know nothin'. Probably don't feel much, either. What I did was different. Entirely different. Jack and Bernice was real criminals. What I did was out of love. There's a fucking world of difference. Jack's the one deserves the lethal injection, not me. And shit, that fucker went free.

———

The next day we went back for the funeral. Now I saw what all them chairs was for. People sat and listened to a minister, just like in church. Except here there was a coffin and dead Harry. After the minister was done, we all had to walk past Harry one last time. I looked at him once more, and he looked the same as last night—just dead. Miss Bernice and Mary wasn't there. Maybe they was afraid to come back again in case there was more kids like Johnnie.

Johnnie and his parents didn't come neither. I called Johnnie when we got back from the wake the day before, but no one answered. My ma called in the morning, and no one answered then, either.

Later, after the funeral and we was finishin' supper, the phone rang. My ma answered it and only talked for a few minutes. It was mostly, "Oh" and "Oh, really?" and "That's awful" and "Yeah, let's talk about it more sometime," and "Yes, let us know." Then she said, "I'll tell C.K. you called and that maybe he can visit him in a couple weeks." I knew it must be Christine or Leland about Johnnie.

My ma came back to the table and sat down. She sighed a big sigh and looked at me. "Johnnie's in a hospital. A mental hospital."

I gulped. I thought, Wow! He really did go crazy. At first I felt kinda bad for him, and then I decided I didn't trust him no more. I sorta imagined he'd turned into some kind of monster. Now that I thought about it, that's how he seemed when his pa carried him out of the funeral parlor. Freaky.

"Christine said maybe you could go see him in a couple weeks."

I thought, Geez! What if he turns into some psycho or something and tries to kill me? I imagined his black curly hair turning long and straight, and his muscles gettin' real big and his eyes all bulgy. Then he'd roar or make some other horrible animal sound. I shivered and tried to make the thoughts go away. I just knew, though, that I didn't like the idea of going to some looney bin to visit nobody. Even Johnnie

"Do you know why he screamed like that?" Ma asked. "What was he talkin' about, killin' a baby?"

"Got me. He's always been a little weird. I mean, I like him, and he's my best friend. But he does strange stuff sometimes."

"Yeah? Like what?"

I wasn't sure I should be telling my ma all of this. She might use it against me. Right now, she was actin' real nice and calm. She seemed interested in this. Kinda like Christine. So, I decided to tell her just a little.

"Well, he gets a little spaced-out sometimes."

"So do you. What do you mean?"

"I don't know. He sorta blanks out, and you can't talk to him. It's like his mind is somewhere else."

She went "Hmm," and didn't ask any more questions. She sat and looked out the window.

The phone rang again. Ma got it. "Sure. Just a second." She handed it to me.

I was afraid it might be Johnnie, and I didn't want to talk to him when he was crazy. I leaned back, away from the phone. But Ma gave me an evil look, like I better take it. So, I did and slowly put it to my ear. I looked at Ma. I couldn't tell by her face who it was. It kinda wished it was Harry.

"Hello?" I sorta whispered.

"Hi, C.K. This is Linda Boggus. I was wondering if you'd like to try sitting tomorrow morning. It'll just be Billy. Only for about an hour and a half. Sandra has a doctor's appointment, and I need to go grocery shopping. Would you be able to come at nine thirty?"

She sounded so happy. I was glad to hear from her. "Oh, hi!" I said. "Yes, I could come then."

"Okay. See you at nine thirty. Thanks!" She sounded so cheerful that I couldn't wait till morning.

Ma was pretty nice the rest of the evening. She was on the phone a lot, and I watched television and went to bed early.

In the morning it felt funny not to call Johnnie or go up there. But it didn't bother me for too long cuz I had my job to go to, and I was looking forward to seein' Billy.

When I got to the Boggus's, Linda was in a hurry. She was going out the door kinda fast, and she said I should just play with Billy and take him to the bathroom if he wanted to go. She said there was juice and crackers if he wanted them. Then she left.

Billy was on the living room floor with his box and shapes. He had the square shape in his hand and was looking for the right hole. I waited till he found it and plunked it into the box. Then I said, "Hi, Billy! It's me, C.K."

He looked up at me and smiled. "Shay shay," he said.

I sat down with him and helped him with the shapes. I pretended to try to get the triangle into the round hole. I pretended that I just didn't understand why it wouldn't go in. He laughed. I pushed and turned and pretended to pound it in, and he laughed harder. Then I tried to put it in the oval hole. He thought that was funny too, so I did the same thing, trying to force it in. He just kept laughin'. So, I gave the triangle piece to him. He tried putting it in the moon shape. And then he tried to imitate me. I was impressed. I thought this kid must be pretty smart. So, I laughed at him. Then he laughed at me laughin' at him. What a neat kid, I thought. Finally, he watched me as he put the triangle in the triangle hole. I acted so surprised when it went in, I thought he was gonna die laughin'. We did all the rest of the shapes like that, and then he went and got a book. It was called *The Little Red Car*. He gave it to me. Then he took my hand and led me to his ma's rockin' chair.

I sat down and he climbed into my lap. I put my arm around him, and he leaned his little body against my chest. He felt nice and warm and cuddly. I began reading to him, and he pointed to the pictures and helped me read. He pointed to Jason, the boy, and he pointed to Jenny, and he pointed to the little red car. When

we was all done, he said, "Again?" so I read it all over again. This time, he leaned his head back against me and just listened. I think he liked the way I read to him. And I liked him.

He never had to go to the bathroom, and he never asked for nothin' to eat or drink. Linda came home before fifteen minutes had passed. At least, that's what it seemed like. She said she was sorry for taking two hours instead of one and a half. She handed me two dollars and said she'd call me again in a few days.

It was over, just like that. I was bummed to leave, and when I walked out on the road and went past their front window, Billy was standin' there wavin' at me. I waved back real hard. He smiled and jumped up and down. I stopped for just a minute and waved some more. Then I felt stupid, so I kept goin'.

I walked down the road and thought about Johnnie and wished he was home like usual and I could go there and play. I thought about goin' to the castle by myself, and I even stopped and turned around to go back up there. Then I thought I'd save that for another day, and I turned back around and walked towards home. What would I do all day? Ma'd left for work. Pa, if he even came home, wouldn't get there till after four.

I heard a rumbling sound behind me, the sound of a car coming. I could hear the thumping clap-clap sound as it went over the bridge. I turned to see who it was. It was Ken Jenkins. I jumped off the road so he could speed by. He did speed by, and then he slowed down after he passed me. He stopped completely and backed up. He backed all the way to me and rolled down the window. He had long dark hair and a red bandana around his head. He had a short beard and looked dirty, kind of like my cousin Skip. He had on a dark blue tee shirt and jeans.

He said, "Hey. You C.K. Bookout?"

I nodded and said, "Yeah."

"I hear your cousin drownded over at Ambrose's place. Was you there, man?"

"Yes. I tried to help save him."

"Damn! What happened, man? Did that Ambrose kid push him in or what?"

"No! Harry fell right through the peat. On the island. He just fell through and we couldn't get him out."

"Wow. Was you two standing next to him? That's what I heard. How come you didn't fall through?"

"We jumped away. And went on our hands and knees. We was scared to death."

"Shit. No kidding." He lit up a cigarette. He set the pack down on his seat, then picked it up again and held it out to me. "Want one?"

"Uh. No, thanks. I've got some at home. I was just heading there now."

"Want a ride?"

"Sure," I said, and went around and jumped in.

He tore down the road, then pulled in my driveway and stopped and looked at me. He smiled, and I thought, He really has a good-looking face. He had nice blue eyes that reminded me of Pa's, especially a few years ago when we used to have so much fun. The corners of his eyes wrinkled sort of twinkly and friendly when he smiled. I looked at his arm on the steering wheel. It looked strong and had deep grooves between the muscles. I hoped I'd have muscles like that in a few years. I opened the door to get out.

"So, what d'ya do all day, C.K.? School don't start for another three or four weeks, right? Me, I don't go to school no more. Got a job workin' nights at the machine shop down the road. Good pay. Benefits. They treat me real good. Respect me. Know what I mean?"

I nodded. "Well," I said. "I used to go up to Johnnie's every day. But now that he's in the hospital, I guess I'll just watch TV and stuff. My other friend, Harry—well, you know where he is. I just really ain't figured it out yet, what I'm gonna do. I got a job, sort of, so that will use some time." I looked at him. I thought he might have some ideas what I could do.

"Your ma works?"

"Yeah."

"So you're just here by yourself all day?"

"Yeah. Except when Linda Boggus needs me."

"Oh. That lady in the house back there? What d'ya do for her?"

I didn't want to tell him I babysat. He'd think I was a wimp. I wondered what I could tell him so he'd think I was cool. I thought and thought, but I couldn't think of nothin'. I almost started to tell him the truth. Then he said, "Yeah, her hubby's not around too much. What d'ya do, help her with yard work and shit like that?"

"Yeah! Yes. Her husband's going to teach me how to run their big tractor so I can help out in the fields, too." That sounded good.

"Wow. Nice job. 'Specially for a kid your age."

"Yeah." Then I didn't know what to say. I wanted to keep talkin' to him, but I knew he didn't have no reason to want to talk to someone just twelve. He must be twenty or thirty, I thought. I started to get out of the car.

"Well, you know, I'm goin' home to an empty house, too. How about you come to my house, and I'll fix you some lunch, and we can watch some TV, shoot some baskets, shit like that?" He smiled and raised his eyebrows. His eyes sure did twinkle like Pa's.

I felt excited and got a little nervous. "Yeah! Great. Love to. Thanks!" I sat back in the seat and slammed the door.

He backed the car out of the driveway real fast. Then he spun the tires and made the gravel fly, and we took off down the road for his house.

22

I was in a bed, and my mom was sitting on the edge of it. Mostly, I wanted to go back to sleep, but my mom was stroking my head and saying, "Wake up, Johnnie. Wake up, sweetie."

I looked at her. Her pretty hair was hanging on her shoulders, and she had her head tilted to one side. She looked so sad. My dad was standing behind her. His hair was black like mine. I knew that's how I'd probably look when I grew up. That's fine, I thought. I like how my dad looks.

"How do you feel, sweetie?" my mom asked.

I tried to sit up, but I felt so heavy. "Tired," I said.

"That's because the nurse gave you some medicine to help you sleep."

"Nurse?" I was surprised. I looked at the room. It sort of looked like a hospital room, except it had blue and green wallpaper with plants and flowers all over it. Being in a hospital room scared me. Had I been hit by a car or something? "What's wrong?" I asked. "Why am I here?" I tried to feel around my body and arms and legs for pain or casts or bandages, but I didn't feel anything. I really felt pretty good. What was going on here?

My mom and dad started to talk to me, but I felt so sleepy, I just drifted away. For just a while, though, because I realized right then that I was very angry at them. So, I woke up again. They were still there. They hadn't moved.

"You assholes!" I yelled at them. "What do you think you're doing!" I mean, really, what did they think they were doing, coming here and waking me up? "Jesus Christ! Get out of here! Go away!"

They didn't move at all. Why wouldn't they move? I looked for something to throw at them. I looked on the dresser and the desk for something like a vase or an ash tray, something I could throw and make them leave. Damn it! Why wouldn't they move?

"MOVE!" I yelled as loud as I could. All they did was squirm around a little. "GO! MOVE!" I tried again. My mom just looked sadder. I hated that sad look.

Then I looked at her right hand. She was holding my blue ball, the one she'd thrown in the pond for Tucker when I was little. I was so happy to see it. "My blue ball," I said. I could feel myself smiling. "How did you get it out? Did you go swimming for it? Did you take scuba lessons so you could go find it for me? After all this time?"

My mother looked like an angel. She smiled and said, "Yes, I did. I never realized how much it meant to you, so, yes, I've been taking scuba diving lessons for six weeks now. I didn't want you to know until I'd found the ball and could bring it to you."

She held the ball out to me. I started to reach for it. Then the ball lifted out of her hand and floated upward. It floated over her head, and she smiled and looked up at it. Then it floated over to me. I held out my hand, and it came right down and settled into my palm. It really was my old ball, with Tucker's and Josie's and Tilly's teeth marks in it. Except it sort of shimmered like it had a light inside. I could feel the electricity, too, in my hand. It tingled and hummed. It was a wonderful feeling. I wanted to just sit there forever and hold the ball. It made me feel the way it looked—sort of tingly and humming. So, that's what I did. I sat there and felt the ball and felt how good I felt. I didn't want to do anything else. My mom and dad seemed to think this was fine, too, and they stayed where they were and smiled at me. I'm sure we stayed like that for hours. No one wanted to move, so no one did, and I just sat and held the blue ball and felt good.

Then, a stupid lady in a white dress came in with a tray of food. She came at me with the tray, and I could feel the ball becoming afraid. It started humming louder, and the tingling started to feel like pins pricking my hand. The pin pricks got stronger and stronger as she came closer. She set the tray on a little table with wheels and rolled the table over to me. The ball got so afraid it leaped into the air and went all the way up to the ceiling. The pin pricks hurt my hand.

"My ball!" I cried. I could see that it was very afraid of the lady in the white dress. It had gotten as tight up against the ceiling as it could, and I was sure I heard it start to scream. So when she got close enough to me with the little table, I slugged her, right in the mouth. Boy, did she yell. My parents leaped up. My dad came over and grabbed my hand, and my mom went right to the lady to see if I'd hurt her. I didn't care about the lady. I was watching my blue ball. It stopped screaming, and I could see that it relaxed a little as soon as the lady got away from me.

It floated down a few inches from the ceiling, and I saw that it wanted to come back to my hand. It would come closer, then shy away again, kind of like a scared horse. I knew it was a afraid of my dad.

"Dad, would you please stand back where you were so the ball can come back to me? See?" I pointed up at it. "It wants to come back, but it won't because you're standing too close." I tried to say this in a nice way so his feelings wouldn't be hurt.

"Johnnie. There is no blue ball up there. There's no blue ball in the room at all." He looked kind and serious, and sad, too, like my mom.

"Liar!" I yelled at him. "It's right up there! Didn't you see Mommy give it to me?"

"No, Johnnie, I didn't. The blue ball is not here. It's still in the pond."

"NO! NO! It's here. Right up there!" And it was there, except now it was frightened and had gone up tight against the ceiling again. "Look what you've done! You scared it again! Go away!" I grabbed the carton of milk on the food tray and threw it at my dad. It hit him in the chin. Then it bounced once on the bed and fell on the floor. When it hit the floor, it sort of went splat, and the milk came pouring out.

There it was—bounce, bounce, bounce, splat! I cracked up. I wished C.K. were here to see that. He'd have died laughing. The way it hit my dad's chin was so funny. The look on his face was funny, too. I started laughing really hard. And I couldn't stop thinking about how it hit his chin and bounced off. And I kept

281

laughing harder and harder. I looked up at the ceiling once at the blue ball, and it was laughing, too. I asked it if it saw what just happened. It nodded itself up and down to say "yes," and it giggled really hard.

"See?" I said to my dad. "The ball thinks it's funny, too. Can't you hear it laughing?" My dad wouldn't even look up at the ceiling. "What's wrong with you!" I screamed at him. "Look up and see the ball laugh!" I looked up and saw the ball jiggling up and down —it was laughing so hard, so I just kept on laughing, too.

Then the door opened real fast, and my mom, the lady in the white dress, and some guy in a white shirt and white pants came hurrying in. The nurse had a shot in her hand. I didn't want any shot. I started to get out of the bed so I could run away. But my dad held my shoulders and wouldn't let me get up.

"Take it easy, Johnnie. This won't hurt very much. It will be over in a flash. Then you'll feel better. You'll feel calmer," my dad said. The guy in the white clothes stood there. I could tell he was ready to tackle me if I fought any more. I looked up at the ball, and it shook itself "no" and let me know I ought to just take the shot. It was no good to fight it.

"Do it quick, please," I asked the lady. I figured she must be a nurse.

"I sure will, doll," she said. She wasn't so bad. She even gave it to me in the arm instead of the butt. Then my mom came and stroked my hair again. She still looked like an angel.

As soon as the nurse and the man in the white clothes left, the ball came floating back down. It sort of hung over my mom's head again.

"Thanks for bringing the ball," I said. "It must have been really hard to find in the mucky water."

She nodded and stroked my head. Pretty soon I fell asleep.

In the morning when I woke up, the sun was shining on the blue and green flowery wallpaper. I think it was supposed to be pretty, but it wasn't. It looked fake, and the green was a pukey color like pea soup. I looked up over the whole ceiling, looking for my blue ball. I didn't see it. Then I checked under my pillow, and

there it was. It said this was the safest place for it until I could take it home, so I said, "Okay" and covered it back up.

Then a different nurse came in with a tray of food. She was young and pretty, kind of like Cross-Eyed Ladonna. She even had crossed eyes and red hair. I blinked a bunch of times. I couldn't tell if it was someone else or if it really was Cross-Eyed Ladonna. I'd never seen Cross-Eyed Ladonna in a dress before, and this lady had on a white dress and white shoes.

"Good morning, Johnnie. How are you doing?" She didn't sound like Cross-Eyed Ladonna, but I decided she looked exactly like her. Maybe this was her twin.

"Are you Ladonna's twin?" I asked.

"Whose?"

"Cross-Eyed Ladonna's."

"No, dear, I'm not. Who is Cross-Eyed Ladonna?"

What could I tell her? I started to giggle. "She's the wife of the Man On The Moon." Then I burst out laughing. C.K. should have heard that one. He would have loved it.

The nurse sort of chuckled. "My name is Nancy." She held out her hand to shake mine.

I shook it. "Nice to meet you, Mr. Fish," I said to her hand, and laughed some more. C.K. would love that one, too. I had to remember to tell him. Nancy laughed only a little.

"Breakfast looks good this morning," she said. "Waffles and sausage. Orange juice and milk. If you don't eat it, I will." Then she laughed just like Cross-Eyed Ladonna.

"I didn't know you worked in a hospital," I said.

"Well, I do."

"How's your mare?" I asked.

"My what?"

"Your mare."

"As in 'horse'?" she asked.

I didn't know what to say, then. I knew this was Cross-Eyed Ladonna. At least, I was pretty sure. Except she didn't talk like her. Why couldn't I tell? I started to feel scared. Then I started crying all of a sudden.

"Where's my mommy?"

"She'll be here later, during visiting hours."

"Visiting hours! Where am I? WHERE AM I?" I felt real scared and started crying real hard. "I want my mommy!"

She came and sat on the bed and hugged me. "Your mother will be here a little later. And Dr. Broward should be here any minute. You'll like him. All the kids do. How about if you eat your breakfast and then get dressed before Dr. Broward gets here? I'll stay here and keep you company."

I felt better. "Okay. Yes, please stay." I looked at her while I ate my waffle. I was sure she was Cross-Eyed Ladonna. "Ladonna?"

"My name is Nancy."

I started to cry again.

"But if you want to call me Ladonna, just for today, that might be okay. We'll ask Dr. Broward when he comes, okay?"

"Okay." The waffle was good. I ate it down and drank my juice and milk. I felt better.

"Ready to get dressed?"

"I guess so." I didn't remember ever being out of this bed. I'd never even stood up in this room. I didn't know if my legs would work. But when I tried, they worked just fine, and I stood up. I had my own pajamas on. That was nice. Nancy called me over to the dresser, and she opened each drawer. There were all my clothes from home.

"How did these get here?"

"Your mom and dad brought them yesterday."

"Why? Why am I here? How long do I have to stay? What is this place?"

Cross-Eyed Ladonna smiled so pretty. "This is Mercy Hospital, and Dr. Broward is your doctor, and I bet he's on his way right now to tell you why you're here. So, you must know something about horses, huh? Do you have one?"

"Why are you asking me such a stupid question? You know Stitches."

"Stitches? Is that your horse's name?"

"Horse? You know he's a pony and not a horse. Geez!"

"How about these shorts and this shirt for today? You go ahead and get dressed, and I'll go see if Dr. Broward is coming. Okay?" She was already halfway out the door.

I didn't like the shirt she'd picked to go with these shorts, so I switched them. I was just pulling my shorts on when someone knocked at the door. Was I supposed to say, "Who's there?" or what? The nurses and that guy had just walked in, so why was this person being so polite? Whoever it was knocked again. I thought, Well, I could go open the door, or I could ask, "Who is it?" Which will it be? If I go open the door, I might not like who I see. If I ask, "Who is it?" they might lie. Or, I still might not like who it is. Maybe it's Dr. Broward. So, do I open the door or do I ask who it is? I couldn't decide. So I finished getting dressed.

The person knocked again. I felt like crying again and didn't know what to do. I started to go open the door, but I stopped. I opened my mouth to ask, "Who is it?" My stomach got all tight, and I just didn't know what to do.

"May I come in?" It was a man's voice.

What if I said "no"? Would he come in anyway? Probably. Everyone else did. He was just being polite. But it would be interesting to say "no" and see what happened. But if I said "no," he might not like me. But I really didn't want him to come in. I didn't want anyone to come in. I wanted to go play with the blue ball.

"NO!" I yelled.

"Please?"

Wow. He said "please." He must be nice. "Okay," I said.

The door opened slowly, and a man stepped in and shut the door behind him. It was Sigmund Freud. I knew it was he because my dad had a bunch of books with his picture on them. Boy! I couldn't believe it! He sort of tiptoed in.

"Are you sure?" he said. "I thought you might still be getting dressed." He pulled the desk chair out and waved his hand for me to sit in the other chair, a big stuffed one in the corner. I sat in it. It felt good. It sort of hugged me.

He had a clipboard with papers on it. He looked at a couple of them and then set the board on the desk. I felt like I was sitting

there with God. I stared at him and tried to see every eyelash and wrinkle and mole on his face. I looked at his hair. It was grey and thin on the sides. He was bald on top. His beard was grey and thick and wavy. I wanted to fit my fingers into the waves. I wondered if the hair would be soft or stiff. His eyes were definitely God's eyes because they were so deep and kind. I could tell he was the smartest person on Earth and that he loved everyone.

He held his hand out to me. His mouth smiled and his face smiled, and his eyes smiled the best. "I'm Dr. Broward," he said.

I started to laugh a little. Who did he think he was fooling? He probably thought I didn't know who Sigmund Freud was. I suppose most kids my age didn't know. But I knew. I wanted to tell him I knew, but that might embarrass him. If I told him, he'd know I thought he was a liar, and I could never insult him like that. He still had his hand out. I didn't know what to say. I was trying to decide whether to let him know I knew or not. I shook his hand, but I didn't say anything.

"I understand you're trying to figure out why you're in this place. Is that right?"

If I said "no," I'd be lying to him, and I didn't want to lie to him. If I said "yes," he'd think I was stupid. I sure didn't want him to think that. So, I didn't answer.

"I understand that your friend Harry died a few days ago. Do you remember that?"

Harry didn't die. Why would he say that? Or maybe he had died and no one had told me. I realized that I really didn't know for sure. I didn't know what to say, so I listened to what he'd say next.

"And you went to the funeral home and saw him?"

No, I thought, the only funeral place I'd ever been to was Grandpa's. What was he talking about? Maybe he had the wrong kid. But I couldn't tell him that or I'd insult him.

"And you saw Miss Bernice and Mary from Little Friends there and they frightened you?"

I hadn't seen Miss Bernice since I was four and a half years old. How could I tell him he had the wrong kid? That would be terrible if I embarrassed someone as smart and wonderful as he was.

Besides, I didn't want to talk about Miss Bernice. I'd told Louise everything I knew about Miss Bernice ages ago. Why would Sigmund Freud want to know about Miss Bernice?

"So, you're not going to talk to me this morning?" He smiled at me. His eyes looked like they were going to ooze out love and smart stuff.

Wow, I thought. Sitting here in front of Sigmund Freud was more than I could handle. I wanted to let him know how special this was, but I just didn't know how. My dad had told me how much Dr. Freud knew about people and how he was a genius and had been the one to discover defense mechanisms and the Oedipal Complex and cool stuff like that. And besides that, he was nice. I couldn't wait to tell my dad that I'd met him. I could feel on my face that I was smiling from ear to ear. I didn't want him to leave. I wanted him to stay right there so I could look at him and watch his eyes look at me. I felt all blown up with air like a balloon. I felt like I was going to float up to the ceiling. Then I remembered my ball. I bet he'd like my ball. I went to the bed and got it out from under the pillow. I held it in my hand and felt it humming. I held it out to Sigmund Freud. The ball was not afraid of him, and it sat there and glowed.

"What do you have there?" he asked.

What dumb thing was I supposed to say, "A ball"?

"Oh, I bet this is the ball your mother and father told me about. What can you tell me about it?"

I tried to think of something to tell him about it, but I couldn't.

"Well, Johnnie, when you're ready to talk to me, let Nancy or one of the other staff members know, okay? I think you're a very intelligent boy, and I think you have a lot to say, and I'd very much like to hear it. But I understand. You're a little confused about what's happened and why you're here. I think that, after a few days, you'll feel better, and things will be easier to understand. There are other kids here, a TV, a Nintendo game, a gymnasium, and an arts and crafts room. You'll be getting together with some groups of other kids to talk about some things that are bothering you.

"In the meantime, know that I'll come by to see you two or three times a day, and I've enjoyed meeting you." He held out his hand for me to shake.

I almost said, "Nice to meet you, Mr. Fish," to his hand, but he might be insulted. I looked up at him and thought, this is what God must be like. Wow. Just wow. He winked at me as he went through the door.

I still had the ball in my hand. It seemed happy and floated off and drifted around the room. It went over and looked out the window, which had bars across it. And it drifted over the bed and the dresser. It looked at itself in the mirror and then floated over the desk. It hovered there for a long time, and then I saw why. Sigmund Freud had left his clipboard. I picked it up and was going to run out of the room and try to catch him. But then I realized what it was. It had all kinds of stuff about me written on it.

The top sheet was all typed in neat boxes and had my name and address and birthday. In the top right corner was a box called "initial diagnosis." Someone had hand printed "Brief Reactive Psychosis." The box next to it was called "DSM No." Someone had printed in "298.80."

I was pretty sure "psychosis" meant "crazy."

They think I'm crazy? And this is a mental hospital? Wow. Why? There must be a big mistake. I wanted to call my dad. He'd straighten them out. But wait. He had already been here. My mother and father think I'm crazy? This can't be. I'm not crazy. Why do they think so?

I sat down in the big stuffed chair. My heart was pounding, and I felt scared—and angry—like someone was playing a dirty trick on me. I got up. I was going to find Cross-Eyed Ladonna or Sigmund Freud and have them call my dad. I went over to the door and pulled on the doorknob, but it wouldn't open. Locked? They've locked me in here? Wow. I sat back down and felt my heart pound through my whole body. My blue ball came over to me. Then it slowly drifted toward the bed. It sat on the pillow. I think it wanted me to let it go back under there. I walked over, lifted the pillow up, and the ball went under. I lay down on the bed and let my head sink onto the pillow. I was careful not to put weight on the ball. I could hear it humming softly to me, and I went to sleep.

23

I guess maybe I, you know, "matured" a little later than some guys. Cuz it wasn't nothin' Johnnie and I ever talked about. Hell, it just never came up. You know—masturbation, sex, girls, boys. Johnnie was too damn proper to talk about it. Sure, he had a thing for Cross-Eyed Ladonna, but I don't think it was a sex thing for him.

Maybe I felt a little something that first day with Billy. I don't remember. And if I did, I probably didn't pay no attention to it. After that, I did. Because of Ken? Maybe. Naw. I think it was cuz Ma smoked dope when she was pregnant with me. You know, the chemicals or genes or whatever goes on in there when the egg gets fertilized must've gotten screwed up. Wasn't nothin' to be done about it, neither. It just happened. Wasn't nobody's fault. And I couldn't change the way I felt.

Ken pulled into his parents' driveway. I'd only been past their house a few times on my bicycle cuz they lived farther on down my road. Their house was a nice red brick one—a one-story with a two-car garage. But Ken didn't pull into the garage. There was a parking space off to one side, and he parked there. He turned off the engine and jumped out. He seemed full of energy.

"C'mon," he said to me. I had to almost run to keep up with him, and I followed him in the front door. He took big, long steps into the kitchen. "Want a coke?"

"Sure," I said. He opened the refrigerator and tossed a cold can to me. Thank God I caught it.

"Come on down to my room," he said, and he walked across the kitchen to a doorway. I hurried and followed him down some stairs. We walked through a family room with two couches and a TV and then through a doorway into his room.

It was awesome. The bed wasn't made, and he sorta had magazines layin' all over. The ceiling and halfway down the walls was painted black with hundreds of tiny white dots. Halfway up, all the way around, the walls wasn't black but was a greyish pink color, just like the sky looks a little while after the sun sets. On the pink part, someone had painted the dark shapes of buildings and trees. On one wall, there was a whole city. It looked just like Chicago. Two other walls had farms with barns and houses and silos. And another wall had almost nothing—just a tree here and there. I looked back up at the ceiling and saw the Big Dipper.

"They're almost all there," he said, pointing. "See? There's the Little Dipper, and there's Orion. And Cassiopeia. The North Star. And can you see the Milky Way? It goes from there all the way across the sky. See?"

"Yeah. Wow! Did you do this?" It looked like a real sky.

"Yep. My ma hates it and wants to paint the whole thing white, but I won't let her. She say's it's stupid. You like it, huh?"

"I sure do! I'd like to paint my room like this."

"It's took three years."

"Three years! Why?"

"Because I'm tryin' to paint every star up there that the naked eye can see—in the real sky. And the planets. See—there's Mars. And Jupiter. Saturn's way over there. And Venus, well, I had to decide if she was in her morning phase or her evening phase. You can't tell by all four horizons because they're the same color, but where the stars and planets are makes a difference. So, I finally decided to make her a morning star. See? Here she is right here. I decided this is east." He stepped to the other side of the room above his dresser and pointed to a white dot.

I thought he must be one of the smartest people I'd ever met. Maybe even smarter than Johnnie.

I sat down on the edge of his bed and started thinking about Johnnie. And about Harry. Being here, they seemed so far away. I tried to imagine what Johnnie was doing, if he was tied up in rags and chains in some white room where he was screamin' and bein' a monster. Or if he was all drugged and sitting in a long hallway

with other crazy people who was naked and moaning and wailing—like I seen in a movie once. And Harry. I thought about him under the ground in his coffin, waking up all of a sudden and not being able to get out. I imagined him clawin' at the coffin and screamin' and no one hearin' him, and then he would suffocate. I pictured him with his short, combed hair and his suit, tryin' to push the lid of the coffin up.

"Hey, man. You all right?" Ken was sittin' right next to me on the bed. He had his hand on my back.

I sorta woke up like I'd been dreaming. "Oh. Sorry. I was just thinkin' about Johnnie and Harry. Sorta wonderin' what they're doin' now." I looked at Ken. He looked like he felt sorry for me.

"You must miss 'em." He started to move his hand around on my back a little.

I shrugged. "Maybe," I said. I didn't really want to be with either of 'em right now, so I wasn't sure I missed 'em.

"Well, I can be your pal." He grinned at me, and those wrinkles came up around his eyes, the ones like Pa's. His hand felt good on my back. It was warm.

"What kinds of things did you and Harry do together?"

"Mostly we fished. Played a few games. Watched TV."

"I'll do all those things with you."

"Really?" I couldn't imagine he'd want to do those things with me since I was so much younger. Maybe he didn't have any friends right now, either. "You got friends?" I asked.

"Used to. They all got married and gotta do what their wives tells 'em."

"Are you gonna get married?" I asked.

"Nah. Women are too much trouble. They want to run your life. I just look at my friends and know I don't wanna live like that."

"How about a girlfriend?"

"Nah. Same thing. Want to run your life. I've got a couple friends I still hang out with once in a while. Mostly I like to be alone. Do what I want. When I want. It's the best way." He was making nice big circles on my back now, and he pressed kind of hard, so I had to tighten up my stomach to not fall over.

"So, tell me about Johnnie. What kinda stuff do you two do together? What's he like? Everybody around here says the Ambroses are real stuffy. Stuck up, you know?"

"Yeah, I know they say that. But they're really nice. Leland reads a lot, and he's gone most of the time. He's always been nice to me. And Christine is a little weird. She makes weird food and believes in astrology. And sometimes they ask Johnnie weird questions. Like when he's mad about something, they try and get him to be madder. I don't get that." Ken's hand felt so good rubbing my back that I wanted to stop talking and just feel it. I started to close my eyes, but I didn't want him to think he was puttin' me to sleep. So, I talked some more about Johnnie.

"Johnnie and I made a real cool castle on the big hay pile. We pulled out a bunch of bales in the center, so we have a tunnel that goes all the way down to the bottom. Johnnie's real smart. He figured out how to use a rope like a pulley to get the bales up. He reads a lot, too. We think the same things is funny, though, and we laugh a lot. And he's got this funny dog named Tucker." Then, all of a sudden I started cryin'. I couldn't believe it. I just started sobbin', and I didn't know why.

Ken moved closer and put his arms around me. He hugged me. Then he went on rubbing my back. "Does this feel good?" he asked.

"Yes," I said and sniffed a whole bunch.

"Here, let me do it with two hands. It'll feel even better." He got behind me on the bed with his legs crossed and rubbed my back with both his hands. I stopped cryin' pretty quick, and since he couldn't see my face, I went ahead and closed my eyes. It felt so good, his big, warm hands on my back.

He patted his pillow. "Why don't you stretch out here, and I'll give you a real, genuine back rub."

I flopped down on my stomach with my head on his pillow. It smelled like cigarette smoke. I could feel him get on his knees over my legs, sorta like he was ridin' a horse. He kept doing the back rub. I started feelin' real relaxed.

"Feel good?" he asked.

"Yes. Great."

"Good. I could do a better job if I could go under your shirt. Would you mind if I did that?"

"No. That's fine." He pulled up my shirt, but it was kind of tight around my arm pits.

"Want to just take it off? Then I can get your shoulders, too. That will feel extra good." He helped me pull the shirt over my head and tossed it on the floor. He went back to rubbing. He sorta dug his thumbs into my muscles and massaged me all the way down to my shorts, then all the way back up to my neck. Then he used his fingers to massage the tops of my shoulders. I couldn't tell if I was asleep or awake. I didn't want him to stop. With my eyes closed I saw big, thick, red waves, and the waves would turn into big, red circles, and the circles would slip away to the right side, then another big wave would come, and it would turn into a circle and slide away real slow. This is what I saw, over and over, and then I think I did fall asleep cuz the next thing I knew, I was on my back, and he was stroking my chest and my stomach. I opened my eyes a little and saw him above me with his long dark hair and beard. He still had the red bandana on, but he'd taken his shirt off, too. The bright light up on the ceiling was off, and he'd put on a little red lamp that was way over on his dresser. Maybe that's why I'd been seein' the red waves and circles.

I wondered how long I'd been asleep. I opened my eyes all the way and tried to look around some more. The room was pretty dark, except I could see Ken above me and his nice face. It was too dark to see the stars and planets. I wondered why he didn't use glow-in-the-dark paint. Maybe he did, and it was still too light with the red lamp on. I wanted to go turn the lamp off to see if the stars would light up.

"Does this still feel good?" he asked. It did, and I just nodded. "Close your eyes again. It feels better that way." He was massaging my arms now, and they felt like they didn't even belong to me. I started to shut my eyes again, and then I saw he'd taken his jeans off, too, and now he only had his white underpants on. Then I knew something was wrong. I mean, why had he taken his clothes

off? But this felt so good, I figured I'd just lay there and see what happened next. He knew I was sad about Johnnie and Harry, and he was just trying to help me feel better.

I kept my eyes closed and felt his warm hands on my chest. They was making hot circles where he massaged me. Each time he made a circle, he moved a little farther down towards my belly, just like he done on my back. I wondered where he learned to do this. Probably in one of those magazines he had layin' around. He was so smart, he probably studied how to do this.

He reached the top of my shorts and said, "I'm going to start from the bottom now, with your feet, okay?"

"Mmm, sure," I said.

He untied my shoes and pulled 'em off. Then he took a foot in each of his big hands and massaged them with his fingers and his thumbs until they didn't feel like they belonged to me neither. Then he did my ankles, then my lower legs. He sorta skipped my knees and used both hands on one thigh, and then the other thigh. He went up under each leg of my shorts until his hand couldn't fit any higher.

He sort of whispered, "Let me slip these off so I can do your hip muscles, okay? Then you'll be all done, all relaxed." He didn't wait for me to answer and started to pull my shorts off. I lifted my hips up so he could get them off easier. I really knew this was wrong, and I knew I was headed for some kind of trouble here, but I wasn't sure exactly what. And I really knew it when he pulled my underpants off with my shorts. It felt so good, and he was bein' so nice, I didn't dare say no. But I did peek at him after he'd gotten my shorts all the way off my feet. He still sat on me like a horse, just below my knees. I could feel his weight, but it didn't hurt.

He went back to massaging the tops of my legs and started to go up to my hip bones. I knew my dick was just sitting there so he could see it, and I wished I could cover it up. I figured he might look at it, and I wondered what he'd think. He moved his hands up on the sides of my hips for a while. Then, slowly, he moved the circles to my lower belly, right above my dick. I thought he kept getting close to it, but I wasn't sure. And then he put one hand right

on it. He sorta rubbed it up and down. It felt real good. It was getting hot and kind of tingly and felt like it was growing. It felt like it was getting bigger and bigger, and I didn't want him to stop.

"Does that feel good?" he whispered.

"Mmm hmm," I said. It felt so wonderful I couldn't believe it.

"This will feel even better," he whispered, and his voice sounded sorta rough and deep. I peeked again and saw him bring his head down to my dick. It was sticking up straight, and it had gotten big. He opened his mouth and put his lips on the top of it. He sort of licked around it with his wet tongue. His tongue and mouth were very wet and hot as he started to go up and down on it. I couldn't help but close my eyes. I was breathing harder and felt my hips going up and down. The longer he did this, the warmer and harder it got.

Then I heard him sort of grunting, so I peeked again. He had pulled his own undershorts down and was rubbin' his own dick up and down with his hand. It stuck up just like mine, except his had a bunch of dark hair around it, and it was bigger than mine. He kept going up and down on me and rubbing himself at the same time. Pretty soon he sort of whined and groaned and brought his mouth off of me. He trembled and shook and kept rubbing himself. Then liquid stuff squirted out, and he slowed way down. He rubbed it a little longer and then he laid down next to me. He fiddled with my dick just a little, and then he stroked my belly.

"C.K.," he whispered. "You okay, man? You feel good? How was that? Did it feel good? You want me to do it some more? I will." He raised up on one elbow and looked at me kind of worried.

I didn't know what to say. Yeah, it had felt good—real good. And I thought he was wonderful. But I knew this was wrong. I liked this and didn't like it all at the same time. The same thing for him. I sorta hated him right then and wanted to get out of there. But I liked what he'd just did, and I liked him. He smiled at me and sorta petted my cheek with his fingers. "Yeah, I'm fine," I said, and I looked up to see if the stars was glowin' yet.

"Hey, man, I want this to be good for you, too. You're a cool guy. I want you to be my buddy, my pal. We can do stuff together,

okay?" He smiled again, but he still looked a little worried. "This will be our special secret, okay? Other people might not understand."

"Okay," I said and sorta forced myself to smile.

He sighed a real big sigh and grabbed my hand and squeezed it. Then he fell asleep with his body up against me.

I laid there and wondered what to do. I moved a little and hoped he'd wake up, but he didn't. I moved some more, but nothing happened. I moved away from him so he wasn't even touching me, and he didn't wake up at all. I sat up and looked at my dick. It was back to its normal size. I wanted to get dressed and leave. Being in this bed with this man felt creepy. I wanted to go home and watch TV. I wanted to go up to Johnnie's and have Johnnie be okay and for us to play in the castle. I moved to the end of the bed and waited. Ken started to snore. He was flat on his back, with his underpants down around his knees. I looked at his dick. It was dark and just sat there on top of all that black hair. I liked it and kinda wanted to touch it and hold it in my hand. But I knew that was wrong, so I got my clothes on real quiet. I carried my shoes and socks and tiptoed out of the room.

I walked through the TV room and headed for the stairs. I wondered what I would say to Mrs. Jenkins if she was up there. She would know what I'd done and she might call my ma and pa. Ma would beat me for sure and tell me I was queer. God! I guess I was—I was queer. Look what I'd just done!

I started to run. I ran up the stairs and ran through the kitchen. Maybe if I ran fast enough, Mrs. Jenkins wouldn't know who I was. I ran out the front door and around the back yard. When I got to the woods, I stopped and put my shoes and socks on. I didn't think Mrs. Jenkins had seen me. I don't think she was even home, but I wasn't sure.

I walked through a little woods. It sorta divided the driveway the Jenkins's lived on from my road. There was a lot of poison ivy, and I had to be careful not to let any touch me. Johnnie said he never got it—that he was immune to it and walked through it all the time. But I remember when Ma had it once, and she was miser-

able. All those red splotches on her legs. They itched like crazy and oozed a clear liquid. I wanted to remember to wash my legs with that strong yellow soap Ma said to use if I ever did touch poison ivy.

I got through the woods and out on our road. It was pretty far to my house. The sun was shining real bright. It seemed like it should be dark cuz so much had happened today. I found a dark blue rock in the road. It was about the size of a golf ball and almost as round as one, and I started to kick it. It would roll along the road and then stop. Then I'd kick it again. It went real far cuz it was so round. Then I heard a car coming. I looked behind me and saw it was a pick-up truck. It looked like Pa's. I knew that all he had to do was take one look at me and he'd know what I'd just done with Ken Jenkins. I wanted to run back into the woods. Maybe if Pa didn't see me for a few days, this would wear off, and he wouldn't be able to tell just by lookin' at me. But there was no woods right here. It was just swamp on each side of the road.

It sounded like the truck was slowing down. I looked back, and sure enough, it was Pa. He stopped next to me. This was horrible. I felt like I had big words written all over me: "I'm queer, I'm queer, I'm queer." I wanted to jump into the swamp. Then, I thought, maybe I can dive under the truck and never come out again. But none of those things happened, and I just had to stand there. I felt like Pa could see right through my shorts and see Ken's spit on my dick. I turned my side to the truck and glanced at him.

He had the window down and smiled real big. "Hop in. I'll give you a ride."

What could I do? I had to get in. I opened the door only as far as I needed to fit through. I slinked onto the seat and sat real close to the door. When I pulled it shut, it didn't catch all the way cuz I was too close to it. I had to re-slam it. I rolled the window down and sort of hung out the door.

"Where you been?" Pa asked.

He knew. I knew he'd know. "Just out for a walk," I said. He'd never believe that. I never just went out for walks.

"I imagine you don't quite know what to do with yourself now, do you? With Harry gone and Johnnie in the hospital?"

I just shook my head.

"I got some free time right now. Want to go shoot some baskets?"

No! I thought. I just want to go hide.

"I really don't feel too good," I said. "I might just go lay down and read."

"That's okay. You got a right to feel poorly. How about an ice cream cone? I'll take you to the Dairy Queen."

"No, thanks. I'm not hungry."

"Okay. Well, you let me know if you change your mind." He patted my leg. I about freaked out when he did that. What if he thought I liked it when he touched my leg? I'd liked it when Ken touched me. Could Pa tell?

It took forever to get home, and I jumped out of the truck before he barely stopped. I hurried into the house and ran up to my room. I had a small stack of books that Johnnie had let me borrow. I opened one and tried to read it. But all I could do was think about Ken. And my dick. I wanted to try rubbing it like he'd done, but I had to wait until Pa left again. Surely he would soon. He always did. I tried to read and listen for him. He would take a shower, and then he'd leave before Ma got home from work. I heard him come upstairs and get clean clothes out of the drawer. Then he went back down and turned the shower on. Then I started to rub. I rubbed gently until it got big. And I kept rubbing. It felt so good. I didn't dare take my pants down in case Pa came in. I wanted to. Pretty soon I heard the shower stop running and Pa come back upstairs. I went back to pretending to read.

He came in after a while. "Bye, son. I'm takin' off now. See you tomorrow."

"Sure," I said. "Bye."

He was hardly gone when I heard Ma come home. I'd have to wait now till she went to bed. I got up and went downstairs. I turned the TV on and watched till suppertime. Ma didn't have much to say, and she talked on the phone most of the time. I didn't want to sit at the table and eat with her, so I told her my favorite show was on, and she let me eat watching TV. I didn't want her to

think I was queer either, except somehow she didn't bother me as much as Pa did.

That night, after Ma was in bed and I knew she wouldn't come up to my room, I began to rub myself. And I thought about Ken. And I imagined Ken making his mouth go up and down on me. And I thought about him rubbing himself and how the stuff came out. First I imagined I was back in his room and he had my dick in his mouth, and then I imagined I was him rubbing my own dick just like he did. I imagined first one, then the other, and back and forth. And then the most incredible feeling came over my whole body. These awesome waves of like dynamite came over me and I felt my dick and my insides pulse and squirt, and it felt hot and wonderful, and I couldn't believe anything could feel this good. And then it slowly died away. I tried it again after a little while, and it took a little longer this time, but it did it again. I started to try a third time, but then I fell asleep.

An itch on my leg woke me up in the morning. I got up and looked out in the driveway. Ma's car was gone already. I went downstairs and looked at the kitchen clock. Ten o'clock. Wow! I usually woke up about seven. Ma'd left me a note that there was frozen waffles in the freezer and to call Linda Boggus. She'd called to see if I could stay with Billy and Sandra this afternoon. I called her right away, and she said she'd like to have me come at 2:00 for about three hours. This time, both kids would be there. I said okay.

I toasted a frozen waffle and sat down to eat. I missed Johnnie. I wanted to call him and go up there. I wanted some of Christine's fruit for breakfast. I wanted to play in the castle and make paper airplanes. I wanted to play Nintendo and just hang out at the Ambrose's house. I decided to walk up there and see if Christine was home. I had to scratch my leg before I got up and took my plate to the kitchen.

On the way up there, I had to stop a couple times to scratch my other leg, just above my sock. When I got up there, no one was around. Not Christine or Cross-Eyed Ladonna or no one. I rang the doorbell, but no one answered. So, I walked home again. I had to stop every few steps and scratch my leg. I kept thinking a mosquito

had bit me, but I didn't see none flyin' around. By the time I got home, both legs was itchin', and then I remembered. Poison ivy. I'd forgot to wash my legs with the strong yellow soap. I looked at my legs, and they was all red and blotchy-lookin'.

Then I started thinkin' about going through the woods behind Ken's house and about Ken and about what we'd done. Pa always said God punishes people for things they done wrong. This must be my punishment, I thought. Now everyone would know for sure that I'd done that bad thing. I went home and found the calamine lotion under the bathroom sink and dabbed it on my legs with toilet paper. There was a rash now all the way up both sides of my legs. It was itchin' real bad now. I went into Pa's room and got his Bible from next to his bed. I took it downstairs and held it in my lap. I thought maybe if I prayed to God and told him I was sorry, maybe he'd make the itching go away. "Dear God," I said out loud. "I'm sorry for what I done with Ken Jenkins. I know it was bad, and I won't ever do it again. Please forgive me and make the itching go away. I won't ever touch my dick again except to pee."

When Linda Boggus answered the door and saw my legs, she sorta screamed, "What's that!"

"I think it's poison ivy," I said.

"When did you get it?" She looked really freaked out.

"Yesterday I walked through the woods. It just started itchin' today." I wondered if she knew about me and Ken, too. Maybe this wasn't poison ivy but was some kind of rash that happened after you did that with another guy.

"C.K., I feel so bad for you. It must be miserable. But you know what? It's contagious. I mean if any of that oozey stuff gets on the kids, they'll get the rash too. Did you know that?"

I shook my head.

"Well, oh dear, I wish I'd known. I don't think it's a good idea for you to take care of the kids for at least a few days. Maybe your mom can take you to a doctor and get a shot. It might go away faster. I really wish you'd told me because now I have these appointments, and I'll have to cancel them. Or take the kids with

me." She looked at her watch and seemed all worried. "Maybe I can get them ready in time." She started to close the door. "Call me when it doesn't ooze anymore, okay?" I barely had time to nod and she shut the door.

I walked home and felt like cryin' the whole way. I looked in Boggus's front window, but Billy wasn't there. I'd watch TV till Ma came home, and maybe she'd take me to the doctor.

24

When I woke up, my mom and dad and Dr. Freud and Cross-Eyed Ladonna were all standing there. I was real happy that my mom could see that Cross-Eyed Ladonna was a nurse here and that my dad could meet Sigmund Freud.

"Dad, see who's here? Isn't this cool? You think he's so wonderful." I nodded towards Dr. Freud.

My dad made his eyebrows go together, like he didn't know what I was talking about. So, I motioned for him to come closer so I could whisper in his ear. "Dad. It's Sigmund Freud. Didn't you know?"

He still looked confused and kind of laughed. "This man?"

I nodded.

He said, "No, Johnnie. This is Dr. Broward." Then he stepped back and looked at Sigmund Freud. "Well, come to think of it, Hank, you do look something like Freud." Then he turned to me. "Good observation, Johnnie. But even though he might look a little like Dr. Freud, he's not."

Wow, I thought. My dad's never lied to me before. I know he just doesn't want me to realize that he knows such a famous person. So, I decided to play along. "Oh, okay. I must have been mistaken." I winked at my dad so he'd know I really knew.

I started to explain to my mom that it was such a surprise to see Cross-Eyed Ladonna here, but I let it go. Then I heard my ball humming under my pillow. I lifted up the pillow and let it out. It floated over everyone's head. Then it just hung up above them and listened to the conversation. I decided not to talk about the ball even though they looked up at it when I did.

"Want some orange juice?" my mom asked and held a small carton out to me. I took it and drank some.

"Johnnie," said Dr. Freud, "we thought we'd try to explain to you why you're here. Or do you think you know?"

I had no idea and shook my head.

"Do you remember my asking you earlier about your friend Harry?"

"Yes. But he isn't my friend. He's a creep."

"Are you aware that something bad happened to Harry?"

I couldn't remember.

My mom said, "Do you remember when you and Harry and C.K. were out on the island and Harry fell through the peat?"

I didn't remember Harry ever being on the island with C.K. and me. "No."

"Let's let him be, then," said Dr. Freud. "It will come within a few days, I suspect. Johnnie, would you like to join some other kids in the TV room? Maybe play some Nintendo? Shoot some pool?"

I really didn't want to go meet new kids. I was happy to be with these adults. But Dr. Freud was smiling so nice, I didn't want to disappoint him. "Sure," I said.

"Nancy, why don't you take him on down and introduce him to a couple of the other kids. Daniel would be a good one." He turned to me. "Daniel's a whiz at Nintendo." He lifted his eyebrows and smiled.

"Why don't you call her by her real name?" I asked.

"Which is what?" he asked.

"Cross—I mean, Ladonna."

My mom said to Dr. Freud, "I see. Nancy looks something like one of our horse boarders named Ladonna." Dr. Freud listened to my mom, looked at Cross-Eyed Ladonna, and then nodded.

"Okay, Johnnie, come on with me," Ladonna said and held out her hand to me.

As I recall, Daniel was a nice kid—a masochist—who enjoyed pushing pins into his toes. He only did it when he was alone, however. He talked about it in group, and the rest of the time we played Nintendo and pool together. We sat next to one another at group meals. By the time I was discharged three weeks later, he was still

wanting to push sharp objects of any kind into his legs, his arms, and his toes. We didn't keep in touch after I left.

One other clear recollection I have of my brief stay there, the adolescent unit of the psychiatric hospital, was of shaking hands with people.

———

Cross-Eyed Ladonna led me down a long hallway with lots of doors. At the end of the hallway there was a real big room. One whole side was all windows. At one end of the room there was a pool table and a TV and a Nintendo game. In the middle of the room there was a bunch of chairs and a couple tables. And at the other end, there were two old couches and another TV. There were about ten kids watching TV and playing games. Cross-Eyed Ladonna took me up to each kid and introduced me. Each kid held out his or her hand for me to shake, like they'd all been trained to do this. And each time I put my hand out to shake one of theirs, his or her hand always looked like a fish. So, I always said, "Nice to meet you, Mr. Fish." The first couple of kids giggled, and I did too because I knew it was funny. And I sort of meant for it to be funny. But I couldn't stop from saying it. I guess after the first few times, the rest of the kids must have heard what I said, and they didn't giggle anymore. They just shook hands because they were supposed to and looked away.

Except for Daniel. He sat in front of a TV with his shoes off. He was playing with his toes through his socks. When Cross-Eyed Ladonna introduced us, I said, "Nice to meet you, Mr. Fish." He kind of scared me because he kept hold of my hand.

"Johnnie," he said. "my hand is not a fish. And its name is not Mr. Fish. I'm Daniel, and I'm pleased to meet you." I liked him a lot right away, and as soon as I'd met all the other kids, I went back and sat down with him.

———

Reactive brief psychosis is what its name implies. It manifests as a result of a trauma or recollection of a trauma, and then it

passes. So, as the days went by, my blue ball became less and less demanding, and one day it just wasn't around. By then, I didn't care about it anymore. My parents, Dr. Broward, and the group therapists helped me remember what had happened to Harry, and I was gradually able to relate the details of the drowning. The more difficult part was accepting the polarity of my emotions—the hate I had for Harry and, consequently, the gratification of observing his demise, as well as the anguish anyone feels when watching another human being die, especially in such a dramatic way that had threatened my own life as well. When they referred to Miss Bernice, Mary, and Little Friends, however, I recalled nothing except that Miss Bernice had been the teacher at my pre-school, and she and the other teachers had made me eat some bad food one day that made me sick. Those details were to remain repressed—safe, put away in some locked corner of my mind. Probably, when Dr. Broward realized the extent of the repression, he let me go home.

———

School started the day before I got home from Mercy Hospital. So, when I got home, we had to hurry up and get ready. We went shopping for paper and notebooks and some new clothes. Mostly, I didn't care about school. I wanted to see C.K. and called his house a few times, but no one answered. Once, Mrs. Bookout answered, but she didn't sound very friendly, and she said C.K. was away for a few days, but he could call me when he got home.

Sometimes I went to Joey's house after school and played, and sometimes he came to my house. But I missed C.K. I didn't even go out to the castle because it was just C.K.'s and mine. I didn't want to spoil it with someone else. And I didn't want to go out there alone. Besides, all Joey wanted to do was play Dungeons and Dragons. So, most days I went to school and then went home and waited for C.K. to call.

25

Ma came home and freaked out at how bad my poison ivy was. She called the doctor and took me in right away. On the way, she started askin' me questions, and I figured she musta found out about me and Ken Jenkins.

"So, what did you do wrong that you shouldn't have?" she asked.

It felt like she'd hit me in the face again, except today she wasn't drunk. She must know, I thought. How could she have found out? Maybe Mrs. Jenkins *was* home that day and had been hiding in the dark and watched the whole thing and then called Ma. That must be it. How else would she know? I didn't know whether to lie or tell the truth. If I lied, she'd be furious, and if she knew the truth—I didn't know.

"What do you mean?" I asked.

"Remember when I got poison ivy that time?" she said.

"Yeah."

"Well, you know what I'd just done?"

I could imagine all kinds of things, like she went out with some other man, or she stole something from work, or she lied to her mother, or she got drunk. But I couldn't say none of those things cuz she'd get mad.

"No. You never do nothin' wrong, Ma."

"Ha!" she laughed. "Well, not too much, but every once in a while we all do something wrong. Well, I'll tell you. I ain't proud of it, and I been feelin' guilty ever since, except it never hurt nobody, so I guess it wasn't too bad." She looked at me and grinned. "You ready for this?"

I shrugged. I knew it couldn't be too horrible, or she wouldn't be telling me about it.

"What'd you do?" I really didn't care what she done. It couldn't be nearly as bad as what I done.

"Remember that beautiful black dress I wore to your rich cousin Angela's wedding?"

I tried to remember but I couldn't. "Yeah. You looked beautiful."

"It was a great dress, wasn't it? Well, what I did wrong was I wore it, spilled wine on it, and then took it back to the store. And never had to pay for it cuz I put it on Pa's credit card. I tucked all the tags inside so no one could see 'em. I about died when the wine spilled on it. But when I got home, I washed that part of it real careful in Woolite, and dried it and ironed it. I was real careful not to get the tags wet. I was scared cuz it cost a hundred and sixty dollars, and there was no way Pa and I could've paid for it. What was bad was that I planned it all. I even picked out a dress that had tags in the right places where I knew I could hide 'em—you know, inside, attached to the label, and under the arm pit. The tags poked me a little when we danced at the reception, but I didn't mind. Everyone said how beautiful I looked. It was worth it." She looked at me and smiled real big. She was happy just remembering.

"But then the very next day I got poison ivy. Your pa said I deserved it. I told him he should've bought the dress for me, then. He just laughed and said I should've gone to K-Mart like we always do. I told him I couldn't wear some cheap dress to that wedding. He didn't care. He wore his same old brown suit and same old funny shoes from nineteen sixty-five."

She looked at me again. "But he was right. I shouldn't have done it. And, like he says, every time somebody gets poison ivy, you know they done somethin' bad. So?"

Maybe she didn't know. Maybe I could make something up. Maybe she wouldn't know the difference. "Okay. I drank three cans of pop yesterday instead of two. You always say I can't have more than two in one day, and I drank three. I even hid the can out in the woods." I looked at her.

She gave me one of those looks that says, "You think I'm gonna believe that!" But I decided to stick to my guns cuz I couldn't think of nothin' else.

"Okay, it was really four."

She gave me the look again. "With as bad as you got poison ivy, it's gotta be somethin' worse than that."

"Well, it ain't." I folded my arms and looked out the side window. I expected her to keep at me, but she shut up and let it go, maybe because we got to the doctor's office right then.

The doctor said it was a pretty bad case. He gave me a shot and gave Ma a subscription to get some better lotion. He said the oozing would be gone in two or three days. When we got home, I called Linda Boggus and told her I'd been to the doctor and that I could babysit in three days. So we made an appointment for four days. She said she hadn't been able to reschedule the things she'd planned yesterday, and she was real glad she could do them in four days. She was real nice.

So, for four days, when Ma was gone, I kept the curtains shut and the door locked and watched TV and rubbed my dick. I thought about Ken when I did it, and then I started thinkin' about Billy and wondered how it would be to do it with Billy the way Ken done it with me. The first day I made the stuff come out seven times. One time I'd think about Ken, and then the next time I'd think about Billy. Back and forth. But on the fourth day, mostly I thought about Billy. I could just imagine his face and how he'd lie there and smile at how good I made him feel.

———

Yeah, hell, it took a while for me to get up the courage to do it to Billy. I held him a lot and read to him and built up his trust. That's the way you gotta do it, you know. I must've just known that, even back then. Linda had me sit with the kids about three times a week for the last few weeks of that summer. The rest of the time, I laid on the couch and jerked off. Not a bad few weeks, eh? Ha ha. Oh, yeah, and the poison ivy was gone in four days.

———

It was the last day of summer vacation. I wondered if Johnnie would get back in time for one last good day before the next year of slavery began. I called his house in the morning. Christine was there. She sounded pretty happy, and she said Johnnie would be home in two days.

"Is he okay now?" I asked.

"Yes. He really is. He's back to normal. I thought he could have come home a week ago, but Leland and Johnnie's doctor wanted him to stay just a little longer. You ready to start school tomorrow?"

"I don't know. I was hoping Johnnie would be able to play one last day."

"Oh, yes. I understand. But there will be time to play after school, you know. In fact, if you want to plan on just coming up after school the day after tomorrow, I know he'll be excited to see you."

"Yeah, okay. I'll do that."

Linda Boggus wanted to go to Chicago with a friend and realized she better do it quick cuz I wouldn't be around after today. She called real early in the morning and asked me if I thought I could handle the kids all day until Mr. Boggus came home at five thirty. So far, the longest I'd sat was four hours. This would be eight hours. She was payin' me a dollar and a half an hour now cuz I always done the dishes and had everything neat and clean when she came home. So, I'd make twelve dollars. Not bad. I said, "Sure."

Sandra was a pain in the neck. Johnnie was right. She wanted me to have tea parties with her and Cinderella all the time. So, when I got there, I told her I'd only have two tea parties during the whole day and only if she was good. She said she'd be good.

Linda said Sandra would take a long nap in the afternoon, and Billy would probably take two short ones. She said she'd call me after lunch and see how things were going, and she gave me Mr. Boggus's phone number at work but to only call him in an emergency. She knew I could call my ma or Christine if I needed help quicker.

The morning was hard because Sandra wanted me to play all her games with her. And Billy wanted to do what Sandra was doin', and I tried to let him play, too, but Sandra got mad at him all the time because he just wasn't old enough to play the games right. She'd yell at him or push him, and he'd start cryin'. So, I'd hold him, and she'd get mad at me cuz I wasn't playin' with her. It was awful. Billy was supposed to take a nap about an hour before lunch, so I told Sandra I'd have a tea party with her then. I think she was getting the idea that I didn't like her as much as I liked Billy. She even said once, "You like Billy best!" and she pouted at me. I didn't know what to say, so I didn't say nothin'.

I was playin' Candyland with her, and Billy was tryin' to play, but when he rolled the dice, he knocked all our pieces off the board. I guess he just didn't have the coordination, and his arm went across the whole board. All the pieces slid off. Sandra screamed and was so mad she pushed his arm away, but she did it too hard and sorta bent his arm back. It looked to me like it woulda hurt. Billy started cryin' and holding his shoulder.

"Sandra!" I yelled. "He couldn't help it. You've really hurt him!" And I picked Billy up.

"He ruined our game!" she yelled at me.

"But he didn't mean to. You shouldn't have hurt him."

"I hate him!" she screamed and kicked the Candyland board half way across the room.

"That's very bad," I said. "You better go stand in the corner for ten minutes." That's what Linda said I should make her do if she was bad.

"I hate you, too! You like Billy better! I'm gonna tell Mommy when she gets home."

"Go stand in the corner or I won't even give you lunch," I said.

She started cryin' real hard, and Billy was still holdin' his shoulder and cryin'. Sandra picked up Cinderella and took her to the corner. I could tell she'd done this for her ma cuz she knew just what to do.

"Okay," I said. "I'll start timing you right now. I'm gonna get Billy some cookies and milk. Don't you move."

311

I got Billy some animal crackers and milk, and he stopped cryin' pretty quick. By the time he was done, Sandra's ten minutes was up. She came out of the corner and wouldn't look at me. She picked up the Candyland game, and I took Billy in his room for a nap. He went right to sleep. When I came back to the living room, I helped Sandra set the game up again. We played a whole game without Billy around. But she still wouldn't look at me.

"Want to have a tea party?" I asked.

She looked at Cinderella. "Do you want to have a tea party?"

Cinderella didn't say nothin' for a minute, then Sandra made her nod her head. So, we went into Sandra's room and brought the tea set out. I got apple juice out of the refrigerator and filled the tiny cups. We sat at the children's table and chairs in the kitchen. I kinda liked sittin' in them tiny chairs, even though I was too big for 'em. Every time I asked Sandra a question, she still wouldn't look at me. Instead, she asked Cinderella the question, and then Cinderella would answer. It was real stupid, and I was glad when it was over. I got her to stop the tea party when I reminded her that Bugs Bunny was on at eleven thirty.

I fixed lunch, and Billy got up. We all ate, and then Sandra took her nap. What a relief! Cartoons was still playin' on TV, and Bugs Bunny was on again. I set Billy on my lap, and we watched them together in the rockin' chair. Billy liked to rock. Each time the chair went all the way back and then started to come forward, I felt his body press into me. And right after we went forward, his body would pull away. I felt his body push close to mine, then away. Close and away. I had my arms around him and rocked him close and away, close and away. I didn't even see the cartoons. I was con-centratin' so much on feelin' his body push into me. I heard all the noises and Bugs Bunny sayin', "What's up, Doc?" but all I seen was Ken goin' up and down with his mouth.

I started to rub Billy's leg with one hand. Then I did both legs with both hands. "Does that feel good?" I asked.

He was busy watchin' the cartoon, but he sorta nodded his head once. I rubbed his legs each time the chair rocked. Pretty soon I just rubbed. He didn't seem to notice the difference. I was gonna start rubbing his little dick, but then I realized he had a big,

I had just finished that point where the stuff squirted out, and I was just sorta windin' down when I heard this scream behind me. At first I thought it was Sandra, and I got real mad that she came out so soon. She was supposed to sleep for a couple hours. I turned my head around, and there was Linda Boggus standin' in the doorway.

"What are you doing!" she screamed.

I pulled my pants up as quick as I could, but Billy's diaper and shorts were on the floor too far away to grab 'em. I knew I was in big trouble as I started to lead him to them, and she shrieked, "Don't touch him!"

I stood there and was tryin' to decide whether I could run past her in that wide doorway to the kitchen and get out of the house. If I just ran away, maybe it would all be okay. Maybe she'd just forget about it.

"Don't you move," she said. She backed into the kitchen and opened a low drawer. She reached in and pulled out a big revolver. "You stay right there. I'm callin' the police. Sit down!" She pointed the gun right at me.

I sat down. I looked at that gun. I'd never had anyone point one at me before. The hole in the barrel looked huge, and I started imagining a bullet comin' outa there and goin' right into my forehead. My heart was poundin' in my ears, and zings went through my chest and stomach. I was pretty sure the bullet would come at me any second, and the whole world would end. I watched her dial the phone. She never brought the gun down. I thought for a minute that it might be better if I tried to run and she shot me. Then this would all be over. Now people would know I was queer. My ma, my pa. I didn't want Johnnie to know, no way. I started to get up to run. I decided it would be better to be dead. But just then, Billy came over to me with his diaper and shorts.

"Need help," he said. He smiled at me and held out the diaper.

"Don't touch him!" Linda hissed.

She was talkin' real fast on the phone and asked someone to hurry. I was startin' to feel shaky. I looked at Billy. "I'm sorry, pal. Your mommy will help you in a minute."

He held the diaper up higher to me. "No. You help. Please?"

Shit, I thought. I wish she'd let me put his diaper on. He enjoyed what we was doin' as much as I did. I didn't do anything bad to him. I didn't hurt him. He liked it.

She hung up the phone, but she didn't put the gun down. "Billy, come here. I'll put your diaper on. Don't talk to C.K. He's very bad."

I couldn't believe she said that to him. I started to tell her he wanted to do it, too, but I didn't. Billy'd been looking at me the whole time, except when Linda screamed. Then he looked at her like she was pretendin'. He almost looked like he was gonna laugh.

"Go on," I said to him. "Go to your mommy."

He started to go to her, and then he saw she was pointin' the gun at me. He screamed and put his hands over his ears. "No! No hurt Shay Shay!"

She held her other arm out to him, and he went over by her. "I won't hurt him. But he's been bad." She hugged him to her leg, but she couldn't put his diaper on or anything cuz she'd have to put the gun down. We had to just stay like that for a long time. She sorta leaned over and hugged him, and he looked at me like he was gettin' scared. The doorbell finally rang. Linda yelled, "Come in!" I heard the door open and heavy feet tromped in. Then I got more scared.

Two policemen came into the kitchen. They looked real big and mean. Linda pointed with her gun. "There he is."

"You can put the gun down, ma'am," one of them said. "May I see it—the gun—please?" Linda looked annoyed, but she gave it to him.

"Please just get him out of here. Get him out!" Billy looked up at her like he was gonna cry.

The one cop came over to me with a metal clipboard and a pen. "What's your name, son?" I was still sitting, and he stood over me. I looked up at him once. Then I stared at his shoes. They were black and so shiny the light from the window made a big white square on each of 'em.

"C.K.," I said.

"What kinda name is that? Give me your full name."

"Clive Kendrick Bookout."

"So, what were you doin' here with this little boy?"

"Nothin'."

"Nothing!" Linda screamed. "He had his mouth on Billy's penis, and he was masturbating. Ohhh! It was horrible. Get him out of here! Why are you questioning him here? Get him out!" She was really screamin' now.

"Yes, ma'am," the cop in front of me said. "Come on, son, let's go out to the car. And no funny stuff or I'll put the cuffs on you." I stood up, and he put one hand on my shoulder. It was heavy, and I wanted to shrug it off. I let my shoulder drop low, hopin' the hand would slide off, but he just dug his fingers in until it hurt, so I walked straight.

Well, shit, lookin' back it wasn't so bad. They called my ma, and she came down, and they just said this sort of thing was to be expected in boys my age, but if it happened again, maybe she oughta take me to see a counselor or somethin'. Then they told me to keep my prick in my pants and not bring it out for the neighbors to see. They laughed a lot and sent me home.

On the way home, Ma didn't say much, except, "C.K., if you keep doin' that sorta stuff, you'll keep gettin' in trouble with the cops." She talked on the phone a lot that night, and the next day she told me to pack my suitcase with four days of clean clothes and my toothbrush. She was sendin' me on a bus to spend a few days with my Uncle Herman in Georgia. He was a guard in the big state prison down there. Ma said he'd talk some sense into me. I hadn't ever met Uncle Herman before.

He was tall and skinny and had blond hair like Ma's. He met me at the bus station. He smiled just once real quick, and then he acted like he didn't know what to say to me. He went to work every

day and left me home to watch TV. He wasn't married or had kids or nothin', so I went for walks in the woods. He lived in a little house in the mountains. He said the Appalachian Trail ran right along his property and said I should go for long walks and think about what I done. He showed me a backpack, a canteen, and stuff to make sandwiches. He said I should be back by dark every day.

I went for a couple walks and found a big creek. I leaped around on the rocks by the creek and looked for frogs and lizards. I seen a few, but I couldn't catch 'em. Mostly, I watched TV. When Uncle Herman came home at night, he fixed supper, and we watched some more TV. He didn't say nothin' to me about what I done. And after the third day, he put me back on the bus. He hardly looked at me when he said good-bye. I guess he was just weird.

When I got home, Ma asked, "You got yourself straightened out?"

I said, "Yeah. Uncle Herman's cool."

She said, "Good," and that was all. I went to school the next day. Before I went out the door to get the school bus, Ma said, "Johnnie called the other day. I told him you'd call when you got back. Why don't you go play with him after school, and I'll call you when supper's ready, okay?"

"Yeah!" I said. That really made me happy. It would be so good to see my best friend again. I couldn't wait. He's all I thought about all day. I thought about the castle and how great it would be to play up there and go down in the tunnel and play sword and Robin Hood and make some more paper airplanes. When I got off the bus, I didn't even go in the house and leave my books and lunch box. I just took 'em with me and ran up to Johnnie's. The problem was I had to go past Boggus's. Before I got to their property, I started lookin' for Billy. I hoped he'd be out in the front yard and wave to me. But no one was out. Then I decided that was better. If Linda even saw me wave at Billy, she might call the police again. So, I ran all the way past their place and all the way over the bridge. Then I was so out of breath, I walked. I wished I'd taken my books home.

I walked up the hill, and I was just about to go up the bank to Johnnie's barn when I heard that rumble. I looked down the road and saw the cloud of dust. Ken was comin'. For a couple seconds, I couldn't decide what to do—run up the path or stay and wait for Ken. I waited for Ken.

He saw me and honked a little and pulled up next to me. He had his window down. "Hey, pal, how you doin'? I ain't seen you in a while. I thought you might come down and see me. Shoot some baskets, you know?" He smiled and made his eyes wrinkle like Pa's. "Hop in."

I felt real excited and ran around and got in. I barely had the door slammed and he drove off. He raced down the road. I looked back once and seen the huge cloud of dust. I couldn't see nothin' behind us it was so thick. He didn't slow down for his little road. I looked at him when he drove past it.

"Ma's home sick today," he said. I want to show you something." He went down the road farther. We went past the swamp and an old burned-down farmhouse. And then on the other side of the cornfield, just before the new expressway, he turned down a grass path. It looked like a path for the tractors that plowed the cornfield. He drove over a small hill and pulled into a little woods. He turned the car off.

"Come on. I want to show you something really cool." He got out of the car, so I did, too. "You been out here before—where the two sections of corn rows come together?"

I didn't know what he was talkin' about. I shook my head.

"Follow me." He went right through a tall row of corn, and we stood in the long path between the first row and second row. The corn plants were a lot taller than Ken, and the two rows made a long, long path that went on forever each way. He said, "One." Then he pushed two plants apart and walked through them into the next row. I followed him. "Two," he said. He kept goin' and called off each one, "Three. Four," and on until he called out, "Thirteen!" Then he turned left and started walkin' down the path. I just followed.

I felt a little dizzy, lookin' up at all them plants. They was all I could see, and it was like I was lost in some strange land, like on

another planet, like maybe one on *Star Trek*. He turned back and smiled at me. He had that same red bandana around his head, and now that I was walkin' behind him, I could see that his hair was real long, past his shoulders. It was shiny and pretty like a lady's, and he had a white tee shirt with no sleeves, so his big muscles stood out. His arms was real tan. He had on tight blue jeans and cowboy boots. Whenever he smiled like he just did, I always looked at those eye wrinkles. They wasn't as long or as deep as Pa's, but they was the same otherwise. I felt like I could follow him anywhere, no matter how long it took. I knew I was special to be his pal.

I kept followin', and I watched his butt. I thought about the front part of him and remembered his dick and the way it looked that day in his room—just after he'd went to sleep. And I wondered if he'd want to put his mouth on mine again, and if he'd let me touch his. I felt mine growin'. I wished he'd stop and do somethin'. But he just kept walkin'. Finally, he said, "Here it is," and he stopped. He pointed. "Look."

Where we stopped, there was a T in the rows. I looked where he pointed, and the path between the corn plants went down a hill, and it went forever. I couldn't even see the end. Then he pointed behind us. I looked back where we had just walked, and that path went forever down that hill. Then he pointed ahead of us, and that path went down a hill, too, as far as I could see. He looked at me with a real big grin.

"See where we are? Right in the middle of this corn field—must be sixty acres or more, and we're right at the top of the hill where the farmer had to make the rows go the other way for drainage—so the soil don't all wash down the hills. Don't you just feel like you're some place besides Earth?"

"Yeah! I was just thinking that. Like on *Star Trek* or somethin'."

"Exactly! Yes! Hey, we really do think alike." He put his hand on top of my shoulder and started massagin' it. We didn't say nothin' for a minute. He stepped closer to me and put the other hand on my other shoulder. Then he stepped behind me and massaged both my shoulders and my neck until I felt real relaxed. I could feel the front of his jeans up against my butt. Then he

319

brought one hand around to the front of my jeans, and he put the other one on my stomach. He massaged both of those parts. My legs was gettin' weak. I wanted to sit or lay down. And I wanted to let my dick out of my pants. I hoped he would undo them. The zing went through my stomach when he started unbuttoning my jeans. Then he unzipped the zipper and put his hand down in my underpants.

"Wow," he said in that low voice. "You're ready for me, ain't you?" I nodded. "Pull 'em down, okay?" I tried to get them down quickly, but I was all sweaty, and they stuck to me. I sorta had to peel them down. He was busy gettin' his own off. I didn't look behind me, though. I just wanted him to rub me. I started to do it myself cuz I could hardly wait.

He came up behind me. "No," he whispered. "Let me." And he reached around and took my dick in his hand and began to go up and down. I thought I was going to squirt right then. Maybe he could tell and said, "Take it easy. Hold on." He let go and took his hand and made his dick go between my legs. It didn't work too good because I was shorter, and he had to bend his knees. "I have an idea," he said. "Kneel down on your hands and knees. Then I'll do you some more."

I kneeled down, and he kneeled behind me. He pushed his dick right up against my butt. He put one arm on the ground to hold hisself up and put the other one around my waist. Then he took hold of my dick. I couldn't help moving back and forth to make it go in and out of his hand. And he started moving back and forth behind me.

"Does this feel good?" he said. His voice was sorta scratchy now.

I nodded and went "Mmm hmm." I started going faster.

"Wait," he breathed real hard. "Let me try it in your butt, okay?"

Then I remembered back at Little Friends when Jack showed Harry's brother, Bob, how to do it in the butt—on me. And I remembered how much it hurt. "No!" I said. "It'll hurt." I could feel my dick start to get small.

"No, no," Ken said real soft. He kept rubbin' me. It won't hurt the way I do it. It will make you feel even better. And next time, you can do it to me. Trust me. I won't hurt you. I promise. The last thing I want to do is hurt you."

I wanted to believe him, but I was still scared. Then I thought about how small I'd been at Little Friends—just four or five—and how much bigger I was now. Maybe it wouldn't hurt as much. And Ken said it would feel good. I believed him. He was very smart. I was still a little scared, but I said, "Okay."

"See," he said softly, "I use lots of spit. That makes it real slippery and makes it feel so good." I could hear him spitting into his hand. Then I felt the end of it against my butt hole, and I got scared and pulled away.

"Relax," he said. "I'll just rub it on the outside, okay? Relax. This will feel good, too." And he did. He rubbed his wet dick under my balls. I did relax and started to get excited again. He rubbed me with his hand and my balls with his dick—back and forth and back and forth. I felt like the stuff was gonna squirt out any second, and Ken was breathin' hard and startin' to moan and whine again. And then he did it. And it only hurt a little at first. He pushed it right into my butt. And he made it go back and forth right away, and he was right—it got to feel real good, and it only took a few seconds, and I squirted the stuff. I think he must have squirted at about the same time cuz we was both moanin' and whinin' at the same time. Then he slowed down, but we kept movin' back and forth, but slower.

He whispered, "Hey, my friend. How was that? Nice, huh? You okay? Did it feel good?"

I was out of breath. "Yes. It felt good," I said. Then he let his dick fall out of me, and I laid on the dirt on my side. He laid behind me and stroked my hip and my leg.

"This is a great spot, ain't it? No one will ever know our secret here, will they?" He stroked my head. Finally, I just wanted to get up and go. I stood up and pulled my clothes back on. When I looked at him, he looked worried. "You sure you're okay? Didn't I make you feel good?"

"Yeah, yeah, you did," I said. Then he smiled a little, and the eye wrinkles made me sure I done the right thing. "I just started thinkin' about Johnnie. He's waitin' for me."

I was surprised when Ken got mad. His face got all angry-lookin', and he said, "What do you need him for? Ain't I your pal now?"

"Well, he's been my best friend forever. And I ain't seen him in weeks—since he went in the hospital. This is the first day we get to play."

"Well, fuck him! Tell him to find another friend. You got me now." The eye wrinkles were gone, and he looked real mean. Then I thought he might think I do this with Johnnie.

"Johnnie and I don't do—this," I said.

The mean look went away. "Oh. Oh, yeah, I get it. Sorry. That's right. You guys been friends since you was real little, right?"

"Yeah. Johnnie and I ain't never even talked about—this."

He smiled again. "That's cool. Yeah, you ought to go say hello to him. Wanna come out here again tomorrow?"

I know he wanted me to say "yes," and I kinda wanted to. But I wanted to probably see Johnnie tomorrow, too. Maybe I could tell him "yes" and then not come. "Okay, sure. I can meet you here. I'll come down on my bike."

"Great. Four o'clock, okay? Good. Well, let's go." I followed him back down the corn path.

26

When the doorbell rang, I knew it was C.K. I ran to the door and opened it, and there he was. My smiling best friend was standing there. Seeing him was the best thing there could be. He looked so good to me, I could hardly stand it. Part of me wanted to just stay there and look at him for a long time—you know, just soak up the picture I was seeing. We probably looked pretty stupid to anyone watching us, just standing there looking at each other and grinning all goofy.

Finally I shrugged and said, "Hi. Come in."

"Hi." He couldn't stop smiling either. "How are you now?"

"I'm really fine. I guess I was just upset about Harry. More than I knew."

"Yeah. Well, it was pretty awful. I still can't believe it happened."

"Did you go to the funeral?"

"Yeah. It was pretty boring. Just like church."

"Yeah, I know. My grandpa's was like that."

We went into the kitchen, and I got us each a piece of cake and a glass of milk. We ate them at the table on the porch.

He said, "So, how was it? In the hospital? I mean, what did they do to you?"

"Nothing much. I just talked a lot to my doctor and to the other kids about Harry falling through the peat, and about dying. I got good at ping pong and pool. Mostly, it was a lot of sitting around and talking to people."

"They didn't chain you or up or nothin'?"

"No. Geez! Not at all. I had my own room, and it was nice. They wouldn't let me call you. I wanted to. I talked about you a lot to Dr. Broward—my doctor. He's a friend of my dad's. He looks just like Sigmund Freud." I laughed a little. "I guess I thought it really was him at first—he looked exactly like my dad's pictures of

him. And I thought the nurse was Cross-Eyed Ladonna, but she just looked like her. Mostly, it was fine. Just a little boring. What did you do the whole time?"

C.K. got a real funny look on his face, like he was embarrassed or something. He moved around on his chair and looked at the bite of cake on his fork. I thought he even blushed. "N-nothing much. Watched TV. And, um—babysat a lot. Hey, you know you were right about Sandra. All she wanted me to do was have tea parties with her and her stupid doll—Cinderella! But I probably won't babysit no more with school bein' here now. I kinda got sick of it, anyway."

"I told you," I said. "Want more cake?"

"Sure," he said. He seemed better now. I wondered if he'd broken something at the Boggus's house and got fired. Something was wrong. I could tell.

"So, what time do you get home from school this year?" I asked.

"We get out at two twenty, but I think I get off the bus about three. How about you?"

"Not till four. Mom has to pick me up in town where the bus lets all the kids off. I actually get out of school at three fifteen, but the bus ride takes a long time."

"Yeah, well that's too bad. I wish your parents would just let you go to school here. We'd have more time to play."

"Yeah, I know. But they won't. They think my school is the best around. I wish you could go to my school."

"I don't know. It sounds hard—all those science projects and book reports. Besides, we ain't got the money."

I hated it when this subject came up about money. It seemed unfair that C.K. couldn't go to a smart kids' school just because his parents didn't have the money. I never knew what to say to him about this.

"Have you been out to the castle yet?" he asked.

"No. I was waiting for you. I didn't even take Joey out there."

He looked at me and smiled. "It's been a long time." We both thought it at the same time and didn't even have to say, "Let's go!" We dashed away from the table and headed for the front door.

"Wait!" I said. Let's get some supplies so we don't have to come back in for a while."

"Good idea!"

We went back in the kitchen. "Let's see, my mom keeps that little cooler in this cabinet," I said, and I opened one of the low cabinet doors. I pulled the cooler out. "Why don't you put some pop and chips and cake—and whatever you find—apples—in here, and I'll run up and get my swords."

"Okay," he said and started filling the cooler. I ran upstairs and got four swords, my bow and arrows, and a catalogue of swords and knives my dad had gotten me. He said I couldn't order anything out of it, but he thought it would be fun to look through. C.K. hadn't seen it yet. I had my arms full, and when I got to the bottom of the stairs, C.K. was there with the cooler. We went out the door and hurried out to the barn. We must have looked pretty funny, trying to hurry, carrying all that stuff. I dropped the catalogue, and C.K. picked it up and put it on top of the cooler.

Cross-Eyed Ladonna's car was there, but Mary's wasn't. My mom said Mary didn't come here anymore. That was okay with me. I didn't like her much.

When we went into the barn, I wanted to see Cross-Eyed Ladonna, but she must have been out on a trail ride. I could tell because her horse was gone and the mare's halter was lying on the floor. That meant she must have the bridle on her. That was probably good because C.K. always got a little mad at me when I talked to her. I kept forgetting why he didn't like her. It was because he'd seen her with his Pa. I never knew what to think about that. It kind of seemed okay to me because C.K.'s mom was pretty mean, and Cross-Eyed Ladonna was always nice.

C.K. and I sort of waddled into the arena with all our stuff. I wondered if we'd make it up the stairs of the castle in one trip. We went through the big doorway from the stall area into the arena and stopped. C.K. gasped and I sort of screamed. Our castle was gone. Well, not entirely—there was a small pile of maybe ten bales left. That was all.

"Where's our castle?" C.K. said.

"Wow! I don't know." It was terrible—that tiny little pile of hay. C.K. started to walk around it, and he looked up at the ceiling, like maybe he'd find the castle up there. He looked all around the barn.

"Where is it?" he said. He looked at me with his mouth open. He looked kind of white.

I thought about it and remembered my mom telling my dad a few weeks ago that she had a buyer for the rest of the first cutting, and she was going to go ahead and sell it because the second cutting would be in soon. I walked over and set my swords and stuff on the little pile of hay bales. "I guess my parents sold it. I forgot they said they might."

"The whole castle? Just like that? Don't they know how hard we worked to build it?"

"Yeah, but don't you remember, we knew it would be gone one day. The horses had already eaten a third of it. But we're going to make that new one, you know? The one with two shafts and a tunnel in between?"

"Yeah—" he said slowly. "But I thought the old one would still be here when we made the new one." He looked so disappointed. I wanted to do something or say something to make him feel better. His shoulders were all droopy, and he looked at the ground. He finally walked over by me and set the cooler on the bales. "When will the new hay be here?"

"As soon as they get three days of sunny weather. Maybe they'll cut it this evening or tomorrow. Then it will be just two or three days."

He stood there for the longest time, I guess just trying to believe the castle was gone. "I can't believe it would just disappear like that. Poof! Gone!" He was starting to sound mad.

"You knew it would happen one day. I told you." I tried to say it gently.

"Didn't you hear me say I thought the other hay would be here first!" He looked at me kind of mean.

He'd never talked to me like that—mad and sarcastic. There was something different about him since three weeks ago. I didn't

know what. I watched him. He started walking around where the castle had been, like he was hoping to find it.

He threw his hands up in the air. "I can't believe it's gone!"

I tried real hard to think of something to say that would make him feel better, something to make him happy again.

"Want to go back in my room and make a drawing of the new one? You know, with all the details? We can draw how many bales wide it will be, and how long, and where the shafts will be. And how many bales deep the shafts will be. And the tunnel that connects them? That would be fun. Then we'd have the plan all ready to go. Maybe, if the hay comes in in three days, we could have the new castle all done in—um—five days from now. Want to?"

He kicked up a big wad of loose hay from the floor. "Oh, I don't know. Maybe we should just stay out here. I guess we could play Robin Hood."

"Sure. That's fine. Whatever you want to do." I pulled the bow and arrows out from the pile of stuff I'd brought. "Who do you want to be? Robin Hood? The Sheriff of Nottingham? Or maybe Lady Marian?" I said this real sweetly, swayed one hip out, and sort of flipped my hand over.

"Why'd you say that!" he yelled.

"Wow," I said. "What? About Lady Marian? I'm just kidding. What's wrong, C.K.? You aren't acting like your regular self."

"Just don't ask me to be no lady!"

"Geez! I was just kidding."

He said, "Maybe we should go in. We can make that plan like you said. Or make the rest of them paper airplanes." His face looked funny—kind of twisted a little. I thought maybe he was still real upset about Harry and just hadn't been able to talk to anybody like I had. Maybe my dad could talk to him sometime.

We took all the stuff back in the house. My mom was fixing supper, and C.K. and I went up to my room. I showed him the sword and knife catalogue, and we just sat on my bed and looked through it. He saw a sabre with a jeweled handle that he wanted. It cost nine hundred dollars. The broadsword I wanted was only eight hundred. We saw some throwing daggers we thought we

could afford. They were three for twenty dollars. But my dad said I couldn't order anything. We sighed a lot and read the description of each sword and knife. Then we'd turn the page and say "Wow!" or "Cool!" and then we'd sigh again.

I heard the phone ring in the other rooms. Then my mom yelled, "C.K.! It's your mother! She wants you to come home for supper!"

"Ohhh, damn," he said. Then he looked at me. He looked like his old self again. "Why don't you see if you can come down to my house after supper? Maybe we can go for a bike ride. I found this neat place out in the cornfield. You know—the big one just before the interstate? There's this cool place where the rows come together, and you can see forever down these neat paths. You really ought to see it."

He looked so happy again, I was relieved. "Sure," I said. "I don't have any homework yet. I bet my mom will let me."

We went down and asked her, and she said, "Yes, as long as you're home by eight-thirty. C.K. left and I ate supper and then I got my bike out. When I rode past the barn, Cross-Eyed Ladonna was standing in the aisle with her mare, pulling the saddle off.

She heard my bike brakes squeak and turned around. She smiled and looked real happy to see me. "Johnnie! Johnnie, Johnnie, Johnnie! You're sure a sight for sore eyes. We missed you around here. How you been? Hey! You look terrific. I like that shirt!" It was a dark turquoise one C.K. had given me for my birthday last year. Her pretty hair bounced around when she talked like that, and she had that nice pink lipstick on.

"You're a sight for sore eyes, too," I said, and then I felt my face get real hot, and I knew it was all red. I'd never said that to anyone before. I pretended my bike tire looked low, and I bent down to look at it and squeeze it so she wouldn't see my face. As soon as I felt my face cool off, I stood up.

"So," I said. "How's your mare?"

"She's fine. We just went on a real nice trail ride. She's great out there. She don't spook at nothin', don't try to run home."

"Oh, that's good," I said.

"Where you headed?"

"Down to C.K.'s We haven't played together in a long time. School started, so now we can only play in the evenings. I'll have homework in the afternoons. We're going for a bike ride now. Where's Mary?" I wondered why I asked that. Maybe because my mom and dad acted so funny about her.

"She moved back to Arkansas. Her dad's got cancer, and she has to take care of him."

"Well, I better go now," I said. I really wanted to stay here with her, but I knew C.K. was waiting.

"Okay. You have a good time. Say 'hi' to C.K. for me. I'll probably see you tomorrow."

"Okay. Bye," I said. I could feel my face start to blush again, so I pedaled away.

C.K. was out in his yard waiting. We rode our bikes down to the cornfield. He wanted to leave them by the side of the road, but mine was a new twenty-one speed mountain bike that had cost almost five hundred dollars, and my parents said I could never leave it anywhere unless I locked it up. They said if it got stolen they'd never buy me another one. I didn't really believe them, but I knew I shouldn't leave it by the side of the road. When C.K. explained that we had to walk down the rows of corn, I said we could ride the bikes. His wasn't a mountain bike, but it was a dirt bike with fat tires, but no gears. He didn't think his bike would work. So, we walked a little ways down a row and felt the ground. It was dry and hard, so he said he'd try it.

He walked along the edge of the cornfield and counted thirteen rows of the tall corn. We took our bikes down that one.

"You go first cuz you'll probably go faster," he said.

I didn't want to go first. This was *his* thing he was showing me. "No, you go first. I won't know where to stop."

He acted kind of mad. "Oh, okay, but don't complain if I go too slow." He went ahead, and I followed him. I put my bike in one of the middle gears and pedaled along real easily. He had to stand up to pedal most of the time, and I could see how much harder it was for him. Every once in a while he'd hit some soft dirt or a hole,

and he'd have to get off his bike and walk it. I always got off of mine, too, so he'd think I was having just as much trouble.

It seemed like we rode forever, and it was getting harder to pedal. I could see we were going up a hill. I downshifted to my lowest gear, and it was a lot easier. C.K. said, "Jesus Christ!" and got off his bike. He turned around and looked at me. He looked mad. I didn't have time to get off my bike yet. "Maybe if I had twenty-one gears, I could ride up this hill, too. It was a dumb idea to take the bikes."

"How much farther?" I asked.

"To the top of the hill," he said, pointing.

I looked up the row and had trouble seeing because the sun had just set below the tassels at the tops of the corn plants, and the gold light was too bright. "I can't see," I said.

"Well, let's just walk from here, okay?"

"Sure." I set my bike against a couple corn plants and followed him. It wasn't that much farther, but it got steeper as we went. Finally, he stopped and pointed off to the right where the rows made a T.

"Look," he said.

I looked down that row, and it was really cool. The path went straight down a hill as far as I could see.

"And look down there," he said and pointed farther on the same path we came up. It went down a hill, too, as far as I could see. "And look back behind us." I turned and looked. It was the same as the other two, except I could see our bikes a little ways down. "We're at the top of a hill, right in the middle of sixty acres. The farmer had to change which way the rows go so the rain don't wash the corn away.

"Do you know the farmer?" I asked.

"No."

"How do you know all this?"

"I-I-I just figured it out," he said.

"I mean, how did you find this spot?"

"Jesus! What are you, my mother or somethin'? I thought you'd think this was cool," he said.

"I do. I really do. It feels like we're in one of those big human mazes like they have in England. How did you find this?"

"I was just passing through. Geez, Johnnie, why do you need to know how I found it? I just found it. I was walking through here and just found it."

"Yeah, okay. But how do you know it's sixty acres and that we're right in the middle?"

"Shit, Johnnie! Why're you asking me all this stuff? I don't know. I guessed! I figured it out! Lay off, okay?"

Something was definitely wrong. I was stupid to ask him all those questions, except I wondered how he knew all this stuff. I really had to ask my dad to talk with him about Harry. I decided to be extra nice and not ask him any more questions.

"Let's just go, okay? I thought you'd really like this," he said, mostly to the ground.

"I do. I think it's awesome. Where would we come out if we took one of those paths?"

He looked down both of them and started breathing kind of hard. He looked at me with a sort of frustrated look on his face. Then he started to act mad again. He held up both hands. "I don't know! I don't know everything! Besides—my bike's way down there, and I'm not dragging it up here."

"I'll go get it. I'll get both of them." I didn't wait for him to answer and ran down and got his bike. Then I ran and got mine. When I got back, I smiled. "So, which path do you want to take? You choose."

"I don't know," he said. "I guess we could just stay on this one." He got on his bike and started down the path. The sun had set all the way now, and I looked at my watch. It said 7:30. Good, I thought, I still have an hour. I followed C.K. down the hill, and then we rode for a long time. The land was flat now, and when I looked ahead, all I could see was corn. The sky was turning grey.

"Where do you think this will come out?" I called to him.

He shrugged. "I said I don't know. We'll find out."

So, we kept riding, on and on. C.K. was still getting stuck every once in a while and had to walk his bike sometimes. Then

he'd get on again and start riding. I made extra sure I got off my bike, too, but he never turned around to look. I looked at my watch again. It said 8:02. I sure hoped this path came out near my house.

Finally, the path ended. It was starting to get dark. We coasted out of the field, right to the edge of a woods. It was a thick, dark woods, and the ground was covered with raspberry brambles and poison ivy. We tried to see through the trees to know what was on the other side. I hoped we'd see a road, but all we saw were more woods, more raspberry brambles, and tons more poison ivy.

"What woods is this?" I asked.

"I don't know, but I'm not walking through that poison ivy!"

"Oh, come on," I said. "You won't get it."

"Yes, I will! I'm not going through it. No way."

"Come on. You're probably immune to it like I am."

"No! Ma had it once, and I remember it, and I'm not going in there."

We looked down the field in both directions, but all we could see was more woods.

"Well, we better go back and take the other path," I said. I looked at my watch again. 8:20. "Geez, I'm going to be late. I bet I get grounded for a month. Let's hurry, okay?"

"Oh, great. Back up the hill with my wonderful bike," he said.

My parents had asked that I not let C.K. or anyone ride my new bike because someone who didn't know how to work the gears could screw it all up. "C.K., why don't you try my bike? It's a lot easier. This was my idea, taking the bikes."

He smiled. "Really?" He let his fall on the ground and came over. I showed him how to work the gears and told him he had to always pedal when he shifted and never go up or down more than two gears at a time. He understood. My parents worried too much. He got on and did fine. But then I had to ride his bike. But that was okay. It was for a good cause.

We started going up the hill. C.K. was way ahead of me because I kept getting stuck. He didn't wait for me. I watched him when he got to the top. He just turned left and went down the other path. When I got to the top and looked down the path for

him, I could barely see him because it was almost dark. I wasn't even sure it was he I was seeing. He was just a blur that moved. I pedaled as fast as I could, but I never did catch up with him until I got to the end.

As I got to the edge of the cornfield, I could see some lights that looked like a house. C.K. was sitting on my bike with his back to me. I came up next to him. "Whose house is that? Where are we?" I asked.

"I think it's Panzerov's house, but I ain't sure. The problem is, there's a big old barbed wire fence here. I don't know how we'll get the bikes through."

I looked at my watch again, but it was too dark to see it. I pressed the little button on the side of it, and the dial lit up. It said 8:45. "Maybe I can call my mom from Panzerov's."

It was totally dark now, and there was no moon. And there wasn't enough light from the house to see very well either. We set the bikes down and felt the fence real carefully. It had four strands of barbed wire. We set the bikes up against a fence post, and I bent over next to the barbed wires while C.K. held the two middle strands apart. I put one leg through to the other side and ducked my head and body through. I'd done this before around my farm. You just had to go real slowly or you'd catch your shirt on the barbs. When I got to the other side, C.K. lifted my bike up over the fence. It was hard to do, and when he had it all the way up, I took it from him. It took all my strength to not drop it on the barbed wire. I had to arch my back and let the pedal rest on my chest. Then I backed away from the fence and let the bike drop down. Then we tried to do the same with his bike.

"Aagh!" he yelled. "Mine's so heavy! I can't lift it over the fence."

"Are you sure? Try again. I'll get real close."

He grabbed it way down low and made all kinds of grunting and groaning sounds. I was right there, almost touching him through the wires, ready to take it from him. But he couldn't get it up the last few inches, and the top strand of wire caught on the wheels. I tried to take it, but it just wouldn't come.

I said, "Just let it go, and I'll catch it."

"You sure?" he gasped. "It's really heavy."

"Go ahead." I had my hands tight around the lowest parts of the frame. He let go, and I couldn't believe how heavy this thing was. I couldn't hold it, and it came crashing down on my head and chest. I fell backwards onto the ground. I thought I heard him scream at the same time.

The bike was on top of me, but I pushed it off. I rubbed my head and felt a big bump starting to come up. C.K. was sort of gasping. "What's wrong?" I called to him.

"I got cut. I think it's bleeding pretty bad."

My head really stung now, and I felt the bump getting bigger fast. My chest hurt, too, where the pedal gouged me. I went over to the fence and held the strands apart for him.

"Let's get over by the light," I said, and he came through the wires.

We left the bikes and walked over towards the house. It *was* Panzerov's house. I'd never seen it from the back, but I could see by the shape that it was theirs. We headed for a window that was lighted up. When we got closer, I could see that the window was open, and I saw some people moving around inside.

I whispered, "We've got to be real quiet. They're in there. The window's open." He was holding the back of his upper arm, right above the elbow. When we got into the light right under the window, I could see that the back of his arm was all bloody, and so was his other hand where he'd been holding it. It wasn't gushing blood or anything, but it was all messy. He held up his elbow and tried to look under it, but he couldn't see the cut.

"Put it down and hold your back to the light," I said as quietly as I could. He did that, and I saw a cut about three inches long. It was oozing a little. "It's not real, real bad," I whispered. "I think the bleeding is almost stopped."

"That's good," he whispered back. "I thought I was bleeding to death." He held up his other hand so the light shone on it. It was coated in blood. He bent down and wiped it on the grass. That's when I heard the moaning. I'd been so busy looking at C.K.'s cut,

I never thought about looking into Panzerov's window. I did, then, and about fell over. I couldn't believe my eyes. It looked like some yucky scene out of an art book that my dad had.

C.K. stood next to me, and we watched without moving an inch. Mr. Panzerov and one of his three grown-up daughters were all naked and lying on a big bed. The daughter was fat and lying on her back with the blubber sort of rolling around. Mr. Panzerov was fat, too, and looked like a whale. He was lying on top of the daughter. Her legs were spread apart, and he was between them, making his butt go up and down, kind of like Tucker did to Lassie. The daughter raised her legs up in the air and moaned a lot. Then she sort of squealed and kind of yelled. Then she got quiet. Mr. Panzerov backed away from her and stood up. His penis was wet and hung there looking icky.

All the children are in a big circle. We're down in the basement, and the spotlight is on in the middle. This time, Miss Bernice is lying there with no clothes on and she's making her finger go in and out between her legs like she does to the girls. Jack is standing there watching her. He's naked, too, and his penis is very big and stands way out.

"Children," he says, "this is what is known as fucking. This is what your mommy and daddy do all the time. This is how they made you."

He's on his knees, sitting over Miss Bernice's chest, and she raises her head and starts to lick his penis. Then she puts it in her mouth and brings it out a little, then puts it back in, then out. She licks it some more and then makes it go in and out of her mouth real fast. Then she puts her head back down and Jack scoots back and kneels between her legs.

"Now, watch, children. You can do this, too. It feels very good, and Satan will love you if you learn to do this." Then he aims his penis where Miss Bernice had her finger and pushes it into her. She moans and he moans. They squirm around and Jack makes his butt go up and down. Then he makes it go faster and faster, and then he starts moaning real loud and then goes, "Ahhhhh." They squirm a little more, and when Jack stands up, his penis is small and hangs there like it's dead.

I glanced at C.K., and he looked like a statue, except his mouth was open. He looked at me and whispered, "Do you believe that? Wow."

"Yeah," I said. "Wow." Then Mr. Panzerov looked right at us and we ducked and ran for our bikes. We grabbed them and wheeled them through the back yard as fast as we could go. When we got out to the road, we didn't know which way to go. My house was to the left, and C.K.'s house was to the right. I thought about going to his house and calling my mom from there, and then I thought he should come to my house and call his mom from my house.

I started to go towards his house, and he started to go toward mine, and we actually bumped into each other. Then I tried to go with him, and he tried to go with me, and it was so crazy for a minute, we finally stopped and started laughing.

"Did you see that!" I said, pointing at Panzerov's house.

He kept giggling. "Yeah, I saw it. One of his daughters! Wow!"

"Should we tell our parents?" I joked.

"Yeah, right away! Wow."

I pushed the little button on my watch and looked at it again. It said 9:45. "Boy, am I in trouble. Why don't you come to my house so my parents can see your cut. Then they won't get so mad at me. My mom will clean it up and call your mom. Okay? Please? I don't want to go home alone. They won't get mad with your arm cut. Will your mom get mad?"

"I guess not, with the cut. Okay, I'll go with you."

We got on our bikes and hurried to my house. After we pushed our bikes up the steep bank, C.K. said, "Well, what did you think of Mr. Panzerov?"

"That was really something," I said.

"Do you ever want to do it?" he asked.

"Sex?" I asked.

"Yes. Sex."

"I-I don't think so. I don't see what's so great about it. It looks yucky. All wet and sloppy and people yelling and moaning."

"But it feels real good. I mean, that's what I hear. Real good."

"I guess so. I just don't see what the big fuss is about."

We got to my house then, and I tried to act like I was out of breath and all scared about C.K. Both my mom and dad were home, and they both came running when they heard us go in. My mom sort of screamed when she saw C.K.'s arm and my forehead, and we told her how we'd gotten lost and then had to go over the barbed wire fence, and that was how C.K. got cut and my head got hit with his bike. My dad called Mrs. Bookout, and she came and picked C.K. up.

PART FOUR

27

Yeah, we built that new castle when the hay came in. Hell, it turned out great, but we didn't play in it much. Maybe cuz I was in middle school then, and Johnnie was still in grade school. Shit, I don't know. Things just wasn't the same after Harry died.

The next four years was pretty damn quiet. I tried to do good in school cuz Pa was payin' me for good grades. I sure as hell wasn't about to try babysittin' for money no more, at least not at that time. I wasn't smart enough yet, if you know what I mean.

Johnnie and I still got together once in a while. Hell, by four years later, I was in high school and he was still in junior high. Fuck, I don't know what happens at that age. It's just not cool to be out with guys younger than you. Not that I had that many friends. Mostly, I didn't like nobody. I was happy bein' at home, watchin' TV, layin' on my bed, thinkin' about things.

For a few years, I met Ken Jenkins different places—the cornfield in good weather, his room, his car, whatever. And then, one day, shit, he tells me he's gettin' married and movin' to Utah. Two weeks later, he was gone. Never even said good-bye. I even seen him drive by my house. His car was all loaded up, and some woman was sittin' next to him. They drove by kinda slow, and I watched to see if Ken'd look at my house, maybe wave. But nothin'. He never even looked over. I don't know why, but I went over and put my foot through one of Ma's dining room windows. I just felt like doin' it. Dang, man. It was a mess, and I had to pick up all the glass and pay for a new window. I told her some car'd come by and some kid had threw a big rock through the window. I went out and found a big rock before she got home, so I could show her, but she didn't believe me.

And then, when I was a junior in high school and Johnnie was in ninth grade, he joined this fencing club at the University.

I thought it sounded pretty cool at first, and I went to one of his classes. I expected the fencers to be like Robin Hood. You know, strong, tough dudes, whacking away at people with their swords. Shit, you ever seen what them fencers wear? Stretchy little white suits, and with their hand up in the air behind 'em, and scootin' back and forth with their swords out in front of 'em. They looked like a buncha goddam fairies. That's when I figured Johnnie knew about me preferrin' boys. And then I realized maybe he did, too. That's why he brought me here to see him and the other guys in the white suits. We'd seen so goddam little of each other since Harry died, I thought, shit, he's like me, and all this time we ain't got together. Damn.

But then, on the way home—I was drivin'—I thought I'd make a pass and find out. When I thought about all these years we could've had somethin' goin', I about kicked myself.

———

I was drivin' us home in my little Volkswagen. Johnnie was lookin' so grown up, sittin' there in the passenger seat. I couldn't believe it. It bothered me that he did. I liked him better when he looked like a boy. Now, he had a strong, mannish face, and his arms and legs was gettin' thick and muscular. I looked at him and imagined him bein' about six again. I liked his face better when he was a boy.

He said, "So, what did you think? Think you'd like to try it? We meet every Tuesday and Thursday evening, and Tim, that one guy, would teach you all the basics. You'd be able to fence with me after just a couple lessons. It's real good for the leg and arm muscles. And if you decided to go to college there, maybe you could be on the team. Most of the competition is out east, and so we'd go out to Yale and Harvard and schools like that. Wouldn't that be cool?"

"Oh, I don't know. If I go to college at all, it'll be the community college."

"No, you're smart. You could go to the University. Are you still keeping your grades up? Is your dad still paying you for A's?"

342

"Yeah, I'm still gettin' A's and still gettin' paid. But I don't think fencing is for me. It's not quite what I expected. You know how we used to play Robin Hood and wave the swords all around and whack each other? And leap up on bales of hay and poke at each other from up there?" We both thought about that and laughed a little.

Johnnie said, "Yeah. We didn't know what we were doing. It's really pretty technical. They do that with sabre fencing, though—whack each other on the side." He laughed some more. "But they don't jump up on bales of hay. We were doing foil tonight, so I guess it looked kind of tame. It really takes a lot of skill, though—timing the parries just right and knowing when to go in for the touch. I bet you'd be good at it. And there's a lot of cool people. And we go away for tournaments. You could get out, see the world, meet new people. Why don't you try it?"

"I'll think about it," I said, and I pulled into the Dairy Queen. Johnnie got a large vanilla malt, and I got a large cone. I was lickin' on the cone kinda like I was thinkin' I'd like to lick his dick. "I sure like eatin' ice cream cones," I said, hopin' he'd look at me and get the hint. He did look right at me, and he watched me eat. I felt myself startin' to get hard.

"You always preferred them when we were kids, too. My dad says that in Jungian psychology, ice cream cones are symbolic of the breast. Did your mom nurse you when you were a baby?" Johnnie asked.

"Shit, I don't know. Probably not," I said and felt my prick go limp.

"He says everyone retains the desire for the breast. That's why we're attracted to mountains and ice cream cones. They represent nurturing. But then there's something some other psychologist came up with called the 'penis-breast' for women. I don't quite understand that."

"Oh," I said. I tried to think of another approach. "So, I might think about fencing. You say it's good for the leg muscles?" I put my hand on his thigh and squeezed. "Yep. Yours feel pretty strong." I left my hand there and moved it just a little toward his zipper. "You

think this is from fencing, huh?" I hoped he would understand what I was gettin' at and look at me the way boys do when they like how I touch 'em. I stared at his face, pretendin' he was six again.

"Jesus Christ, C.K.! What the hell are you doing?" He threw my hand off his leg and jumped out of the car. "Shit! What're you queer or something?" he hissed at me through the window.

I couldn't think of nothin' to say. He just glared at me. Then he went and dumped his malt in the garbage can. He came back, grabbed his fencing gear out of the back seat and said, "I'm walking home."

I watched him walk away from me. He was tall and strong. He looked like a jock, and I decided I didn't like him anymore. I sat there and took my time finishin' my cone.

A mother had her boy with her at the order window. It seemed kinda late to have a kid out. Maybe he'd had a long nap that day. He was a beautiful boy, maybe six or seven. He had real light blond hair, almost white, probably from bein' out in the sun all summer. He was tan, and his body was perfect—not too fat, not too thin. I sat there and imagined havin' him on my lap, right there in the car. He'd probably like sittin' in the driver's seat and steerin'. I'd stroke his legs, and he'd tell me it felt good. And then, if he let me, we could do more. I daydreamed about the things we could do together—right there on the front seat.

I sorta woke up, and the boy turned around and looked at me. He smiled, and I knew he'd been thinkin' the same thing. When his mother turned around, I recognized her, but I didn't know from where. She looked right at me and smiled. I smiled back. Then she came over to my window.

"Aren't you C.K.?"

"Yes." My heart was poundin' cuz I was afraid she knew what I'd just been thinkin'. "You look familiar to me, too," I said. "But I can't remember from where."

"From church. Your pa's church. I don't see you there very often. How long's it been?"

I did go to church with my pa and Ladonna sometimes, just so I could be with him. They'd got married a couple years ago, and Ladonna'd had a baby girl.

344

"Yeah, it's been a while," I said.

"Well, we'd like to see you more often. Maybe, if you don't want to attend service, you could help out in the nursery. They's always needin' help in there. The kids' Sunday school only lasts a half hour, and then they all go in the playroom and wait for the parents. They's real short-handed. I think they even pay somethin'. Not much, a couple dollars an hour. Last Sunday the preacher asked us all to try and recruit some teenagers to help out. So, I guess I'm doin' my part askin' you, huh? Give it some thought." She smiled and said, "Come on, Kyle," and she and Kyle went and got in their car. I knew Kyle wanted to have sex with me cuz he looked at me that certain way and gave a little wave as they drove off.

I drove home and wondered if I'd see Johnnie on the way. I guessed I wouldn't offer him a ride. It was only about a mile, and I didn't see him and figured he'd gotten home already. I thought about Kyle the rest of the way home, and that night, I thought about him and imagined having sex with him while I jerked off. This was Thursday night, and I'd get to see him on Sunday.

The next day after school, I called Pa and told him I'd run into that lady and that I'd been thinkin' about goin' to church anyway and how she said they was payin' teenagers to watch the kids. He told me to call the pastor and tell him, so I did. The pastor asked if I'd had any previous experience takin' care of small children. I told him I'd babysat every summer since I was twelve. He acted real happy and said I could start the next Sunday for two dollars an hour. All the rest of the week I thought about Kyle.

On Sunday, I knew I'd made the right move. The nursery was filled with about thirty little kids. Two girls who must've just been in junior high was tryin' to run the place. Things was pretty wild. But within minutes I had the whole place in order, playin' games, readin' stories and shit like that. The little kids loved me. I gave them horsie rides and let them hang all over me. I let the two junior high girls do stuff with the little girls, and I took charge of

the boys. It worked out great. One little boy named Brian said his tummy hurt. I had him lie down on the cot, and I rubbed his belly with my hand. He said it felt good. Then I put my hand under his shirt and rubbed. He said that felt good, too. Kyle stood by me and watched.

That's all I did the first time. I intended to let them trust me and love me first. The next couple times I hid candy in my pockets, and every time one of my favorite boys did somethin' special, like spell Jesus right or name all the colors on the color wheel, I'd give him a piece of candy. Of course, then all the boys was eager to give the right answers, and they all paid attention real good. I had no trouble controllin' 'em. The two junior high girls still had a lot of trouble with their little girls, but I didn't care. They'd look over at me and the boys sometimes and look frustrated, like they wondered how I did it, but as far as I was concerned, they could figure it out on their own. Little girls was snippy and sassy, and they could keep 'em. My boys was well-behaved and good little pals.

All I did with Kyle them first several Sundays was to give him a wink once in a while cuz we had a special secret. I just couldn't do nothin' yet until I'd been there longer. But I was just about ready to make my move. I'd gone exploring in the church building and discovered the basement. The door to it was just down the hallway from the kids' playroom, and it looked like all they did was store stuff down there—chairs, card tables, a couple pews, and huge boxes of paper towels and toilet paper.

One Saturday afternoon when I was watchin' TV and Ma was outside rakin' leaves, the phone rang. It was never for me, and I almost didn't answer it cuz I didn't want to have to get shoes on and go outside to get Ma. It rang and rang like it wasn't never gonna stop, so I couldn't stand it no more and got up and answered it.

"C.K., it's me, Johnnie."

"Oh," I said. I was surprised. But I was happy that it was him. "How're you doin'?" I got a little nervous cuz I thought maybe he was gonna tell me what an asshole I was.

"I'm calling for two reasons. One is to apologize for my reaction at the Dairy Queen that night. I thought about it later, and I realized I may have misread you. I may have gotten the wrong impression and jumped to conclusions. I'm sorry —if that's what it was. The second reason is to say good-bye. My dad got invited to join the faculty at Yale University—in Connecticut, and we're moving out there. We're leaving tomorrow. I just couldn't go away without saying good-bye, especially with the way we left things."

"Wow. You're moving away. I thought you'd be here forever. Well, do you wanna come down here for a while, or I could come up there? We could go for a bike ride or somethin'."

"I'd like to, but I have to help pack. I just want to say that— that I'm sorry we—that our friendship fell apart. You were my first and best friend. I—I don't know why we didn't stay as good of friends as we used to—probably going to different schools, and you being older."

"Yeah, I think that's it because, well, you were my first and best friend too," I said. Shit, I was startin' to feel choked up.

"I know. But I guess people grow up and have to do their own thing, or something like that. I, um, worry about you a lot. I see you every once in a while, and I guess I think you don't look very happy. And, um, I don't know, sometimes I feel like I did something wrong—let you down or something. I don't know. I guess I just hope that—your life goes well. I'd say come visit me out there, but I think you probably won't. And besides, I mean, maybe we just have our own lives and have to live them our own way. I'm having trouble saying what I want to say." He laughed a little and sounded kinda nervous.

I laughed a little, too. "You always been good with words, Johnnie."

"I mean, is everything okay with you? Are things going the way you want them to? Are you really going to college?"

"Yeah, shit, things are great. Beautiful. I hope you like Connecticut. Somehow, that sounds like the right place for you instead of stuck on some farm in Indiana."

Susan L Metzger

"Well, I don't know. Maybe. Yale has a fencing club, too, and who knows, maybe I'll get a scholarship for college and end up back here. If I do, I'll look you up. But just take care, And, um, I don't know. Be good, okay?"

"Yeah, I'll be good. Thanks for calling." I wanted to say more. I wanted to run up to his house so we could go out to the hay pile and play our evil warrior games. I wanted to be with him and laugh real hard like we used to and just giggle about nothin'. But I didn't.

"Sure," he said. "Say good-bye to your mom for me."

"Yeah, me too—your ma. Tell her I miss her weird food." I giggled a little and hoped he'd giggle too, and then we could just start laughin' real hard and not be able to stop.

And then we hung up. The next day was Sunday, and I took Kyle to the basement. I told him I had some very special pieces of candy I didn't want the other boys to see. I sat down on a chair and put him on my lap. I gave him one of the pieces of candy. While he was unwrapping it, I started stroking his thighs. I asked him, "Does this feel good?"

He said, "Yes."

Then I stroked his hips and belly and asked him if that felt good, and he said, "Yes." And when I started rubbin' the area over his crotch, he didn't pull away. So, I put my hand down inside his pants and fondled his little dick. He still didn't pull away. He was busy eating his candy. I asked him if that felt good, and he squirmed a little, but he said, "Yes." I gave him another piece of candy. I had him stand up in front of me, and I unzipped his jeans and pulled them down. His little dick was almost hard, and when I fondled it some more, it got real hard. I asked him once more if it felt good, and he said, "Yes." But he was startin' to look a little scared, so I quit right there.

"I like to make you feel good," I said. He smiled a little and nodded, and I gave him one more piece of candy and said this would be our special secret. I asked him, "Okay?" and he nodded.

"Your mommy and daddy probably wouldn't appreciate all the candy I've given you, so you won't tell them about this, will you?"

He shook his head no.

"You got to promise me, okay? Or the pastor will fire me, and I won't have a job. Okay?" He nodded again and pulled his pants up. I gave him a big hug and tickled him till he laughed. I held out my palm for him to slap. "Secret?"

He giggled and slapped my hand real hard. "Secret!"

"All right! Let's go back up."

This went on for a few months. He let me go down on him all the time, and I jerked off. He didn't want to go down on me, though. That was okay.

When Kyle stopped comin' to church, I got Brian to go down in the basement with me. He let me stroke his thighs and put my hand down his pants, but when I stood him in front of me and tried to take his pants down, he said, "No."

"This will feel very good," I told him. "I won't hurt you. You'll be glad."

He still said no. I told him he was a good boy for saying no, and he should always say no when anyone tried to do this. "I was just testing you," I said. "And I'm very proud of you that you passed the test. You're a good boy." I gave him a piece of candy and told him this would be our secret. He agreed.

Timmy was next. He was a scared-lookin' kid with straight brown hair and great big brown eyes. He let me do it in his butt. He never complained, and he loved the candy. Timmy was my pal until I graduated from high school.

Pa said he'd help pay for college if I got at least a part-time job. The YMCA had an ad in the paper for a janitor twenty hours a week, so I went and applied. They liked it that I was goin' to college and hired me that same day. My main responsibility was keepin' the locker rooms, showers and pool area clean. This meant I got to be around the pool when all the little kids was takin' swimmin' lessons, and I got to be in the boys' locker room whenever they was takin' showers and changin' clothes. But the littlest boys, the three, four, and five-year-olds, went in the girls' locker room so

their moms could help 'em change. Once they was six and seven, they changed on their own. And if they had trouble with a zipper or some buttons, I was usually around to help. They always seemed glad when I was there, so I made it a point to clean the locker room when they had their lesson times.

When they took their showers, I was always there to help them get the water temperature just right. The swimming instructor, Josh, used to have to do this, and he was real glad that I did it for him. It gave him extra time to talk to his girlfriend on the phone in the office. Josh and I went out for beers sometimes. I even let him fix me up on some dates with friends of his girlfriend. They always thought I was such a gentleman cuz I didn't try to take their blouses off or screw 'em. I got careless once and went out with the same girl—Sally—six or seven times. I liked her because she thought I was smart. I helped her with her computer a couple times, but she kept actin' like she wanted to kiss me and sit close.

So, I let her. I kissed her in the back seat of Josh's car. She got real carried away and started french kissin' me. I got pretty excited. She took my hand and put it inside her blouse. She didn't have no bra on, and I felt her breasts. I rubbed my thumb across her nipples. She got more excited, and it felt kinda good to me, too. She put her hand down my pants and rubbed my prick. That felt damned good, and I decided I wanted to have sex with her. So, when we got to Josh's house, Josh and his girlfriend went in, and Sally and I stayed out in the car. It was a big, old, '76 Pontiac Bonneville, and the back seat was real big. I let her do it to me. I laid on my back, and she pulled my jeans off and gave me a damned fine blow job. When she pulled her own pants off and got on top of me, I thought, This is gonna be interesting. When she put my prick in her cunt, it felt pretty good, but there was something about her breasts in my face and her cunt bein' kind of big and sloppy that wasn't exactly awful, but was just kind of pig-like or somethin'. I did come, but it took a little while and only when I pretended she was Timmy from church.

I didn't go out with Sally no more and was real careful after that to take the same girl out only once or twice so she wouldn't expect me to have sex with her. It showed the people at the Y that I was normal. They all liked me and trusted me, and that's how I wanted it.

In college, I took a math course and a computer course. I got A's in both of 'em without tryin' very hard. My computer instructor was real excited about my ability to understand programming, and he said I should become a programmer. I enrolled in two more computer courses second semester, but the week after the semester started, the Y lost their other janitor and offered me a full-time position. They said it would include drivin' the bus for summer day camp, and they said I'd have to get a commercial license. So, I dropped the computer courses. I studied for the commercial license test and passed it. Then I got an apartment and moved out of Ma's house. She was goin' with some guy now who was there all the time, and she didn't need me around. I got an apartment just a block from the Y.

By summer, I had two little pals, Christopher and Adam. Both of their moms and dads worked late, and both of 'em had babysitters that dropped 'em off for their swimmin' lessons. And both of 'em always had to wait for their parents about a half hour after all the other kids had left. So, I started takin' 'em down to the little grocery store for candy and ice cream. Sometimes we'd go to the park and swing on the swings. And sometimes I'd take them to my apartment.

———

Yeah, shit, by then I had the system down pretty good. A couple months later, Adam told his ma what we been doin'. They'd had some little play at school about "good touching and bad touching." Shit. The problem with them motherfuckers is they don't understand what good touching is all about. So, Adam goes home and tells his ma that C.K.'d been doin' bad touching. The damn police came to my apartment accusin' me of molesting some little kid at the Y. I told 'em I'd never do such a thing,

351

that all the kids was talkin' about "good touching and bad touching" these days on account of that play, and Adam must've gotten confused. I said maybe it was his pa or his uncle done it to him. The people at the Y all said I was great, and they'd never had no trouble with me, so the District Attorney finally dropped the charges, and his parents took Adam out of swimmin' lessons, and the police went away.

But goddammit, that summer at the Y day camp after I'd dropped the kids off, another boy, Eric, liked to stay on the bus and talk to me. He hated camp and didn't want to go. So, I'd keep him on the bus with me, and we'd go for rides and shoppin' and out to lunch, and other things, if you know what I mean. I had to put in extra hours durin' the summer cuz I had all that free time between the bus rides, but that was okay. I did the cleaning at the Y in the evenings. Well, like I was sayin', dammit, one day Eric's Aunt Myrtle—shit, she must've been ninety years old—saw me and him at a truck stop. We'd gone in for lunch, and she came in after we did. She sat down for a cup of coffee at the table right next to us. At first she was happy to see Eric, and then she started askin' who I was. Of course, Eric told her I was the bus driver, and damn if that old bitch didn't put two and two together. She made Eric go with her and went home and told Eric's parents, and they called the police. When I pulled the bus full of campers into the Y parking lot that afternoon, the fuckin' cops was waitin' for me.

That damned little Eric testified against me, and I was sentenced in criminal court for child molesting. The Y fired me, and I moved out of my apartment. I didn't have to go to jail or nothin', but I did have to go to the mental health center for group counseling twice a week. I moved to South Bend. There was a nice little apartment right above a Montessori daycare center. And I got a job at a spring and wire factory doin' data entry on their computer. The group counseling was okay. There was five of us all convicted of the same thing. The therapists was pretty cool. It was like they understood us and even cared about us. But it was pretty damn clear to me nobody was

gonna "fix" us. We couldn't make ourselves not think certain thoughts.

So I didn't do nothin' with a kid for a year or more, but I did make friends with the teachers and the kids at the Montessori school. First, there was Roy. And then Mark. And James. And—

28

I didn't understand at the time why C.K. began to withdraw from me. It was as though the two of us had reached a fork in a road right after Harry died—a road that we'd started on together but were branching off from. C.K.'s body and his mind were pulling him down one of the roads, the road that doubted, the road that was not supported by his parents—and I took the other. But he'd only gone a short distance, and I wasn't aware of the fork in the road at all.

I recall my excitement when they began to harvest the hay the next day. I called C.K. the minute I saw the tractor out in the field, and I called him the following day to tell him they were raking it, and I called him the third day when they were baling it. It was a spell of hot, dry weather, and the harvesting went smoothly. The fragrance of the cut alfalfa drifted over the field, over the pond, up the hill, and through our windows. The rich, sweet aroma is one that I still savor today. I try to get out of the city every week or so during the summer to drive through the farmland, sniffing the air, hoping to catch a whiff of that divine perfume. It triggers a *deja vu* of fun but also of sorrow.

———

I thought C.K. would want to come up and see the hay being harvested. It wasn't because he hadn't seen hay harvested before but because this was very special hay. This was the beginning of our new, grand castle, the one with two shafts and a tunnel. But he said he had a bunch of homework because he was in junior high school now. He was still getting money from his dad for A's on his report cards, and he said he'd be getting more report cards in junior high school than he did in grade school. He said he really wanted the money.

Susan L Metzger

When I saw the hay wagons coming up the driveway after school a few days later, I called him again.

"It's here! It's here!" I shouted.

He said, "Oh, good. I've got a few more math problems to do, and then I'll be up."

I went out to the barn and watched as the guys unloaded the bales. The hay was a dark green and smelled so sweet I thought about trying to eat some myself. I watched them lay one row down with the bales on their sides so the twine wouldn't rot next to the ground. Then they put the second row down with the bales lined up going the other direction. The third row was laid like the first, the fourth like the second, and on and on until they had made a huge square. Then they started the second layer. They set the bales down flat, and then they alternated the direction every two bales, so the second layer looked like a checkerboard. Every time a guy would set a bale down, he'd push it and kick it into place, so it was a nice, tight fit. I knew this was good because it would make the castle real strong and make it easy to pull exactly four bales out at a time when we made the shafts.

I watched the men, but I kept turning around to look out the big door to see if C.K. was coming. I kept an eye on the bank of the road where he would come up the path. I looked at my watch. It had already been a long time since I called him. I guess I didn't understand because I thought he cared so much about building this new castle. He sure was mad when the old one was gone. And now he was taking forever to get here. The hay guys were stacking the fourth layer now. I figured there would be about twenty-five layers. I turned again to look at the edge of the bank and saw a blond head bobbing up the hill. It was C.K. pushing his bike.

I ran out and said "Hi!" and told him to hurry. He came into the barn. He took one look at the big, flat square. It wasn't quite as tall as we were. He frowned.

"Smell it?" I asked. "Doesn't it smell wonderful?"

"It's not even a pile yet. I thought it would be as tall as the other one. You didn't say they was still stackin' it."

"I thought you'd want to see it from the beginning."

356

He shrugged. "I hurried up here. There's nothing we can do with it now."

"Boy! Does that alfalfa smell sweet!" It was Cross-Eyed Ladonna standing in the doorway behind us. C.K. rolled his eyes when he realized who it was.

I turned around right away. "Hi!" I said. I sounded out of breath, even to myself. She looked beautiful, as usual.

"Them horses are gonna love this stuff. Just look how green it is. Makes me want to eat it myself," she laughed.

"That's just what I was thinking!" I said. C.K. stood there and looked at his feet.

"You guys gonna make another castle?" she asked. Her hair bounced around on her shoulders. She had a dark pink tee shirt and jeans on and that pretty lipstick. She looked fantastic.

"Yeah! We're just waiting for them to get done stacking it," I said.

"That's gonna take a while, with three wagon-loads. You boys might be waiting all night. They might have to finish it tomorrow."

"Oh," I said. I hoped they'd be done in a half hour. C.K. was sort of swaying back and forth and looking restless. He wouldn't look at Cross-Eyed Ladonna.

"I'm sorry," I said to him. "Want to do something else?"

He looked at me. "Yeah. Let's go in the house." He walked away.

"See you later," I said to Ladonna. She grinned, and I hurried and caught up with C.K.

I almost asked him what was wrong, but I knew. We didn't talk while we walked to the house, and he stayed just a little ahead of me the whole way. When we got inside, I offered him some cake and milk, and he said, "Sure" and walked into the living room and put the TV on.

He ate his cake and watched TV—an old rerun of *The Dick Van Dyke Show*. But he didn't talk. He got involved in the show and laughed at all the funny parts. When it was over, he said, "Well, I might as well go home. I've got more homework to do. I'll come back tomorrow, and we can make the castle then."

Susan L Metzger

I was surprised that he wanted to leave, but I couldn't argue with homework. "Okay," I said, and he left.

The next day after school, he came over and he was more his old self. We worked hard with the lunge lines and got the two shafts made. We put all the extra bales around the top edge like before. We were all sweaty when we were done. He stayed for supper, and then he went right home.

The next day he wasn't home after school. I called a bunch of times, and no one answered the phone, and he never came over. The day after that, he just showed up, but he seemed like his mind was on something else. We tried making a tunnel to connect the two shafts, but we couldn't pull the bales out. They were just packed too tightly. He seemed only sort of disappointed, but it was a big let-down for me. The whole idea of having two shafts was to be able to go back and forth between them. So, after all that work, having two shafts wasn't really much better than having one. We'd go down in one, and then we'd go down in the other, and they were exactly the same.

Finally, he just stopped coming over. I'd call sometimes, and he was either busy doing homework or he didn't answer the phone. Then I joined the soccer team at school and had practice three afternoons a week, and I didn't get home until suppertime. I had homework then and just didn't bother calling him.

The year went on like that, but every once in a while, he'd call, usually on a weekend, and we'd go to a movie or he'd come up and we'd watch TV. Mostly, though, he seemed to have something on his mind, but he didn't want to talk about it. One day, when we were watching TV, I said, "What are you thinking about? You always seem to be thinking about something."

He didn't take his eyes off the TV. "Nothing," he said. "Really. Nothin'."

———

During the next four years I developed other friendships at school. I became part of a circle with four boys I really enjoyed. They were all sons of college professors and doctors, and we all

358

had similar values. I believe that sharing similar values is the basis of most friendships. One or another of my friends would often spend a night or two on the farm on the weekends. They liked getting out of the city, and I enjoyed going to their houses and experiencing the stimulation of urban life. We were all avid Dungeons and Dragons players and became interested in fencing as a result of that. The university had a fencing club for fencers of all ages, and we all joined. I excelled at it, and it became a major focus in my life. I went to tournaments and competed very successfully.

By the time we were freshmen—ninth grade and still in junior high—the pressure to have a girlfriend was strong. I interacted with girls easily enough, but when I thought about getting intimate with one, I became tense and avoided situations where that might occur. And then I got to know Shelley. She was a cheerleader. She had light brown hair that hung in loose curls around her shoulders—something like Ladonna's— and a pretty, round face.

I guess it was the way she always looked at me. She had a smile in her eyes, and she'd cock her head to one side and sort of cock her hip to the other side and just look into my eyes like there was nothing else that mattered to her. She was so interested in what I thought and what I said. She always laughed at the right times and looked concerned at the right times, but she never seemed to expect anything from me. If I met her in the hallway after school but had to hurry off to soccer practice, she'd smile and say, "Have fun!" I guess she wasn't the jealous type like some of my friends' girlfriends.

If I asked her to go with me and some friends to the movies, she seemed happy to go. And she always wanted to know what I thought about the movie—the plot, the acting, and whether the story was realistic. Sometimes she had her own opinions about these things, but she always wanted to know what I thought. Even when I took another girl out once in a while, she acted like it didn't make any difference.

We held hands a lot, and I kissed her sometimes. But as soon as I started feeling other feelings, sexual feelings, I stopped. I know

359

my friends were all excited about doing more with their girlfriends, and most of them were figuring out ways to get the girls to have intercourse with them, but I just couldn't do it. I mean, it was always on their minds. They'd joke with me and say, "Come on, John, how often do you and Shelley screw?" I used to be honest and say "never," but they just laughed and said I was lying. A couple of them had already done it and said it was the best thing in the world.

I wondered what was wrong with me. I knew I felt the feelings because I'd get erections when I was kissing and holding Shelley, and sometimes all I had to do was think about her and I'd get one. I had some wet dreams, but my dad explained it and said it was normal. I was still embarrassed when it happened, but my dad was pretty cool and told me about when he'd had them. He also talked about masturbation and said it was normal, too. He did it when he was my age. He said he still did it sometimes now, and all boys and men do it. But he said it's a private thing to be done only in the shower. So, I did. But not a whole lot. There was some kind of weird, bad feeling that always happened when I did it. The feeling was bad enough that sometimes, when I'd start to masturbate, I'd want to stop what I was doing. It was like two forces were fighting with each other. My penis wanted me to continue, but some other force was saying, "No, no, this is wrong." Actually, more than wrong—evil, somehow, and I tried to make that force, that other feeling, go away. And the closer I got to coming, the more awful the other force became, until I wanted to scream.

One time in the shower when I was doing it, a picture appeared in my mind, sort of like a movie screen. I was little, like three or four years old, and I was naked, and I was masturbating myself. A big man was standing next to me, and he was naked and masturbating too. He was showing me how. The picture wasn't so terrible, but the feeling that went with it was. I wondered who the man was. He wasn't someone I recognized, and I didn't understand why the feeling was so bad. It wasn't horrible because I was masturbating; it was horrible because of the bad feelings. I hated it. I tried to push the picture and the feelings away because I liked masturbating. It felt good, and I always felt real good afterwards. But each time I started doing it, the picture of me and that man would come into my mind.

After a while, I just stopped masturbating, but then I had more wet dreams. Finally, I asked my dad about it. We were up late one weekend night watching a movie. Mom was in bed. It was a sexy movie, and I started thinking about the picture I saw in the shower every time. My dad wasn't home very much, but whenever we were together, he was terrific. He was always interested in what I thought—about all kinds of things, and I think he talked to me about some stuff that most dads don't, like masturbation. He made it seem really okay and normal. Most of my friends were uncomfortable letting their parents even know that they knew what it was.

"Dad?" I said. I guess I was a little nervous about bringing this up because I guessed there was something weird about it. So, I asked the question during the movie itself, rather than a commercial. Maybe he wouldn't give me his full attention, and I wouldn't be so embarrassed.

"During masturbation, is it normal to see pictures of other things—while you're doing it? I mean, do all guys picture something else—during it?"

He never looked away from the TV. "Of course. Most men picture a woman they're attracted to, or we imagine having intercourse with her. It's probably abnormal not to create an image. I think masturbation in and of itself probably isn't nearly as fulfilling as having a fantasy to go along with it. Why? You got Shelley on your mind a lot?"

"Well, no. It's something different than that. It's something I don't like. I hate it, actually." He turned his attention to me so quickly, I got scared. He looked real serious, and I got scared that he knew something was wrong with me—my sexuality or my mind. I wished I'd never brought it up and wanted to leave the room. He must have read my mind because he tried to make himself look more relaxed. But he was very interested in what I'd just said and totally lost interest in the movie.

He tried to back off a lot. He forced himself to look back at the TV. "Is it something you'd like to share?" He stretched out his legs and fluffed up his pillow.

"Maybe. I'm not sure." I laughed a little. "I don't know. It sort of feels like you think there's something wrong with me. Like I'm one of your patients."

"Don't be silly. You're my son. I love you. I hope we can always share this kind of stuff. I'd like to hear about what it is you picture, but only if you want to tell me."

"Well, I do. And I don't, I guess."

"Okay." He smiled at me. "You decide. You know I think this stuff is kind of interesting, and I'm always willing to listen." He went back to watching the movie.

At first, I thought I'd just let it go. I looked at him lying there. His wavy black hair was turning grey, and his wire-rimmed glasses made him look extra intelligent. I just watched him and thought about how cool he was. He knew so much about people and why they did what they did. Wisdom. That's what he looked like. Mr. Wisdom. But Mr. Kindness too. How silly, I thought—I sound like a little tot. Mr. Potato, Mr. Hot, Mr. Cold, Mr. Tooth Decay. I laughed a little.

"It's that funny?" He glanced at me and smiled. "Humorous masturbation. Now, that's a new one. Most men lose their erections when they laugh." He chuckled and kept watching the TV. A commercial came on, and he got up and went in the kitchen. He called to me from out there. "Want some popcorn?"

"Sure!" I yelled. I heard him open and close the microwave, and after a few minutes, he came out with two bags of hot popcorn. He handed me one and sat back down. Before he fully reclined again, I said, "Okay. I guess I think that my image is a bit strange. It's sort of freaking me out."

He looked at me, but not like he was as interested as before. It was like he was thinking, Okay, I'll act like this is no big deal. If he wants to tell me, fine. If not, fine.

"When I do it. In the shower. I get this picture—this image of me being a little kid—doing it. And some guy—some big guy is standing next to me, showing me how. But it's not you. Some guy with sandy-colored hair. And it's not the doing it that bothers me. It's a bunch of feelings that freak me out. It's like they're good and

bad at the same time, and the feelings are fighting each other. And the closer I get to orgasm, the more they fight and the more I can hardly stand it." I took a deep breath. "There. I told you. Is it weird?" I expected him to say something like, "No, it's not weird at all. The images we see are simply representative of the collective unconscious, and the collective unconscious calls forth all kinds of archetypal images that are often nonsensical to us." But he didn't say that.

He said, "Johnnie, I've been waiting for this to come up." He took a deep breath. He looked real uncomfortable for a few seconds, and then he faced me, sitting on the edge of the couch with his elbows on his knees and his face resting in his hands. "Do you have any recollection of the daycare center you were in when you were about four? Any? Do you remember the teachers or the other kids or any of the stuff you did there?"

I tried to think. "No. Nothing. Oh, there was something about some bad food once. I think I got sick. That's all."

"Do you remember C.K. from there?"

I thought and tried to remember. "No. I only met C.K. when he moved in here. We were, what, six and seven when we met? In grade school, not daycare."

"How about Mary? That friend of Ladonna's that was here for a while?"

I thought about Mary for a minute, and my stomach got queasy. "I always had a bad feeling about her, sort of like I'd met her before, but I never knew where. I didn't like her. Why? What are you talking about?"

"Do you remember when Harry fell through the peat out here and going to his wake? Do you remember seeing Mary at the wake, and Miss Bernice?"

"Sort of. Yeah, I sort of remember seeing Mary there. And Miss Bernice? The daycare center owner? She was at the wake?"

He sat up real tall and took a deep breath again. Then he let himself sink back against the couch and exhaled real hard. He leaned forward and put his elbows back on his knees. He looked into my eyes. "Do you know that you were abused at Little Friends—the daycare center?"

"Abused? What do you mean? Beaten?"

"No, I don't think you were beaten. Worse."

"Worse? What could be worse than beaten? Murdered? Obviously not. What? What!"

He stood up and started pacing around the room. He said, "The guilt I felt then is all coming back now. I can't believe this." He seemed to be talking to himself instead of me. "I hated myself so much then for taking you there." He turned and looked at me. "We thought we were doing you good. That you needed to interact with other kids, that being in a social environment was the best thing for you. God damn it!" He threw his hands up in the air. "We needed a lot more money to make the mortgage payments on this place, so your mom took a nine-to-five job before she got hired at the university. We put you in the daycare center. Everyone thought it was a great place. The director—Miss Bernice—had a masters degree in child development. They had a music program, their teaching materials seemed good. The fact that her husband worked there bothered me a little at first, but then I saw how tender he was with his own baby, and I shrugged it off."

I didn't care about all that. I wanted to know what horrible thing had happened to me. Why was he so upset? I'd never seen him like this. His fists were tight. His shoulders were all drawn up. His face was angry. And he took these big, heavy steps like he was about to grab someone and kill him. I wanted to say, "Stop! Just tell me how I was abused. What did they do to me?" But I didn't interrupt him.

He stopped pacing and looked at me. "You were there for nine months. Nine fucking months. And we didn't know what they were doing. We took you out of there because you were beginning to use improper English—double negatives. Do you believe that! Only afterwards—a month or so later—did we get the call from the police. They had been told by another kid that Jack had— had done some stuff to you." He took big strides over to me. He grabbed my hands and pulled me up out of the chair. He threw his arms around me and hugged me hard and long. Then he held my shoulders and looked into my eyes. "I'm sorry. I'm so damned

sorry. I wondered how long you'd repress it. I figured it would start to come out about now. Sit down. And I'll sit down. And I'll stop ranting."

We sat down. My heart was pounding, and I was getting the shakes a little. He sat like he did before, with his elbows on his knees, and he looked at me. "They were a God damned satanic cult. You, all the kids, were exposed to all kinds of shit. You talked about it for a while to Louise. Remember her? And then you clammed up. You just put it in a box, sealed it up, and put it away. And now the God damned box is beginning to open. I wonder how much you'll remember." He stood up and started pacing again. "Maybe it won't be too bad." He stopped and looked at me. "I'd like you to start seeing Dr. Broward again. Two, three times a week. I suspect that you're going to start remembering more and more of the stuff that happened to you. And you need to process it with someone. And Broward's great. He understands it all." He paused again and sort of squinted and bent down. He looked into my face like he was trying to see right into my brain, like my mom used to do. "Am I scaring you?"

Yes, I was feeling scared, but I shrugged. "I guess so. A little. I mean, I'd like to know what happened. Is this what the picture in the shower is all about? Did that really happen and I'm just now remembering?"

"Yes. Yes, I think so. And," he started talking slower, like he was thinking about each word before he said it. "I think you may have more images—flashbacks. And I imagine that some of them might be, um, unpleasant—possibly scary. But I think if you understand what's happening—and have someone—Dr. Broward—to share them with and discuss their meaning, you'll pull out of this just fine. I mean, it's not like you were traumatized by your parents. You got all the good stuff from us—all the unconditional love and all that. We never hit you or said anything to damage your self-esteem. There are other kids who were at Little Friends whose parents dealt with the whole thing by hitting the kids and telling them they were stupid for letting Jack and Bernice do that stuff to them. Those kids were a mess, and most of them probably still

are." He stopped and looked at his feet for a minute. "I'm afraid your friend—C.K.—is one of them. Though he's done awfully well. I don't understand how he's done so well." He looked at me again. "Am I scaring you? I mean, how are you reacting to all this?"

I was scared. It sounded like I was on the verge of some sort of psycho hell. I almost wished he hadn't told me. I nodded hard. I didn't feel like talking. I sort of felt like crying. I sort of felt like I was a little kid again and just wanted to cry and have my daddy hold me. My upper lip started trembling, and the corners of my mouth pulled down. I couldn't stop them. I took deep breaths and tried not to cry. I held my breath when I felt sobs starting to come out. I got up and walked into the kitchen. I still felt like crying and fought it with all my strength. I wanted to get out of the house. I wanted to go outside and walk. Just walk and clear my head.

"I'm going out for a walk," I said to him and burst out the door. It was dark and cool outside. I wanted to go running through the woods like a wild man and scream and wail until all these feelings—this pressure in my chest—were gone. I took a couple running steps into the woods, but then I decided to just walk up and down the driveway. I took long, strong strides and breathed deeply. I was starting to feel better already. I walked down to the mailbox and then turned around and walked back up, past the house. I walked out to the barn, around the cul de sac, and back down to the mailbox. I must have done this four times, two or three miles' worth. Then I heard my dad's voice.

"Johnnie? Johnnie, are you still out here?"

"Yeah," I called to him.

I saw his dark form in the driveway. We walked toward each other, and then he walked next to me. He said, "I just want to say a couple more things. First, I know you'll get through this just fine. It really might be pretty smooth. Maybe you won't have flashbacks. Maybe it will be gentler than that with some memories just coming in slowly. I don't know. Second, it may take some time, maybe a few years, to process it all. Maybe you'll do it in just a week or two. I can't predict that. Third, you will be so much stronger for having gotten through this. You'll be wise and strong. You're those

things now, but you'll be even stronger and wiser. And fourth, I hope you realize that we love you more than anything and did not know what they were doing to you. None of the parents knew. I think the teachers probably told you we knew, but we didn't. They were very, very good at what they did. You know, there was a whole rash of these daycare cases that happened at the same time. They were popping up all over the country—Boston, Miami, Chicago, St. Paul, California, Louisiana, and they were all the same. They were all doing the same ugly things to the children and fooling all the parents. I know some experts are doing follow-up studies on the victims, and there are probably some groups of victims that are getting together. I'm going to check that out. That might be real helpful for you.

"Also, I want to make it very clear that there's nothing wrong with you. You're not sick or psycho or any of those things. You had a traumatic experience, and now it's time to process it. That's all. Your mind did what it was supposed to do—it protected you from the unpleasantness. It repressed all the intolerable memories. And now that you're older, your mind must feel ready to deal with it, so it's letting some of the stuff come through. Does that make sense?"

I had to think about that for a minute. It was a lot to keep straight—something about having had a real bad experience and my mind forgetting it, and now my mind was starting to remember. "Yeah. I guess so. I wish it hadn't happened. I have a feeling this is going to be awful."

"Maybe. But maybe not. It might not get bad at all. You might just have a few memories—enough to deal with it, and that's all. I'll call Broward in the morning. Were you comfortable with him four years ago? Do you remember him?"

I did. I also remembered that I was pretty mixed up and thought he was Sigmund Freud. I felt embarrassed about that. I wondered why I did that then and thought maybe it had something to do with the daycare center, too. We went back in the house, and two days later I saw Dr. Broward. I talked to him for a long time, but I still wasn't remembering anything except for that one picture in the shower.

Susan L Metzger

A couple weeks later, Shelley and I went to a party. It was at a guy's house who we didn't hang around with too much, and he always seemed a little on the wild side. It turned out his parents were gone for the weekend, and he had all kinds of beer and wine and hard liquor. I drank some. We all did. And there was some marijuana there, but Shelley and I didn't try it. And then we danced. It was really a pretty cool party, and nothing had gotten wild, except that none of us was used to drinking, and we were feeling it. Most of us were pretty careful, and we each had maybe only four cups of wine or cans of beer.

Shelley and I were dancing a slow dance, and we pressed together like we never had before. I could feel her breasts against my chest. I'd never touched them with my hand before. But I started thinking about that, and I started wanting to run my fingers over them. I began to get an erection, especially when I could feel her pubic area rubbing against the top of my thigh. We felt dreamy together, like I couldn't tell where my body ended and hers began. I decided I loved her. I started kissing her neck, and then her cheek and her lips. We kissed and kissed and felt each others' bodies. I whispered, "I love you" to her, and she got real passionate. I think we weren't even dancing anymore, but just standing there kissing and hugging each other.

I put my tongue into her mouth a little ways and found it incredibly exciting. I put it in farther. My penis was totally erect now, and I had a real strong urge to make love to her. It seemed natural that we should do that, and I felt that nothing should stop us. It was supposed to be. Nature had taken over. I took her hand and led her upstairs, through the house, looking for a bedroom. I found one, and we fell onto the bed in each others' arms. We began unbuttoning and unzipping, and pulling at each others' clothing until we were naked. It only took a minute before I did what Nature instructed, and I was on top of her, making love. My penis knew where it should go, and my friends were right. It was the greatest feeling to be inside her.

And then it wasn't Shelley beneath me but little Annie. *Little, four-year-old Annie. And Jack is beside me, coaching me.*

"That's right, Johnnie, you're doing it. Good job. Now come up just a little so I can take a picture." A bright light flashes, and I hear the camera make the whirring sound when it spits the picture out the bottom. I want to stop what I'm doing, but I want to keep on, too. It feels good and bad at the same time. I look down at Annie's face, and she has her eyes scrunched closed.

"One more," says Jack, and he crawls around by our feet. "Lift up just a little, Johnnie. 'At a boy! Good!" Then the flash flashes and the camera whirrs.

Shelley said, "What's the matter, Johnnie? Is something wrong?"

"Shelley!" I said. "Oh, it's you. Thank God, it's you. I—I—I just thought. Oh, never mind. It's okay. It's okay. Are you alright?"

"Mmmm. I'm very much alright. This is wonderful, isn't it?"

I was suddenly sober. "Birth control," I said. "Are you using any?"

"No. I forgot. I mean, I didn't think about it. I mean, I did at first, and then I guess I got carried away. I better get it. Is it too late?"

"No. No, it's not. Go. Go get it." I pulled myself off of her, and she fumbled around in one of her pockets. I heard the ripping of heavy paper. "Here," she said. "Put this on." She handed me a condom, and I fumbled with it—a lot—until I managed to roll it onto my penis. She lay back down on the bed. She reached up and kissed me some more. Then we went back to making love.

I forced myself to look at her and think, "Shelley, Shelley, Shelley. This is Shelley. I'm fifteen, not four. I'm not at Little Friends. This is not Annie. Jack is not here." The picture tried to come back, and I'd see Shelley's face and then Annie's, and then Shelley's. Then I came, and I didn't see either of their faces.

I told this to Dr. Broward and he seemed interested. He wondered what I had remembered around this image. Who was Annie? Why was I being asked to do this? How did I feel back then? I didn't know the answers to any of these questions.

I thought about C.K. more these days because my dad had said he'd been abused at Little Friends, too. I wondered if he

remembered any of it. I called him one day and asked him to go to my fencing class with me. He seemed pretty interested. I thought he would be because of our Robin Hood sword fights when we were kids. I hoped he might get involved in fencing, and we could get our friendship going again. I sort of wanted to ask him about Little Friends to see if he remembered anything.

He picked me up in his car, and we went to the class together. He sat on a chair at the edge of the fencing gym and watched. But he was strange. He watched me only a little. I kept trying to get his attention so I could show him what I was doing. But he kept looking at the younger kids' group. I didn't get it because the little kids could barely hold the swords, and they didn't pay attention. I had taken my turn trying to teach them a couple times, and it was awful.

When the fencing class was over, C.K. said it just wasn't for him. I didn't know how he could know that when he hadn't even tried it. He would have been able to get instruction the next time and start training, but he wasn't interested.

On the way home, we stopped at the Dairy Queen. His mom had bought him an old, used VW Rabbit, and he'd wanted to show it to me and give me a ride. This gave my mom a break, and I think she would have been real happy if C.K. had decided to join fencing so she wouldn't have to drive all the way back up to the university twice a week. Anyway, we were sitting there eating our ice cream when C.K., for no reason at all, put his hand on my thigh, way up high, real close to my fly. He made a pass at me! I couldn't believe it. I couldn't believe this was my old best friend. Right then, I knew my dad was wrong. I knew something *was* wrong with C.K. because of being at Little Friends. And he had the nerve to come on to me! I freaked, I guess, because I got out of the car and walked home. I never wanted to see him again. And as I walked along the highway and thought about what he'd just done, another image hit me. I mean, this one hit big.

I'd been thinking about C.K. being gay, and I started imagining him having sex with other men and what that must be like. I thought about Shelley and how wonderful it had been to make

love to her. I tried to imagine making love to a man. My friends had all made lots of jokes about queers and about ass-fucking, and I'd laughed along with them. But now, all of a sudden, it was real. Someone I knew really did that. I couldn't help picturing some guy's penis in C.K.'s mouth or in his rectum. That's when the image hit.

I was about four, and C.K.—Clive—was just a little older. We were both naked, sitting on a little green rug. The room was in some farmhouse way out in the country. Jack had taken us there. There were men in the room—about six of them. I'd seen some of them before, and some I hadn't. Jack had his camera ready, and there was a video camera on a tripod that some guy was fiddling with. First, Jack made Clive and me lie down, and then he had Clive get on top of me, front to front, and rub his penis against my penis. Then, he had me get on top of Clive and rub mine on his. Then, Jack told Clive to roll over on his belly. Jack took his pants down and kneeled next to him. He masturbated himself until his penis was erect. Then he put some kind of clear jelly on it and put it into Clive's butt. Clive cried and screamed. After a while he stopped. That's when the video guy started running his camera. Someone else had Jack's camera and was taking pictures. When Jack was all done, he told me to lie down on my belly, and he gave the tube of jelly to one of the other men. And the man did it to me. I yelled and screamed. It hurt so bad.

I was walking alongside a big, open field when this image hit, and before I knew it, I'd dropped my fencing gear bag and was running through the field screaming, "NO! NO!" I tried to make the image go away. I stopped in the middle of the field. I was sweating and breathing real hard. All I could see was the green rug in my face and feeling that horrible man ramming his penis into my butt and looking at Clive, who had a different man on top of him now.

I held my hand out in front of me and tried to focus on it in the dark, anything to get the other picture out of my mind. Dr. Broward had told me to do this if I saw an image that I couldn't stand. I tried so hard to focus on my hand. The yard light of a

house across the road was so bright I could see it. I looked at my hand and started counting my breaths. Dr. Broward had said to count my breaths up to fifteen and then start over. He said to keep track of how many times I'd counted to fifteen.

I just took big steps through the field, staring at my hand and counting to fifteen. I did this seven times, and then I began to feel calmer. Finally, I walked to the edge of the field and found my fencing gear bag. I walked home, holding my hand out in front of me the whole time, and I kept counting.

When I walked into the house, my mom came to the front door to greet me. She stopped in her tracks, and her mouth fell open. "What happened? You look terrible!"

"Is dad here?" I asked.

"Yes. He just got home. Leland!"

He came with me up to my room, and I told him what happened. He hugged me for a long time and said he was sorry. He asked if I were seeing Dr. Broward tomorrow. When I said no, he picked up the phone and called him.

"Hank? Leland. Johnnie's just had another flashback. A sodomy scene. He and his friend C.K.— yes, he did the counting. Yes, it worked for him. Yes, I think you're right. I'll call them tomorrow. I know. They've been after me a long time. Guess they'll get what they want, huh? Funny what it will take to motivate a person sometimes. Yeah, thanks. At four then? Okay, good."

He hung up the phone and turned to me. "Dr. Broward will see you tomorrow at four and then I think you, your mom, and I need to talk about moving to Connecticut."

"Moving! Connecticut?" I said. "Why do we need to move?" I didn't want to leave my friends and the fencing club.

"Yale has the number one fencing team in the nation right now," he said. He must have read my mind. "The other thing they have is an excellent academic position for me. They've been asking me for years to take it. But the main reason I want to go, Johnnie, is that in Boston—about two hours' drive from Yale—they're running a group for kids your age who were victimized like you were in their daycare centers. It's being run by several professionals who

have been on top of this crisis since the beginning. I think they can help you better than anyone right now."

I thought about Shelley and about my school and my friends. I didn't want to leave them. And then I thought about what I'd just been through and about my flashback when I made love to Shelley. I knew that this stuff was going to get worse, and I wanted to be done with it, to be rid of it, to get it out of me as soon as possible. I guess I realized that getting this horror expelled was the most important thing right now.

My dad was standing there, waiting for me to say something. He looked sad and tense, and maybe hopeful. I looked at his face. "Okay," I said. He smiled and then hugged me for what felt like an hour.

FINAL WORDS

29

Each time I got a new pal, I was happy. Things would go along real nice for a while, and then, every fuckin' time, the kid would change his mind. Or he'd just disappear. I didn't get it. Kids liked me, man. I was good to 'em. I played games, I took 'em to carnivals, out for ice cream, gave 'em candy. And gave 'em good feelin's, too. And every damn time, they quit on me. I always started slow, you know, strokin' their legs, askin' 'em if this or that felt good. If they was at all hesitant, I'd slow way down. Didn't want to scare a kid. That never works for you.

I wasn't finding one to stick with me from that Montessori school. Shit, they all started sayin' no. So, I moved. Down in a nice trailer park on the south end of town. Bunch of nice people there. Everyone was friendly. And there was a bunch of kids. And the kids all liked me. I got a night job doin' data entry for an RV company—went in at 11:00 p.m. No one was in the office at night 'cept me, so no one bothered me. Stayed there twenty years. Was makin' good dough, got good benefits, built up a dynamite retirement account. Had some lady friends, too. Even married one of 'em, Amanda. Turned out she really preferred women. That was cool. We stayed married for thirteen years. She didn't say nothin' about what I did; I didn't say nothin' about what she did. Only thing was I wanted to have some kids, but she went and had her damn tubes tied. So, we never seen each other much. I worked nights, she worked days and waited tables in the evenings, and instead of havin' kids of my own, I took care of all the neighbor kids. I was around when they got out of school when their parents wasn't.

The parents was all pretty glad they had me. I had the kids all over for football games and badminton and videos. Sometimes there'd be twelve kids at a time in my trailer. Then, about five o'clock they'd all leave. 'Cept for Ricky. His ma worked second shift. She offered to pay me to take care of him after school until

suppertime. She had a teenage girl who was supposed to come and feed him his dinner and put him to bed, but a lotta times she didn't show up. Finally, when Ricky was about seven, and I'd been takin' care of him for almost two years, and his stupid sister didn't show up—and when she did she was strung out on somethin'—then Ricky's ma asked me to take the girl's place. I was glad to do it. Ricky was my own little pal, and we was tight, man. There wasn't nothin' I wouldn't do for him and nothin' he wouldn't do for me. I went to his school for Parents' Day and class picnics. I even went to a PTA meetin' a couple times. His teacher was impressed that I came and said how lucky Ricky and his ma was for havin' me.

So, I grew to love that boy. And he loved me. Like I said, we was tight as hell. Got him on the Little League team and practiced with him every afternoon after he done his homework. Went to every damn game. After a while folks just thought I was his pa, and I never told 'em any different.

Only part that was tough was takin' him to his ma's trailer every night, tuckin' him in, and waitin' for her to get home. Then I'd have to leave him. She got to get him ready for school every morning. Sometimes on weekends she'd let him stay at my place cuz she had a date. I gotta admit, there was times I thought about just runnin' off with him so we could really live together—full-time. I asked him about it sometimes, and he said he'd kinda like that, except he'd miss his ma.

By the time Ricky was in sixth grade, he was about the best damn player on the Little League team. And it was on accounta my coachin' him and practicin' with him. The next step was Babe Ruth hardball. That would take him through high school, and I was plannin' on him becomin' a pro. By eighteen or nineteen he'd be gettin' all kinds of offers from the major leagues.

I didn't think about it at the time, but along with Babe Ruth hardball came junior high school. And with junior high school came growin' up. And with growin' up came wantin' to do his own thing. He started askin' me if he could go home after school with this kid or that kid or go to a movie or a goddam party. I put my foot down with parties. I told him he was too young to go. But his goddam ma

said it was okay. I don't know how she got the idea she could start tellin' him stuff different than what I was tellin' him. So, I tried to reason with him. I sat him down one evenin' after he'd gone to some kid's house for supper. First, I made him do his homework, and then the two of us sat down for a talk. He was a damn good-lookin' kid. He was gettin' taller now and kinda lanky. His legs was gettin' real long, and his hands and feet was gettin' big. He had real nice dark brown hair, almost black, and it was kinda wavy, so I had to keep it cut short or it went all wild. And a sweet face. And big blue eyes. Gorgeous boy, and he still had that boyish face. So sweet.

"Ricky," I says, "you gotta keep your mind on two things: homework and baseball. There just ain't no time for partyin'. Besides, you're too young. Shit, I didn't go to parties till I was in high school."

"That was a long time ago," he said. "Things is different now. Kids do things at a much younger age than when you was a boy." He looked so damned innocent. God damn, I loved the boy. But I was gettin' a little nervous, man, like he was startin' to slip away. I had to clamp down on him quick before he got any ideas. We'd been best pals for too long.

"Now, listen," I said. "I know what's best for you. Don't even be thinkin' about parties till you're in ninth grade. And that might be too soon. How you gonna be an All-Star if you go and get wild, huh? The two just don't go together. Now, don't you think I know better? Don't you think I love you and know what's best? Huh?"

He was fiddlin' with a ballpoint pen and wouldn't look at me. "Answer me!" I said.

He shrugged. "It's just that the guys are startin' to ask questions. They want to know who you are. Their own fathers don't hang around them as much as you do with me. It's just startin' to look—you know—funny." He looked up at me to see what I'd say.

I slammed my hand down on the coffee table and made a glass fall off and break on the floor. "No! The answer is no! Now, get ready for bed. I think you better go to bed a little early tonight."

And damn if he wouldn't do it for me that night. Said he felt sick to his stomach. Pissed me off, man. So, that night I didn't wait

in his trailer for his ma to get home. I left him there alone to think about things. He'd come to his senses by morning.

And sure enough, he straightened up. Came right to my place, didn't go to no boys' houses for supper. Did his homework, and things was just fine between us. I knew a little firmness would work. And then one day in the middle of winter when there wasn't no baseball practice, I was sittin' in my trailer, waitin' for him to come walkin' in as usual after he got off the school bus. And he didn't show up. At first, I figured somethin' must've been wrong with the school bus. They break down sometimes, like any vehicle.

So, I waited. After 'bout an hour I tried callin' the school and the school bus garage, but no one answered. Then I figured maybe he missed the bus. Maybe he was gettin' help from a teacher after school and missed the bus. So, I went lookin' for him. Drove to school and went walkin' through the halls. I went to his homeroom, but no one was there. So, I figured maybe he decided to walk home, so I drove back real slow, expectin' to see him walkin' along the streets. No Ricky. Then I got worried. What if someone stole him or somethin'? Some weirdo could've made off with him in his car. You know, tricked him into ridin' with him somewhere. It happens, man. Guys in here done it. They're sick, though—really fucked up.

So I starts drivin' up and down every damn street between his school and home. There was a park about halfway in between, so for the hell of it, I drove through there. And I see a bunch of kids walkin'—kids about his age. Maybe eight of 'em, so I looked each one over real careful, lookin' for Ricky's red baseball jacket. And damn if I don't see him. And damn if he ain't holdin' hands with some girl. Some flouncy-haired blond thing—she was leanin' on him and shit. That did it. I stopped the car and jumped out. I was gonna go grab him and beat the shit out of him. Then I stopped. No, I thought, that would embarrass him in front of his friends, and then they'd make fun of him, and he might not do so well on the team in the spring. So, even though it took every fuckin' ounce of will power, I got back in the car and drove home. I hated that little blond bitch. He'd sure have a lotta talkin' to do when he got home.

So, I went home and waited. And damn if the kid never fuckin' showed up. Never showed up! I had supper waitin' for him and his study desk all cleaned off with the light on. All ready, and he didn't come home. How could he! is what I was thinkin'. Did he think I did all this work for him for the hell of it?

So, then I figured it out. Maybe he'd taken the little blond bitch to his ma's trailer. Maybe he was fuckin' her. I walked over there fast as I could and damn if the fuckin' lights wasn't on and music was blarin' so loud I could hear it through the goddam, fuckin' walls. I turned the door knob, and the damn door was locked. "Open up!" I shouted. But the stereo was on so damn loud he didn't hear me. So, I used my key. I threw the door open, and there they was—on the couch, all over each other, kissin' and huggin'. At least they still had their clothes on.

I looked at my boy—my best pal, who I loved more than anything—lovin' on that girl. And she was all over him. I couldn't stand it. It was like he'd fuckin' thrown a brick in my face. I guess that's when I lost it, man. I went over and grabbed the bitch and threw her across the room. Little thing was light as a feather. And then I started slappin' Ricky across the face. At first he held his hands up and tried to protect himself. The little bitch started moanin' and cryin', and we both looked over at her real quick. She had blood all pourin' down her face. That's when Ricky tried to kick me in the nuts. He just missed.

I couldn't do nothin' about it, man. I grabbed that big brass table lamp and started swingin'. I hit him in the head over and over. Even after he fell on the floor, I kept hittin' him with it. I never even heard the door open and shut, but the little bitch had run out and got help. I was still smashin' Ricky's head when two big guys came rushin' in and pulled me away. And then the cops came. I saw Ricky—beautiful, gorgeous Ricky layin' there with his head all bashed in and blood all over the place.

"Ricky!" I called to him. I tried pullin' away from the cops, but they had a tight hold on me. "You okay? I'm sorry. Get up. It'll be okay. Ricky—" But he didn't move. The cops hauled me out to

the car. It was three days before the damn pigs even told me he was dead.

My lawyer, the best damned defense lawyer my folks could buy, argued that this was a "heat of passion" murder, not pre-meditated, so I could avoid the death penalty. He tried real hard to convince the judge and the jury. But that goddam judge said that because the relationship between me and Ricky wasn't—in his fuckin' language—a "legitimate love affair," I was not allowed to use that as a defense. He and the jury both fuckin' ruled that it *was* a pre-meditated murder. Fuck, I didn't think about it ahead of time. Damn. And that's why they's executin' me, man. Lethal fucking injection.

But ya know, maybe I deserve what's comin'. Beautiful Ricky is dead, and I killed him. But it *was* outa love. Why can't no one see that?

30

At the time, moving to Connecticut was extremely painful for me because it meant leaving behind my high school friends, Shelley, and the fencing club. Looking back, I see that the move to New Haven was for the best. Shelley and I kept in touch by letters and occasional phone calls, but the romance waned after time. However, getting away from both her and C.K. eliminated the triggering of those particular flashbacks. The fencing club at Yale was every bit as good as the one back in Indiana, and since I'd trained with top-notch coaches already, I was immediately respected and welcomed by the club members at Yale. And the daycare victims' group was the ultimate in therapy.

Although I was no longer having those violent, barely-controllable flashbacks triggered by C.K. and Shelley, I was thrown into a storm of recollections that were just as horror-filled and maybe more so because of the satanic, ritualistic nature of many of them. Each of the other victims, teenage boys and girls who were having the same symptoms because of similar experiences, told about different images they were beginning to recall. And each time a group member related a new recollection, most of us also recalled, however vaguely, a similar one, even though we'd been abused at different schools. We related memories of having to eat feces, eat insects, drink urine and blood, shoplift, take part in every imaginable sexual deviancy known to man, and worship the devil with various chants, phrases, and songs. Some of the memories remained fuzzy and vague, and others would spring forth with a clarity that rivaled reality.

Our group facilitator, Karen, was everything she should have been. She was a woman around fifty with short, greying hair. She'd taken part in nearly every daycare-cult investigation across the country. She'd done research on similar incidents in Europe, some of the tropical islands, and other small countries. Karen was so

warm, intelligent, supportive, and nurturing that we felt we could share any memory or emotion that came up.

I guess my most horrifying memory was the one I must have re-experienced at Harry's wake. The nature of it was so completely forbidden by my conscious mind that even when it was triggered by the presence of Miss Bernice, I repressed it instantly again, leaving my emotional being in total upheaval. It was as though the flashback had emerged and struck for all of a couple seconds, found itself defeated by my defense mechanisms, and retreated once again to wait until it was invited to be released years later. It heard its invitation some two years after we'd moved to Connecticut. The group had been able to talk about the sexual abuse, about the graveyard experiences, about the drugs, the captivity, the bestiality, the religious rituals, and the defiling of the children with excrement, but none of us had been able to talk about the murders.

Perhaps I began the process to release that last, most hellish exorcism when I told the group about my pet rabbit, Fluffy. We'd been given Fluffy just before we moved to the farm that summer of 1983, and my dad had built a nice A-frame hutch for him. When winter came, we weren't sure where to put Fluffy, and Miss Bernice asked if they could keep Fluffy at the school. It seemed like a great idea. Fluffy would be indoors, and the children would have an animal to take care of. It took two strong men to carry the hutch inside, and they made a place for it in the playroom. When spring came, they moved his hutch back outside and later told my parents that Fluffy had escaped. The truth, however, was that Fluffy was plunged live into a huge pot of boiling water as a sacrifice for Satan. And it was Fluffy that we ate for a snack that day.

My story triggered a memory for a girl who'd been victimized in Chicago. She recalled her teachers plunging a baby, live, the same way, into a pot of boiling water. This, in turn, released the memories of several other group members. One recalled her teachers baking a baby in the oven and another recalled the children being directed to hammer nails into one. A fellow from Minnesota had trouble recalling whether he saw a movie or

whether one of the male teachers really did saw a boy named Jason and a girl named Jenny in half with a chain saw. Horrible as it was, once the ball began rolling, nearly all of us began to regurgitate similar scenes.

I was still having trouble with whatever flashback had caused me to scream, "Don't kill the baby!" at Harry's wake. My mother and father told me about this once I'd been in the group for nearly two years. I shared this with the group members, and I was struggling to recall the exact scene. It just wouldn't materialize. I had a vague image of a pregnant woman, perhaps one of the teachers, and a contiguous image of a pointed boot, like a cowboy boot, aimed at the woman's huge belly. But that's all that would come, and that's all that ever has come. The group surmised the rest and tried to help me fill in the details. All I could recall was knowing that a baby, still inside a woman, was about to be kicked to death by the pointed boot, even though I was never able to say with any certainty that that's what really happened. Nonetheless, the feeling of horror is still vivid. Perhaps the rest will present itself one day, or perhaps my most protective defense mechanisms will never allow that repressed material all the way through.

The group therapy lasted three years. I don't know how I managed to do school work through it all, but I did, and I managed to do well enough to earn an academic scholarship as well as a fencing scholarship to Yale. I avoided dating until my senior year of high school, and I did not have sexual intercourse again until my junior year of college. When I did, it was with a clear mind.

Now, I read and re-read the article about C.K. and realize with a heavy heart that I am one of the lucky ones.

EPILOGUE

Walter Bookout and C.K.'s attorney were not able to convince the Governor's office to extend a pardon. However, C.K.'s defense attorney arranged a meeting between C.K.'s psychiatrist and the Governor. The psychiatrist was able to convey to the Governor his belief that C.K. was in a state of brief reactive psychosis leading to temporary insanity when he murdered Ricky. They were able to persuade the Governor to have mercy and commute C.K.'s sentence to life in prison.

THE AUTHOR

Even though *Two Boys* is the first novel that Susan Metzger completed, she began writing her first one when she was ten. She was the assistant editor of her high school literary magazine and won numerous fiction contests as a high school and college student, but she pursued careers in counseling and business before returning to her true self when she completed her third masters degree, an MFA in Creative Writing at Western Michigan University. Prior to the publication of *Two Boys*, her *Spirit Dogs Trilogy* was published under pen name Susan Kelleher. Her fifth book, *Beringei: A Modern Fairy Tale*, will be published in 2013.

Ms. Metzger lives on the Front Range of Colorado where she teaches college-level writing and literature, hikes and showshoes the mountains, bicycles the plains, and plays viola in a large orchestra.

www.ingramcontent.com/pod-product-compliance
Lightning Source LLC
Chambersburg PA
CBHW060145260626
47160CB00001B/126